Two's Company...

Christie H. Lovelace

JL

Published by
Jennifer Lovelace
Lydd, Kent, United Kingdom

Printed and bound by Lightning Source

First Edition

ISBN: 978-0-9926126-0-3

British Library Cataloguing in Publications Data available

Cover design Jon Evans
Cover photos Christie H. Lovelace

www.christiehlovelace.com

For my family

For my friends

For those of you who
were there for us

For love
X

Acknowledgements

To Tom, for lending us his body - you look great from ALL sides.

Jon, who achieved in fifteen minutes what would have taken us a lifetime.

Flavio, for lending me his name, and who I should point out is firmly heterosexual and always has been.

Anna, for being enthusiastic.

Sam, the technical man.

Proof readers, well done!

Ben, so generous and who is such a loyal friend to my girl.

Bonnie, so brave and inspiring.

Maggie's, though it didn't exist in 1977, it was our refuge in 2010.

Sir Richard Lovelace, for his sublime poetry, and Richard Lovelace, for your unfailing humour in dark times.

Jenny, my brave baby.

John, the love of my life.

And for everyone who inspired this novel...

Part One
September 1976

Chapter 1

Dawn

What was I doing? I was staring into the face of a person I didn't know. She was confident with a determined look and it was someone I just did not recognize. I looked beyond my reflection in the bus window and tried to focus on the dark shapes flying past. I felt sick on one hand, yet so excited on the other. Oh God, how had I got myself into this situation? I was just acting on impulse. I was like two completely different people. Me, the shy wouldn't say boo to a goose, be a good girl, do as you're told girl, and this other crazy stranger who seemed to know exactly what she was doing, and didn't give a second thought to how it looked or what anyone might think of her. Someone super cool, super confident, that wasn't me at all! I was fluctuating between exhilaration and out-and-out terror. 'Fight or flight' I think they call it, and I didn't have any control over that either. I was just being pulled along by this insanely calm person. What the hell did I think I was doing? What if I was making the biggest fool of myself ever? I looked at my reflection for help, and there it was, that calm almost defiant expression. *What the hell does it matter? You are going to see him again and then you'll find out!* My stomach lurched as the bus went over a large pothole, and I clasped my hand over my mouth. I really was fighting not to throw up, whilst all the while she was watching me with no sense of fear in her eyes just a steely determination.

The bus was groaning now as it began the ascent of the steep hill. *Oh God, only a few more minutes on the bus and then what?* My stomach lurched again as the bus roughly changed down through the gears. I was up on my feet, making my way to the front, ensuring that he didn't drive past my stop, somehow running on automatic. It was a good job I couldn't see my face any more, couldn't read the fear I was feeling inside. But this other person was taking me over now, and I was calming down. I knew my purpose, so I locked away that mousy girl, stepped off the bus and strode away determinedly down the driveway of the school.

I was late, I knew it. Sarah was supposed to meet me on the bus but my train had been delayed, so I guessed I was about an hour out. Panic began to bubble up in my chest, what if it was all over? What if everyone had gone? *What if you just shut up and get on with it,* my alter persona replied. I didn't even have a plan. I crossed the empty quad, a large parade ground or car park, I wasn't sure what it was for, but right at the end of it there was a sign pointing towards a door. 'Schools' Industries Conference This Way', with a nice, helpful arrow. I grasped the polished brass latch and the huge door swung open, revealing a wide corridor with polished floors. On either side were glass cases containing photographs and an assortment of highly polished silverware, gleaming in the light. My high heels echoed as I strode down the passageway towards another helpful arrow, pointing this time to a pair of large double doors, beyond which I could hear someone in full flow. Well, new found confidence or not, there was no way I was going through those doors on my own. I envisaged the whole hall's audience turning around at the sound of the latch and hundreds of pairs of eyes landing on me. No, that was definitely a step too far. *Go home*, said the voice in the back of my head. Tempting, but no, no way, not now I was so close. I pushed all negative thoughts back. *I will just wait here until the lecture finishes and when they all come out hopefully I will spot Sarah*, I told myself. So I waited.

After about twenty minutes there was muffled clapping and the unmistakable sound of a room full of people rising to their feet. I took a deep breath as the doors opened and pressed myself against the wall opposite, so that I would have a good view of the people as they emerged. They were mostly male, groups of about seven or eight, chatting. A few of them eyed me with a curious glance as they passed, but they continued on their way seemingly knowing where they were going as they flowed out along the corridors. And there it was again, surprising utter confidence. I met their eyes briefly but moved on, looking for Sarah, whom I spotted with a large group of girls. Clustered together they flapped in a flock of femininity, chatting rather too loudly with occasional nervous giggling, but all immaculately turned out, make-up, nails, hair etc.

"Hi where did you get to?" Sarah seemed genuinely delighted

to see me. She wasn't a really close friend. We had known each other years ago in Primary School, but we weren't particularly good friends even back then. Later I had met up with her again at sixth form college. I didn't have any subjects with her, but she had been the only girl to sign up for this conference whose name I knew. I had a major attack of cold feet after initially signing up but wasn't allowed to back out of it. The words of my Headmistress, echoed in my head.

"This will be a good opportunity for you Dawn. I know it is difficult for young girls to meet members of the opposite sex, but it is something that you are going to have to do at some point. I know that you are shy but this will be an interesting experience. You will go to the conference and that is an end to it." Little did she know the other Dawn, the confident Dawn, who on hearing there was to be a conference with the local boys public school, had perused the lists looking for the name Lovelace. Once having spotted it, flashing as if it were written in neon, she had signed herself up without a second of doubt, just in the hope of seeing him again, leaving shy retiring Dawn to deal with the practicalities and consequences. I had been mercenary enough to phone Sarah and arrange to go with her.

"Sorry my train was late, did you wait long?" I hoped she hadn't, I was beginning to feel even more guilty about using her, but Sarah was cool.

"No," she replied casually, "when the bus came I guessed your train was delayed or something, I knew that you would catch up at some stage." Great, well at least that was something I didn't have to feel guilty about. We followed the crowd of boys in front of us and they led us out of the main block, back across the quad, to a large refectory building.

As we entered cups of tea or coffee were thrust into our open hands, it had to be a quick decision because of the people pushing in from behind. The refectory itself was enormous and far too big for the numbers in the hall, so it had been strategically chopped in half by a row of refectory tables, designed to keep us all down one end. Despite this, the boys were standing along the edge of the tables in large groups, in what was the middle of the hall, and the girls were all hanging about by the entrance. In between the two groups, inmates and visitors, was about thirty feet of clear empty space, far too intimidating for anyone to enter.

Sarah was now chatting excitedly to the other girls in our group, whom she probably knew far better than me. They were giggling in a flirty way which gave me some time to stand back, sip my tea, and look up at the boys at the far end of the room.

He wasn't hard to spot, it was as if a magnet were drawing my eyes to him. He hadn't seen me and was chatting easily to a group of his friends, some of whom I recognised. There was Moli, an Italian Count no less, who Kelly, my friend from my old school had told me about. She had been dating him since our last school dance. There were the twins, a lot shorter than the others, but they had so much self-assurance I doubt they ever noticed they had to look up to their peers. There were a few others I recognised but didn't know their names, and then there was Lovelace. He was standing sideways on with all his weight on his back foot giving him a casual air, but also showing off his slim physique. He was looking down, listening to something Moli was whispering to him, his cup almost to his lips as he began to laugh. His eyes creased up with laughter lines as he chuckled and made a remark in response. He was devastatingly good looking, well to me anyway. He reminded me of a Dickensian character, David Copperfield, or was it just that he looked quintessentially like a hot, English public school boy? I couldn't see his eyes from this side, but I remembered how blue they were, an intense blue, not the usual run of the mill blue grey but the colour of the sky in summer. He was wearing his uniform, but it did not mark him out as a schoolboy like some of the rest. He was definitely a young man. Black trousers and jacket, which looked as if they had been tailored for him, they probably had, and a crisp white shirt that gave him an official air, as if it were something he wore to the office. With no school badge on the pocket he could have been a master had I not known differently. That and the fact there were probably seventy other people in the room all dressed identically to him.

It was then it happened. I looked at everyone chatting around me, looked again at his group, and I just walked. I hadn't meant to, and had I thought about it I never would have, but it was like I was being drawn to him. Something was taking control, pulling me to where I had to be, next to him. I think I began to be aware of where I was when I heard the silence. Everyone had stopped talking and was looking up at me in astonishment, including Lovelace. I was halfway across the no man's land between the two groups when all the teacups seemed to land on their saucers as everyone stared at me crossing the room.

What? What in God's name was I going to say to him? I hadn't the faintest idea and I had no choice but to carry on. It was only when I was within about six feet of him that I pulled my eyes away from his to Moli and smiled at him instead. *Brilliant idea, I could introduce myself to him.* I held out my hand, whereupon everyone else in the room resumed their conversations.

"I don't know whether you remember me or not," I said, "you're Moli and you were going out with my friend Kelly from Lillesden?" Moli, having looked shocked to begin with, recovered himself quickly, taking my hand. He didn't shake it but held on to it, which I was glad about, as I am sure had he let go my knees would have buckled, or I would have passed out on the spot. I could feel Lovelace's eyes burning into the side of my head, but I couldn't look around at him, not yet anyway, and besides, I didn't want to be *too* obvious!

"No, I don't remember, I'm sorry, but yeah I'm still seeing Kelly, or rather we're writing as it's term time." He smiled warmly with his enormous mouth, oozing charm. At which point the twins interrupted and introduced themselves, taking my hand and turning me still further away from Lovelace. I was relieved as this gave me a bit more time to compose myself before the inevitable introduction to my left. Those few seconds were all I needed, and I wanted to get in first, after all, I had come here for this specific purpose. I took a deep breath, spun around, smiled and said, "And you're John." His mouth dropped open ever so slightly, as if he was going to say something, but he didn't. He closed his mouth in a gentle smile and his eyes seared into mine.

Moli

We whisked her away from the hall. Rob, being head of house got in first, inviting her back to the boarding house. She probably didn't realise this was forbidden territory for anyone in the other houses, let alone a member of the opposite sex, and we neglected to inform her. She was lovely. I could see what Lovelace had been talking about, he had been rather quiet since the Lillesden dance. I knew something had gone down there but details had been few and far between. Rob oozed charm, well, as did we all. Lovelace was unusually quiet though. We bombarded her with questions and made her coffee, told her about the house and about the school a bit. She had charmed us all. She was a stunner and obviously bright and intelligent. I think we all fancied our chances a little, and we arranged to meet her at the bus stop the next day and take her into the conference. En masse we escorted her to the quad and then watched her disappear down the drive in her dad's MG. I turned to walk back across the quad and noticed Lovelace was still standing there in the middle of the space staring after her. I walked back to him and blew in his face.

"Sod off Moli."

"Is that any way to talk to your best mate?" I enquired trying to sound hurt. He didn't move. "Ok… what am I missing here? Did you ravage her at the dance or what then?"

"I don't know…" he left it hanging.

"God you weren't that drunk, you must know what base you got to."

"You know Moli, it's not always about sex for Christ's sake!"

"Bloody hell! Snappy or what?" I was a little taken aback. I tried a gentler approach. "It isn't? So, what is it about then?"

"I don't know… I really don't… something weird happened at the dance, and it happened again today."

"Well tell me then…" I said exasperated, "cause from where I was standing you said bugger all to her."

"I didn't have to… it was weird, it was like some kind of connection… I don't know how to explain it to you."

I looked at his face, pained and confused.

"Well, there's only one thing for it then…"

"What?"

"Copious amounts of vodka, my show Lovelace, you need to get drunk and bare your soul."

I smacked him on the back and we sauntered off back to the boarding house, back to my show, to plan our strategy for the morrow.

Chapter 2

Lovelace

Thinking back it had all begun with a van load of over sexed, testosterone fuelled seventeen year olds, some of whom had been a little too heavy handed with the aftershave!

"Christ Almighty!" yelled Matt, one of the twins. "At this rate all the great girls will have gone so what's the point in going?"

"Don't be an arse!" exclaimed his twin in a bored tone. "Do you want to go back to school and do Prep Duty?" The minibus had broken down again so we all tumbled out of the side door onto the grass verge running along the edge of the road.

"Don't worry," said Mr. Brown in his New Zealand twang, "I think I know what the trouble is." Everything he said sounded like a question. We all groaned, we had heard this one before and had missed a rather important rugby match a couple of weeks previous. Still, it wasn't raining, the sun was shining, and the verge where we had stopped was wide with a gentle slope, so we stretched out on the grass for the duration. It was just good to be out of school and out of our uniforms. We were on our way to a school dance with one of the all girl boarding schools several miles from ours, which at the worst would mean we could get drunk, with any luck we might pull, or even strike it extra lucky and get a snog and a feel, and who knows what else? Moli had thought ahead and was quietly passing round a small bottle of vodka. Moli's my best mate, a rather rakish looking Italian Count; tall, slim, probably handsome with wild blonde curly hair (odd for an Italian), and a mouth a little larger than the norm, which always reminds me of the Cheshire Cat in Alice. Bodies honed on the rugby pitch, circuit training and in the pool, we were all toned, and that makes you pretty confident if you feel good about yourselves, especially when facing the opposite sex.

"Hey, Lovelace? Fancy a chaser?" We always referred to each other by our surnames or nicknames in school, it was part of the accepted school tradition, except for the twins that was; Green and Green would have been far too confusing. I propped myself up on one elbow just in time to see a small bottle hurtling towards my head. I caught it in two hands defensively which sent me flat on my back.

"Cheers," I called out, feeling in my top pocket for my cigarettes which I in return threw to Moli's expectant hands. I removed the screw top, propped myself up on one arm, and took a swig. It caught in the back of my throat and made me gasp slightly, at which point the packet of cigarettes landed in the front of my chest. Moli attempted to light his cigarette by flicking the wheel on his lighter, over and over to no avail. I leaned forward, and with one click, my Calibre lighter sparked into life.

"You want to get one like mine," I said.

"Where'd you get it from?"

"Nicked it off my dad," I laughed as I lit my own cigarette.

"It's ancient!" snorted Moli.

"1930's dress lighter… and it works every time!" I retorted, snapping it shut and pushing it into my pocket. "Have you ever known me without cigarettes or a light?"

"Have you ever known me without a drink?"

I nodded with a chuckle in agreement.

"Who knows, maybe we'll get lucky on the side of the road here?" Rob exclaimed standing up, hands on hips surveying the road they had just come down.

"Well I don't think much of yours," Matt replied to his twin brother, nodding in the opposite direction to where Rob was looking. Cycling slowly towards us was a little old lady who vaguely looked in our direction as she passed. We all chuckled and then turned in surprise as the old van spluttered into life.

"Well that was quick! I thought we were here for the night," said Hedges as he pushed past to get back onto the van. Hedges was very dapper, a good cricketer, great scores in Wisden every year.

"Well done Sir. Saved me from a fate worse than death!" chuckled Rob as he climbed in beside Matt.

"What?" said Mr. Brown confused, as he was head down under the bonnet when the local talent was passing.

"Never mind Sir," I said, patting his shoulder as I too clambered back into the thick claustrophobia of clashing colognes.

We were late. We could hear the music from the gymnasium as we arrived and there were at least seven or eight vans from rival private schools parked up next to ours. Moli groaned as he jumped down from the bus.

"Oh God! Look who's here." He indicated towards a van with a large heraldic crest upon the door, rivals from the ill fated rugby tournament.

"Bastards have a head start on us again!" remarked Moli. "Still, no match for us, eh Lovelace?" he added as he checked himself out, turned his cuffs and rearranged himself for comfort.

"Lose the cigarettes!" ordered Mr. Brown, but with good humour. Being an overseas exchange tutor he was rather lax on school rules about smoking. As one, the cigarettes were adroitly flicked over the top of the bus to the far side of the driveway, like a small shower of arrows shot from bows. I slid my arms inside my jacket and shrugged it up over my shoulders. Mum had it tailored for me, it fit like a glove, Moli gave me a nod of approval.

"Lets go get 'em then?" he said, and we followed Mr. Brown into the gym.

Once inside we made a rapid recce of the situation. It was quite apparent that, though we were late, the other schools had not yet pressed their advantage. They were still hanging back around the drinks table, or were in small groups gathered together discussing which girls they were interested in, but none really having the courage to approach anyone. Wasting no time, en masse we honed in straight away on a large group of girls talking together excitedly to one side of the hall. They were thrilled to be approached, moving straight into coy shy mode, giggling and batting their lashes. Moli had picked out his mark almost immediately, a tall red haired striking girl, who seemed to be the centre of attention. He got straight to it, oozing Italian suave charm, and without taking his eyes from hers, took her hand and bowed very slightly to her.

"Flavio Olivari de Molina, Moli to my friends." She was taken aback. This was not the usual approach, corny maybe, but it was so Moli; she was dancing with him in seconds.

I was drawing out some of the rest of the girls in the group in conversation. They fluttered their eyes and responded to my questions. Things were looking very promising, when suddenly I spun around. Someone had pinched my bottom. I was surprised but not sure who it was. To one side of me was Hedges. *Surely not, but then again not altogether out of character.* To my other side was a rather pretty looking girl. There was no competition, I certainly didn't want to spend the evening with Hedges discussing cricket averages, so I addressed the girl. She didn't seem at all shy, but then again she didn't look confident enough to begin a conversation with physical contact. But hey, what the hell, this *was* an all girls boarding school what did I know? She seemed nice enough and we began to chat about the usual things, what's your name? Gillian, John etc. etc. I got her a drink and things had progressed far enough for me to put my arm around her on the dance floor.

The music was slow and my gaze wandered around the room over the top of her head. As I turned her round I found myself gazing at a young woman who had just entered the room. She wasn't a girl, she was somehow more mature than the others. Perhaps she was a young teacher, but no she couldn't be, because in her wake was a day boy I recognised from St. Quentin's, only a year younger than myself. He was obviously with her as he was holding her hand. Instantly I was angry, this was a sixth form dance what was he doing here? And what the hell was he doing with someone like her? They looked incongruous together. I turned Gillian, so that I could follow her as she skirted around the outside of the dance floor. There was something about her. *Did I know her? No*, I knew that I didn't even as I thought it. *Did she remind me of someone? No*, I knew that was a non starter as well. But wow, I gasped and the intake of breath made my partner look up. Embarrassed, I looked down at her and smiled. She smiled back and looked down again. In those seconds this other girl had disappeared. A shot of adrenaline flew up the inside of my chest as I scanned the room for her, *ah*, there she was, talking quite animatedly to Mr. Brown. The track changed and I let go of Gillian. She stepped back and looked up at me. I wasn't sure of my next move, I must have paused a little too long, uncertain what to do next, so she took my hand and led me towards the back of the room where the table of drinks was located, and in the direction of the group with Mr. Brown. On drawing nearer it was obvious that Gillian had recognized the girl chatting to the master.

"Dawn!" she exclaimed, "what are you doing here? It's so great to see you and...?" She looked at the boy standing next to her, and then to Mr. Brown and pulled me like a trophy nearer to her, obviously proud of her acquisition and eagerly awaiting her turn to introduce me to the others. Dawn put her arms up to Gillian and hugged her tight around the neck. Her perfume wafted towards me and I breathed it in surreptitiously. It was light and fragrant and as her sleeve brushed mine, my stomach lurched involuntarily with excitement.

"This is my boyfriend Pete Penfold," she indicated to the junior at her side. I felt my eyes narrow ever so slightly as Penfold and I exchanged nods. Penfold was looking smug, not only was he at a sixth form dance, he was with a gorgeous girl and he knew it. What also puzzled me was that I knew Penfold as a bit of a weasel, definitely trouble, and couldn't for the life of me see what the attraction was for her. "And this gorgeous guy is Mr…?" she turned a flirtatious smile to Mr. Brown who was obviously flattered.

"Err Brown," he stuttered, flushing a rather deep shade of pink. He had been more than charmed by her too I noted. "I'd best go and check on the others," he added, as he stepped backwards out of the circle. It turned out that Dawn had left the school in the summer and had been invited back for the dance as she lived locally, and as her 'boyfriend' - *uh I hated the thought* - was a Quentin boy she had thought it ok to bring him along. Now it was my turn to be introduced.

"This is John," Gillian announced proudly pulling at my sleeve. She thrust her arm around my waist leaving me nowhere else to put my arm other than around her shoulder, which now I felt a little awkward about doing. It was then that Dawn met my gaze. It was an 'Oh my God' moment. I was aware that I was talking, making such remarks as, 'So you're an old girl' and 'Why did you come back if you've already managed to escape?', but I was even more acutely aware of her dark eyes staring back intensely at mine. It was as if we were removed slightly from the people around us. All my other senses seemed dulled and I had the impression that my vision had blurred around the edges, leaving just a clear tunnel from my eyes to hers, a thrill rushed up from below my navel into my chest. Gillian shifted position under my arm, but I was only vaguely aware of her and her odd comments. Penfold too seemed to have disappeared into the periphery, and it was just her and me in this quiet personal space. I watched her mouth as she replied to my questions, how her teeth caught slightly on her lip as she paused over a response. The shape of her lips, and her eyes, *God her eyes*. She seemed to be reading my soul, and I was completely unguarded as I responded again and again, urging her to tell me more about herself. It was so intense and private but that didn't seem to matter. I became aware that I must be appearing extremely rude to the others. I could feel the tugging on my arm and the shifting of Gillian's body weight against my side, but I couldn't take my eyes from hers, I was mesmerised. Did she feel the same? She couldn't possibly not have noticed, or maybe it was just me and I was deluding myself. Maybe it came from being deprived of female company for so long, but each time I looked across at her she was looking back at me, and there it was again, this intense connection between the two of us. Gillian dragged at my arm and I found myself unwillingly dragged onto the dance floor again. Pete was now staking his claim too, encouraging Dawn to dance with him, but even as we danced to the music, over twenty feet apart, our eyes kept locking. Although we were dancing with our partners there was a whole other level of communication going on between us, at least that was what I felt.

I watched Dawn wander over to the drinks table. Penfold had gone to the gents, and she had ladled out two glasses of punch…

Dawn

"Hey, can I get some of that?" I knew who it was instantly and turned my head. He was so close to me and his eyes were so intense, capturing my gaze. He held out two empty glasses and smiled warmly.

"Sure," I couldn't help but smile back at him. *Must be just one of those charming people that absolutely everyone finds attractive*, I thought, *and the poor guy has no idea why girls throw themselves at him*. I sighed as I filled the ladle. I was concentrating hard on filling his second glass when he suddenly moved it from under the stream and the punch cascaded onto the table.

"Oh I'm so sorry," it had gone all over his hand. I looked up into his eyes, they were shining and such a vivid blue, and he was smiling, almost laughing. "You did that on purpose," I said laughing back at him. He shrugged in acknowledgement then he looked up at me through his amazingly long eyelashes, eyes smouldering, but before he could say anything else Pete's arm descended on my shoulder. Lovelace bristled, he looked me seriously in the eyes, gave a final slight smile and backed away without saying another word. I was lumbered with Pete again.

Lovelace

It was getting hot in the hall and a slow record had come on. Gillian turned to me eagerly but I wasn't interested. Dawn had exited out of the side door with Penfold to get some air, so I grabbed Gillian's hand and nodded my head in the direction of the exit. Gillian eagerly nodded back, hopefully she would think that this was better than a slow record, I was taking her outside. The night air was cold compared to the interior of the hall, and there was not much room on the steps outside the fire exit. There was a small platform and then the steps dropped away to a terrace below. Dawn and Penfold were only just outside the door and it was obvious that he wasn't pleased to find us following them outside. I hoped Penfold was beginning to feel more than a little uncomfortable in my presence, he certainly looked it. Even though he was a good two inches taller than me, he was skinny, and hadn't accumulated the muscle that would have made him look a little more mature.

Penfold

I wasn't stupid, it was obvious, well maybe not to that gooey eyed girl he had in tow, but anyone could see that Lovelace found Dawn attractive. *Greedy bastard,* I thought, *what was wrong with the girl he had?* She was stunning with her long blonde hair and thick lashes, and on top of that she was obviously smitten with him. *What was it with these handsome guys? Did they have to go after every girl regardless? Or was it personal vendetta?*

Lovelace had been one of the prefects that had caught me

after the break in at the school tuck shop. I had been caught red handed and had been mortified when they had passed me over to Tubby, the housemaster. I had been caned the next day, but not before I had managed to freeze my backside. My dad was a dentist and I had managed to steal some gum freeze from the surgery prior to my punishment. Then I had, with considerable difficulty, injected myself in the cheeks with a good dose of novocaine. It had been really weird sitting on the bus to school on cheeks I couldn't feel. I had to act like it hurt as I was being caned, and I didn't think I was much of an actor. There was something even more humiliating about the whole thing without the pain that went with it, and then when my cheeks thawed out…! Still, I held Lovelace personally responsible for the whole incident. God I hated Lovelace, but now revenge was mine, I had something that he obviously wanted and I was going to make sure he knew that Dawn was mine, someone he couldn't get his filthy hands on. This was a fight I had already won.

Lovelace

He pulled himself up to his full height, puffing out his chest a little, and then leaned against the metal handrail next to Dawn. Looking me straight in the eyes Penfold smirked as he draped his arm over her shoulders. I leaned against the opposite rail and reached for my cigarettes, I wasn't rising to the bait. I flipped open the top and pulled a couple forward so that the lid was jammed and then I offered one to Pete. This took Pete off guard. Surprised, he took one, well he wasn't the type to pass up a free ciggy from anyone. I offered the packet next to Gillian.

"No thanks," she said, and then I offered one to Dawn. She smiled widely at me, her eyes shining.

"No, thank you, I don't smoke either. I sing." I had by now put a cigarette between my lips and was holding the lit lighter up cupped between my hands to shield it from the wind. I held it out to Penfold who bent to the flame.

Her reply made me smile, and raise my eyebrows. I was surprised at her answer. I lit my own cigarette and drew deeply. Still on the intake of breath I said "What? You sing in the bath or in the choir?" Then I blew my smoke out of the side of my mouth, diverting it away behind me on the breeze.

"I sing opera," *whoa,* that was a surprise.

"Not the most popular music at the moment?" I said with a question in my voice.

"Maybe not, but I can do it and I love it. I tried smoking once," she said, "but it knocks about four notes off the top of my register." I listened attentively. "Anyone can smoke," she continued, "but not everyone can sing. I reckon that if I don't make it as a singer then I can always become a smoker, but I doubt that it's possible the other way around." I looked down snorting a snigger down my nose and nodding in agreement, and then I looked up at her.

Dawn

He was looking at me through those long eyelashes, eyes smouldering. *Oh boy*, it was another of those really intense moments and my stomach did a back flip. Had he any idea of the effect he was having on me? *And why was it,* I thought, *that great looking guys have the longest eyelashes?* I felt a little self conscious, mine only approached half his length with copious amounts of mascara carefully applied.

"So what do you sing, are you a Brunhilda or a Queen of the Night?" I was impressed, he not only knew some operas but the characters as well.

"Neither, maybe one day the Wagner. I can do the Queen of the Night but it's not really me, my voice is a lyric soprano, more of a Mimi, Puccini's my thing." He nodded like he had some idea what I was talking about. He looked into my eyes again and smiled at me.

Lovelace

I hadn't a clue about opera, little did she know Brunhilda and the Queen of the Night were it as far as I was concerned. They were the only characters I had heard of and that was from an old compilation of my fathers'. I could very quickly find myself right out of my depth here and end up looking like a complete dork.

"Do you sing?" she asked me smiling. I gave a startled laugh blowing all the smoke out in a blast of exhalation.

"Err no," I laughed out, "no I don't think you would call what I do singing by any stretch of the imagination. Rather people would pay to get me to stop." She laughed, along with me. Penfold snorted, he was obviously annoyed that I was even talking to her.

"But I love modern music," I continued, "and I generally

groan along to it… the walls at school are thin, I have had complaints!" She laughed again and her eyes seemed to intensify as she captured my gaze, I took another drag on my cigarette. The breeze blew and she shivered. I started at this, I was making a move to do something but Pete was there ahead of me, throwing his arm dramatically around her again and pulling her into his side. It was only then that I realised that Gillian, who was standing right next to me, had her arms across her front and was rubbing them up and down in a bid to keep herself warm. She looked up at me expectantly, I popped my cigarette between my lips and shrugged out of my jacket and draped it around her shoulders.

Pete looked as if he had sucked a lemon, I think he was wishing he had thought of taking off his jacket. Still I was upset that I hadn't noticed Gillian was cold, I had been so preoccupied with Dawn. I didn't want to encourage Gillian any more and lead her on by putting my arm around her, but I didn't want to go in either, not as long as I had an excuse to talk to Dawn. Gillian seemed thrilled with the gesture, and was busily rubbing her lips against the lapel of my jacket, feeling the soft plush of the brown velvet.

Dawn

I had noticed the gesture with the jacket and smiled sadly, I was pleased for Gillian but now I was feeling a little self-conscious. Gillian was my friend and here I was flirting with her guy, a guy I didn't know. And what the hell was Pete up to? He had plonked himself in front of me now and was becoming very free with his hands.

Oh for pity's sake Pete, I thought in my head I didn't want him touching me. I wriggled free only to find that Lovelace and Gillian had gone back inside.

It wasn't difficult to escape Pete's advances, it really was getting cold outside and Pete was beginning to feel it too. Back inside, Gillian had got John back on the dance floor and was now wearing his jacket properly with her arms inside the sleeves. I leaned against the wall of the hall watching them. He wasn't the greatest dancer but even the way he moved made my insides churn. I could have cried, I was jealous and angry about how I was feeling. I was also confused, was I mistaken about the way he had looked at me... was still looking at me now? Perhaps he was just conditionally polite, hadn't the jacket incident just proved that? He wasn't even aware of my existence, why should he be? Gillian was very pretty with her long blond hair, mine was short and a boring shade of brown. Sickening disappointment flooded through me, I was a fool.

Lovelace

And then the dance was over, how could it have come to an end so soon? Hadn't we only just arrived? Panic and adrenaline flooded my body, the overhead lights were turned on and the Quentin boys were gesturing to me to join them. Moli was locked in a major snogging session with Kelly outside, and Gillian was urging me in the same direction. Dawn was trying to avert her gaze, and Pete was doing his best to put his arms around her, but without much success. Our eyes met briefly for the last time, there were no smiles from either of us. We had spent a whole evening together, though with other people, shared the most intimate of moments, though never touched, and now it was over. Gillian was now pulling at my collar raising herself onto her tiptoes, I looked down at her eager face and pulled back slightly. It was enough to make Gillian raise her eyes to mine. She let go and looked down with disappointment. I quickly looked over to where Dawn had been only a few seconds ago, she had gone. Physical pain hit me in the belly, I looked down at Gillian, agonised that Dawn had gone. I guess that Gillian misread this and thought my pain was for our parting. She pulled at the collar of my shirt and pushed her lips against mine. I opened my lips in surprise, to talk, but she pressed further against me and then I was kissing her back, hard. She wasn't what I wanted, she was intruding in my confused thoughts. I thought for a split second it was Dawn I was kissing, but no, there was no connection, no spark. It was just an action with its own rhythm, that would very quickly reach its end, which it did. Gillian looked like she was up for seconds but I held her forearms by the elbows whilst I caught my breath, and my thoughts, this kept her back from me. I raised my eyes to hers, and as kindly as I could, smiled and said, "Gillian, it's been a pleasure, you're great, but I have to go." She reluctantly shrugged out of my jacket. I took hold of her two hands, raised them to my lips, kissed them, then swung my jacket over my shoulder and ran off to the minibus without looking back.

Dawn

"Is that you Dawn?" called Mum from the living room as she heard the front door open and then close.

"Uh huh," I replied as I entered through the door from the hall into the lounge. Mum was laying out on a bed in the living room. She was recovering from a spinal operation and was spending her time confined to downstairs.

"What have you done with Pete? Was it a good dance? Did you see your friends?" Loads of questions all at once. Well it was hard when you had to spend most of the day and night on your own staring at the ceiling or the TV in the corner. Dad had taken a job in The Hague and only came home for brief periods at the end of each month. Mum was therefore not only immobile but lonely to boot.

I didn't want to think about Pete. I never wanted to see him again. It had been a very ugly end to the evening. He wasn't who I thought he was, but I had discovered that even before the dance. *How on earth did I let him talk me into taking him?* But now I hoped I was free of him, and things had changed from this evening on. I didn't want just anyone now, not after tonight.

"I met a guy," I spurted out.

"Oh really, I thought you were with Pete?" replied Mum.

"I was," I paused. *How could I explain it?* "And he was with Gillian."

"Oh yes?" my mum was immediately interested, she rolled painfully onto her side. I imagined his face as I talked about him, I felt lit up from the inside. Mum's life was such a vacuum without Dad being there that she hung on my every word. Not that she wouldn't have been interested anyway, but she was hungry for anything that informed her that somewhere, beyond the living room, interesting lives were being led.

I ignored her questions. "His name is John, John Lovelace, and he has the most incredible eyes, Mum. They were sooo blue... and we just looked at each other, and I couldn't see anything else. It was just him and me. I don't know, it was weird, it just felt so fantastic, and even though we were with other people, it felt like we were alone and we were talking just to each other and..." I paused and suddenly tears were pouring down my face as intolerable sadness struck me. "And I'm never going to see him again... what am I going to do?"

"Hey, hey," Mum waved a hand at me indicating for me to come over to the bed. "Why can't you see him again?" I knelt beside the bed, arms on the mattress but not touching Mum for fear of hurting her.

"Because he doesn't know my full name or where I live, and I only know where he goes to school... and he was with Gillian, and we're never going to meet again, and I don't even know if he liked me..." I trailed off and sobbed into the mattress. Mum rested her hand on my head.

"Sounds like you're in love to me," she said gently. She patted my head to get my attention. "I felt like that once..." she confided, whispering slightly. "His name was Dane, Dane Crosby. He was a lot older than me, but I thought he had the most wonderful eyes too, they were grey, dark grey. He only went out with me for a bit, I was too young for him I suppose, so we split up. He had a new girlfriend but he used to chat to me a lot even so. He probably just humoured me but I was besotted, I'd never felt like that before." Dawn looked up.

"What happened?"

"He was in the merchant navy, he was a signals officer. His ship was torpedoed and he was sending signals to the last… he went down with his ship… I was at school when I found out." She trailed off obviously remembering.

"Oh Mum…" I sympathised, sharing her pain, we held hands. "And Dad?"

"Well that's another story, but I've never forgotten Dane…" she said brightening her voice, "I believe in fate, and if it's meant to be, then who knows?"

"That's no help," I replied dejectedly. "What about Gillian?"

"What about Pete?" she countered.

"Well that's very much over," I said quietly.

Mum picked up immediately, there was something I was not saying, well, I wasn't going to tell her about that one.

"Dawn? Has something happened? Are you all right?" I shook my head dismissing it, I didn't want to say anything more about Pete. So Mum changed tack.

"Tell me more about this John then."

Moli

We were up in the prefect's bathroom.

"Come on Lovelace, how far did you get with that girl then? She looked like she was up for it, you looked like you had it on a plate there."

"Huh? Oh yeah," he didn't really seem as though he was paying any attention to me, he was miles away.

"Like that was it? Are we a little bit smitten then?"

"Did you notice that other girl? You know the one with Penfold?"

"Yeah… bloody sneak, what the hell was he doing there then? God knows how he managed to pull someone like her."

"Her name was Dawn."

"God Lovelace, how many girls did you get through then? First there was the group at the beginning, then the luscious blonde and now the dark little beauty with the turd in tow." I took a drag on my ciggy. I had my feet up on the side of the bath watching Lovelace gazing out of the bathroom window. He was pulling hard on his cigarette deep in thought.

"Did you notice anything strange?" he asked, still not looking at me.

"What, like she had three heads or something? No, I was a little preoccupied myself if you remember, and you haven't asked me a thing about how I got on, I'm wounded!"

"I mean did you talk to her? Did you notice anything when she spoke to you?"

"Are you going to give me some kind of a clue here?" I asked, not having the blindest idea what he was on about. He looked around from the window and to the side, snorting an embarrassed laugh. He obviously wasn't going to say anything else on the subject so I gave him a blow by blow account of my activities with the rather promiscuous Kelly.

Chapter 3

Lovelace

The Lillesden dance seemed ages ago now, we were all waiting for the number eleven bus as it pulled in opposite the school gates.

"I thought you said she was on this bus Lovelace," accused Rob as the bus pulled laboriously away from the bus stop. There was still a quarter of a mile to the crest of the hill, and the bus stop was on almost the steepest part of the climb.

"Must of got it wrong," I replied, trying to sound nonchalant about it, but sickening disappointment was flooding through me. It was the beginning of the conference and about ten of the Lancaster house boys had flocked to the bus stop with me, on the promise that one of the girls attending would be on the bus. I'd worked out the times, it had to be this bus, if she was coming that was. Moli pushed my shoulder with his in sympathy. I looked up and acknowledged the gesture with a slight grimace. I knew all of them fancied their chances with her.

As we strolled back down the school drive a mustard coloured

MG roared past us into the quad. I would have known her anywhere, even from just the back of her head. And then we were suddenly running, all ten of us in our bid to be the first to open the door for her. Hedges got there first and opened it with a flourish. Her dad seemed somewhat surprised to be surrounded by so many youths, he looked at us all dubiously. She got out to a hand held for her by Matt and span around to her dad, grabbing her bag.

"So, I'll see you later, I'll catch the bus home." Her dad nodded, now amused at the flurry of boys all around the car, and roared off again, spinning the car around adroitly in the quad and holding his arm upright in a farewell salute.

"Thought your dad was in Holland?" Rob had been paying attention when she had been chatting to us the night of the refectory meeting, and I knew he was hoping that she would notice.

"He came back last night, he's home for the week and then he's off again," she replied.

"Nice car!" said Day, another of the lads that had been introduced to her.

"Yeah, it's actually my mum's, but she's had a back op so she can't drive. Dad drives it as an excuse to keep the battery charged up, but really he wishes it was his. He tends to thrash it when he uses it though, which infuriates my mum." We all flocked around her shepherding her towards the main block.

Dawn

The talk was of cars. I knew Lovelace was there, I was aware of his presence even though he was standing back. A big butterfly got caught right in the back of my throat as our eyes met, but he said nothing. The boys were leading the way to the main hall again, where the introductory talk for the day was to take place. It was great for my ego. All these gorgeous guys currying for my favour, but there was only one person I was interested in, and he was keeping remarkably quiet. He wasn't even really keeping pace with us. I was suddenly full of self doubt again, I swallowed, maybe I had got it wrong after all. I looked wildly around for some sanctuary in the form of someone I knew and there was Sarah. She had seen me arrive with all the guys and she and several of the girls were making their way towards me, obviously eager to cut in on the action and grab their slice of male attention. I introduced Sarah to the boys, well those names I could remember. I deliberately left out Lovelace, I wasn't being that selfless even if he wasn't interested in me. The guys were hoping for this very moment, all their dreams come true in one introduction. They took their opportunity and moved in, escorting one or other of the girls to the chairs, each trying to bag a girl for himself. I was feeling so unsure and disappointed. The crowd around me had thinned and I felt a hand on the small of my back. What surprised me was the proximity of his face, his lips were almost on my ear. I jumped sending my heart hammering in my chest, as if it was about to beat its way out. He started back in surprise at my reaction too.

"Sorry," he said apologetically. We both laughed as we gazed at each other. "I was going to say, it's better to sit at the back, it's easier for a quick exit at the end." He smiled, his eyes creasing up again. *Dear God, did he know how handsome he was?* He knocked my breath away when he smiled. I felt myself staring at him, but it wasn't embarrassing because he was doing the same.

"Shall we?" interjected Moli, shattering the moment and bringing us both back to the present. He swept past us both taking a place two rows from the back. I followed, but as I turned around I was disappointed to find that Lovelace had slid into the row behind us. I turned around with a raised eyebrow, questioning. He smiled again and popped a polo mint into his mouth. He leaned forward holding the packet over the seat next to me.

"Would you like one?" He smiled again holding the packet up. His eyes captured mine throwing me into confusion.

"Err yes… thank you," I said as I took the packet from his fingers.

"Moli?" he said, indicating that he could have one too. I held the packet out for Moli but he waved his hand. I was about to turn and hand the mints back when he leaned over and gently took my hand, there was a slight pause and then the mints had gone. *Did they give them lessons in this sort of thing,* I thought. Or were all my nerve endings strained so tight that I was reading too much into his every movement? I couldn't be sure of myself, I had to try and calm down. *Come on cool it Dawn*, I told myself. The speaker was beginning. I was curious to know why he was sitting a row behind, so I picked my moment and turned around quickly to try and catch him out. He was sitting with his foot upon his knee, slouched down in the seat, propping his head on his hand, body turned, not to the speaker, but towards me. He was staring at me, not smiling, his face was serious, but he wasn't embarrassed that I had caught him, he just continued to stare. I turned around feeling myself going hot and red in the face. He leaned forward, resting his arms flat along the back of the seat in front of him and propped his chin onto his hands. Oh my God he was so close my heart began hammering again. He then turned his head and laid his cheek down on the back of his hand facing the side of my face and whispered.

"Are you interested in industry then," he paused briefly, "being a singer?"

My mouth dropped open and my breath shot out in a gasp. *Sussed!* I looked at him trying to read his expression. His blue eyes seemed to penetrate into me. I felt a stab in my chest and looked away. I felt like I was burning. So he knew all along how I felt. He was a player then, and I was what? Being played, his next mark? Tears pricked the back of my eyes and I felt sick. Panic was setting in and I couldn't breathe, all I wanted to do was to run, to get away. What a bloody little fool I was, how utterly naïve to have left myself so vulnerable. I had to get out of there, I just had to, either that or I was going to make a complete job of it all and break down in front of him. Too late, I could feel the first tear racing down my cheek, and I knew he had seen it. I stood up and started moving towards the end of the row.

"Excuse me, excuse me," I muttered to a group of boys who were sitting several seats along. *Why wouldn't they get out of the way faster?* Waves of adrenaline were shooting through the middle of my chest, stabbing up the inside of my throat. They pulled their legs back to let me through with puzzled expressions on their faces. Too late, he was there at the end of the row before me. His expression was confused. He held his hands up as if to say 'what?' *Yeah right, what indeed.* I looked down from his face and pushed past him as tear number two slid onto the floor. Moli was only just becoming aware that I had got up, and concerned he came fast after me down the row. As he passed Lovelace I heard him whisper.

"What the hell did you do to her? Poison her?"

It wasn't far to the doors at the back of the hall, but it seemed to take forever to get there. I fumbled for the latch, but a steady hand had got there before me. I looked up quickly, it was Moli, concern all over his face, he pressed down the latch and held the door open for me.

"Thanks," I muttered, looking down again as I ducked under his arm. And then I just ran. Down the shiny corridor, past the cups and flying out the doors at the far end. I turned, still running, to find a large expanse of grass in front of me with two large trees on the far side, and beyond that some gates to a road. I headed straight across the lawn, jumping the wall at the far end as it dropped down to the path below. The drop was greater than I had imagined and I jarred my shin bones. I ran straight out of the gates to find myself on a track. I slowed down to a walk breathing heavily, the tears now coming thick and fast.

"Oh Christ!" I said out loud with sudden realisation that I had left my bag behind in the hall and with it all means of escape. No bag, no purse. No purse, no money and definitely no bus home. Just how much more embarrassing was this going to get? Well I couldn't return now. I would just have to wait until the hall was empty. I reckoned the coffee break would be at about 11.00, and it was now? I looked at my watch. 9.30. Dear God, what the hell was I to do for one and a half hours? *Get a grip of yourself for a start,* said a voice in the back of my head. I bent over resting my hands on my knees, trying to catch my breath. What did it matter? *You don't know him. You've hardly even met,* I thought to myself. This brought on a fresh wave of tears. *But it does matter because you're a stupid, stupid little girl. You've gone and fallen in love with him.* I wrapped my arms around myself for comfort.

I seemed to have wandered out onto some playing fields and to my right was a steep drop, like the edge of a cliff, into which there seemed to be set some steps. I turned towards the steps and sat on the third one down. It was very high and my legs dangled without touching the step below, but I was well hidden from anyone, other than someone using them that is. No one could see me here, so I just sat in silence, tears streaming down my face, feeling my heart breaking. *What an idiot he must think I am.* How was it that falling in love happened so fast? How was it I hurt so much for someone I didn't even know? I gazed out from my hidden seat, I could see for miles from up here. The fields spread out below me, a bright patchwork quilt of colours as far as the eye could see. I pulled my knees up and hugged them resting my chin, trying to calm down, but I just couldn't. The tears flowed in a silent never ending stream.

"Are you ok?" a concerned voice came from behind me. *Oh God,* which one of them had found me? *Please God, oh please don't let it be him.* I buried my face in my knees and tried to sound light without looking around. There must have been several millions of places I could have been, how was it he had found me so quickly?

"Yeah, yeah I'm fine, don't worry I just needed some air it was a bit hot in there, I'll be back in a bit." *Like hell I would, just go away and leave me alone please, please,* I prayed in my head. Any minute now I was going to have to sniff and it would give the game away big time. Whoever it was wasn't going away though. I heard him starting down the steps behind me, but he had the grace to sit on the step above my head, his legs resting on the step I was on. I glanced over, that didn't matter I still couldn't tell who it was, they all wore black shoes and black trousers. *Oh God, horror!* Now my nose was running, this was just getting worse and worse. Humiliation complete, not only tears but snot as well, just terrific!

"I thought you might be needing this." My bag was slowly lowered onto the step by my side. *Thank you,* I thought, *there is a God!*

"Cheers," I said and without looking up, grabbed it and pulled it onto my lap, diving in straight for the tissues. I really wanted to give a resounding blow, but that would have been too embarrassing, so I kept wiping and dabbing, hoping he wouldn't see, trying all the while to staunch the flow of tears, which for some bizarre reason were still flowing freely down my face.

"You had me worried then," he paused. "I thought you were going to throw yourself off the cliff."

Christ! a joker, that was all I needed, but it made me laugh and the tears had stopped. I sighed. He interpreted it as a comment on the view, and I was just happy not to have to say anything.

"We tend to take it for granted you know, it's not until someone else points it out that we can appreciate it again." I didn't comment I just gazed out to the horizon. "Look… back in the hall…"

I froze, I knew exactly who it was sitting beside me now, and yes, throwing myself off the cliff was looking like my only option, but I knew I would probably make a mess of that as well. It was obvious there was no way to save face, so I took my tissue and did myself a favour giving the most almighty blow!

"Whoa!" he commented.

"Just don't," I snapped, and held up my hand to stop him saying anything further, "I don't think I need another crass comment right now." I paused and sighed. "Look, I'm an idiot, just toddle off would you and find someone who knows how to play your games, I don't know the rules, you have an unfair advantage."

"Dawn, I don't know what you're talking about." God, he'd used my name, there was definitely something alive and hopping about in my stomach. He clambered down onto the step next to me, but I still couldn't look at him. I had my hands either side of me pressed down onto the step. He laid his hand upon mine and squeezed it.

"Look, I obviously said something to hurt you back there, I'm really sorry." I looked down at his hand on mine. Were boys really that thick or was I a complete pushover? I looked up at him and I just didn't care. His glorious face was level with mine.

"Come on," he said slapping my hand, "it's coffee break, I'll make you some tea in my show if you'd like?" He jumped up on the step and held out his hand to me smiling warmly. I took his hand and he helped me to my feet. Pushover, I was definitely a pushover!

Lovelace

It just seemed the logical place to take her, somewhere I could talk to her and get to know her better. I knew I must have said something crass and needed to make amends, I had to be the perfect gentleman. Getting her to my show was really a piece of cake, there were so many strangers, mainly female, around the school what with the conference going on, that no-one really even batted an eyelid as I led Dawn through the boarding house. *Dawn,* I said it over in my head, *I could call her Dawn.* We climbed the back stairs above the housemaster's flat to the 'lighthouse', which was my room, or rather we called them our 'shows'. It was away from the others at the top of the stairs below the tower. I opened the door and backed into it encouraging her in with my arms open wide. I was praying I hadn't left anything laying about. There was a shirt and a pair of jeans draped over the desk chair, but otherwise my show was pretty tidy. I had the reputation of being the neatest in the house, it was born by my upbringing. Mum had always thrown out anything I had forgotten to put away. Consequently, it was either tidy up or lose my toys forever, that is if I didn't retrieve them from the side of the bin before Monday mornings when the refuse collection was made. It had made me pretty careful. Apart from the chair there really wasn't anywhere else to sit except for on the bed. I turned the chair around for her but she had already sat down on the edge of the bed, probably because it was right next to the door, and then she wriggled her way back until she hit the wall behind.

"Not bad," she said looking round in approval. I went straight to the kettle, filled it at the sink, plugged it in, then slung my jacket off onto the back of the chair.

"So… what's your preference then?" I asked her, indicating to an array of boxes lined up along the window ledge. "Lapsang, Earl Grey, English Breakfast or bog standard PG?"

"What do you usually have?" she asked.

"Depends on how I feel," I replied honestly.

"Well how do you feel today," she enquired.

"Mmmn… well I feel like Earl Grey today. How about you?" I turned to her. She pressed her lips together and shook her head.

"A little too much like smoked kippers," she said, "do you have milk, or do we have to drink it black?"

"No, no, I can do milk," I said, opening the window and pulling in a carton which was standing in the shade.

"How old is it?" she asked dubiously.

"Not that old," I said with a snigger, but I gave it a sniff just to be on the safe side.

"Then I'll have bog standard please." I looked into her big brown eyes, it was great to see her smiling again, made me start smiling too.

"I can do toast too if you'd like. I have butter, marmalade, marmite, and a few other things if you prefer." I made to go over to the toaster, but she stopped me with her reply.

"No, no, tea is just fine. Good God!" she exclaimed, "do you do self-catering?" She had got up and was eyeing up my array of marmalades jams and spreads over my shoulder.

"No, it's just a long way to the refectory from here and we're allowed to keep a few things." She was standing so close to me now. I swallowed hard, aware of my Adam's apple bobbing in my throat. The room was narrow and to pass her she would have had to sit down on the bed. Either that or I would have to hold on to her to spin her around and I didn't think that touching her would go down too well. She realised that she was blocking the way to the cups, so she backed up towards the far end of the room so that I could reach them.

"So… do you make a lot of tea?" she asked. I knew what she was getting at, she wanted to know if I had lots of girls up in my show, drinking my tea. I laughed nervously.

"No, just for my fellow inmates," I said truthfully meeting her gaze.

"Mm," she said nodding knowingly, I couldn't tell if she believed me or not. "So you don't make tea for Gillian?"

"Err…" gosh I didn't see that one coming. "No I have not had the pleasure of making Gillian a cup of tea." Oh God, that wasn't a good reply, did it sound as if I'd been doing a lot more than making tea for her? I grimaced slightly as I thought about that one, head down hands on my hips. I looked up at her, she seemed amused, though she wasn't letting it go.

"So… do you make toast for Gillian?" I'd better watch my reply this time. I hesitated looking down again for inspiration.

"Well I don't see Gillian at all, so there's nothing on that menu." Did she get that? Or was she reading something more into that reply? She was nodding again, thinking.

"Do you write?" she continued.

"Well, we have written, but we don't any more." I hesitated. "Look," I thought I had better draw a line under this, "there is no Gillian and I." I tentatively added, "Ok? Does that help you out any?" Oh boy, I hoped this didn't make me seem callous.

"Mm… maybe" she said, she twisted her mouth up and then smiled at me. She was so beautiful, I caught my breath, I covered it with a cough. Well at least I hoped I had. What was that about a watched kettle? I needed it to boil now. There was a knock on the door. Dawn froze.

"It's all right," I said, confident in the Lancaster secret knock, "it's only one of the guys." I went to the door and opened it. There were about five Lancaster House sixth formers outside, they barged past me pushing their way into the room.

"Come in," I said to their backs.

"Got the kettle on Lovelace?" asked Matt. "Ah, tea for two I see!" He smiled and raised his eyebrows as he looked at the two cups set out ready. "Hi Dawn," he said cheerily and sat down on the bed.

"We brought biscuits!" added Rob immediately on his tail. Plonking himself down as well.

"Shove up," he elbowed his brother in the ribs. Hedges was behind, then in came Day, and Moli bringing up the rear. I saw Moli and Dawn exchanging looks, checking if she was ok I guessed. I hoped she was, I glanced over to see for myself. Yeah, she was smiling and nodding. They all started passing round the cigarettes and biscuits whilst I tried to make tea around them. Just about everybody had lit up when there was a further knock at the door. We all stared at Dawn in panic. The cigarettes flew out of the window en masse and she was bustled over to me by the door. I pushed her behind it and, with a reassuring smile, put one calming hand on her shoulder as I opened the door. It was Tubby the Housemaster.

"Ah, you're all here I see. Good time to have a little house meeting I think," and he made to come through the door. Quick as a flash Moli was up on his feet at the end of the bed pushing straight out of the door and taking Tubby with him.

"Oh there's much more room in my show Sir, come on everyone," and they all streamed out of the door pushing Tubby back into the corridor.

I took a quick look at Dawn behind the door. She looked horrified and then she relaxed with sudden relief. I winked, squeezed her shoulder and said, "Back in a tick, help yourself to biscuits," and was off down the corridor chasing after the others.

Dawn

Show? What a strange name for someone's room, well maybe it was not such a strange word. It was *his* room, what better way to present your personality. He was obviously a very tidy person. I had far more on the floor at home than he did. Though it was small he had made it really cosy. The duvet cover on the bed was bright orange, which made the whole room look warm. He had Escher posters on the walls, you had to look at carefully to see what was going on in them. There was the water going uphill, I knew that one, crocodiles moving from 2D to 3D, and a rock that looked like a person in a reflection. *Dalí!* that one I knew too. Everything was neat and tidy, even the papers on his desk. What with the teas and marmalades all lined up, it *showed* up his personality pretty well. There was a wide dado rail running all along the wall behind the door and neatly stacked one on top of the other and side by side, were row upon row of Newcastle Brown Ale cans. I was admiring how attractive they looked what with their labels all lined up, when I had a terrifying thought. *Christ!* I was in the tiny space behind the door. Had I leaned back too far when Tubby came in the whole lot would have come crashing down around me, giving away my hiding place. Was that why he held on to my shoulder? I had thought that it had been rather sweet, and that he had been keeping me calm but now… And how much tea or beer can one person drink, I thought suspiciously? Was this Svengali's lair?

I looked along his bookshelf. There were some boring Advanced Level economics books, *Further Maths, yuck!*

History, better - oh Poetry? Mmmn… interesting, whose poetry? What was this? A book by Lovelace? I took it down from the shelf immediately. Looking back at me was a rather handsome cavalier dressed in a shiny suit of armour. I screwed up my eyes up trying to see a resemblance, it couldn't be just a coincidence could it? I tried again, this time trying to imagine the cavalier in a white shirt and black jacket, give him a modern day hairstyle and… possibly. I flicked through the well thumbed pages;

'Stone walls do not a prison make nor iron bars a cage'.

Mm, page 53 seemed very well thumbed and worn. This Lovelace must have attended a boarding school too, it was a very apt description of a school or a prison. My eyes travelled on;

'I could not love thee, Dere, so much, Lov'd I not Honour more'.

Hey I recognised that one, must be quite famous if I'd heard of it. I placed the book carefully back onto the shelf and looked about. *What else did this show tell me about the person who inhabited it? Cards! Several packs – maybe he was a bit of a gambler, no, there was a book on contract bridge. Pictures, school team pictures, where was he? Ah, right, in the middle with pads on, plays goal in hockey, oh and plays rugby too.* My eye had been caught by the next picture along the wall. Looking on down the wall the pictures continued. *Mm, plays a lot of rugby.* His physique wasn't lost on me either. *Nice body.* My insides were melting. *What must it feel like to touch him,* I wondered. *I mean I had touched him but to put your arms around him?*

What else? There were pictures of who I presumed were his parents, possibly grandparents, they looked to be a little old, especially when I could see the same person in a World War II uniform. *Must be grandparents, but where were the pictures of his parents then? Oh God! He wasn't an orphan was he?* My stomach lurched in pain for him. *Definitely an only child, no evidence of sisters or brothers, so all alone in the world except for the old couple?*

There was an electric fire on the floor with about four electric bars and a false plastic coal effect. *Must be for extra warmth, always useful in a boarding school, the heating isn't ever on at the right time,* I mused. He had a turntable, speaker system and hundreds of LP's all arranged in alphabetical order. *My God how long would it take him to listen to this lot end to end?* I had a quick look at some of the titles; Elton John, Free, Led Zepplin, Thin Lizzy. *Mmmn, I agree with those. Oh, and a large box of cassette tapes. No classical music,* I noted, *ah well, no one's perfect I suppose.* And that was about it. I wasn't about to pry inside his cupboards, that would have been an intrusion too far, but I could have bet that they were as tidy inside as was the outside of his room. I liked it, yeah, I really liked it and I really, *really* liked him. And if his room was anything to go by, he seemed straightforward, nothing hidden, just a genuinely nice guy who liked to drink tea, eat toast and marmalade, and listen to music.

The kettle was boiling its head off, so I poured it out and made myself tea. I wasn't sure how long they were all going to be so I didn't bother with making any more. I set the mug down on the side table and curled up on his bed to wait for their return. My head rested on his pillow, *oh my,* his cologne was amazing. I buried my face in it breathing in the delicious fragrance. I imagined him with his head on the exact same spot.

Lovelace

Why wouldn't Tubby shut up? He was droning on about making guests welcome and how St. Quentin boys must have impeccable manners. He must have outlined our duties several times over, how many people were needed to usher the groups to different areas etc. etc. on and on. I kept flipping up my watch, I didn't wear it on my wrist since the strap had gone over two years ago. I kept it on my trousers, on one of the belt loops. I had to remember to take it off when they went in the wash, but otherwise it was a good place to keep it.

I kept worrying about Dawn. What was she doing up there? Would she be all right? Or would she have got fed up and made her way back to the conference on her own? It was getting on for 11.30 now and the group sessions would be starting. Tubby was passing out lists of groups. I quickly scanned the list of names passed to me. How lucky was this? Dawn was in my group, in fact she was the only girl in the group. Well that was good news, I could make sure I looked after her. It was no good, I had to get back to her.

"I think I may have left the kettle on in my room Sir." Was that the best I could come up with? But it worked, Tubby was waving his hand dismissing me. I shot off back through the house and up to the lighthouse, pausing at the top to knock. Well I didn't want to scare the poor girl out of her wits. There was no reply. *Well there wouldn't be if she was hiding,* I thought. I slowly opened the door. She was in there all right, curled up on my bed fast asleep. I crept into the room and tilted my head on one side to see her face more clearly. She was stunning, just stunning. I couldn't believe she was here in my room on my bed. I just stood there like a lemon, staring at her, watching her sleeping. I don't know when it happened, but one minute she was asleep and the next she wasn't, and I was staring into her big brown eyes. She didn't move or say anything she just kept staring up at me.

"Hi," I whispered, "all got a little too boring for you?" She smiled at me and God what it did to my insides! It wasn't just my insides either, I shifted uncomfortably. What is it we men do? Think about sex every 15 seconds? *Jesus think about something else, dear God help me think about something else!*

"Sorry," she said sitting up quickly. I think she was a little embarrassed. Then she pointed to the wall behind me. "You should have told me about those" she said. My head flung around in panic. *What? What had I left out?* Now it was me that felt embarrassed, but I couldn't see anything amiss. I looked back at her puzzled. "The cans, you should have told me about the cans."

"I'm not an alcoholic" I said defensively.

"No I don't suppose you are," she said with a slight laugh, "but I might have brought the lot down earlier!"

"Oh!" I said relief and understanding colouring my voice. We laughed together. "We've got a group session if you're up for it?" I informed her. God, I hope she didn't think that statement was full of sexual innuendo. "You're in my group," I added quickly. She looked pleased. Well I hoped that was the look I was getting. I grabbed my jacket and flung it over my shoulders, another fifteen seconds had passed and I needed a distraction. "Come on then let's go," and we left my show together, and I escorted her back to the hall.

Chapter 4

Dawn

I had a date! I was going on a date with John. We had spent three whole days together at the conference but it hadn't been a date, not a proper date. Now the lines had been drawn and it was official, I was his girlfriend. Well for at least an evening. He had waited until the last day to ask me, and to be quite honest, I had been feeling the weight of not knowing what I was going to do after the conference was over. The days were fantastic, I was completely besotted with him, but once alone in my room at night, doubts had been creeping in. Maybe it was just a great friendship. After all he hadn't made a single move on me and it wasn't as if he hadn't had the opportunity on several occasions. I had been alone with him many times, drinking tea in his show in between lectures and group sessions, but he was ever the gentleman. He had been in my group and looked after me the whole time. We talked and laughed. *Oh God* I had so wanted him to touch me, but the conversations stayed safe, never betraying any feelings he might have for me. But every now and again there had been a look between us which had been just enough to keep me hoping that he felt the same way I did. That last afternoon as the time ticked away and the speaker made his closing remarks I realised that this was it. This was the last time I would sit this close to him. My heart was in my boots, I was going to have to smile and say 'well it's been great…' Despondency was washing over me and I disappeared into the loos to try and get a grip on my feelings. He was waiting for me outside with the others. I looked at my face in the mirror. Where was that confident girl now when I needed her? I had to somehow find a blistering smile, and then I imagined his eyes, his blue beautiful eyes. I could cry tonight but not now, not whilst I was still with him, breathing the same air. How could I not be happy? It was impossible to contain what I felt for him, so when I came out of the door and our eyes met I just felt lit up from the inside. His smile back was dazzling and he held out his hand to me, in front of his friends. I didn't hesitate, it just seemed so natural.

"Look chaps…" said Moli addressing everyone, "Tubby's called a meeting, so we'd best say goodbye to Dawn here. Lovelace can walk her to the bus stop." The guys were lovely, they all took turns to kiss me on the cheek and say 'farewell but come back soon.' John kept hold of my hand the whole time, that is until it was Moli's turn. Moli put his arms around me and gave me a big hug, then he whispered in my ear, "If he doesn't ask you out let me know will you? Cause I will." I laughed, then he kissed me on the cheek and let go of me. John immediately took my hand again and a thrill shot up inside me.

"See you Mols," it was a friendly but firm dismissal from

John. Moli turned and left us to walk down the drive. At first the silence was comfortable, we walked hand in hand and I occasionally looked up at him smiling. His head was bent looking down but he was grinning from ear to ear too. But he didn't speak and we were at the end of the drive, turning to walk down the hill, and now my smile was wilting. Happiness was deserting me and it seemed the longer the silence, the less likely he was going to say anything to me other than goodbye. I couldn't look at him now as I didn't have any happy reserves left. If I looked at him I knew I would make a fool of myself and cry. The silence lengthened and even holding his hand seemed uncomfortable as his fingers were twisting in mine. Suddenly we were at the bus stop and he let go. I looked down and bit my lip.

"It's been fun hasn't it?" he said. He was obviously looking at me but I wasn't composed enough to meet his gaze.

"Yeah, it's been great," I said, nodding then clenching my jaw so as not to start trembling. I scuffed my shoe on the ground. God this was awful, maybe I should let him off the hook. "Look it's ok," I said, "I've caught buses before."

Lovelace

"Oh" I replied, I was taken aback, *was she brushing me off?* I was so nervous now. Talking to her before was so easy, but now every way of asking her out seemed wrong. I couldn't seem to string a sentence together. Then suddenly I could hear the bus coming down the hill and my time had run out it was now or never.

"Look I was wondering… I was wondering…" *For Christ's sake man spit it out!* "I was wondering… if you'd like to go out with me? I mean for a drink or something." She wasn't looking at me and she wasn't replying. *Oh God,* I felt sick. Then she started nodding, she raised her head and looked at me. She was laughing. *What did that mean?*

"I thought you'd never ask," she said smiling at me. I laughed with her. "When?" she asked.

"Saturday? 6.00? I'll meet you in the quad? That is if that's ok? Or I could come to you?"

"No, the quad's great! It's a date."

"Ok then!" I replied, grinning like a monkey at her. The bus doors hissed open and she stepped on board. I think I floated all the way back to school.

Dawn

I don't think I'd ever been that nervous. I pulled out outfit after outfit onto the bed but there was something wrong with everything. Well, we were going down to the pub so jeans were a definite. That was the easy part, but what top? I finally settled on the blouse he had seen me wearing when we had met at the Lillesden dance. Bright red, a good colour on me with my dark hair. I paused applying the mascara. All I could think about were his eyes and the length of his eyelashes. I felt sure that if he had mascara on they would curl right up and touch his eyelids. I stabbed myself in the eye with the brush and then had to start over. My stomach was gurgling and churning, was I going to be sick? I was to meet him in the tower. I knew where that was, and Moli was going to escort me to make sure that I didn't bump into anyone or get lost.

Dad drove me right into the quad and Moli appeared from his hiding place against the wall in the bushes by the chapel. We watched the MG disappear then, smiling, Moli took my arm in a very old fashioned manner. He held my hand in the crook of his elbow. He wasn't hurrying, but he was keeping a good lookout all around.

"Tubby is on duty tonight," he said, "but we've posted a couple of juniors on the doors to the house and got a couple of runners if we need them. Matt and Rob are covering prep, and Day is on hand for any emergencies."

"My God!" I said in surprise, "It sounds like a military operation?"

"Well it is a bit," he said, smiling and looking around again. "But no-one minds, we all rather like you, and we know what you mean to Lovelace so…" *Oh God,* I thought, my stomach doing cartwheels, *don't stop there, tell me what I mean to Lovelace?*

"So…?" I tried to encourage him to talk on, using my eyes. He just gave a muffled laugh down his nose, he wasn't going to say any more. Besides I suspected Lovelace would have him later if he did. Suddenly we veered off to the left, up some steps around the far side of the chapel, away from the quad and into the shadows beyond.

"What?" I said in a hushed tone.

"Tubby!" whispered back Moli. We stopped for a moment, Tubby and some other masters were loitering over the far side of the quad over by the entrance to Lancaster House. There was no way we could get to the tower from here.

"Plan B," whispered Moli into my ear steering me back around the far side of the chapel. Having gone completely around the chapel, he shepherded me along the grass lawn that sat to one side of the drive.

"We'll have to go all the way around," he whispered again. I was just glad I had worn sensible shoes. Although the boots under my jeans did have slight heels they were quite thick so I wasn't in any danger of sinking into the grass. We emerged at the entrance to the school, whereupon a small junior boy popped out next to the gate. I jumped in surprise but Moli was obviously expecting him.

"Tell him, Tubby's in the quad and I'm taking her to the George." The little junior set off at a trot puffed up with the importance of his task, whilst Moli and I walked down the road and around the pub on the corner.

"So, you and Kelly?" I asked as we wondered down the road. "Is it still on? I mean I don't mean to pry but…?"

"Yeah, it's still on," he replied happily, "but then we never really get to see each other, and Lillesden is a hell of a long way away you know."

"Term's ending soon." I said trying to be helpful.

"Yeah," he sighed, "but then she lives in London and I'm going home to Italy for most of it, so you know…" he shrugged his shoulders and left his sentence hanging. "And then again…" he added looking up cheekily through his blonde fringe, "it's not like you two."

"You two?" I repeated questioningly.

"Yeah, aw come on… you know," he said playfully walking backwards down the road now looking me in the eye.

"Huh?" my breath rushed out in almost a gasp. "No I don't think I do know." I said not sure what he was alluding to.

"Mmph," he snorted with a laugh, obviously not believing me, and spun around facing forwards again.

"You know this isn't something we've ever done before," he continued.

"Oh no?"

"No definitely not," he said firmly. "I mean, give us a break, we don't exactly get out much!"

"And if you did?" I was doubting now. Was I just available then?

"Listen," he said spinning around again and stopping right in front of me with a serious expression on his face, "you've got nothing to worry about." He took a couple of backwards steps and then paused. "Jesus Dawn, don't make me say things for him. You know you've got a really great guy there, just don't break his heart eh?" Turning around again and walking on he added, "At least not before he's finished his A's."

We were still walking down the middle of the road, down past the lower part of the school and on up into the village. The pavement was all cobble stones so walking was easier in the middle of the road. There was no traffic though there were lots of parked cars along each side of the road. The road rose uphill again and The George pub came into view, sitting on top of the pavement, which was now some three feet above the level of the road. We climbed the series of steps up to the pavement and I turned to go up the further flight of steps leading to the front door of the pub.

"Not that way," said Moli, "we have our own entrance." He smiled and tossed his head indicating around the side of the pub. It was dark around the back and I kept as close to Moli as I could. It was pitch black and I couldn't tell what the ground was like or where we were going. I followed him inside the back door.

"Mind the step!" he called back.

"Ouch!"

"Oh, and the beam. Sorry I forgot you didn't know." We stepped down into the back of the pub. In front was the entrance to the rear of the bar. Moli greeted the landlord. "Harry."

He replied with an acknowledging nod, and said "Bar's clear."

"This way," said Moli holding another door open for me. We stepped down into a room. "We sit over here," he indicated to some high backed benches, "that way we can't be seen. What can I get you?" he inquired.

"I'll have a pint of lager please."

"Oooh, impressive, a pint girl!" he said grinning, "I'll just be a tick," and he disappeared off to get the drinks. I sat down on the bench, feeling protected by its high back. It was a little gloomy back here, but there were a few candles lit casting a warm flickering light. The benches were covered with long thick cushions and so were quite comfy. And then the nerves started to kick in. I thought about John up in the tower waiting. *Had he got the message yet? What if something had gone wrong? What if he had run into Tubby? And if he did come, what the hell was*

I going to say to him? It wasn't something I ever usually worried about, I always seemed to have something to say in all sorts of situations, but what if tonight I ran out of words? Would he think I was a complete idiot?

Lovelace

I leaned my head against my arm which was framing the window. *God, how long was it now?* I shot a look to the makeshift ashtray into which I had been flicking my discarded cigarette butts to gain some sense of time spent. It was impossible to say which were mine. The sixth form had, for some time now, taken over the prefects' bathroom in the tower, making it our smoking room. Long disused, it now housed the world's largest ashtray; it was our bid to see how full we could get it before we left at the end of the summer. At this time the butts lay only about an inch deep, having just crept over the plug hole. My dog ends however, were lost in the myriad of brands littering the stained enamel. I drew deeply on the cigarette still burning in my hand and strained my eyes as if to make them see further through the small window which, in daylight, gave the most stupendous panoramic view. Set as it was atop one of the highest geographical features in the county, the tower's view was unparalleled. A scuffling sound of feet climbing the stairs outside was enough to set the well honed survival skills in place. With a swift flick, the lighted ember was knocked off and, as my boot quenched the still burning core, the rest of the corpse was landing amid its fellows in the bottom of the bath. A quick exhale and a brush of fingers raking my hair from my eyes, I rushed to the door.

It wasn't who I had been expecting, or a master, it was Perkins, pink faced and breathing heavily from his ascent. Flushed with the importance of his clandestine task, he was eager to deliver his message and be on standby for further orders.

"They're in The George, Tubby was crossing the quad so…"

"Great," I interrupted with a broad smile flashing across my face. I grabbed Perkins' face in my two hands as I passed him and slapped him playfully on the cheek, then raced down the steep steps.

No slouch on the rugby field, I was flying now across Prefects' Lawn. Prep had begun so the area was empty of boys and masters. Within seconds I was through the main part of the school and running along the track below the headmaster's house. Out onto the corner of the rugby pitch, to the top of the scarp where it fell away and became a cliff come series of terraced gardens, which dropped down into the village below. I had to slow, the descent down the scarp face upon which the school was built was perilous in daylight, let alone in the pitch black. The pub in question lay at the foot of the slope nestled in the centre of the village and, between me and it, lay a decent of over seventy feet of roughly hewn crumbling steps. This was, however, a well used path between the school and the village, and we boys learnt the sequences of steps in our first year. We could all do it, even in the dark, without thinking. I was already reeling out the step sequence in my head, five then three, all the first ones were very steep and very high. The next series of seven was more even. *Look out for number three*, and so on down the slope getting ever nearer to my goal. I could see the lights of the pub below me and a man exiting from the back door. I froze as the man paused to light his pipe. As he began to draw on it I could see the embers glowing. The unknown man steered off away from the bottom of the steps. *Good, not a master then,* I didn't relish the prospect of having to go back up again to avoid an encounter. The steps were narrow and passing someone would not be possible without being recognised. Though I was now seventeen and had long passed that gawky adolescent stage, I was still immediately recognisable as someone from the school. However, dressed in jeans and a jacket, I could possibly have passed for one of the new young housemasters.

Dawn

Moli was back with the drinks.

"Sorry Moli, I should have got these…" he cut across me.

"You're joking aren't you?" he seemed a little affronted. "It's *my* pleasure. Anyway, I've got you all to myself. For a little while at least," he added. I smiled and grabbed my pint holding it up to him.

"Cheers," I said. He saluted with his and I took a long deep drink. Lager was a brilliant thirst quencher, and my throat was bone dry with nervous anticipation. I was aware that he was watching me drink. I paused and looked at him raising my eyebrows. He didn't say anything. "Tomboy!" I replied to his unasked question.

"Uh huh?" he replied.

"Well either that or an alcoholic like your friend. Quite a

collection of cans hasn't he?"

He laughed. "Well I can't say that he did it alone. You know there were quite a few of us willing to help him out, although he did pay for them all." We both laughed.

"How long have you known each other Moli?"

"Since the first year, we went to different prep schools but we've been together since the beginning." I nodded. "That was pretty gutsy of you, you know," I looked up and raised an eyebrow in question. "You know walking across the empty hall like that, seemed like you knew where you were going."

I looked at him over the rim of my glass and then said playfully, "You drew me to you Moli!" and I laughed.

"Yeah, that's what I was thinking… at first!" He eyed me with a wistful look. I changed the subject quickly.

"What's that you're wearing then?" I indicated to a bright blue bead around his neck.

"Unpolished sapphire," he said touching it with his free hand.

"Yeah right!" I replied with sarcasm, it was huge.

"No really, it's the genuine thing." I laughed disbelieving.

"So how did you come by that then?"

"It was my mother's, my father bought it for her." I didn't want to pry so I changed tack.

"What sort of music do you listen to?"

"Elton John. The man is an absolute genius. I have all his albums and go to every concert I can."

"Interests?"

"Flying."

"Really? Are we talking jumbo jets here?" *What a joker!*

"No small stuff."

"Remote control?"

"A little bigger, big enough to get in!"

Was he having me on? Time to steer the conversation in another direction again. "So what's *your* show like Moli?"

"My show?" he said surprised. "Well a bit like me really, I'm scatty."

"Untidy," I said, sure that it was. He smiled and nodded.

"Yeah, not at all like Lovelace's."

"Posters?" I asked. "Girl with the tennis ball scratching her arse?"

"Yeah, now you come to mention it," he laughed a little taken aback. "How...?"

"No I haven't been in, it was just a good guess. It's very popular at the moment."

"Aaah," he said, nodding and understanding.

"Guitar, I bet. Acoustic?"

"Electric," he replied. "Fender !" he added proudly.

"Fender copy, surely?" Thinking he must have made a mistake.

"Whatever!" he smiled mischievously.

"Exceptionally large amplifier," I stated adamantly.

"Exceptionally small amplifier. It is a boarding house, I do have neighbours you know."

"Mmm," I said thinking. "What next…? Whiskey bottles?"

"Vodka," he corrected.

"Lots of Vodka," I added.

"Lots and *lots* of Vodka," he chuckled taking the final swig of his pint. "I think you had better stop there before it gets a little too personal and embarrassing," he said laughing.

"Just one more," I pleaded.

"Go on then," he said begrudgingly.

"Teddy bear?"

He smiled a wide cheeky grin.

"Doesn't everyone?" he asked.

Lovelace

Thoughts of being caught were now secondary. My stomach was beginning to tighten and churn, and the saliva was thickening at the base of my tongue. My heart was hammering on the inside of my chest. I paused at the back door, took a deep breath to steady myself, and stepped into the darkened rear passage of the pub. The door direct to the bar was open ahead of me and the large frame of Harry, the landlord, blocked the light. He looked up from his work and acknowledged me with a nod of his head in the direction of the saloon bar. Harry was an old boy of the school and more than willing to turn a blind eye to any members of the sixth form who frequented the back room of the Saloon bar. The masters tended to frequent the other pub at the far end of the village, probably because it was nearer to their accommodation. We boys felt we had the best of it though. The George was much cosier, with the added advantage of a long saloon bar beyond which was an archway of beams and, if you could be bothered to go beyond the end of the bar, there appeared to be another room. Few ventured this far as their main aim was the bar and there was plenty of seating around the large, homely log fire. Further back, beyond the arch, the seating had been arranged so that the high backs of the benches hid you from the rest of the Saloon. Here we could relax with our pints, safe in the knowledge that we could not be seen, but also knowing that Harry, ever vigilant, would come and warn us should a master come into the bar. Then it would be a mass exodus out the back door, up The George steps, and safely into our shows before anyone was any the wiser. I dipped my head to avoid the door jamb and the low beam beyond it and stepped down into the rear of the saloon room.

Moli jumped up at the sound of the back door opening. “Lovelace.” It was a statement for those hidden behind the curtain of wood, and an acknowledgement to me that he had Dawn safe. Moli smiled knowingly at me and pushed past, empty glass in his hand.

“I’ll get you a pint,” he said looking sideways at me, as he passed on his way to the bar. I nodded, my face serious with apprehension and then I rounded the bench. My eyes met hers full on.

Dawn

Was it only two days since I had seen him last? It had seemed forever. His eyes met mine and my insides were turning over and over. He broke into a blistering smile, his handsome face was just alight and I guess mine was too because I couldn’t help but respond with my own joy at seeing him. *Great*, I thought, *no point in trying to be coy about how you feel, only an idiot couldn’t read that one.*

"Escaped from your tower then Rapunzel?" I said. He laughed out loud and replied narrowing his eyes.

"Sorry, weren't you the one that was supposed to come and rescue me?" he answered. I laughed and shifted up along the bench so that he could sit down next to me.

"Do you want another?" he asked, pointing to my half empty glass.

"Well I usually wait until I've finished," I said, picking up my glass in my hand and tilting it so that he could see how full it was. "But if I have to keep up with an alcoholic?"

He laughed again. "No, don't worry, I'm not working on the next wall for a couple of weeks." Moli returned with only one pint in his hand and placed it in front of his friend. "This one's on me, you can make it up to me later. I'll leave my window open Cinders and stand down the troops. Dawn, you are a delight," he said turning to me. "Should you realise the error of your ways you have only to let me know. By the way, after midnight he turns into a pumpkin." Moli turned to go and John slapped him on the arse as he went. "Thanks Mols!" he called after him.

"Moli says you don't get out much. That's pretty sad considering you're only what, seventeen?"

"Well they lock us in at night, but that's not true, we do escape sometimes." He took a swig of his pint and continued. "A couple of weeks ago Moli and I went up to town to see the Peter Frampton concert. We've been to a few concerts recently."

"You what?" I asked flabbergasted. "Do the school know?" He shook his head.

"We're what you call a captive audience. They think we are captive so they assume we are there." I couldn't believe this.

"But don't they notice you're missing?" He seemed to find this amusing and sniggered.

"Well, not really, you see we prefects run the school, the housemasters just think they do. We cover for each other and no one really bothers much." He continued. "It *is* what they train us for you know?" He looked at me like I was expected to know. I didn't, so he filled in the gaps for me. "Officers and gentlemen? Running the show? Lay down your life for Queen and Country?" I swallowed in response to that.

"So is that what you're going to do then? Join the Army?"

"Probably," he smiled, "though the Lovelaces' do have a nasty little habit of leaving men on the battlefield, and I don't fancy that scenario much," he smiled. I didn't want to think of him lying on some bloody battlefield, all that seventeen year old perfection...

"So we're talking London here?" I asked getting him back to the subject, shocked or impressed, I wasn't quite sure. I had never been so far afield on my own before.

"Yessss" he said slowly, pulling out the word. "We don't do it all that often," he said seeing the horror on my face and trying to reassure me, "just when there's something good on. Moli saw Backstreet Crawler the other day and didn't tell me he was going." He was obviously still smarting from that one by the way he said it.

"But, you can't get there and back in an evening, where do you stay?"

"Moli has a sister with a flat in Mayfair, so we bunk on her sofa."

I couldn't take it in, the thought of them casually skipping off school and dashing up to London on the train, like it was nothing at all, and no-one seeming to notice them missing.

"I go and watch the football too sometimes. Chelsea," he added as if that was a foregone conclusion. "Only I don't tend to do that anymore," he said putting his pint down. He turned his head and smiled at me, his eyes twinkling with mischief. "I was a bit of a bad boy see."

"Ooh, now I'm intrigued" I said hanging on his every word, urging him on to furnish me with every little detail of the story.

"Well there was a little bit of trouble with some skinheads, and I got slightly involved."

I was shocked. "You don't look like a typical football hooligan," I said.

"Well I'm not really. It's just I was in the wrong place at the wrong time. It's difficult trying not to retaliate when someone is trying to kick your head in, and I sort of got picked up by the police along with everyone else."

"Oh my God! What happened?"

"Well they phoned my parents."

"Oh good," I said relief saturating my voice.

"Good?" he asked, surprised.

"Yes, good." My voice dropped, I shrugged embarrassed. "I couldn't see any pictures of your parents in your room." He shook his head not understanding. "I thought you were an orphan," I confessed.

He spurted out a laugh. He nodded to himself. "There were pictures..." he said quietly looking down and flicking a crumb across the table. He seemed for a second to be far away.

"Anyway," he pulled himself back from his thought with a big intake of breath. "I had to find my way back home and present myself before my father's desk. He gave me his 'very disappointed speech' and packed me off back to school."

"I'm amazed you weren't expelled," I said.

"The school never found out about it." He stretched his back. "But I tend not to do the football matches any more." He turned his eyes on me full blast and gave me one of his devastating smiles.

"What about you?" he asked. "Are you a good girl?"

"Depends what you mean," I said dropping my eyes. I didn't like the way this conversation was turning. My stomach did a back flip, and it wasn't because of him for a change. He picked up on it straight away.

"Come on," he said "I've told you all my dirty secrets. You're what seventeen?"

"Sixteen," I interjected.

"Sixteen then, you haven't had much time to do anything too bad. Weren't you locked up in a boarding school too until quite recently? You can't have had time to murder anyone just yet."

"I wasn't a boarder, I was a day girl. So you see I've had plenty of time to collect a past." I said playfully. *But if you think I'm telling you anything you've got another think coming,* I thought to myself. *Besides, I don't think you would like me very much if you knew my past.* I must have looked a little sad as I thought this to myself because his smile vanished and concern flashed momentarily across his face. At that moment the back door opened and Harry the landlord appeared and whispered loudly over the back of our seat.

"Masters in."

"Come on," whispered John, and he jumped up grabbing my hand pulling me after him towards the back door.

I was acutely aware that I was holding his hand as I followed him out. I hadn't touched him since the walk to the bus stop. Outside we didn't go round the front of the pub, John was towing me to the right.

"We're going up the steps," he said, "they're pretty steep, they come in sets. Put your hand on my belt and I'll call them out to you." I didn't understand what he was talking about so he grabbed my hand and placed it on the belt on his waist. I felt him going up the steps in front of me.

"Three," he called out, and there were three steps. We continued up the steps with John calling out the numbers, I was very impressed as it was pitch dark. He paused half way, "You ok?"

"Yep," I replied, I didn't have any spare air to say more and I didn't want him to think me unfit. Towards the top though they became much steeper and I was puffing like a steam train by the time we emerged. It was stunning up here. The sky, free from any light pollution, was a mass of stars. It was so clear you could see the Milky Way.

"Wow," I said looking up. I still had hold of his belt and he turned around to face me bringing me in close to him. My arm was now wrapped around his waist. We were both breathing heavily and I could feel his breath in waves on my face. He touched my forehead gently brushing my hair from my eyes, and then pulled me even closer.

"Wow," he whispered looking down at me. My heart was in my throat, I felt like I was hyperventilating. I looked up at him, then he bent his head down and gently kissed me.

His lips were so soft, I opened my mouth slightly and he pushed his tongue gently inside. *Oh my lord, he was kissing me, touching me.* All kinds of thrills were running up and down my spine. My breath was ragged now and so was his. I pulled myself closer, he kissed me harder and harder. I didn't want him to stop. I could feel his strong arms pulling me tighter. *This was incredible.* We moved as one. It was so intense, so sensual that I was lost from that point on. Time, what was that? I just wanted to stay in his arms forever.

Eventually we had to stop to catch our breath, to pause. We rested our foreheads against each other's gasping for air. I clung onto his belt. I was so light headed and on the point of fainting that I gripped his belt tighter with one hand, trying to steady myself and his arm with the other, unknowingly pulling his hips into mine. His arms were wrapped around me.

"Dawn," he whispered, "I love you."

"You want me," I replied with slight sarcasm in my voice.

"Yes," he breathed out on a chuckle, surprised by my answer, "but I love you," he said seriously. There was only one reply I could make.

"I love you too," I confessed, and he kissed me again.

God she was wonderful, soft and warm, and her kiss, well I had kissed girls before but there was a sweetness and an intensity that heightened all my nerve endings, and I hungered for more and more. It was such a powerful feeling and I wanted her so much, but I was scared of the power of it too. *And God what did she smell of?* I rubbed my nose up and down the side of her neck breathing in her incredible scent. And then I froze I could hear someone coming up the steps behind us. The master in the pub! I squeezed her shoulders and held her still.

"Get down," I whispered in her ear. *Wrong thing to say. Big time!* It was just about the most tactless two words I could have possibly picked. As soon as I had said it I heard her brain click and she turned to stone in my arms. I had two choices, neither of them good. Either clamp my hand over her mouth to stop her screaming or let her go and pray to God she saw the master before she let fly at me. I hadn't time to think, I chose the latter knowing that she would move backwards away from me and away from the top of the steps. I let go of her and she instantly stepped back. I followed her quickly back towards the shade of the trees. She held up her two hands in front of me as if to fend me off. She hadn't made a sound yet, but I knew it was coming. I turned around away from her, dodging to the side and kneeling down on one knee, hoping she could see enough of me to get the message. *Thank God she'd cottoned on.* I looked around to see if I could see her in the dark. She was there crouching a bit behind me.

Whoever it was stopped at the top of the steps, hand on

his back, snorting, puffing and grunting with the effort of the climb. We held our breath, which seemed like ages. *God this person was unfit.* He had his back to us.

"I'll expect to see you in my study in an hour," he said calmly without turning around. "After, that is, you've seen the young lady home." He didn't turn around, he just stood up straight and walked off down the lane back to the school.

"Christ," I said putting my hand on the top of my head and pulling at my scalp in frustration. "Pri… errr, Mr Rogers" I said realising that his nickname wasn't polite in the company of a lady.

I looked around at Dawn. My eyes were so accustomed to the dark now that I could see her face quite clearly, but I couldn't read her expression and didn't know what she was thinking. How must she be feeling? I had put her in a horrendous position.

"I am so… sorry," I said lamely. She looked down not meeting my eyes. I wanted to take her in my arms, but a few seconds ago she must have thought me some sort of rapist and the gulf between us was getting bigger and bigger. I just didn't know what to do or say to her. I felt as though some huge hole had been ripped through me. I'd blown it, I had so blown it, and I was in agony for her as well as for me.

"What will they do to you?" she asked quietly, looking up at me again.

I shrugged. "Not a lot," I tried to be casual.

"Will they expel you?"

"I doubt that, it's not that they've got much on me. Well

except for the smoking, underage drinking, and the visitors on school premises without permission." I smiled sideways at her in a sort of apology.

"Don't join the army," she said in a small quiet voice looking down. She looked up at me, and a tear slid down her cheek. "Please don't join the army?" She looked me in the eyes and added, "You don't seem to be terribly lucky." I put my hands around her face cupping it gently. And I didn't care if it sounded corny but I just felt if from the bottom of my heart.

"I'm the luckiest guy in the world."

Chapter 5

Dawn

"We'd better phone my dad then, he'll come and pick me up."

"How long will it take him to get here?" he asked.

"About twenty minutes," I answered.

"Then we'll call him from the school in about forty minutes, we have an hour." He said flipping up a watch attached to the belt loop on his trousers and checking the time.

One hour, I thought to myself, *and then what? I might never see him again.*

"Are you ok?..." he stuttered. "With me I mean?" he asked concerned. "Or would you like to be around other people? I mean… I must have sounded like… you know… yet another crass comment."

"No… I think I'm pretty safe, though I doubt if you are," I added with a smile. "Where do you want to take me?"

"Well I'm sure I can't get expelled twice in one night so… how about the tower?"

"Ok," I said, "lead on." He took me by the hand and led

me back along the track. He didn't seem worried about being caught, now that he had been, and we walked right through the school grounds without bumping into anyone.

"Where are they all?" I asked.

"Supper… in the refectory," he added, "we're ok for about forty minutes."

He held the door to the tower open and I went inside. It was dark inside and the wrought iron, circular staircase went up and up. I stopped at the first landing.

"No, not there, that's the smoking room. You wouldn't like it in there," he said "keep going."

The stairs wound up and up until we came out into a largish room filled with old trunks. There was a small electric light on and as I rounded the pile of trunks I could see one of them had been set out like a table with some mugs, and the kettle was standing on the floor plugged in over by the wall. There was a lot of dust but this area had been swept clean.

"Someone's gone to a lot of trouble I see?"

"Well I don't know about you but I like tea," he said coyly.

"Earl Grey today is it?" I asked.

"Bog standard," he replied.

"So you were planning on kidnapping me and taking me up to your tower then?"

"Err no…"

I looked around, and asked, "So other than tea, what were you going to do with me?"

"I hadn't got that far," I answered truthfully, "just talk I guess." *Oh no,* it looked like I had got her up here to take advantage of her. God I was so bad at this, and after my remark by the George steps I half expected her to turn tail and run. I put my hand to my forehead in despair and then ran my fingers through my hair onto the back of my neck. "Look I'm sorry," I shrugged giving up and sitting down hard on the trunk, head down fingers in my hair. "I see what this looks like now… I didn't mean anything like that… I just thought it was somewhere to go… and have tea… and talk … you know … in case it rained." I trailed off, and laughed at myself in despair. God it sounded so limp, I was a completely useless arse. I hadn't thought this through from her point of view at all. I must seem like the biggest player of all time, either that or the biggest idiot, and only I knew which of the two it was. I sat with my elbow on my knee and my chin in my hand totally dejected. This had to be the worst date in history, apart from the kiss that is. I seemed bent on wrecking the whole thing, lurching from disaster to disaster.

She came and sat down on the floor by my feet leaning against the trunk both legs tucked up to one side.

"You've *obviously* never done this before," she said kindly. *Wham!* That was a blow in the chest. *Yeah, I'm a right idiot,* I thought in agreement with her. "You need to know something… about me I mean," she continued.

I looked down at her.

"I'm not a virgin," she said looking me straight in the eyes.

Woah, I wasn't expecting that, it knocked me backwards for a moment.

"You need to know that, in case it's important to you." She didn't blink she just stared at me.

I thought about it for about a micro second and looked her straight back in the eyes, shook my head and said truthfully, "It's not important to me."

"You might need some time to think about that one," she said again not taking her eyes away from mine. "He's a Quentin's boy."

I looked at her blankly trying to fill in the missing information. I dropped my head and nodded biting my lip as I did, the realisation striking me.

"Penfold," I said nodding my head. I looked straight back into her big brown eyes shaking my head. "It's not important to me," I repeated.

She screwed her lips up still not taking her eyes off me, looking dubious.

"You hate him," she said.

I nodded, I couldn't deny that.

"But I love you," I had never been surer of anything in my life.

I swallowed and took a deep breath, well if it was time for confessions… "You need to know something about me too," I said, looking into her eyes. God I was actually shy. I gasped, I couldn't believe I was about to say this but I carried on. "I *am* a virgin… Is it important to *you*?" I stared into her eyes.

"No… no that's not important to me." She smiled gently,

"I love you too," she said and her voice broke slightly with the weight of her emotion. I bent down and kissed her softly.

Dawn

It was time to call my dad. There were only twenty minutes left before John had to go before Mr. Rogers.

"You know I could wait until after, I could stay up in the tower and then call my dad."

"No, they'll ask me if you're home safe, and I don't know, I just don't want to lie about that one," he replied.

I was having to use the boy's phone in the boot room. Tubby had met us at the main house door and had a quick quiet word with John before sending us along to make the call.

"Dad," I said, "can you come and get me?" I put the phone down. "He's on his way." I said glumly. Moli came to the door looking sympathetic.

"Tubby says you can wait in his office for your dad. Do you want me to wait with you?" he asked helpfully.

"No it's ok," John replied. "I'm allowed to stay with her until he comes. Can you put a junior on the door and come and tell us when he's in the quad?"

"As good as done." He stopped as if to say something else but just gave a sympathetic shrug and went. John took my hand and led me through the boys' boarding house to the flat down by the back stairs. I looked up in the direction of John's show and then down at the large office door which was standing open.

"Don't worry," he said, "it will be ok."

"It'll be ok for me but what about you?" I asked. He just smiled and shrugged. We went in.

Tubby got up from behind his desk, smiled gently and held out his hand for me to shake. That was a surprise. He looked at me with sympathy and said "I'm sure you will appreciate the necessity for this." He smiled again at me and then addressed John. "You may see she is returned to her father and then I'll meet you in Mr. Rogers office Lovelace." It was all quite gentlemanly. I reckoned the fireworks would follow after I had gone. He left leaving the door ajar. It was a warm office if a little spartan. There was a fire in the grate and a pot of tea on the table with two cups and some biscuits. I started to shake. I was terrified for John. I grabbed him around the waist and held on tight. Goodness he was slim, but all muscle. He held onto me too, resting his head on the top of my mine.

"This is all my fault," I said shivering.

"Hey, no it's not," he replied, pulling me closer still.

"I feel sick," I said.

He took my face in both his hands pulling me up to look at him. Then he turned the full force of his dreamy blue eyes on me again and smiled brighter than I had seen him do so before.

"It's going to be all right, really," he urged, "and I don't care what happens, because I have you now, right?"

What a silly question. He had me the first time I set eyes on him, that very first time at the Lillesden dance, when Gillian had introduced him to me. I just gazed into his eyes and tears started to fall down my face.

"They can't kill me you know," he said holding me close

again. "Hey, they've left us some tea," he said, trying to distract me and nodding to the teapot, but not letting go of me. "Would you like some?" I couldn't reply, I just shook my head. Then he suddenly let go of me and grabbed a pen off Tubby's desk. "Here," he said, scribbling down on a piece of paper which he had torn off a spiral notepad. "This is my number, my *home* phone number and this is my parent's address, I'll give you the school boot room number as well," he said eagerly. "Tell whoever answers that you want to speak to Lovelace and they'll come and get me. If they won't let me talk to you ask for Moli, he'll relay messages for me. Curfew is at 10.00, after that we can't take calls." He held out the piece of paper and then turned the pen around to hand to me. I turned to the desk and scrawled out my number and address and then gave that to him. "If all else fails I'll leave a message with Harry at the pub, ok?"

"Ok," I said trying to pull myself together. I thought how brave he was being, after all this was the worst that was going to happen to me, well Dad might have something to say, but this was only the beginning for John. And his exams weren't too far away either. *Oh God*, what a mess I had made for him. I tried to smile at him but just wanted to feel his reassuring arms around me again. He read my mind and pulled me close again kissing my forehead, then my nose and then my lips.

"Mhhhhm..." came a forced cough from the open door, and a junior announced, "there's an MG in the quad."

"Thanks," said John looking up. He didn't let go of me, he looked down and asked, "Are you ready then?"

"No," I answered but smiled at him. He smiled down at me, let go and took my hand.

"Ok then," he whispered to himself and led me from the office.

Out in the quad, it was quite obvious that no one had approached Dad, so John walked me up to the MG and opened the door for me. The roof was up so he squatted down by the door. I introduced them. "Dad, John. John, Dad." Dad addressed John briefly with a nod saying his name. John replied to him "Sir," then he looked at me with a tight lipped smile and nodded. He stood up and slammed the door shut, and we roared off down the drive. I looked back at John in the wing mirror. He was standing in the middle of the quad with his hands half in his front jean pockets watching us go, and then he turned to face the music.

*

"Had a good time chickie?" Dad asked lightly. He didn't wait for a reply. "He seemed a nice lad."

"Oh Dad," I said, bursting into tears.

"Hey are you all right?" he asked sternly slowing the car down with concern, trying to see the road and my face at the same time.

"Oh God Dad, it's such a horrible mess," I broke down into uncontrollable sobs. Dad found a place to pull over and turned off the ignition.

"Want to tell me about it?" he said gently, offering me one of his big white hankies he always kept in his pocket.

So I told him all about it.

"Mmmn," he said thoughtfully after a while. "So let me get this right. Your date was to meet him down the pub, then you left when a master came and got caught canoodling in the school grounds, that about it?" he asked. I nodded. "Well, the first thing is to stop crying, that isn't going to help anyone," he said gently. "The second thing is that he's right, they can't kill him, it's not allowed." He continued. "It isn't a capital offence you know. He isn't the first and he certainly won't be the last to have a drink in the local pub. It's been going on for generations, you can bet the school has faced that one before. As to the 'canoodling', well, I don't think he's the first to be caught doing that either." He sniggered, which caught me off guard. "Got caught myself once, with your mother," he added. "Not by the school but by her mother. God it took me a lifetime to live that one down, you should have heard her." I laughed for the first time since I had entered Tubby's office. "However," he continued, "you are my daughter."

"Aw Dad, come on," I said.

"And you say you love him?"

"Uh huh."

"What are we talking here Dawn, a crush? Or something more?"

"Something more, definitely something more," I said quietly.

"Well then!" he paused for me to look at him. "He deserves a damned good thrashing then," and he laughed his head off, turned over the engine and roared off down the road.

*

The wait was agonising I sat at the bottom on the stairs in the hallway with the telephone next to me and watched the clock ticking round. *Oh God, what were they doing to him, caning? Or had he been expelled?* I was so deep in speculation that when the phone rang I actually screamed as I jumped at the sound. I picked it straight up after the first ring.

"Hello?"

"Dawn?"

"Moli? What's going on?"

"Well I'm sorry to say that Lovelace was beheaded at 9.45," he said in a serious voice.

"What?"

"Well don't worry, he's still alive. They couldn't get through his thick skull," he joked, "but he can't come to the phone right now."

"Why ever not?"

"Because he's been gated."

"Gated? What's that? Sounds horrendously painful."

"Yeah it is," he said trying to sound serious. "They chain you up by the wrists to the school gate and then we all shout rude things at him," he fell about in a fit of giggles. "No, just means he's banished to his show at the moment pending further punishment. He's not allowed to make calls home," he added. "He's not allowed out at all and it's ixat next weekend." It sounded like he was hiccupping!

"Dear God, what's ixat?" Although I'd been at a boarding

school I wasn't party to some of the odd things the boarders got up to.

"It's a long weekend at home, you know, Friday night to Monday morning. If you live nearby like Lovelace does, you get to go home. I can visit my sister in London or other overseas boarders get to go to their guardians. But poor old Lovelace has to stay in school. So does a master to look after him, so he's not popular all round at the moment."

"You mean exeat you moron!"

"That's what I said!" he said, getting a fresh attack of the giggles.

"They haven't expelled him then?"

"No, not likely to either this close to exams. Anyway it's not like he's taken off to London to a pop concert or a football match, or been arrested or anything serious like that eh?" Moli seemed to find this highly hilarious and was now wetting himself at the other end of the phone.

"Bastard," I said laughing down the phone too. "You told me he didn't get out much!" I said in an accusing tone.

"Well he's not now," he said, going into fresh hysterics.

"By the way, he gave me a message to pass on to you but I'm too embarrassed to say it," this brought on a fresh wave of hysterics. He sounded as though he was doubled up on the floor crying.

"Have you been drinking?" I asked. The laughter was becoming contagious.

"Clear liquids only," he said, hardly able to contain himself or to make the words audible.

"Dear God." I sighed.

"Have you any messages for the condemned man?" asked Moli pulling himself together a little.

"Yeah, I have actually. Tell him, 'Lovelace page 53.'"

"Page 53?" he said questioningly, sobering up a bit more.

"No." I paused "'*Lovelace*, page 53.'"

"Got it!"

"Got it?" I was dubious to say the least! "Then repeat it," I instructed.

"Lovvvvelaaaaaace," he drew this out dramatically, "page 53. What's that, some sort of code then?"

"I'm sure he'll tell you, if you remember the message that is."

There was a crash on the other end of the phone.

"Oops."

"What was that?"

"I dropped my cup of 'water,'" he replied seriously and then began giggling again.

"See you Moli."

"See you Dawny," he replied cheerfully.

I shook my head in disbelief. *Jammy bastard,* I thought, *and there I was thinking it was the end of his school career.* Maybe he was lucky after all!

Lovelace

"Page 57?" I said to Moli, "What do you mean page 57?"

"Oh, it could have been page 53 now come to think of it," said Moli through the open door to my show. I wasn't allowed out and he wasn't allowed in so we talked through the open door.

"God Moli you are such an arse. That doesn't help me any," I complained. "You've been drinking too much 'water' again, you should stick to the Vodka," I told him crossly.

"53, yes it was definitely 53… or 57? God Lovelace, I try to help you out and all I get is complaints."

"Did you pass on my message?" I asked eagerly?

"No! I said I refused to pass it on because it was embarrassing." He replied adamantly.

"Saints preserve us," I said in a tired response. "So what do you think it means then 53 or 57? Do you think it's the bible? Maybe its Psalm 53 verse 57. Do you have a Psalter Moli?"

"Don't be stupid, all I possess is the Gideon Bible, as do you for that matter." He started lighting up a cigarette.

I went in search of my Gideon Bible.

"Could be Psalm *57* verse *5, 3*" Moli called out from his perch in the hall.

"Very helpful," I called back sarcastically.

"Hey!" He shouted out. "Maybe… maybe," he said slowing down for dramatic effect "it's a grid reference? Yeah, who's cooking now baby?" He was congratulating himself on his new theory. *Come on think, think Lovelace what could she have meant?* I thought to myself. It can't have been that difficult, she wouldn't have had time to plan it out. I looked around my room for inspiration. *Records, what about my records?* I looked for one sticking out maybe. No, they were all neatly stacked where I had left them. *Number 53, what album would that be?* Right, number 53 was The Doors – 'Waiting for the sun.' I pulled it out and looked on the back of the label. Track one was 'Hello, I love you.' *That could be it,* I carried on looking at the titles of the tracks, the last one was called 'Five to One.' *Right!* Five to one was a euphemism for masturbation! What was she saying 'Hello I love you but go play with yourself?' No I don't think so. Five to one odds, I was barking up the wrong tree here. *What about album number 57?* That was the Eagles Greatest Hits. No, nothing obvious there either, anyway how would she know the numbers of my albums, unless she was looking and spotted her favourite or something? Then I remembered that she was a classical music fan, opera. Possibly not a Doors fan then, or the Eagles for that matter. We hadn't really talked about music anyway, *so yes I think I am barking up the wrong tree.* Maybe it was an opus number? Well I was stumped there then as I didn't have a clue what opus 53 or 57 would be. *How about?*

"Shakespeare," Moli shouted loudly from the hall outside "What about a sonnet or a verse Lovelace?" I leaned against the door jamb looking down at Moli.

"What *exactly* did she say Moli? Come on think man."

"You know Lovelace I think she loooves you, looooves you Loooovelace, loves Lovelace," he was messing about in a sing song voice. I laughed at him, God he was crazy. I threw a book at him, which caught him smack in the back of the head.

"Ouch," he said looking round at me over his shoulder. "She said it you know." He was dragging on his cigarette now. He passed it to me. I took a drag and handed it back to him.

"What? She told you she loved me?"

"Yep."

"So? How did she say it?"

"Looovelaaaace page 53." I went straight to the bookshelf and took down my copy of Poems by Richard Lovelace. *Page* 53, that was it! '*To Althea, from prison*'. The rest of the poem was on the previous pages, but this was the verse she wanted me to read:

Stone Walls doe not a Prison make,
Nor Iron bars a Cage;
Minds innocent and quiet take
That for an Hermitage;
If I have freedome in my Love,
And in my soule am free;
Angels alone that sore above
Injoy such Liberty.

"Moli you're a genius!"

"Yeah, you know it man!"

Chapter 6

Dawn

There was a letter lying on the mat for me. I bent down to pick it up. It could only be from one person, John. Moli must have posted it for him as he wasn't even allowed to post his own mail. I hadn't heard much for a while and all this waiting was killing me a little bit each day. I was having trouble concentrating in school, I just couldn't think of anything else but him. I was obsessed and miserable. I ripped open the letter.

Dearest Dawn,

I'm sending this out via 'Moli mail', so I hope it actually makes it to the letter box. You can never be entirely certain! It's exeat this weekend and I'm being allowed out after all on compassionate leave. My mum has been taken ill again. I hadn't told you she was sick. Dad is picking me up in about an hour so I'm rushing to get this off to you. I'm probably going to be at the hospital a lot. She's been taken up to Guy's. I miss you, God how I miss you. If only I could see you. I may get home before I have to be back at school so if you're around? I'll call you when I can,

I love you xxx John

Oh God, poor guy. What could I do? I didn't want to call his home in case I was intruding. I thought about the conversation in the pub when he had talked about his parents' photos. 'There were photos,' he had said, and then he had gone all silent. They must have been the old couple I had seen, and the chap in the WWII uniform must have been his dad then. Strange, how did that work out? Was he an accident late in life or perhaps he was adopted? It didn't matter, I felt so bad for him. I went to the phone to see if I could catch Moli before he disappeared off for exeat.

"Can I speak to Moli please?" God I hope the others knew him by his nickname because I couldn't for the life of me remember what his real name was. The little junior who answered sighed on the other end of the phone. I knew why, Lovelace and Moli had the shows furthest away from the phone and he would have to climb all those stairs. I waited for ages and could hear his feet coming down the empty school corridor long before he picked up the phone. "Hi is that you Moli?"

"Yeah, who is this please?"

"It's me, Dawn."

"Dawn, oh hi," he didn't seem his usual chirpy self. "Look Dawn, Lovelace isn't here, didn't you get his letter?"

"Yes, that's why I'm phoning, I don't know how to contact him."

"Listen, he's got rather a lot on his plate right now, I think it might be a good time for you to give him some space." He seemed rather cold.

"What? I don't understand," I was shocked and I have to say a little hurt.

"Listen Dawn, he's in rather a lot of trouble right now, and hanging on to his place in the school by the skin of his teeth. And now this with his mum, and his exams, the last thing he needs right now is more agro… ok? Time to back off baby and let him get over you."

I couldn't speak, I was completely choked.

"Are you there?" he asked.

"Um, yes," I managed to whisper. "Have I done something?"

"Oh I think you've done plenty. Look, he thinks he's in love, maybe he is, but your timing is way off. Anything more and he'll be out and God knows how that will affect his mum in her condition. He's a bloody mess so I suggest you call it off sooner rather than later. Sorry baby." And he put the phone down.

What was that all about? Tears were streaming down my face. What had I done? What sort of trouble was he in? They must have done more than gate him over the date. And his mum must be seriously ill. But what was so wrong about him being in love with me? Well I knew the answer to that one there and then. I had never been so miserable in my life. He had snuck out to the phone a few times, but the phone calls were awful. We spent the whole time misunderstanding each other because we couldn't see each others facial expressions or reactions. Half the time we spent them in silence, and it had only been a couple of weeks. It was like a slow torture, and I knew he was miserable too. I didn't dare go near the school for fear of getting him into any more trouble. I cried myself to sleep every night because my whole being ached to be with him. I couldn't eat, I couldn't sleep and I certainly couldn't concentrate on my school work, but luckily for me, I didn't have final exams coming up. Mine were only mocks, but his were finals, and on top of that his mum was ill. How ill I didn't know, but it must be bad for her not to be in the local hospital.

Oh my God what was I to do? Why was Moli so upset? He must really care for John. My chest was full of butterflies from sheer panic. 'He *thinks* he's in love,' wasn't he sure any more? Were his feelings changing for me? 'Back off baby!' Was it all me? Was I suffocating him? Was I too needy? 'Your timing is way off.' This wasn't a time he could afford to be anything more than 100% focused on his work. 'Let him get over you.' So there was still time for him to get over me before his exams got too close. Then he couldn't feel the same way as I did, because I was never ever going to get over him. 'He's a mess,' and it's all my fault. *Oh God Moli, you just don't know what you're asking of me.* And I cried and cried and cried.

*

John called me on the Sunday morning really early. It was about 8.00 in the morning. Mum took the call on the telephone by her bed. She whistled from downstairs. She was able to do that ear piercing two fingers in the mouth thing, but it was a while before I woke up and heard her. I had a knot in my chest as soon as I heard his voice. I hadn't heard him for ages and as soon as I did tears began to fall down my face. But I managed to keep my voice bright and nonchalant. "Hi," I said, "how's your mum?"

"She's ok, she's out of danger now," he said. God he sounded really tired and strained. "Listen, I really need to see you," he said. "Can you catch a bus to Ashford and I'll meet you half way at The Phantom pub?" *Here goes,* I thought and I took a deep breath.

"You know I don't think I can today," I said, "I'm rather tied up here."

"Oh…" he said, rather taken aback. "It's just I won't be able to get to see you otherwise as I have to be back in school by 7.30 tonight."

"Yeah I'm sorry but you know how it is. Maybe we can meet later on." The tears were just a waterfall down my cheeks now and my nose was getting blocked.

"Dawn, are you ok?" he asked.

"Yeah, I've just got a bit of a cold and a blocked nose."

"Dawn, look I don't mean to push you but I really do need to talk to you."

"Yes, well maybe now is as good a time as any," I said, "I need to talk to you too. You know my timing isn't probably great, but I don't think I can do this any more." My heart was breaking, and I was just wiping tissue after tissue across my face.

"What do you mean? Dawn? Are you all right?"

"Yes – look I'm sorry for all the trouble I've caused." There was a pause at the other end.

"Oh you heard about that?" he said. "You've been talking to Moli."

"Yes and I'm not happy. I think we ought to call it a day."

"What? Look Dawn I'm sorry it just happened. I couldn't help myself," he was pleading now.

I didn't answer, I was too busy dying inside, trying to breathe though there seemed little point.

"Dawn? Please talk to me Dawn… Dawn are you there?"

"Yeah, well it's a little too late for that now." I hadn't a clue what I was saying or what I was talking about. I had my arm pulled tight into my stomach to stop the pain, when the door opened and my mum was standing there. She had dragged herself out of bed, she had been listening to my conversation. I looked up at her in surprise.

"What on earth are you doing Dawn?" She asked looking at me. I was shocked to see her standing there. "Give me the phone Dawn," she said. I just sat there. "Give me the phone now," she said and held out her hand. I passed her the phone.

"Hi, is that John."

"Yes," replied John, desperate and confused.

"Well this is Dawn's mum. Look, I don't know what's going

on here but is there any way you can get yourself over here?”

“Mum,” I said pleading with my streaming eyes, she ignored me and carried on.

“I think you need to come and sort this out face to face.”

“Err yeah, I’ll have a word with my dad.”

“Good.” She handed me the phone back, left the hall and shut the door.

“Dawn? Are you all right baby?”

“Oh God John, I’m so so sorry.”

“I’ll be over as soon as I can, ok?”

“Ok,” I said and put the phone down.

I went into the lounge where Mum was laying on the bed and looked at her with my tear streaked face.

“You love him,” she said, looking at me under her eyebrows, unapologetically. “Don’t throw it away love. You may never ever feel like that about someone again in your whole life.” And I knew it then that she had never felt about my dad the way she had for Dane.

Lovelace

There had been an incident as I had been coming off the rugby pitch. The whole school was out playing, as we did every Tuesday, Thursday and Saturday afternoons. Today it had been a really good game. I was trying to get off to the showers early as I wanted to try to phone Dawn before prep. I was just walking around the side of the changing rooms when as I rounded the corner, a rugby boot hit me, studs first, smashing, with terrific force, into my face. I could feel it had sliced me, warm and wet blood was freely flowing from the bridge of my nose. I staggered back under the force. Immediately anger rushed up inside me, my lungs were pumping overtime, feeding the oxygen into my system as my body began to power up ready for a fight. I clenched my fists into balls as I rounded the corner to face my attacker. It was Penfold, he was hopping about in delight at having got me. I was immediately enraged with disappointment. Penfold was a junior and though I would have paid good money to beat his brains out, it was not something that I would ever do; you never fought Juniors. He could see the fury I was in, but he was safe and he knew it.

"She's mine Lovelace. I got there first. Why don't you just back off and leave her alone? We were fine till you showed up you bastard!" He sneered at me.

"*She* has a name but I'm not going to discuss this with you, you little piece of shit." I hated him, slimy worm. *How could she have ever cared for him?*

"Not getting it yet then, eh? Not putting out for you like she did for me?" I felt the red mist coming over me, my nails were digging into my palms with the force of my restraint. I wanted to pummel him, to annihilate him. I made a slight movement towards him. He saw it immediately and jumped back, brief panic on his face. Then as he saw I wasn't going to hit him he sneered even more at me. Feeling braver in the knowledge that he was completely safe, he moved within my reach.

"She likes it rough you know," he was breathing in my face now."Well, no you don't know," he was laughing now. "Had to teach her a lesson or too though, make her behave. You have to know how to do it though, can't mark her."

That was it. Something, somewhere in my brain just snapped, blind rage and fury took over me and I launched myself bodily at him. Grabbing him by the neck I dragged him to the ground and began beating the hell out of him. I wasn't really aware of anything he was trying to do, whether or not he was fighting back I didn't know. I was just consumed with rage at the thought that this worthless piece of shit had beaten my Dawn, *my* baby. *Well come on then, let's see how you like it,* I thought.

I was vaguely aware of more bodies getting involved, they were getting in the way. I was hitting anything and anyone that came in reach until my arms were pinned back behind me and I was being dragged across the ground by many hands. I was panting and shouting but I couldn't break free and now someone, or rather a few somebodies, were sitting on me, pinning me down. My fury abated slightly, enough to make out what was going on. I could hear whimpering from the direction Penfold had been and I could hear a master shouting. One by one the boys peeled off me and I was left panting and spitting blood from my mouth. I looked up and Tubby had obviously caught one of my blows. He had a swollen lip and was issuing orders.

"Study Lovelace, five minutes, and this had better be good." He stormed off in the direction of main block.

Dawn

A large Daimler pulled up outside my house about two hours later. The car was almost as long as the front garden which ran the full width of our house. John got out of the back seat and he held the door open, talking to someone who had obviously been sitting next to him. He closed the door and the car slid off silently purring down the road. I put my hand up to my head as a fresh wave of nausea rolled over me. I watched him looking the house over. *Yeah probably not as big as yours,* I thought. He came towards the front door, and I opened it for him before he rang the bell. I couldn't look at his face. I lowered my eyes and indicated with my hand that he should come in and the direction he should go. But he didn't go through. He stopped next to me, stroked my hair and bent down looking up into my face, making me look at him.

"Dawn? Are you ok? What's going on?" His face wasn't the same, he had a split lip which appeared to be healing and a nasty looking cut held together with butterfly stitches over the bridge of his nose.

"What? What have you been up to?" I asked surprised, I forgot about everything momentarily.

"Football match?" he said it as a question to see if I believed him. I didn't. It was obvious that he was lying and both of us knew it.

"Come in here," came my mother's voice from the living room. I twisted my mouth up, raising my brows and led the way into the living room. John shut the door behind him, wiped his feet on the mat and followed me into the living room.

"Hello John," greeted my mother. "Look, let's not beat about the bush here, you two need to talk, and I can't really get out of your way, so Dawn, if you want to take him up to your room to talk I don't mind." I looked at John and he shrugged, so we went back into the hall and I led him upstairs to my room.

My room was much larger than his show and I was suddenly ashamed of the state it was in.

Lovelace

"So, this is *your* show?" I said, smiling at all the mess.

"Yeah," she said sounding more than a little ashamed, "it reflects my personality!"

Her bed was unmade with an old crocheted quilt on it. On the floor was a pile of records stacked one on top of the other all higgledy piggledy. Next to the vinyl was a stack of old shellac records and an old wind up gramophone player with a little horn on it. She caught me looking at the records.

"No they're in no particular order," pointing at the shellac ones and said quietly, "they're all people like Caruso and Gigli, they're original recordings." I nodded.

Her clothes were everywhere, and she had a large desk in the corner raised up like an architect's drawing board, covered with pens and papers. She was obviously quite an artist, the walls were covered with paintings and drawings. I was rather surprised to see the same Dalí picture that I had in my room, with a rather odd original interpretation of it to the side. She put her hands in her front jeans pockets and said, "I'm doing A level art, free drawing, calligraphy," she indicated to another pile of papers with beautiful neatly drilled handwriting on it, "and life drawing." I turned behind me to where she was pointing and stacked against the wall were twenty or thirty oils, water colours, charcoal and pencil life sketches of nude men and women. This was obviously her best work of the three, I was impressed. I wondered over to her bookshelf. It was filled with opera scores and piles of music. "Those *are* in order," she said quietly. "Puccini is my favourite so they come first and then Verdi, Mozart..." her voice trailed off. There were some other books as well, a *Collection of Poetry by the Metaphysical Poets*. She nodded her head in the direction of the books. "Page 53," she said, "quite a coincidence." I laughed. She smiled at me a little shyly.

"Tea?" I asked. She shook her head.

"Fizzy water," she said looking towards a couple of large bottles on the floor. "Tea with milk thickens the saliva," I raised my eyebrows questioning. "Not good for the voice," she explained. I nodded in understanding.

"Toast?" I asked. She shook her head.

"But I can do chocolate," she said, now smiling much wider. "That thickens the saliva too, but nobody's perfect."

Despite the mess I liked the room, it suited her. There was nowhere to sit so I just sat down in the middle of the floor propped up by one arm. I rested my elbow on my raised knee and ran my fingers through the front of my hair. She joined me on the floor about three feet away from me. I looked into her eyes.

We just stared at each other, pain on both our faces. The distance was horrible. I knew what was coming. She was dumping me and I felt like the world was coming to an end.

"Look, about the fight," he said.

"What fight?" I was surprised.

"I thought you talked to Moli?"

"Yeah I did, but not about a fight." I frowned.

"Well, he was goading me."

"Who? Moli?"

"No," he said. "Penfold."

I gasped and shook my head, hugging my knees to my chest.

"So you hit him," I said. It wasn't a question. "Why?"

"You know why," he said, tilting his head and levelling his blue eyes at me.

"But you said it wasn't important."

"It isn't," he said gently.

"Then…? Oh!" I said realising that he must have found out other details of our relationship. I covered my face with my hands. "How did you find out then?"

"He told me… not in so many words, but he made it quite clear what he had done and I just lost it."

I didn't say anything.

"Dawn?" he said gently, again trying to catch my gaze. "What were you doing with a guy like that?" His voice was urging but pained.

My eyes were watering and my chin was trembling, I couldn't look at him.

"They don't come with instructions," I said, big tears now falling in my lap. I looked up at him and laughed at myself through my tears. "I thought… I thought he was sweet and kind..." I looked up at the ceiling for help. "I tried to finish with him but he wouldn't let me go, then he didn't like what happened at the dance so he took it out on me."

"Oh my God Dawn," he leaned forward and pulled me into his lap and just held me.

He rubbed his face and lips in my hair soothing me.

"What's all this about?" he said rocking me. "What is going on here? I feel like you're slipping away from me and I can't do a damned thing about it." I looked up at him and his eyes were full of tears too. And then we were kissing each other desperately, it was as if we were trying to force ourselves into one being. The pain of being apart in separate bodies was unbearable. He pressed down on top of me and I pulled him closer still. His weight pinned me to the floor but still he wasn't close enough. I pulled at his belt wanting him to push down onto me more.

It would have been so easy. We both wanted to make love, to join together into that one entity. He pulled his head away from me still holding me tight and we looked at each other, bodies still locked together.

"I want you so badly," he said, and he looked so sad. We lay there on the floor until the fever ebbed still holding on to each other. "Do you love me?" he asked.

"You know I do," I answered.

"Then why is this all so difficult? Why are we tearing each other apart?"

"I don't know," I said, though I knew he wasn't asking for an answer he was searching for one of his own.

It was some time later that we went downstairs in search of a cup of tea. Well we had sorted one thing out, we were still together. Her mum was really nice and really concerned.

"How are you two doing?" she asked, "are you getting anywhere?"

"I think so," I said, "I hope so."

"You know if I can help in any way?" she offered. "There really isn't any problem that great that it can't be got round somehow, but I don't want to pry," she added.

We sat on the settee and Dawn curled up under my arm. I decided to give it a try. What could it hurt? After all we were making rather heavy weather of it all by ourselves.

"I'm on a final warning," I said. "I got caught fighting and I can't put a foot wrong, so that means Dawn and I can't see each other."

"And?" said her mum.

I looked down and laughed as she seemed not too impressed with that problem.

"And if we can't see each other, we can't seem to do anything else either, like study."

"And?"

I swallowed and said "And my mum was revived three times at the weekend," I laughed nervously. It was weird to say it out loud and panic shot through me.

"Oh John I'm so sorry," she said with genuine concern in her voice. Dawn sat up immediately and took my hand.

"It's ok," I said, "she's a lot better now," and I laughed again.

A tear shot down my face.

I turned my head away before they could see and quickly wiped it away with my forearm. I looked at Dawn, worried she would think badly of me. She hadn't seen, either that or she was pretending she hadn't. She put her head on my shoulder and I rested my head against hers.

"Well your mum is a very lucky lady to have a son like you. No one would have known that you were coping with that one. She really is in the best place though, where she can rest and get the medical attention she needs. That's an awful lot of pressure you're under there. And on top of that you have your exams looming. You know your biggest problem here is your age, and there really is nothing you can do about that one."

I looked up at her not understanding, what had our age got to do with anything? She looked at me and continued. "Most people just can't recognise this," she said, "and it's only when you are a lot older that you'll be able to turn around and tell them 'I told you so.' I'm sure something can be done about the rest though, is your dad aware of all this?"

I grimaced.

"I think you need to talk to him, or someone at the school if you prefer. Do you have a housemaster?" I nodded.

"Then please talk to someone." I nodded without saying anything. There was no way I was going to talk to my dad he had enough pressure at the moment, but perhaps Tubby. He had been really understanding about my mum, and I knew he was doing everything he could. He really had been going out on a limb for me lately.

Chapter 7

Dawn

The long black Daimler slid in front of the house and we walked down the path to meet it. Mum had agreed to me spending the rest of the day with John at his house so that we could have some time together, and then he was going to drop me off before he had to be back in school at 7.30.

"Come and meet my fa…" he said holding my hand and towing me along the drive.

I didn't hear the rest of the words because at that moment a large Alsatian having a walk gave an almighty series of barks at a cat crossing the wall nearby, just opposite the car. I was suddenly terrified at the prospect of meeting his father. God knows what he thought his son had been doing for the last hour. *What had he told him about me?* What reason had he been given to make him drive over here with his son, and when his wife was so ill? But the driveway was short and we were already level with the back door of the car. The window slid smoothly down with a small whirring sound. I was bracing myself for the meeting, when Moli's head stuck out through the window.

"Hi guys," he said smiling, looking a little sheepish.

"Moli?" I was so surprised, and turned to John. "I thought you were taking me to meet your father!" John laughed.

"No, I said my fatheaded friend! Budge up Mols," he said taking the door handle in one hand and holding mine with the other. He held the door open for me and Moli slid over to the far side of the car. Bending low I and climbed in next to him, then John stepped in beside me. It was quite dark in the back of the car, the seats were shiny red polished leather with thick, deep creases, very slippery. In front of us was a pull down cabinet which had inside some glasses, with a good slug of some form of liquid in the bottom of one. Whiskey I suspected. It was obvious that Moli had been making himself at home during John's absence. There was a walnut table which folded up and down into place from behind the drivers' seat. John leaned forward and slid the glass panel between us and the driver open.

"Home please," he said, and the almost silent engine took us off down the road. John slid across the leather as the force of the acceleration moved him into the back of the seat.

Moli moved forward so he faced me, his back against the side of the car.

"I owe you an apology," he said through his fringe. "I should have kept my humungous Italian nose out of it... What do I know?" He said shrugging. "I was just trying to look out for Lovelace here, but he put me straight." He glanced away from me to John with a slightly wary look. John was sitting with his foot on his knee, resting his arm on the edge of the window propping up his head, with his other arm along the back seat behind me.

"Yeah, cheers for that," he said sarcastically to Moli. They grimaced at each other like naughty children. It was impossible to stay cross with Moli he was just so, well so Italian I suppose, whatever that meant. He had looks, grace, style and charm, with the addition that he was like an over effusive puppy. If he had had a tail it would be permanently wagging, especially when he had had a bit to drink, which he obviously had. I slid under John's arm and he let it fall onto my shoulders.

"How comes you're here then and not up in London with your sister?" I asked.

"I was but, well, Lovelace needed a chaperone and I volunteered so I came back down with him. Besides," he added turning serious, "I owed him." He smiled gently at me. "Anyway," he said picking up the cut glass tumbler, "it does have its advantages," and he polished off the slug. The car slid silently along the country lanes and I stretched out my legs diagonally across the back of the car.

"This is a little bit over the top isn't it?" I said addressing John but without moving. "Company car," he replied. "Anyway, you can talk what with an MG in the drive."

"Its hardly the same, the MG is really old."

"The MG is class," replied Moli, "not like this old tub."

He leaned forward and was putting a cigarette between his lips when John stopped him. "Not in the back, eh Mols?" he said.

"Huh? Oh yeah, right." He said returning the cigarette to its packet and then away into his top pocket.

"Just what exactly does your dad do?" I asked.

"He works in a garage," he replied, "car wheels mostly."

Moli didn't look at him but I saw him raise an eyebrow.

"I don't believe you," I said. "You don't drive around in cars like this if you work in a garage."

"Depends on the garage," replied Moli under his breath but loud enough that I was sure to hear him. John made to kick his leg out from under him. He tried to kick him back.

"Hey watch out!" I said leaning forward between them. They tried unsuccessfully to grab each other around me. I pushed back into John's arms moving him away from Moli's reach.

"What about your dad Moli?"

"Books," he said leaning back too, "bird books." He snorted out a laugh. "Well one bird," he continued, "penguins!" He and John burst into fits of giggles, and he turned his face to the window unable to contain his mirth.

"What's the joke?" I asked. I couldn't help but be affected by the hilarity. I looked at John for enlightenment.

"Penguin? Penguin books."

"No!" I said in disbelief.

"Or rather he did." There was a pause. "Let's get this old tub rocking," said Moli, "got any music Lovelace?" Moli leaned forward and tapped on the windscreen to the driver and twisted his fingers as if turning a knob. The driver smiled and leaned forward pushing a button on the cassette player in front of him. Music appeared out of somewhere and as the intro played I yelled out the title in joy.

"Wishing Well."

"Thought you were a classical girl?" John said surprised.

"I am, but I'm also sixteen and can appreciate other music, besides, you can't dance to La Boheme." Moli laughed.

"Oh I don't know," said Moli, "caught Lovelace trying to dance to some God awful racket the other day." He then began a take-off of someone singing 'O Solo Mio' and tried to gyrate his hips at the same time. John put both his arms around my waist and pulled me close to him again.

"Yeah well it's a darned sight better than your dancing Mols," and he kissed me lightly on the cheek.

"Oh God , no sex, I'm young and impressionable and likely to get extremely horny if I have to watch you two," said Moli smiling. "Besides which," he said, leaning over and knocking on the glass again to attract the driver's attention, "I am suffering from acute oxygen poisoning and need to have a fag before I expire." The car drew to a stop and Moli got out crawling past us, flying out of the nearside door in a most ungainly manner. He lit a cigarette, then opened the front door and jumped in next to the driver. He offered him one by shaking the packet at him. I saw the driver hesitate flicking his eyes towards John in the back, looking at him in the mirror. Moli said something to him and he urged him again with the packet to take one, which he did.

"Are they allowed to do that?" I asked, remembering John's earlier comment about smoking.

"Yeah, it's ok that side of the glass."

"He's great isn't he?" I stated.

"Yeah, he's really been looking out for me lately." He looked into my eyes, "maybe a little too much recently?" I got his drift.

"It's ok, I don't want to come between you and your friend." The car started up again, Moli was now wearing the driver's hat. He was singing the next Free track at the top of his voice. "Thank God for the glass," I said. "What did he mean about what his father *did?* I mean, what does his father do now?" John looked uncomfortably out of the window.

"Moli's the orphan," he replied, then turned and looked at me, "not me." I held my breath in shock. "By the way, I liked your show," he said, changing the subject. I let him.

"Oh God," I said. I paused and slid around on the leather seat pulling my legs up off the ground in front of me, holding onto one ankle with one hand and supporting my head with the other. I could look into his eyes better like this.

"You lie a lot, I saw you were itching to tidy it up."

"I like your mum too," he continued. "What did she mean about our age?"

"She had a boyfriend before Dad," I explained. "She was in love with him and he went down with his ship. She thinks that we've got something special… like they had at a young age." He swivelled around a bit too, facing me more.

"Okay?" He drew out. "And what do you think about that?"

"You tell me?" I said, not wanting to put words in his mouth.

"Well I think it's pretty special," he smiled. His face was glorious.

"You are so… pretty," I said focusing on his eyelashes. He laughed out loud.

"That's *not* a compliment!" he said continuing to laugh.

"It's true though," I said smiling. "I have a theory," I said rummaging in my handbag.

"What?"

I found what I was looking for and held it up.

"That if you wore mascara your eyelashes would be so long that they would touch your eyelids." I waved my mascara backwards and forwards in the air, teasing.

"You reckon?"

"Yeah, are you game?"

"Oh hell," he said, "what if you stab me in the eye?"

"Oh that's all right, I do it to myself all the time," I said teasing further.

"Well how about after you've met my father," he said. "We don't want him to think I've been getting in touch with my feminine side."

"Will he be there then?" I asked, butterflies flying all around my tummy. I dropped the mascara back into my bag looking down as I did.

"Yeah. Hey don't look so worried, I'll protect you," he said keeping it light.

"Ok, what am I in for then, you'd better warn me. Age?"

"Sixty-eight."

I raised my eyebrows.

"I was adopted," he smiled happily.

"Oh how exciting," I said. "A mystery."

He laughed again.

"What about the garage?" I said suspiciously.

"It's a foundry really, he makes bits for aeroplanes and the wheels for the Formula One racing cars. Means I get to hang around airports and racing tracks occasionally."

"Very flash."

"Very noisy," he added.

"You don't live in a castle do you?"

"Good God no," his eyes shone as we chatted. "I live on a housing estate actually."

His eyes were twinkling again, I was beginning to recognise the look.

"Yeah right!" I snorted.

"No really," he laughed lightly.

"Will he like me?" I said losing my cool a bit.

"Who wouldn't?"

"That's not very reassuring, you're biased."

"Dawn, he's going to love you, just like I do. Stop worrying."

Lovelace

I squeezed her hand, gazing at her, drinking her in. Suddenly I found my body flooding with adrenaline and my throat became all dry and tight. I was acutely aware of how uncomfortable I was. All these powerful surging emotions, I wanted to throw myself at her and take her there and then on the back seat of the car. My eyes had moved to the base of her throat and as she swallowed, I swallowed hard too. Her shirt buttons were loose, down to where they disappeared into the low v neck of her jumper, and her breasts rose and fell with each intake of her breath. *Oh, how embarrassing, how long had I been staring at her breasts?* I hoped it was just a second and that she hadn't noticed. I looked up again at her eyes, she'd noticed all right. She had a playful smile on her lips for a second. Her mouth opened slightly, as if to speak and then she slowly dragged her teeth across her bottom lip. Did she know how my body reacted to her every gesture? I looked at her eyes. Yeah she knew. We both smiled in acknowledgement. Then there it was again, this tunnel between our eyes. The surroundings of the car disappeared and we shared one of those really intense intimate moments together. From one second to another I went from feeling the most glorious deep warm joy between us. The next it was if we were standing on a precipice and were about to part forever. We seemed to be on a huge rollercoaster ride with no control over this force that was possessing us, and again we were left at the bottom of the ride in a pool of pain and despair.

I pulled her hand and she thumped onto the middle of my chest. We slid on the leather of the seat and ended up slumped down across the back with her on top of me. I took hold of her and the tidal wave of lust and wanting washed over the both of us as we kissed.

The car was slowing, the glass slid back and Moli shouted out over his shoulder. "We're home children." Then as he couldn't see us he turned around looking. "Oh for God's sake, you two need to get a room." He laughed out. "Come on put her down before your dad sees." She pulled away from me breathing hard, her weight on her two arms, and smiled hugely. She wasn't embarrassed. So I grabbed her again for one last quick kiss.

Chapter 8

Dawn

'Housing estate,' he had said. With a big stretch of the imagination you could possibly call it that. More like, a house on an estate!

Turned out to be a house with a farm at the back, with a good few acres which the farmer now looked after. The house itself was a medium sized Georgian mansion with a circular shingle drive in the front and large mature horse chestnut trees planted around it. It was side on to the small lane where it was situated, so it wasn't until you were in the drive that you could see the front of the house clearly. As we swung onto the drive I could see 'LOVELACE' written on the large white gate which was standing open.

"That's a bit O.T.T. isn't it? Naming the house after yourself."

"Well the house on this site has been called that for about six hundred years, that we know of, it just also happens to be our name too."

"So what? It's a coincidence then?"

"No, Dad had wanted to live here for ages so he bought it

about twenty years ago when it came up for sale. I'll give you a potted history later, come in and meet the old man."

John led the way into the house with Moli bringing up the rear. I held on tightly to his hand, I was terrified. John's dad was in his study. He was sitting in a round backed rattan chair stuffed with gold cushions at a rather ornately carved desk with ball and claw feet. He rose to his feet when he heard us coming and turned around with a smile. His face was round and he had dead white hair at the temples, and his eyes crinkled just like John's when he smiled. Then I remembered that John was adopted. He was obviously very fond of John because it was written all over his face.

"John," he said with profound joy as his son came towards him. What surprised me was that he grabbed his arm and shook it and clapped him on the back. Was this a bloke thing? I didn't have any brothers to compare with, only an older sister and I certainly wouldn't have greeted my dad like this. It was so formal, especially when John replied "Sir." It was with deep emotion, but it still stood out as odd and very alien to me. He had after all just been spending a lot of time with his dad in the hospital and had only just seen him that morning. I would have expected at least a hug under the circumstances. He turned to Moli whom he also knew.

"Moli." He too stepped forward and shook his hand. *Definitely a bloke thing.* Then he turned his crinkly eyes on me. They were the same blue as John's, *must be something in the water,* or maybe I wanted them to be like John's. He was like my imaginary picture of a granddad, not ever having had one myself. John introduced me as his girlfriend. Whoosh, I felt light-headed. I was a girlfriend. Well I knew I was. It was just that he'd never referred to me as that before and it caught me off guard.

"Hello," was about all I could manage though.

I was wondering if I should have added the 'sir' at the end, when he said "My dear girl, what a pleasure it is to meet you. John talks very fondly of you."

What a charmer, I thought, *know where John gets that from then.* The charm, the manners, it was a prime example of nurture, well it couldn't be genetics. We sat in a small leather Chesterfield whilst Moli and Mr. Lovelace, I didn't know what else to call him, sat in matching old leather chairs. We passed pleasantries together for a while with him asking me all sorts of questions. Then he said that he had to go soon as he was going back to London. Meaningful glances were exchanged with John, and then Moli and I were instructed to make ourselves known to Mrs. Brownie, who was in the kitchen baking and that she would sort out 'Something for your lunch.' His dad stood up and held out his hand for me to shake again, and then I followed Moli out of the room leaving John with his dad.

It was obvious Moli had been before, and he led the way towards the kitchen at the back of the house. The kitchen was not as big as I had been expecting. It had a very large Aga along the centre of the back wall and in front of it was a huge oval oak gate legged table with chairs all around it. Mrs. Brownie greeted Moli warmly. She flapped her hands, which were covered with flour, indicating that she expected a hug from him. He put his arm around her back and kissed her on the cheek.

"And who is this delightful young lady?" she said, indicating with her eyes that I might be something to do with Moli.

"This is Dawn," he said, "John's Dawn." He coloured John's name with innuendo and grinned.

"Oooh, how lovely," she said flapping her hands at me too, so I too went over and was given a hug, minus the hands as they were still covered in flour.

"We were told we might get a spot of lunch?" Moli was using all his Italian charm on her. It turned out she was midway through making Sunday roast and just needed to get the apple pie trimmings finished.

"It will be ready in about an hour, but help yourselves to tea or coffee if you wouldn't mind whilst I get this in the oven." Moli dodged in and out of her as he passed back and forth for cups, milk, and the kettle, which was sitting on top of the Aga. I sat down and did my best to answer as many of the hundreds of questions Mrs. Brownie had for me as I could. She was lovely, if a little incessant. By the time John came in tea was definitely drunk and it was time for lunch.

"Ooh I've met your lovely young lady," Mrs Brownie gushed.

Lunch was scrumptious, I felt full to bursting. John's dad had left us to go back to London and Mrs. Brownie was now tidying up in the kitchen. Moli was having a post prandial nap and was snoring ever so quietly, his legs both up on the end of the settee arm as he was too tall to fit onto it properly.

"Come on," said John, his eyes shining, "I want to show you something."

The churchyard was down the lane and could be easily seen a short distance away, atop a small hill in what appeared to be the middle of the village. We walked up the hill holding hands. At the bottom of the churchyard was a series of narrow steps which acted like a stile up into the churchyard. We picked our way up through the headstones and then on around the side of the church to the main entrance. The door was slightly ajar, well it was Sunday. We went into the porch and then into the main part of the church. Inside I have to admit I was a little disappointed. All the old box pews which would once have stood in the aisle were gone. They had been replaced with what were obviously expensive, but more contemporary benches. Probably more comfortable than the pews, but not as aesthetically pleasing, well at least not to my eye. John took me by the hand down the aisle towards a very small chapel to the right hand side of the altar. The chapel itself was tiny but somehow very sweet and intimate, despite the fact that it was open to the rest of the church on two sides. The main window was a modern representation of the Madonna and child with smaller pictures around it. The carpet was pale blue and gave it a tranquil air.

Lovelace

The organist was gently fiddling around the keys having a little practice and the sun was shining in through the windows.

"I know this piece of music," she whispered to me. "It's Faure, Faure's Requiem."

"It is?" I said, it was obvious that I didn't have a clue who

Faure was, or his requiem.

"I'll sing it for you if you don't look at me. I'll get all shy and self conscious if you do. That is if the organist doesn't mind."

"You're on," I said. She disappeared out of the lady chapel and I sat down on the step near the altar, this took me below the level of the pews so that I could not be seen. I waited. I couldn't see her chatting to the organist but the music had stopped and I heard their voices. Then the music started again, a pattern of four notes repeated three times and then one long note. I had to admit it sounded pretty, and then she began. It wasn't what I expected at all from her speaking voice, the notes just seemed to float on the air held suspended. It was a beautiful haunting tune, and her voice spun the notes like silky threads through the chapel and the colours, the colours of her voice were like the lustre on a pearl. The piece built in intensity in the middle and I could hear the control she had over what was an incredibly powerful instrument. The ending of the piece became hushed and it was almost as if she were whispering a prayer in my ear. Even as the piece ended I could feel the air gently pulsating on my drum. I didn't realise but I was hardly breathing. The church itself felt like it was holding its breath. Then the voices resumed and I could hear her footsteps echoing on the flags as she returned. She looked at me and shrugged her shoulders. I couldn't say anything to her, I didn't have any words of my own to tell her what I wanted her to know.

"Page 54, verse 3," was all I could say. She smiled as she sat down.

"I'll have to look that one up," she said, so I translated.

"Such sweet command, and gentle awe,
As when she ceas'd, we sighing saw
The floore lay pav'd with broken hearts."

"Ooh that's beautiful," she said. "I'll take that as a compliment then."

Dawn

I sat down on the altar step and looked at his eyes. It was turning into one of those really intense moments again. The organist had resumed the rest of Faure's Requiem and John was beginning to look nervous, so I thought I had better say something.

"This is a really pretty chapel."

"It's called the Lovelace Chapel," he replied.

"Really?" I said, not believing him for a moment and looking for the twinkle in his eye to see if he was teasing. He wasn't.

"Look," he said, "this morning I said I needed to talk to you."

"I remember," I said thinking back to the morning and our near break up and then the encounter on my bedroom floor. "I've had a lot of time to think whilst being locked up and it's just been hell not knowing from one moment to the next whether it's the last time I'm going to see you. I need to be close to you even when we can't be together. I need you to have something that shows you how I feel about you."

He was swallowing hard, and then he took my wrist, his hand slid down mine to the end of the fingers where he stopped and held onto the tips. I watched intrigued as to what he was up to. He turned my hand over and then with his, dropped something into the centre of my palm. Sitting in the middle of my hand was a circle of silver metal. I looked at it for a moment wondering and then saw it was a ring. I looked up at him suddenly, shocked.

"Will you marry me?" he asked. Still holding my hand, his soul laid bare before me in his eyes. There was no doubt in my mind, not even for a second and my smile must have blinded him because he was instantly reflecting back my joy like a mirror.

"Are you going to do it properly?" I said, still radiating. His eyes creased up even more and he slid the two inches necessary for his knee to reach the floor.

"Dawn Hillary Armstrong, will you marry me?"

"Yes!" I said throwing my head back and looking to heaven. "Yes!"

He grabbed me tight around the waist and hugged me to his chest, and then we kissed.

*

"Don't tell me," I said, "it's an heirloom and it's worth a fortune," I said joking, but I wouldn't have been surprised with an affirmative answer.

"No, I bought it in London from a street seller near the hospital. It is hand made though," he added, "but it's only silver, and that's a semi precious tourmaline," he said rubbing his thumb over the stone. "But I bought it with my own money," he added proudly, "strawberry picking in the summer." He sniggered a little with embarrassment now. I looked at the ring on my finger. It was slightly lopsided and the stone wasn't perfectly level but it was an incredible deep blue-green. It was the most beautiful ring he could have chosen for me, it was perfect.

"Do you like it?" he said sounding uncertain.

"I love it," I said fluttering my fingers. "You can't have it back now."

"What do you think your mum will say?" he asked.

"She'll be thrilled," I said with absolute certainty.

"And your dad?"

"He'll be shocked, and think we're too young, but he won't object. What about your dad?" I asked.

"Well he'll probably have a fit," he said, "but I don't care."

"And your mum?"

"She'll have a fit too!" he said, "but I still won't care, you have to start forever somewhere!"

"What do you think Moli will say?"

"Oh he'll think were mad, but I'm sure he'll also take it as an excuse to get legless."

Lovelace

"You never cease to amaze me Lovelace. I mean you haven't even escaped from school and you're engaged pending the hangman's noose. Of course I like her and everything, but God MARRIAGE?"

"I don't see it like that. I love her, I can't exist without her."

"You've been reading too much of that damned poetry. What you need to do is to shag her and then you'll recover your sense of proportion."

"I don't want to shag her, I want to make love. There is a difference you know."

"Yeah well you don't have to get engaged to do it."

"That's not why I got engaged."

"You mean there's more?"

"Yes there's more, but there seems little point in explaining it to you."

"Christ man you're seventeen! You haven't even lost your cherry yet. Think of all the girls you're gonna miss out on."

"I don't want any other girls, I just want her."

"You know you may not like it, when you get to it that is. Oh My God!"

"What have you thought of now?"

"What if she's frigid and you never get any at all? It'll be too late then Lovelace. Think of it… a whole life time of masturbation. It'll be like being in school for the rest of your life!! Oooh," he had obviously had another thought, "and then it will drop off!" He grabbed his groin and started mock pained noises.

"She's not frigid."

"Oh ho ho!! Have you been holding out on me then? Have you something you'd like to confess Lovelace?"

"No, but it wouldn't be any of your business if I had."

"Confess! Lovelace, confess!"

He grabbed my pillow and started to hit me over the head with it. I batted him away with my hands.

"Look Moli, can't you just be pleased for me?" I so needed an ally. "I've got my dad going ballistic at me, telling me my mum will have a relapse when she finds out." I sat forward on the bed my head in my hands. Moli sat on the bed next to me, fag in his mouth, glass of 'water' in hand and took a swig. Then he patted me on the back sagely.

"I am happy for you, really. If that's what you want. Look if I'm absolutely honest about it I'm jealous."

"Who of?"

"You…" he began hamming it up. "It's you Lovelace," he said playfully trying to grab me. "I'll never find another love like you. Don't leave me, please don't go."

"For Christ's sake Moli, you raving homosexual. You really are the limit. That's all I need." I put a foot up and kicked him off the end of the bed.

"Is that any way to treat your lover?" he wailed.

"Sod off and good night Moli," I said, getting up and shoving him out of the door.

"Think! They'd have a good reason to expel you at last… Ooh!" another thought was occurring, "you could bugger the Bursar, that'll have you out in no time!"

I shut the door on him."Good night Moli." I leaned my back against the door suppressing laughter. *Silly arse!*

Chapter 9

Lovelace

It was the weekend and we had just finished our Saturday afternoon rugby match. Dawn and I had to be together it was so unbearably frustrating for us both. We had talked about sex, and it was perfectly clear that we were of one mind on the topic. I had to create an opportunity for us somehow. We decided to enlist Moli's help. I wanted her so much but we had very few options as to when and where. This weekend I had invited Moli over Saturday night and most of Sunday, returning to school in the evening. He was going to help so that this would be the most perfect evening it could. Well under the circumstances that is, but when you're seventeen and at boarding school what choices do you have? The back of a car? No, not never, not for our first time. I didn't want her to feel in any way that the circumstances were cheap. Other options? Somewhere in the school? Well no, outside was freezing and the weather unpredictable and inside? No, the whole house of boys would know what 'Lovelace and his floozy' were up to. I didn't want anyone thinking badly of her, she was so precious to me.

It would also mean instant expulsion, not that I cared too much about that, but being caught in those circumstances just didn't bear thinking about. There was the option of abstinence and I suppose that is the road we morally should have taken, but it never even came up in our conversation or to be honest our consciousness. We both knew that what we felt for each other was special. This was something so right between us and as necessary as the oxygen we needed to breathe, we had to join as one. So that left us with her house or mine, talk about a rock and a hard place. It was the flip of the coin really but my mum was still unwell and Dad was staying 'up in town'. This left an empty house with the exception of Mrs. Brownie in daylight hours. As perfect as it was going to get.

I would distract Mrs. B to get Dawn into the house and Moli would take her up to the attic above my room. I hated the thought of sneaking around but we had no choice, not if this is what we both wanted, and it was. Moli was to stay in the guest room, which happily was located between my room and my parents' room, not that they would be there. We would be near the back stairs and, if it was needed, we could escape outside to the garden. I hated the deception but the whole thing was taking on a life of its own. If I am perfectly honest, neither of us really gave a damn about any of the consequences. We had to be together, that was all there was to it.

We left the school together, all three of us in the car. I knew Carl, our driver, would not even think of mentioning picking us up to Dad. I'd called him to pick me up, he would just assume that Dad knew about it, and if he did happen to mention it, well, I just didn't care about that either. Dawn had told her family she was staying over at my place straight out and that Moli would be there too. What she left out though was that my parents would not be there and that they didn't have a clue that she would be staying over. She knew there would be no circumstances under which her parents would phone the house to 'speak to Dawn', so what could go wrong? Mrs. Brownie? Well she would only be there at supper and lunchtime the next day so it would be easy to hide Dawn from her. And then what? Carl would drive Moli and I back to school and Dawn home. Mission accomplished.

*

Dawn was delivered to the quad by her unsuspecting father. I was worried, thinking that she might have changed her mind. Suddenly now the time had arrived, I had begun to get stage fright and worry about the consequences for her of getting caught. But when I saw her face all doubts vanished from my thoughts. She was absolutely glowing with excitement, and there again, so was I. There was no exeat and the other boarders were covering for us. Moli and I had told them we were going to a concert in London, so it was just us three who knew what was really going on. Carl picked us up in the quad and, what with all the day boys being picked up, no one noticed our car, however ostentatious it was, sliding out of the drive. Dawn and I were just blissed out and because we had the evening to look forward to we just had fun chatting and catching up on a week's antics at school, with jolly banter all the way to the house with

Moli. On arrival I went straight to the back kitchen to find Mrs. Brownie. She was where I expected she would be, cooking supper, I kept her chatting whilst Moli whisked Dawn upstairs and into the attic. She was surprised to see me as she wasn't expecting me but then I had done this sort of thing many times before, taking her off guard turning up out of the blue, she wasn't that put out either. Then Moli joined me in the kitchen and we began to persuade Mrs. Brownie to make up a 'picnic' supper for us as we 'wanted to watch the match' on TV upstairs in my room. I left Moli with Mrs. B whilst I shot up the back stairs to check Dawn was ok. She was making herself comfy checking out the room and sitting on my huge old rocking horse riding backwards and forwards just like a little kid.

"This is absolutely amazing," she said. "Is it yours?"

"Yeah they're made locally in the village. It was bought for me when I was very small, I've always loved it."

"It must have cost the earth. It's all real horsehair and leather! I love it too!"

I didn't like to tell her their was a weight restriction, I was trying my best to 'Think Before You Speak!' and banish the crass comments once and for all. Anyway I thought the horse must have a safety margin built in. "Does he have a name?" she wanted to know.

"Champion," I replied shrugging, well I was young at the time. "You know Champion the Wonder Horse?" *Gosh how embarrassing,* I felt really silly. *If this is bad, how embarrassed am I going to be later on?* I didn't like to think.

"Mrs. B is making a picnic supper for us," I informed her.

"Moli is making her think we are really hungry after the rugby so that she does enough for three."

"This is a lovely room," she said climbing down from Champion and beginning to nose about. "Was this your show when you were small?"

"Well, yeah, when I was very small," I said looking about me and remembering back. It had been ages since I had been up here. I had forgotten how I loved it. The roof was all funny angles where the different levels met and there was a big window which led out onto the valley of the roof. There was no view from it other than the different pitches of the roofs opposite. *Why had I abandoned it for the room below?* Well that was because I had been in boarding school since the age of six, and as I had got older it was probably easier to bring my trunk up only two flights of stairs instead of the three it took to get up here to the attic. The stairs were really narrow and my trunk was huge. I tried to imagine Dad struggling up the stairs. No, that was probably the reason.

The room had yellow wallpaper with ribbons painted on it and baby lambs up and down at various angles. My old cot was dismantled in the corner by the wardrobe which also boasted a little lamb on each door. The floor was polished wood around the edges with a very thick pink rug which almost reached to the walls. It had a symmetrical design in the centre and another pattern around the edges in all manner of different colours. Most of all it was soft to walk on with bare feet at night. I remembered the feel of it on my toes on my trips to the bathroom as a child lit by the night light, a plastic picture and frame with the 'Little Bow Peep' nursery rhyme depicted on it.

Dawn wandered around the room. She looked at me as if for permission to look in the wardrobe. I nodded. My games were stacked neatly in the bottom of the empty wardrobe. Monopoly, Cludo, Chinese Checkers, Kon Tikki, *that was an odd one*, and a huge Hornby train set, all in their original boxes. She moved on to the corner of the room where a large suspension bridge stood on the floor. It was pristine, made from metal strips. "Meccano," I said as she looked to me with a question. It was my favourite toy and had beautiful brass washers, screws and tiny round headed bolts.

"Did you have help?" She enquired.

"To begin with," I answered, "but later on I was able to make things on my own. Dad helped me mostly." I remembered the hours he had spent with me patiently explaining and helping me to build things. "Dad liked my train set best. I hated it." I explained. "When other children came home with me on exeat I used to leave them with him and the train, whilst I went out and played football with some of the lads from the village."

Then there was the bed. Single with a white painted ironwork bedstead. The cover was patchwork, it reminded me of the one in Dawn's room. We both looked at it. I felt uncomfortable and put my hands in the back pockets of my jeans and looked down at the floor. She came straight over to me and put her arms around me wedging her hands too into the same back pockets. I raised my head to look at her.

"It's perfect," she said eyes shining smiling up at me. She looked so beautiful it was a moment before I realised I had stopped breathing.

"Unless we fall out of it," I said looking into her eyes. She laughed and kissed my bottom lip, holding it between hers. My hands were trapped in my pockets and I couldn't get them out fast enough to hold onto her. She backed away from me teasing, smiling and moving towards the bed. She had her hand on the front of my belt now and I willingly followed her like an eager puppy as she towed me along walking backwards towards the bed. Then the moment was broken as the sound of Moli's feet came thumping up the back stairs. Moli took in the mood as soon as he entered the door, looking at us under his curly fringe.

"Look guy's, I'm sorry to interrupt but I've got some bad news." We were shocked for a moment as Moli's face was so serious. "Just Joking!" He looked very pleased with himself. "Mrs. B has had to leave early tonight due to some relatives or some such thing, I wasn't really paying attention, but she's left supper and we have the house to ourselves until mid morning. How about that then?"

"God I thought you were going to say something awful then," I said, realising I was braced for some dreadful news.

"Listen," he continued seriously, "you really don't need me any more. I'm sure you can take it from here." At this point he broke into a huge smile almost laughing at me. "I've already called a taxi and there's plenty of time for me to catch the next train up to town, I might see a show and my sister will put me up. I can catch an early train back down tomorrow morning and see you then, so until then you two can… play scrabble?"

Dawn ran up to him and threw her arms around him and kissed him on the cheeks. "I love you Moli," she said.

"Hey steady!" He said jokingly taken off guard. Moli gave her a huge hug lifting her off her feet as he did so and kissed her back on the cheek.

"You know you picked the wrong guy here, don't you?" he said smiling down at her. For a moment I thought he wasn't joking, well maybe he really wasn't? Then he kissed her on the forehead and dropped her from his arms. He looked at me seriously, almost severe and said, "Take care of her," and then turned and ran down the stairs shouting, "Be good children!" And we were left alone.

Oh God, then this is it, I thought. *We're alone, just Dawn and I.* I felt suddenly panicked with stage fright. After all the planning here we were and I hadn't a clue what to do, and she had. What if I failed miserably?

"Are you hungry?" I asked her, hoping for some time and swallowing like a maniac. What had happened to all my saliva? It felt like my mouth was made of sandpaper. She shook her head looking at me seriously.

"Are you?"

"Not really." It came out a bit shaky. Oh God I looked like a moron already. She had picked up on it though and went and sat on the bed closing the distance from me a little. She sat down with one knee up and the other leg dangling off the ground. She dropped her head down to speak. Her body language wasn't inviting me over, I stayed where I was near the end of the bed.

"This is all new to me too you know," she raised her head and her eyes were intense like liquid chocolate.

"But you said…?" I didn't understand, I was confused.

"I know what I said. I said I wasn't a virgin, and I'm not," she added. God this one had really got me.

"Then what?" I asked still clueless. She looked down again and then pulled both knees under her chin hugging them, she rocked slightly like a child.

"I've had sex precisely twice, but I've never made love." My heart was melting, she looked so small, so vulnerable. I wanted to wrap my arms around her. I walked up to her slowly and sat down next to her on the bed. She tipped her head onto one side on her knees and smiled at me, tears were glistening in her eyes. "I wish I'd waited… waited for you!" A large tear held in by her lashes plopped out onto her cheek and ran slowly down the bridge of her nose. I put my hand up to her head and ran it down her hair, stroking her.

"So are you as scared as I am?" I asked smiling at her.

She didn't say anything she just nodded vigorously and smiled, still hugging her knees.

I took her hand and held it and looked into her eyes. This wasn't the right time, it needed to be natural. I didn't want to rush this and in the light of our conversation I was feeling less pressured.

"Come on," I said, "let's go and see what Mrs Brownie has been up to and get something to eat."

Her head popped up off her knees.

"Sounds like a great idea!" She said eagerly, so I led her by the hand through the house to the kitchen.

Down in the kitchen Mrs. Brownie had left out a wonderful spread. She had cut some slices of her famous gammon, well I say slices but they always tended to disintegrate into strands of meat not holding together as a slice, but the taste... oh the taste was morish. I always had trouble restraining myself with Mrs. B's roasted ham. She had left some home made bread thickly buttered and a wonderful potato salad, another of her specialties.

"That has garlic in it," I warned Dawn, indicating towards the potato salad.

"I'll have some only if you do then," she beamed. There was an amazing green salad with all sorts of wonderful things in it. There was a cake stand with a variety of yummy looking cakes and meringues on it, all my favourites. Mrs. B was a genius.

The kettle was on the Aga to one side, keeping warm but not boiling. Dawn went over and put it on the plate whilst I sorted the teapot. I looked at her enquiring and waved a teabag at her.

"Whatever, you choose," she said smiling. I chose bog standard.

"Where do you want your picnic?"

"Oh, I don't know, wherever you think. In here is rather nice."

It was, so we stayed in the kitchen savouring the delights Mrs. B had assembled for us.

I felt so relaxed in the cosy warm kitchen, sitting just across the table from Dawn. We chatted about all manner of things. It was amazing how much we didn't know about each other. But I loved it, finding out about her, watching her as she chatted and laughed. Looking at the way her eyes shone when she talked about her singing, and her serious frown when she talked about her art. I washed up, she was no help whatsoever. She spent the entire time cuddling me from behind just leaning her face against my back. But she did help me pack away the left over food into the fridge. Well, she carried it over to me whilst I arranged it all inside.

"I would have just piled that on top of that," she said, indicating and looking at the neat way I had arranged the items on the shelves.

"Yes you probably would," I laughed. We were complete opposites, chalk and cheese.

"What about you," she said seriously, "do you know anything about yourself, you know... why you were adopted? I mean you must have been a beautiful baby, I can't imagine anyone giving you away."

"I know a few bits," I said matter of factly. "I was a private adoption, it was allowed back then. I was an advert in the Chiswick Gazette."

"You know you don't need to tell..." I interrupted her.

"I really don't mind," I said looking at her worried face. "I have no problems at all with this... really. My parents love me and that's all I need to know. Whoever it was that had me didn't, and I don't need to know about them."

"Are you really that well adjusted?"

I thought about that for a moment. "Yeah, I really am," I said convinced. "Anyway, my Uncle Paul was a doctor and he arranged the adoption and collected me personally from the hospital, then he delivered me to my parents. They were in their fifties then. They tried to adopt a few years later but the laws had changed, and they were deemed to be too old to adopt again."

"How long have you known you were adopted?"

"Since I was about seven. A lady in the village had a very large family of all creeds and colours. I asked my dad about it one day and he informed me that she fostered children. I had to get him to explain that and what adoption meant, and then I asked him straight out if I was adopted. I remember he almost choked on his dinner and then he answered 'yes.' I replied 'Oh Goody, that means I'm different then,' and that was an end to the matter."

"And you've never been upset about it?"

"No, why should I?" Dawn just shrugged. "Dad has tried several times lately to show my birth certificate to me and talk it through, but I'm really not interested. Besides, he and Mum really love me. I just feel somehow that no matter what they say to the contrary, they would be really hurt, that it would be a betrayal somehow for me to ask. I have no reason to want to know so I can wait. I'll find out one day anyway."

"I couldn't do that, I would want to know who I was, where I came from, it's just too enticing."

I shrugged. "I could find out any time I choose," I said.

"Huh," she sniggered disbelieving, "What, like now?" I nodded. "How?"

"Dad has a file on me in his desk drawer. He's shown it to

me many times. I don't know why he keeps trying, I'm just not interested. They didn't want to know me so I don't want to know them."

"So you do feel some sort of rejection then?" she asked.

"A little bit maybe, but nothing more, no raging anger or anything."

"One day you may need to know." I shook my head not understanding. "You know if you wanted to get married or something… I could be your sister," she said looking a little surprised at her own suggestion. I laughed hard.

"I don't think so."

"But you don't know so," she said seriously, "what if we're related, it's a long shot you know, but it happens. And what if you have children," she pressed.

"What…?" again I didn't understand.

"They ask you, you know, if you have any medical problems, if you have inherited anything you might pass on." I snorted a laugh down my nose. "So why do you think he has been wanting you to know lately then?" she continued. I shrugged.

"Probably because I'm approaching eighteen? And he thinks it's about time?"

I had both hands on the table spread out, leaning my weight forward onto them, I put my head down to think. "So what are you saying… you think I have a reason to know?"

"I'm not saying anything… Listen to be honest I'm curious as hell but it's not my business it's yours and…"

"And?"

"And now I'm scared… it's silly I know, but I'm scared… and

now I don't want to know anything. Now I wish I didn't know that you were adopted either." I looked at the panic on her face. I wrapped my arms around her.

"You're not my sister... do you have any idea what the odds are? They are infinitesimal." I stood hugging her for ages rolling things around in my brain. "Ok, come on..." I took her hand and led her to my dad's study. She pulled up outside the door when she realised where I was taking her. She stood there shaking her head.

"You don't want to know... I'm making you... I don't want to know either, I really don't."

"Dawn... you're everything to me... and I now have a reason to know the whole story... will you help me find out?" I held out my hand to her. She took it and reluctantly followed me into Dad's study. I knew where he kept my file. Many a time he had left his drawer open to me and invited me to look. "It's here for you any time John, any time you want to know you have only to ask. I'd like to talk to you about it, I'd like to explain it all to you. You know your mother and I don't have a problem with this, it is your right to know about yourself. One day you will need to know." His eyes had crinkled up and he had smiled kindly at me indicating with his hand where it was. But I couldn't, I couldn't take the chance of hurting him and Mum. I could see the love in his eyes. I just couldn't bear to cause him any pain by taking that step, by admitting to him, acknowledging by my actions that I wasn't his.

But he wasn't here, he need not know that I had looked, and now I did need to know, I really did. I pulled the desk drawer open and there it was in place, just where he had left it on the last occasion. I took a deep breath, and felt Dawn's hand on my shoulder. I took it out and laid it on the desk.

The top paper was my birth certificate. It had my name John Richard Elliott and the name of my mother and I stopped breathing. My mother's name was Juliet Lovelace, and my father's name was Brian Heaton, manufacturer. I was shocked, Juliet Lovelace was a name I knew. Dad's brother Walter was in bomb disposal, he was killed during the war. Apparently there was only enough time to tell everyone to get down, as the bomb stopped ticking just as he reached it. There was very little found of him to bury. His wife, my Auntie Freya, gave birth to Juliet several months after that. Juliet, had married Brian many years later. I knew the story, Juliet had left Brian and married someone else but she had lost contact with the family. This made Juliet my dad's niece. How did that work then? Had she had me with Brian and then left? Or was there something else? Why was I adopted? Why did she leave Brian? It didn't really matter, what did matter was that Dad was Juliet's uncle and he was therefore my great uncle. He was bringing up his brother's daughter's child, me!

"What?" said Dawn, she sounded terrified.

"Well, I sighed, that's good news, you are definitely NOT my sister!" and I laughed. There were lots more papers, but I had found out all I needed to know for now, so I closed the file and placed it carefully back in its place in the drawer and shut it. I turned to her still terrified face and smiled.

"It's ok you know, at least I know where I get my blue eyes

from now!" I explained what I had found out, and what I knew of my father's family.

"You mean you're not upset," she urged.

"Not in the least! In fact I think my dad is amazing! Good on him! It's great… you know it's really great." I felt really warm inside knowing that I really did belong to him. Did Mum know though? Ah well, best leave that, I didn't need to know that one. Now I knew for certain that nothing could come between Dawn and I, I just needed to hold her. I held out my arms to her and she jumped into my lap clinging to me like a small child. I hugged her tight and she rested her head on my shoulder.

After a while I said "Come on, I need to look at something." She climbed off my lap and I took her hand to the main staircase. I switched on the landing light.

"Oh…" she gasped. "Richard Lovelace."

Hanging from the picture rail on the landing were two enormous illuminated portraits. One was the picture of Richard Lovelace in his armour that was on the cover of my book, she had recognised him and the other was his grandfather William Lovelace. We climbed the stairs almost to the top until we were level with them.

"Are they real?" she asked, "they must be worth a fortune!"

"Well they cost a fortune, but no, they're not real, they're copies my dad had done. The originals are in the Dulwich Picture Gallery, I'll take you to see them sometime." We both looked at them hard.

"I thought you said that you weren't related to them, that it was just a name."

"That's right," I continued. "But now I'm beginning to know how Dad feels about them. I want to be related, I want to find out, to try to make the connection with the past. Think about it, this is their house, well only part of it is original…" she stopped me with her raised eyebrows.

"The kitchen," we both said in unison, and then laughed together.

"And my attic possibly," I added.

"I like that," she said.

We had sat down on the steps, me at the top and her further down. We looked up at the portrait of William.

"He looks friendly I can imagine him in contemporary clothes… I may have a go at painting that one myself," she mused. "Tell me about Richard then, I know he wrote poems and that he ended up in jail…" She trailed off and looked up at me expectantly.

"Well… he was reputed to be the most handsome man in England." She looked over to the portrait, screwed up her eyes and started moving her head about.

"What are you doing?"

"I'm trying to imagine him in your school uniform and if you blink and go from one eye to the other very fast repeatedly his face changes expression, it kind of brings him to life a bit."

I copied her. It did he became animated in a staccato way and his face did change, he suddenly seemed to come alive.

"Not so sure about the most handsome thing though, but if he is related to you he must have been."

"Biased!"

"Truthful!"

"Anyway," I continued, "he got his degree at Oxford at eighteen and became one of the Queen's favourites… the court was up in Oxford. He wrote plays and poetry, one of them the most popular of its day, but Cromwell banned theatre and dancing, so a lot of plays were lost. Now only his poetry survives."

"That's appalling, destroying a man's work."

"Yeah but I suppose it was like sweeping the decks with the new 'roundhead' regime. A lot of his poems were set to music so they were a lot more difficult to eradicate because people knew them by heart."

"Like pop songs today I suppose," she said. "Good! Music was as important back then just as it is nowadays."

I laughed gently.

"What else?" she urged.

"Well, he raised two regiments for the king. He was imprisoned, that's where he wrote a lot of his poetry, you know, *Stone walls...*"

"*Do not a prison make!"* We said in unison.

"And he was extremely brave in battle. At the Battle of Maidstone, one of the bloodiest battles of the Civil War, they were driven back down Gabriel's Hill. They had set up a canon at the top of the street. Well… it was carnage. They fought for five hours at the entrance to the town losing two hundred men. They were fired upon from the top of the hill and snipers picked them off from their vantage points, from the houses lining the street. They fought hand to hand until they were driven back to the church down by the river. It was only when their backs were against the wall of the church, when they were completely surrounded and so hard pressed that they could no longer swing their swords, that they were forced to surrender."

"Wow... so handsome, talented, a ladies' man, loyal to his king and a brave soldier. I wonder what his show would have been like?" She mused.

I laughed again.

"What happened to him?"

"Well, the family went to America where his brother Francis was the first Governor of New York."

"Impressive!"

"New York then was not like New York is now you know."

"Still he was the first."

I nodded.

"And Richard?" She asked.

"Well he died in 1658, a pauper. He gave everything for his king. He contracted consumption and died in Gunpowder Alley, rather apt for a soldier, and was buried in St Bride's church Fleet Street, but that was destroyed in the Great Fire of London in 1666. I think his friends helped pay for the funeral."

"What a sad end."

"But here we are three hundred years later and his poetry is still being studied and read."

"That's true. Tell me some then. You seem to know an awful lot."

I looked down at her shining eager eyes. I knew the poem but I changed the first word from Amarantha to hers.

Dawn sweet and faire,
Ah brade no more that shining haire!
As my curious hand or eye,
Hovering round thee let it flye.

Let it flye as unconfin'd
As its calme Ravisher, the winde;
Who hath left his darling th'East,
To wanton o're that spicie Nest.

Ev'ry Tresse must be confest
But neatly tangled at the best;
Like a Clue of golden thread,
Most excellently ravelled.

Doe not then winde up that light
In Ribands, and o're-cloud in Night;
Like the Sun in's early ray,
But shake your head and scatter day.

See 'tis broke! Within this Grove
The Bower, and the walkes of Love,
Weary lye we downe and rest,
And fanne each others panting breast.

Heere wee'l strippe and coole our fire
In Creame below, in milke-baths higher:
And when all Wells are drawne dry,
I'le drink a teare out of thine eye.

Which our very Joyes shall leave
That sorrowes thus we can deceive;
Or our very sorrowes weepe,
That joyes so ripe, so little keepe.

She knelt upon the step below facing me. I was sitting with my knees apart facing her. She moved in close to me and put her arms around my neck and said quietly, "I don't have long hair," I snorted a gentle laugh and smiled, "and it's not golden it's dark brown." I laughed a bit more smiling widely now.

"Details, mere details," I suggested.

"I am interested in a couple of the lines though," she said seducing me with her eyes.

I raised an eyebrow questioning 'which ones'?

"*Weary lye we downe and rest, And fanne each others panting breast,* oh and the bit about *Heere wee'l strippe and coole our fire!*"

Ok so my fire was beginning to burn!

"Come on then," I stood up towering above her on the penultimate step of the stairs and held out my hand. She smiled up at me, took it and followed me to the attic.

*

She was giggling as we picked up the pace, up the narrower back stairs to the attic and she had put her hand in the back of my belt again, like when we had climbed the George steps in the dark. I was chuckling too, I felt light-hearted and giddy with excitement. When we got to the attic we both stood just inside the doorway looking at the room. The bed looked tiny.

I looked at her and said, "I don't fancy falling out of bed, do you?" She laughed and shook her head. "Here," I said, "give me a hand." We pushed the bed to near the middle of the room and then I pulled the mattress lock stock and barrel onto the floor. Then I discarded the bed frame in the far corner of the room. She threw herself onto the mattress giggling, and I joined her. She snuggled into my side and I pulled her close whilst we stared up at the ceiling.

"Do you think he brought her here?"

"Who?"

"Richard and Amarantha." She replied.

"I thought you didn't know the poems," I hadn't mentioned the title of the poem… *had I?*

"Well I've been doing some research recently, having a little bit of an interest in one particular Lovelace," she explained, "and although I couldn't quote them, I do know the titles… and a couple of the most famous lines," she added.

"Oh you have, have you?" I said rolling over to face her. I propped my head up on one arm so that I could see her better. "And I do know that he didn't write one to 'Dawn'." She was teasing me.

"Poetic licence, anyway he couldn't have brought her here because he was only a child when he lived here, he met Amarantha years later."

"So this would have been his show, his nursery, like it was yours."

"Possibly… anyway, if he had of met you the first word would definitely have been Dawn." My voice became suddenly flooded with emotion as I looked at her lying there, the last letters of her name disappeared almost inaudible.

The mood changed in an instant, one second it was cosy and relaxed, the next it was as if electricity were emanating from every part of our bodies. What was a happy eager look on her face became tormented, pained to the point of agony, and that's how I felt too, pain at the need to have her. She threw herself onto my lips bruising herself and me in the severity of the blow. Adrenaline surged through my body, and I was aware of how slight and fragile she felt in my embrace. I didn't want to hurt her but it was so all-consuming and she didn't seem to be worrying about hurting me either. I kissed her hard, thrusting my tongue into her I wanted to possess her in every way. She was pulling my shirt frantically out the back of my jeans and she plunged her hands up to my shoulders and then raked my back along its length with her nails. The pain made me gasp. I looked into her eyes, she was defiant and smiled severely egging me on. I pinned her shoulders down with my weight surveying briefly the buttons on her shirt. They appeared tiny and seemed to multiply before my eyes. I grabbed the bottom of her shirt and pulled it up. She helped and made it easy for me to get it over her head. Her arms were left trapped inside. I held her hands above her head with one hand whilst I reached under her back for her bra strap with the other. She raised her chest slightly to help, all the while gazing severely into my face. Her breasts fell heavily from their confinement spilling into my hands which were now exploring their weight and exquisite texture. Her nipples rose hard under my finger tips which sent a surge of adrenaline from my groin to my stomach. I put my mouth on them, sucking. She let out a surprised startled cry. I was enveloped in a mixture of her perfume and her own incredible sexy scent which was exciting me even more. She had obviously managed to free herself from her blouse as she was pulling at my shirt again. Most of the buttons had mercifully come loose, but she was impatient and I felt the fabric tear as she pulled at the cotton. I moved up her neck, her scent was heavier here and I must have bitten her slightly as she yelled out again in surprise. She grabbed the back of my hair in her hand, pulling it by the roots, forcing my head back and then thrust her lips onto mine pushing my head hard against her now. She pulled back a little, my lip in her teeth and she bit me slowly looking at me as she did it. I took her wrists above her head again and pinned them with one hand and then I felt for the button at the top of her jeans. I looked at her eyes to see if there was any doubt, any flicker of objection. There wasn't. I pulled down her zip, it slid easily. She lifted her hips up the bed slightly which had the effect of moving her jeans downwards. Putting my hands either side of her hips I pulled her jeans down further, again she raised her hips to help me. I ran my hand over the smooth flat of her stomach and down under the flimsy material of her knickers. Exploring with my fingers. She smiled and obligingly moved her legs further apart. She was warm and wet, gosh she was wet, and she was making small moaning noises and rocking her hips. My shirt was so getting in the way, it was still attached at my wrists but had come off now completely over my head. She was exploring my back with her hands pulling and squeezing my torso. Now her hands were in front, I lifted my weight up and she found my belt. She fumbled with the clasp. *Why had I pulled it so tight.* I had to help her to get the buckle free. Then she pulled at the leather running it through her fingers and with her thumb she easily flicked open the button on the top of my jeans. The pressure was so great that the zip descended on its own with very little help. I could feel her fingers running up and down my length. *Oh God,* I felt like I was going to come there and then. To begin with the panic of it was enough to stop me, but then she was stroking me urging me on. I tried to think clearly… now what was she doing? She was pulling me to her, guiding me towards her. *Oh no!* I couldn't come now, that would ruin everything. *Cold water, think of cold water, diving into the pool at school, cold icy water.*

In the split second of sanity that followed I remembered precautions. I fumbled in my back pocket and rolled onto my back, tearing the plastic wrapper with my teeth whilst I wriggled my jeans down further. Oh my God I was all fingers and thumbs, I was shaking and my damned shirt was in the way, I was desperate… and then I dropped it. I froze and shut my eyes, this was where it was all going to fall apart. *This is where I fail,* I thought.

I tried to steady my breath as disappointment began to flood through me. I couldn't breathe properly, but when I opened my eyes she was above me looking down at me tenderly. She picked up the sheath and sensually guided it into place. Somehow she had managed to get rid of her jeans whilst I had been wrestling with the remnants of my shirt. She sat astride me, I looked down, she was still wearing her underwear, sexy and lacy. She had her hands on my shoulders and she nudged me gently enticing me, thrusting her hips forward. A surging force shot through my body wedging itself in my chest. I couldn't breathe, I was panting so hard. I took her shoulders in my arms and rolled her underneath me, my legs between hers and as we did so we slid off the edge of the mattress onto the carpet. I looked into her eyes, they were shining with excitement mixed with amusement, and we laughed. *That was the moment we would have fallen out of bed,* I guessed she was thinking the same thing.

Then suddenly the violence was gone and in its place was heartbreaking tenderness. I touched her gently slipping my fingers up and down. With her eyes she let me know she was ready. Her lacy pants moved aside easily for me and I pushed inside her. *Oh my God* it was so amazing, I could have never imagined anything like this, the feel of her, her softness her warmth and it just built and built in intensity. She was pulling my hair and moving with me. I was enjoying it so much, I looked into her face. *Was she? Was it this incredible for her?* She pulled my forehead to hers and closed her eyes, at each thrust the intensity built and built, climbing higher and higher until I exploded with joy and orgasm and everything... and I collapsed shaking but sated in her arms.

We lay welded together and she clung to me tightly. I looked at her suddenly worried. *Was she ok?* The actual event was rather short, I should have made it last. *Oh no, how was she feeling? Did she enjoy it? Did I hurt her?* So many questions that were answered with her look. She smiled at me, tears flowing down her cheeks.

"I love you John, I love you," and I kissed her as if she were made of some unimaginably fragile material.

"I love you too," I said and held on to her tight, listening to the pounding of both our hearts.

*

We managed to divest ourselves of our clothing sometime later I was worried about her because she had bled, something else that I hadn't given a thought to. I felt really bad about that because I thought that I must have hurt her badly even though she tried to reassure me. I felt guilty about that though too, because secretly I was also pleased, I felt somehow like it had been her first time too. Later we made love again, this time I knew what to expect and it was everything the first time had been but more. It was more exquisite, more intense and I hoped for her it was more fulfilling. I didn't expect to be great at this, but it was just so incredible for me that I wanted her to enjoy it every bit as much as I did. I tried to make it last longer for her, urging her towards her own ecstasy but I really didn't have a clue how it was for her in reality. She moaned and squirmed under me and I heard her cry out at the end, but I was lost at that moment myself.

The night stretched out into periods where we rested sleepily in each other's arms, followed by gentle explorations of each other's bodies. And kissing, *my oh my,* passionate, passionate kissing, followed by fits of the giggles and silly messing around. Every emotion that you can possibly think of we spent a whole night exploring, until unbeknown to us, daybreak began to creep over the windowsill. This time we made love without using anything. Well she was on the pill, she had told me that, and I was until quite recently a virgin so… Anyway I had no idea about the practicalities of all this and I had run out of the damn things.

I was so exhausted, so was she. We moved slowly together, not intending on getting anywhere just enjoying the kaleidoscope of sensations which were flooding our senses. There was no more tender expression that I could give of my love for her, and this time, skin on skin was so sensual. The best yet and I knew that she came just before me as she shuddered and pulsed beneath me. Then eventually she fell asleep and tears of complete happiness fell down my cheeks and I wept silently with my sleeping lover in my arms.

It was about 9.30 when I awoke. She was still tucked under my arm. *God she was so beautiful.* I gently kissed her eyelids, then her nose and by the time I had reached her mouth she was smiling and kissing me back, even though she had not opened her eyes. It was morning, well you know, and she had noticed my problem too.

"Your stamina is amazing," she said opening her dewy eyes. I laughed.

"You're pretty amazing yourself." I didn't want to press her, but she was already wrapping her legs around me, when we heard a door slam somewhere in the house down below. We both froze and looked at each other.

"Moli… I hope." I jumped up pulling my jeans on and doing up my belt as I moved towards the door. I went outside and made my way down the back stairs to the kitchen. It was indeed Moli looking rather harassed.

"You owe me big time Lovelace," he said from under his curly fringe. It turned out that the really early morning train from London had been cancelled and he had hitch hiked down from London all the way to here. Luckily one lorry was able to take him within spitting distance of Ashford, and then he had managed to get a ride along the main road with a local. "I'm knackered and hungry," and then looking me up and down he added "and you look like hell too," he said eyeing me with a grin.

"I know Moli, I owe you heaps." I rattled around putting the kettle on the Aga. "Look Mols, help yourself to eggs, bacon, whatever you want will you? I'll be back."

"So? How was it then?" he asked.

I was making for the door, I turned around to speak and then thought better of it. I looked down smiling, laughed and ran off to find Dawn.

"I'll take that as FANTASTIC then," he shouted after me. "Joined the club at last!"

Upstairs Dawn was surveying the evidence of our night together. What had been for me the most ecstatic and powerful experience of my life, also had sobering consequences both physical and emotional. My shirt was torn, as was the sheet we had been lying on. There were smears of blood and stains upon it. She was on the verge of tears. I went straight to her and held her.

"Look, it's ok I'll take care of it, it doesn't matter, I love you silly. Last night was wonderful, so please don't be sad."

"But what about your parents?" she asked.

"They'll never find out. Really, it's ok I promise." I held her and kissed her until she seemed to relax.

I took her down to the shower and plied her with lots of soft towels and lotions and left her looking much happier, then sorted the room out whilst she was gone, pushing the sheet into my bag to dispose of later. My shirt, well that could be disposed of too. It was just another school shirt after all, I had plenty and I took off to the other bathroom to have a shower myself.

Downstairs Moli was making himself at home. He was in full flow apparently when my dad walked in.

Dawn

I was mortified as I sat surveying the wreckage and evidence of our night together. Strewn about me was soiled and torn linen. I had bled and I was a little sore. I had been surprised by this. As I had told John I had had sex twice previously, though

I had only really bled on the second occasion, neither one of which I wished to recall ever again. With John it had been a joining of the two of us into one. 'Making love,' what a perfect description. It had been the most wonderful experience of my life so far. He had taken me and now I was his forever. I could still feel his touch deep inside me and sticky and wet on my thighs. But alone in the room I was beginning to feel panicked. *Why was he taking so long?* I needed to feel his reassuring arms around me. I didn't know what to do. I knew I had to tidy up, to hide the evidence of our beautiful night together. Others wouldn't see it as we did, and I didn't want to see it through their eyes. What if his parents found out? What would they think of me? They wouldn't understand what this meant for us, they would only see this as grubby. What about the sheets and his shirt? And then he was back, holding me, reassuring me, and my world was on its axis again.

Chapter 10

Moli

"Moli!" Surprised he greeted me, taking off his gloves as he entered the kitchen. I was so taken aback that I dropped the egg and shell I was breaking into the frying pan and, catching the edge of the pan in my panic, I burnt my finger.

"Ooww!" I said sucking on my finger ends. *Fuck!* was my first thought, Mr Lovelace! *Where the hell was Dawn? And where the hell was Lovelace, and what the hell were they up to?*

"Morning Sir, errr, would you like some tea, breakfast?" *Jeeesus...* adrenaline was pumping through me and my heart was going like the clappers. How was I going to get Lovelace out of this one? *Think, think, think!*

"John?" he enquired, shrugging out of his Crombie coat and putting it over his arm.

"Errr... in the shower I think." *Yeah,* I thought, *but doing what?* By the state of his apparel the last time I had seen him he hadn't looked in any hurry to put things on, in fact I think he was still taking things off. *Shit!* What was I going to do? I had to get up there and warn them fast!

"Yeah… I'm just taking him up a cuppa, wake him up… you know!" I said, grabbing my cup of half drunk tea and moving straight for the door, when smack, I bumped straight into Dawn coming in from the other side. I closed my eyes and froze in front of her.

"Dawn?" he said surprised. I looked at her checking her out. *Thank the Lord she had her clothes on.* Then I remembered that she knew I was here. Well that was something at least I suppose. I smiled at her and rolled my eyes. The flicker of horror was instantly gone and she smiled pushing up her sleeve, and walked into the kitchen. "I'll take this to Lovelace," I said, backing out fast leaving Dawn with his dad. I raced up the stairs spilling and slopping the tea as I went in pursuit of the missing dick! "Lovelace!! Lovelace!! Where the fuck are you?" John appeared in the doorway to the bathroom wrapping a towel round his waist as he did. "Get a move on, your dad's downstairs and Dawn has just walked into the kitchen! What do you want me to do?" He had frozen to the spot and was running his fingers through his hair, then he paused and shrugged.

"I haven't a bloody clue Moli, and I don't really care… play it by ear I suppose?"

"Well you might not care about yourself but what about Dawn?" I said, my temper flaring.

"What do you mean?"

God, was he being thick or what? Was this a new Lovelace, a Lovelace I didn't know? If so I suddenly didn't much like him?

"You bastard… You fucking bastard… I thought you loved her… I thought this was special…" As I gesticulated the tea was flying everywhere. "If I'd for one moment thought you were as shallow as me I'd... I'd..." Dawn was gorgeous, she was special, and if he had just used her...? I was ready to knock his lights out. I knew Lovelace would win in a fight, but I just wanted to get in one good punch before I went down. I felt the mug in my hand and tensed my fingers around it. It was as good a weapon as any, and I lunged forward at him.

"For Christ's sake Moli," he said, angrily dodging to one side, leaving me sprawled down the landing, mug in hand and contents slopping about, though miraculously still inside. "I do love her," he said quietly, "I love her more than you can possibly imagine, and she is special... too special to have to apologise to my dad, or anyone else come to that." He raised his eyes and looked at me. And I knew what he was seeing on my face. My feelings for Dawn, which I hadn't really been aware of up to now, were out in the open.

"Yeah well I was just checking," I said trying to cover up. I looked at him again and there was a sympathetic smile on his face. I laughed, embarrassed acknowledging it. "Anyway, what do you want me to do?"

"Just go and be with her, don't lie, just tell him I'll be down he won't be questioning her. If he's got any questions he'll wait for me. I'll be there when I'm decent."

"Can't remember you ever being decent," I retorted, getting up to my feet. I looked him straight in the eyes. "Can't remember you ever not being decent," I mumbled. I smiled at him and he hit me on the shoulder. I shoved the remnants of the tea at him and went back to help Dawn out in the kitchen.

Dawn was continuing where I had left off and was now plating up the food. I have to say she didn't look like she was having any difficulties at all with his dad, and he seemed to be chatting easily with her. He was asking her about her singing and her studies. It looked like she was working her magic on him too. Well how could he not be captivated by her? I allowed myself a moment of indulgence as I watched. She looked different today, there was an underlying calm about her and she somehow glowed. She was absolutely radiant and a pang of jealousy stabbed me in the chest as I realised why. Still there was Kelly. Maybe we could have something like that? Maybe it was time to stoke up the fire there and see where it went?

"So how are the studies coming along Moli?" his dad asked.

"Oh you know not too bad, gets in the way of the rugby a bit."

"What about John? Is he working hard?"

"Yeah actually," I replied sincerely. Well, he hadn't been specific about what he was working hard at had he?

"Good," he said satisfied, "you know you've only got a very short time to make this count," he added. "What do you intend on doing over the holidays?"

"Do you know, I was thinking of planning a little trip. Not sure where yet but it'll be about the last real break we get before we'll have to get stuck in for the exams."

"Sounds fair enough, you need to have a *little* relaxation… Ah John, good to see you son." He paused infinitesimally looking at him as if something was slightly amiss and he was trying to work out what it was. John stood in the doorway, hands in his jean pockets. There was something about his bearing, his stance. I knew what it was, he had made that shift from youth to man and it was almost tangible. “I want to have a chat with you if you don’t mind, after you’ve eaten. Your mother’s fine, should be coming home tomorrow. We need to talk about a few things though, when you’re ready, don’t rush. He rose from his chair and picked up the mug that was in front of him. “I’ll be in my study, come and find me. Dawn,” he bobbed his head at her and then again his head to me, “Moli,” and as he passed John he smiled, “John.”

“Dad,” John replied. There was ever so slightly a pause as he heard the word and then he continued down the hall to the study.

“Don’t you normally call him Sir?” Dawn asked.

“No, don’t think so,” he replied shrugging.

Lovelace

“Ah John,” Dad raised his eyes to me as I entered his study. “I was surprised to find the three of you here this morning, it’s not an exeat is it?”

“No Dad, it’s not.”

“Do Dawn’s parents know she’s here?” I sat down on the sofa, it looked like it was going to be a long chat.

“Yeah, they know… but they don’t know that you weren’t here.” I confessed sighing.

“Look John…” he was trying to tread carefully, “you say you love her, and I know you’ve gone and got yourself engaged, but this isn’t right, this isn’t putting her first. Can you imagine what her parents are going to say about this? A girl alone in a house with two young men all night. Have you thought about her reputation at all? I presume you two didn't…?"

"Didn't what Dad?" I challenged him. I wanted him to say it, I wasn't going to make this easy for him if he really wanted to know. He didn't say anything though, he just looked at me with an expression of total miscomprehension on his face. I sat forward legs apart with my arms resting on my knees, hands clasped together, head down. "Look, I get it that you don't understand this, that you think somehow in a few months time I'll have moved on, that it's just some passing crush, it isn't." I looked him in the eyes. "I love her Dad. How else can I put it? I love her in every sense of the word. I know that this would be a hell of a lot more convenient for everyone if she and I were older, but then what age would suit you Dad? Twenty? Twenty one? No, you'd all still think that was too young. Twenty four? Twenty five? They're just numbers. You still wouldn't be able to see what we feel for each other because you're not looking, no one's looking." I dropped my head down, how could he understand? He got up from his chair, and came and sat next to me, resting his hand on my shoulder. We sat in silence. It was Dad that broke it.

"You're right, I don't know how you feel, I don't know what I'm supposed to see here. I see you're in pain, I believe you think you're in love and you think a ring proves it, but that doesn't give you rights."

"The ring was never for her, she didn't need a ring, it was for me, I needed it. I wanted her to have it, to have some tangible proof of how I felt, but you're not going to understand that either." I looked down again.

"But going behind people's backs doesn't make this right. You've abused our trust John, Dawn's parents and mine."

I felt desperate. He was right, of course he was right. I nodded, and tears ran down my nose. I pressed both thumbs into the sides of my eyes to try to stop the flow. His words were like a knife in my stomach. I didn't know what to say to him. I thought of Dawn, my beautiful Dawn, and our wonderful night. What had I done? Now it was being trailed through the mud. I looked up at him and shook my head.

"And if I'd asked your permission? What would you have said?"

"I'd have said wait, if it is right then later on..."

"But when Dad?" I interrupted "When would you have thought this ok? Would you ever?" I could hardly see him through my tears. "When did you love *me* Dad?"

"What?" he said, taken aback, not understanding the connection.

"When did you love me? Was it when I was two, or was it when I first went to school? Was it the first time I scored a try or when I was naughty? Did you prove it then when you forgave me? When did you know? Or was it the first time you saw me? The first time you held me in your arms? Did you just know in the deepest part of your soul that this love was forever, unconditional?" He was completely startled by this and didn't say anything.

"I knew the first moment I saw her," I continued, "before we had even spoken, when our eyes met for the first time. That's when forever began for me, and miracle of miracles she feels the same. I can't prove it Dad, I can only tell you how I feel. I'm so sorry you feel I've let you down, but we can't be apart and if you can't see that then I can never explain it to you." I could hardly breathe now. I stood up, pain was stabbing in my lungs with every breath. I looked him in the eyes and pulled myself up as best I could. This was so hard for me to say and after everything he had done for me. "Its ok Dad, don't worry, I understand how you feel," I said, tears still leaking down my face. "We'll be at Dawn's until I can figure out what to do." I smiled weakly at him and I noticed that tears were sliding down his face too.

"It was when I first saw you. You were in your mum's arms. You were wearing a lemon pixie hat and you opened your eyes, and then she put you in my arms and my heart was your's forever." I looked down at him, he suddenly looked very old to me.

I smiled at him. "I knew it," I replied in a whisper.

He stood up and awkwardly opened his arms to me. I don't think I had hugged my dad in years, not since I was very small, but it was wonderful and we both hugged each other tight.

"John, you know you don't need to go anywhere," he said awkwardly. "I need to think about all this, but please don't leave. Just give me some time and then we all need to sit down and talk. Please don't go." He put his hand on my arm. I nodded and left him. At the door I turned, he had his back to me, head down, both hands on the back of his desk chair. His shoulders were shaking as he wept silently.

Dawn was in the kitchen with Moli. When she saw my face she just ran to me and put her arms around me. Moli discreetly backed out of the room and left us. She didn't say anything, she just held me.

"He knows," I said. She didn't respond. "I'm..." she cut straight across me.

"Don't say you're sorry, please don't say you're sorry," she looked up at me, "because I'm not." She was searching my face. I stroked her hair from her forehead and I finished my sentence, looking into her eyes "I'm so in love with you." We both smiled and then I kissed her and the power of our love consumed us, leaving us breathless.

"What are we going to do? We could go to my house?" she suggested. "My parents will understand."

"He wants some time to think, he's trying to understand. Don't forget there's a generation missing here, he was brought up in a different era. Lets face it he's an Edwardian, it's hard for him. But he doesn't want us to go." She buried her face in my chest and hugged me tight. I rubbed my face in her hair and held on to her. She was the most precious thing in my life, she was exactly that - my life.

*

My dad was in the doorway, I don't know how long he had been standing there watching, but I think this was the first time he had seen me with her, other than holding her hand. Dawn was not aware of him. I just held on tight to her. He looked me in the eyes with a gentle smile on his lips and nodded his head in some form of acknowledgement and then he backed away down the passageway.

We made tea and were sitting around the table when he returned. I got up to get him a mug. He sat down on the opposite side of the table from us. He put his hand up to his head and pulled at his eyebrow. He looked into his mug.

"I nearly lost the most important thing in my life today. I thought I didn't understand how you two feel, but then I was reminded that I do." He looked up at me and smiled, his eyes creasing up at the sides. "I can't agree with the way you've gone about this, but then, if I'm honest, you haven't had many choices either. You are both so young," he looked at us both in sympathy, "you have no idea what an important stage of your life you've reached at the moment. Your exams John. You say you want a future together but how well you do now determines your future, how well you can provide for yourselves." He put his hand to his forehead. "What about college? Have you thought about that? Dawn is a year behind you. What are you going to do then?" He clasped his hands together and placed them flat on the table in front of him and looked down. "And what about consequences…?" He flushed pink, he had never talked to me about sex in his life. "What if you two make a mistake? I know that it's the modern age but accidents do happen?" He didn't look up.

"Well I wouldn't marry him," said Dawn.

I was shocked, taken aback. This is something that we had never discussed, I just assumed that we would marry anyway. I looked at her.

"If John wants to marry me it will be because he loves me, not because he has to! And as for the rest of your questions… the answer to all of them is, we don't know," she replied hotly. "How are we supposed to know? But we'll work it out. We may make mistakes, but we'll work it out. On our own if we have to, but we'll work it out together." She stood up. "I don't care what you think of me." Tears were rolling down her cheeks. "John loves me and I love him and that's all that matters, we're not planning it but if we have a baby then it will be something wonderful not something shameful and… and…" She looked at me for help, tears pouring down her cheeks. I stood up and held her.

Dad looked shocked, he hadn't expected this reaction, well neither had I. I knew she was ballsy but I was quite impressed with her conviction. Dad stood up too and held up his hands in apology.

"You're right… I'm sorry… I'm so sorry to have offended you. How can I expect you to know the answers? Dawn I am sincerely sorry, please sit down. I do want to help you both. Please." He held his hand out to the chair. "Please…" We sat down.

"Ok," he sighed, "well from my point of view I need to put things straight with your parents Dawn. When you came here you involved me and I have to know that they know everything." He looked up at her trying to read her reaction. She didn't say anything. "Either I can talk to them, or if you would prefer…"

"I'll talk to them," I interjected.

"*We'll* talk to them, together," she butted in and squeezed my hand, looking up at me with a slight smile.

"Ok," he sounded somewhat relieved. "The next thing is school. John, there's only a few weeks left. If you're in school that's where I expect you to be, studying hard… for you both," he added. "Call each other by all means, write to each other, but unless it's an exeat then I want you studying. The term is nearly over and then you can be together. I want your word on that." I looked at Dawn and put my arm around her, she looked into my face.

"I want to say yes, I want to give you my word, but I can't, I just can't, if I did it would be a sham. You're asking something of me that I just can't give. You may as well ask me to stop breathing I could no more do that than what you're asking."

"Help me out here John, I'm trying to reach a compromise."

"But it's not a compromise. You think that by not seeing each other I can just cut off and get on with my work. That the odd phone call will somehow keep us happy. We've gone way past that, we are one whether we're married or not, and if you force us apart then…"

"Then?"

"I don't know Dad… you tell me?" I felt so tired, suddenly weighed down. "What do people do when they are desperate?" I put my head on my hands which were flat on the table. My brain hurt with all this. "I suppose they lie and cheat. I suppose that's what's happening…"

"But John, you can't just give up, you have to go back to school, all I'm asking is for a few weeks."

“I’m not giving up on school, but I can’t give up seeing Dawn either…!” I looked at Dawn. *‘Just lie,’* said a voice in the back of my head. *‘What does it matter? He just needs to be reassured so what’s a little lie? Then we can meet in secret.’*

“No!” I blurted out in answer to the voice in my head. I shook my head. “I won’t give you my word. I’m sorry I just can’t”.

“Dawn?” Dad turned to her. “Talk to him, try and make him see sense. I’ll leave you two to talk it through.”

I looked at her pain and knew that she was a reflection of my own feelings.

“I can’t lie to him Dawn, even if it’s just to make him feel better. I don’t want to be sneaking around trying to find stolen moments with you.”

“I don’t want you to either,” she said, taking my hand. “But I do want you to finish school and I don’t want to come between you and your family. You have to go back to school, and I have to go back to mine. We could phone in the week.”

“But to go week after week without seeing you, I just can’t. And it’s not just about sex. Well if I’m honest that does come into it somewhere, but it’s about needing you, holding you, just being with you.”

“I know,” she whispered. “If we could only be together at the weekends, we could study together. It’s a pity you’re not a weekly boarder.”

“But I could be,” I said, seeing the glimmer of a plan. “I only live half an hour away from the school, and if I pass my test in a few weeks’ time I could drive myself to school. Then we would be able to have the weekends together, even if we have to study. What do you think?"

"I think you might have something there John," Dad said later when we explained our plan to him. "But this is all dependent on how Dawn's family feel, and of course the school. But if you hold up your side of the bargain and talk to Dawn's parents, I'll talk to the school. No promises though, and I still have to explain all this to your mother too. I have no idea how she will feel about all this." He paused thinking, then he seemed to make up his mind. "All right," he said, "and the rest we'll take as it comes." He smiled at us both kindly and then he got up and went out.

Chapter 11

Lovelace

So I went back to school and as I failed my first and then second driving test, it was back to being apart. Being engaged to each other helped somewhat, but it was hell being apart, the agony of not seeing her was as acute as ever. The phone calls made it better, and although we were still on this crazy fairground ride lurching from agony to ecstasy, we both knew in our hearts that this really was a forever thing. The fact that we both knew that, made it easier to deal with other people's doubts and pessimism. How could we prove to anyone that this was the real deal? We couldn't. Only we could see into our souls at what must seem like a transient crush to them, but we two knew it as something rare and precious, and I realised what her mother had meant that day in her house. "Most people just can't recognise this," she had said, "and it's only when you are a lot older that you'll be able to turn around and tell them 'I told you so'." She was right. How could we expect people to realise how we felt? All we could do was wait for time to show them but I so wanted them to know, to stop having to justify it to people. Why couldn't they see, wasn't it written in the sky above our heads wherever we went? It certainly felt like it was to me. Dad at least was trying to understand but my mum was a different matter.

Forever – how did I really feel about that? Well if I was really truthful, forever really wasn't going to be long enough. I had thought about what Moli had said but I knew that she was the one, the *only* one. I would never want anyone else as long as I could have her. And the sex thing? Well the sex was just amazing. Not that I thought I was the greatest stud on the planet, but it was like some other world that just we two inhabited, where we were learning and growing together. That too was its own ride, moments of exquisite gentleness and tenderness I really couldn't have imagined before. Sensations that were new to me as well as her and other times of wild desperate, almost violent, passion that was hard to control but just left us wanting more. Finding opportunities was the hardest thing though, and desperation drove us. For me, it was the ultimate expression of our love for each other and I didn't want it to be tainted and become sordid by my inability to provide a safe haven for us to be together.

So when Moli had the brilliant idea of a 'little trip' we were certainly up for it.

I had only recently passed my test. Well as a matter of fact I had to retake it twice. There was the slight problem of reversing around the corner.

"Well, to be perfectly honest, I can't see that there's anything wrong with your driving John," Dawn's dad informed me as he sat next to me. I was taking my test in my mum's old Morris 1000, named 'Moggy.' She had it since new, about twenty years ago but had given up driving a few years previously, when she had her first stroke. She had lost the sensation in her left hand side and her foot had become numb. Her walking had been really bad at first but she had got better and better and was recovering nicely, until her recent fresh attacks that is. The car had been standing in the garage unused for some time. Dad kindly got it up and running for me and I had had some lessons with a local motoring school.

"Lets see you do the maneuver then." It was very kind of Dawn's dad to take me out. There had been a little bit of trouble between Dad and me over an incident whilst driving and he was now refusing to sit with me. Well it's not that great when you are learning to drive and your 'co-pilot' decides to panic and pull on the handbrake, putting you into a 180 degree spin where you end up facing the traffic behind! It had put the wind up me and I had got out and refused to go with him. After that little episode he had also refused to go with me and now becoming a weekly boarder was looking further away than ever.

I selected reverse, checked all the mirrors, etc. and began my maneuver. It always started all right but I ended up miles from the kerb and that was not good enough to get me through the test. Yet again, I mucked it up. Three times I did it until Dawn's dad told me to get out and he would have a go. We swapped seats and, lo and behold, he made the same cock up as I did.

"Well it's not a problem with your driving," he had said, "it's the car." It turned out the webbing under the driver's seat had perished with age and the whole seat sunk when you sat on it, leaving you less than nil chance of seeing through the tiny window in the back of the Morris, unless you were seven feet tall that is. With a cushion strategically placed, I was off and reversing round the corner with no problems at all – and finally passed my test!

Moli's little Easter adventure was the perfect time to get away and spend some quality time with Dawn on our own. Well, having Moli and Co. along was going to be fun and we would still have the evenings to ourselves. The idea was to go camping. I should have known that it had not been thought out properly, but then I was used to going camping with the school CCF so I was prepared for anything. Moli and Co. however were not. We intended to go as soon as we broke up from school. We knew that it would be cold but I was confident that we would be fine. Moli had asked Kelly if she would come along, it seemed that they'd had a resurgence in their relationship, which up until now had been mainly letter writing. Although recently Moli had been putting in a bit more effort to see her. Despite comments to me such as, "I like the fringe benefits of having a girlfriend Lovelace!" he did seem to genuinely care for her.

We were taking two tents, one for the girls and the other for the boys. Really though, it beggars belief that anyone was falling for that one. Mum was in denial and I didn't want to push her after her recent bout in hospital. Dad did seem to genuinely like Dawn very much but I still think that he was finding the whole thing very stressful, being caught between Mum's health and trying to support us. If it all went away then he would feel much happier, if it would just 'wind down and fizzle out,' I overheard him say.

Mum and I were at an impasse. She had made it perfectly clear that she was not fond of Dawn, but she too could see that she was coming up against a brick wall with me. Not that she was unkind to her at all, it was rather her indifference that was noticeable.

Dawn's family, on the contrary, were far more enlightened and modern thinking. They really had embraced the 1960s sexual revolution and had taken me in with open arms. Her mum was treating me like the son she had never had and her dad, having had two daughters, was enjoying a bit of male company. Except for that is, when he challenged me to a game of chess. I'd had a few games with him and he usually won, however I had begun to notice a pattern. He always followed the same format, and once I had grasped this, it was a piece of cake to beat him. Now he was more than a little reticent to repeat the experience.

I had made a list of everything I thought we might be needing and Dawn was sitting cross legged on the kitchen floor crossing off all the items. All the tent equipment was to one side, then the blankets and sleeping bags. I had a section for food, etc. all arranged neatly.

"This is really great," she had said. "Surprisingly it makes life so much easier to be organised!"

"Do tell?" I replied to her, a sarcastic tone in my voice. "How would you have done it then? Put everything in a heap and wait until we arrived to find out that we had forgotten something vital, like the tent?"

She laughed at me. God I loved the sound of her voice. I wanted to go over and give her a cuddle but there was so much equipment surrounding her on the floor. She was sitting in a little island of her own personal clutter and it looked like she was fenced in. The Morris only had a small boot and what with all the camping equipment, Moli and Kelly were going to have to sit with some of their gear around themselves. I had attached a roof rack to take the larger bags of clothing.

I was rather dubious when we arrived at Moli's place in London and surveyed their idea of what they would be needing to camp in the cold, in April. Moli's main contribution to the trip seemed to be a large quantity of 'things to warm us up,' aka Vodka and a single sized duvet. Kelly had a suitcase, a very large suitcase, and a big bag which was reportedly to contain shoes. *Shoes! How many pairs of shoes was she going to wear camping for God's sake!* And a large vanity case which I was reliably informed by Dawn, contained only a small portion of her cosmetics collection. God knows how the poor old Morris managed to struggle up the motorway with all that paraphernalia. I had a theory about that, I reckoned that once it had built up speed it just kept going under its own sheer inertia. Stopping it was a major problem though. There were a few hairy points where I had put on the brakes and absolutely nothing had happened! I had, through necessity, found out that pumping them with my foot helped.

We came to a place called Honister Pass. Dawn had lived in the Lake District as a child and remembered it well.

"It's really steep," she said. Three times we attempted to take a run at it. Twice the poor old Moggy just petered out coming to a stop and we had to roll back and take another go at it. The third time, another car was coming down the other way, so we had to pull into a passing place and then we couldn't get started again.

"Fourth time lucky, otherwise you lot will have to get out and walk," I said. Hill starts had not been a strong point on the test and I was a little rattled by now. Moli and Kelly had spent a good proportion of the trip 'getting reacquainted.' "Give us a break Mols," I laughed. "You're steaming up my windscreen and I can't see a bloody thing."

"Revenge, for all I have had to put up with from you," said Moli, ignoring me completely.

We stopped on the top to have a look at the view. It was breathtaking, though Moli's interests were otherwise occupied in the back seat of the car. It was freezing so we were soon back inside and on the downward slope. We were heading for a campsite on the other side of the pass down by the lake, Buttermere. What a lovely name for a lake, or rather a mere. It was getting really steep and I was trying to keep Moggy in a low gear, but the car was so heavily laden that it kept jumping out into neutral. The brakes were smelling something awful. Dawn was looking more than a little concerned as every time we jumped into neutral the car began speeding up again.

"I don't mind how slow we go," she said as she stomped for the hundredth time on the imaginary brake she thought was beneath her foot. Yeah right, now we were really in trouble. It had come to the point where it didn't matter how hard I pumped the breaks, nothing, absolutely nothing was happening. At the bottom of the pass was a right hand bend with a bridge over the river, and on either side of the bridge were, *Oh My God,* dry stone walls! All I could do was to give up with the brakes and hope like hell that when I turned onto the bridge at high speed, I got it right and didn't either skid or hit the bridge side on!

I have to say Stirling Moss would have been proud of me. We shot over that bridge like a bullet from a gun, taking the chicane on the other side. Dawn went all silent, shock or fury, I couldn't tell, and Moli and Kelly, well they were still inspecting each other's tonsils and were oblivious to the whole incident.

Dawn

Campsite! Well that was one word for it I suppose. A farmer's muddy, wet field, was more apt a description for it. As for the amenities, they consisted of a dry stone wall built toilet block, which looked as if it had, in the not too distant past, been a cow byre. But I was absolutely thrilled to be able to spend a few nights with John. Just us two, on our own, in total privacy, without any threats of someone discovering us. Kelly was absolutely horrified, and she and Moli had had a few choice words about it already.

"Bloody hell, women!" said Moli to John, whilst Kelly was in the toilet. "You offer to show a girl a good time and she has to get picky about the facilities." John was very amused by the whole thing and was trying not to laugh at him. He had his arms folded across his chest and lifted one hand to cover his mouth so that Moli wouldn't see.

"Have you tried pointing out the view to her?" asked John smiling under his hand.

"Yeah I have, and you know what? You know what?" he repeated in an astounded tone. "She said 'I've seen better'. Seen better, I ask you? Time for a fag Lovelace, there's too much pure oxygen up here." He lit up a cigarette and dragged on it deeply.

"Time to get the tents up, it's going to take a while and it looks like it's going to rain." I nodded to the gathering gloom ahead of us down the valley and we discussed where we were going to position the tents. Well there wasn't much choice really. Much of the field was very muddy and waterlogged and then it rose steeply to one side, which was also no good for pitching a tent. John and I chose a level-ish spot for our tent and Moli and Kelly selected one a little further away where the land was beginning to rise to a slope. We set about erecting the tents and Kelly, who was now talking reasonably again to Moli, was helping him put up theirs. It took a while.

John really seemed to know what he was doing and we were soon inside sorting our things out. I was busy zipping our sleeping bags together whilst John was arranging blankets and foam to go under us.

"Won't we need the blankets to put on top of us?" I asked "It's going to be really cold out here tonight."

"You need more layers underneath as insulation," he informed me. Well, who was I to argue, he seemed to have done this before and had a large quantity of kilt pins which he was using to make our nest. "Besides, you'll have me to keep you warm," he said eyes twinkling.

"And what are you two up to?" said Moli in a knowing, sing song voice. He had popped his head in through the tent flap and was grinning at us like a Cheshire cat. "Damn no action then yet?" he pretended to be disappointed.

"Sod off ," said John.

"Come in," I invited.

"Nah, Kelly and I are off down to the pub. Wanna join us?" John and I exchanged glances, we read each other's expressions immediately. I let John answer.

"Were having a cup of tea and then an early night."

"Why bother with the tea?" said Moli.

"Why bother with the vodka?" John replied raising his eyebrows.

"Touché," he replied. "See ya!" and off he went.

I made tea whilst John finished off the sleeping arrangements and we sat in our little make shift home, his things neatly arranged on one side, and mine piled up on the other.

There was plenty of room and we had been careful that nothing touched the sides of the tent so water wouldn't be drawn inside in the night. We had a gas light which was warming us up, and along with the gas burner we were quite comfortable as the light began to fade.

John had made himself comfortable stretched out on our little bed. One arm tucked up behind his head, his mug of tea in the other hand resting on his chest. He was wearing his school CCF clothes, his army sweater and thick warm camouflaged trousers. All the boys had to belong to one or other of the cadet services in the school, John was in the Army Cadet Force. Our boots were at the end of the tent near the entrance, covered in thick mud, well away from anything else. There was a full moon which meant that though it was dark, I could still see John's face clearly. I crawled up his body to his chest and took his mug away from him. He didn't object, his eyes were shining, anticipating me as I approached. I snuggled down onto his chest. He brought his hands down on my shoulders and rolled me over pinning me with his leg in one swift, strong movement. We didn't kiss, he just smiled at me. It was contagious, we just grinned at each other. For the first time ever there was no time pressure, no one to disturb us, we could take our time and enjoy each other as we wished. The temperature in the tent was dropping fast as I had extinguished the gas light, and already my nose was freezing. I rubbed it on his cheek.

"You're cold," he said and took his fingers and pinched my nose. Then he kissed me gently.

"It's too cold to get undressed," I complained.

"It'll be warmer without our clothes on," I acknowledged this with a smile.

"You first then," I encouraged. I was not keen on this at all.

"If we do it fast it won't be so bad," he said challenging me with his eyes. They creased up as he grinned.

"Oh God," I moaned. "I'll race you then."

We sat up and went into a frenzy of pulling off our clothes, jeans and pants together with socks in one swift movement. Then jumpers, T-shirts, and bra all wildly flung to our allotted sides of the tent. Then we quickly climbed into the freezing cold double sleeping bag, grabbing tightly hold of each other under the covers. It was so cold that my teeth had started to chatter long before I got inside the bag. We clung onto each other rubbing our backs with our arms until the temperature inside began to pick up.

Then the rubbing slowed and John began to tenderly kiss me underneath my ear and down my neck. The softness of skin on skin amazed me. I hadn't ever really appreciated how incredible it felt. I brought my leg up, rubbing it up and down his, feeling his skin on the tenderness of my inner thigh. He rolled over on top of me. His mouth was on mine now and our heart rates were picking up. He pulled my arms up above my head. I could feel how strong he was as he held my wrists tight and pressed his hips down on me. It made me feel vulnerable, exposed somehow, but I liked it. His hands trailed down my body, stroking me and then his mouth was on mine. I played with his tongue sucking, urging him on thrusting my hips into his. He nudged himself against me, tantalising me and then slowly and sensually he pressed into me. I wanted him to push more and more, deeper within me. I raised my knees to bring him further in. My every movement he responded to. When I thought it was amazing and couldn't get any better he moved, changing the rhythm and with it the sensation. It became even more intense, more erotic. It was like he was reading my mind. Could he really be this in tune with me? Was this connection between us guiding him or was it that I was just alert to any movement he happened to make I was so turned on by him?

The answer didn't matter, he urged me on higher and higher in intensity and pitch. *Oh please, make me yours, make me yours forever.* We reached our climax together and were left shuddering and panting in each others' arms.

We stared up at the tent above our heads, watching the wind play on our ceiling. I lay warm and snug quietly in his arms, our legs entwined and twisted together immobile, whilst he gently played with my hair, curling it slowly and repeatedly around his fingers. It was so blissful and quiet, we didn't need to talk. We could hear footsteps approaching from a long way off and voices. They weren't whispering, it was Moli and Kelly. We knew they wouldn't disturb us, but I turned around to look at John who was also listening, alert to their approach. We held our breath straining our ears to hear what was being said.

"These shoes will be ruined, there's all this mud."

"Well it's a bloody field, what do you expect?"

"I expected a nice warm camping site."

"Just how did you expect it to be warm, pray?"

"Well I didn't expect it to be like this, I can't see a bloody thing? Where are you going?"

"You're going in the wrong direction. We left the tent over here, that's John and Dawn."

"Oh it's all slippery."

At which point something struck one of the guy ropes of our tent followed by a loud heavy splattering as something, or rather someone, had tripped and fallen face first into the mud. John and I held our breath looking at each other waiting for the next sound. It started low, rising in pitch and intensity.

"oh.... oH...OH...OOHH..."

"For God's sake woman, pull yourself together. Here give me your hand."

There was a lot of squelching muddy slipping sounds.

"This is the worst night of my life."

"Just shut up and come to bed."

"If you think..."

Their voices trailed away on the wind as they faced away from our tent until there was silence. John and I began to giggle, silently at first, and then more and more until we were weeping with hysterics.

"Poor Moli," said John, unable to contain himself.

"Poor Kelly," I struggled to reply.

I don't know whether or not we slept and I lost count of the times we made love but each time it was like a new adventure, a new scene, a different series of colours, and though we exhausted ourselves over and over, we were always wanting more. Was this what it was always like, for everyone?

Lovelace

They were such a sorry sight in the morning. They hadn't risen so we decided to go and check on them. Their tent seemed to have collapsed on one side and it had all sort of slipped down the hill into a small ball.

"Looks like he got some action after all!" I said to Dawn. "Hey you two. Do you intend on getting up at all today?" There was some low moaning and spotting what was the tent flap, I grabbed it and pulled it back.

Dawn

Moli and Kelly were curled up under the duvet they had brought and Kelly was shaking violently. So was Moli for that matter. We could see immediately they were in a serious state. We managed to get them over to our tent and put them into our sleeping bag, their duvet was soaking. John lit the gas stove and light to warm up the tent and I poured out tea. We had already boiled the kettle for ourselves.

Their tent, having been pitched badly on the slope, had collapsed during the night. They had sleeping bags but the zips had broken so they couldn't secure them together. They had also slid down the slope leaving the pair of them lying for most of the night on the groundsheet with no insulation beneath them. To top it all, because they had been touching the sides of their tent, condensation and dew had wicked into it and they had both been sleeping in a soggy puddle. Well not sleeping, they had been awake all night trying to keep warm. They were both seriously cold, but as they began to thaw out, John and I couldn't help catching each others' eye and chuckling.

"All right clever bugger, bet you were cold last night too."

John twisted his lips. "Can't say that I was Mols, sorry."

"It was sooo cold, I never thought a night could last so long," Kelly said.

"You should have taken your clothes off, you'd have been much warmer," I said.

"I couldn't have removed so much as a sock," said Kelly. "It was the most miserable night of my life."

"Doesn't say a lot for your technique does it?" John said

teasing.

"My technique is fine, as long as you don't have a mud bath before bedtime," he said grumpily, looking at Kelly.

"Err yeah, we did hear something last night," said John looking at me and grinning.

"I'm surprised you heard anything with all that sweating going on!" He snapped.

John and I couldn't contain ourselves any longer and we burst out laughing. Moli looked furious and then he began to laugh too, even Kelly began to chuckle.

"Were you really warm?" He changed, sounding serious, as though being warm was something he hadn't experienced for a long time.

"Yeah, I'll help you sort out your tent later," John added with sympathy.

Unfortunately their tent was a disaster. They had broken poles and there was clearly no way that they could sleep another night in it. Their duvet was useless too as there was no way they would be able to dry it. What with that and the fact that they had sleeping bags they could not zip up, they ended up having to make up their bed in our tent. John surrendered some of our blankets and helped them pin their bags, and that was the end of our alone time.

Chapter 12

Lovelace

The return journey took us back over Honister Pass. I hadn't told anyone that the brakes had failed on the way up to the campsite, and had passed off my rather speedy descent on 'misreading the road conditions.' Well, what was the point in scaring everyone when I knew full well that the only way home was back the way we had come. Although the ascent and descent of the pass was again traumatic, for me, we emerged unscathed on the other side. That is however, until we hit some black ice at the bottom. Moggy sailed majestically into a dry stone wall on the far side of the pass. At which point a wheel must have given way, a common fault of Morris Minors we were later to find out. She tipped alarmingly, and then very very slowly started to roll over onto her side.

Dawn

I was absolutely terrified of going over the pass again. John had been rather reckless and driven much too fast the first time we drove over. I was apprehensive of having to go back via the same route, but to go around would have taken us forever. As a child I had lived in the Lake District and been oblivious of such things as road conditions and weather. Now however I was developing a raging aversion to heights and did not like the fact that the road dropped down what seemed to me sheer cliffs to the river below. Each time a car in the oncoming traffic approached us it was our car that had to pull into the passing places. It was unnerving to say the least. We had all but escaped from the confines of the river and hillside when we seemed to be sliding, with no control across the road. Kelly started to scream in the back and I was hanging on to the door strap as if my life depended upon it.

The impact of hitting the dry stone wall was not too severe really, but then we felt the wheel give way and we dropped down at an alarming angle. Still skidding on the ice slowly to the edge of the road, Moggy began to turn over. I could see John out of the corner of my eye but didn't dare to look properly. I got a vague impression that he had hold of the steering wheel and that he was staring out of the front windscreen unmoving. In only a fraction of a second I had, in my imagination, envisaged him knocked unconscious, head streaming with blood, in the seat next to me. When I could steal myself to look though he had only a slight bump on his forehead and was staring out of the windscreen in disbelief, wide awake.

Being trapped in a car is a scary thing, especially when it has turned onto its side. I was trapped in my seat on the upward side of the car and the seatbelt was holding me firmly in place.

It was most uncomfortable, but worse than that I was worried, firstly about John and then secondly, the possibility of fire. It was obvious that the two in the back were still alive as Kelly was screaming her head off and Moli was trying to calm her down. I used my arms against the side of John's seat to try to relieve the pressure of the seatbelt on my chest so that I could undo it, but it was no use. John seemed to come around from his shock and turned off the ignition. I was relieved, as with the cessation of the engine so went the threat of fire. But we were at an incredible angle. Kelly was becoming hysterical in the back and as cooing at her to calm her obviously wasn't working, Moli leapt to the other extreme.

"Will You Bloody Well Shut The Fuck Up!"

I think she was so shocked she did exactly that and there was instant silence. Then after a few seconds, she burst into tears.

Considering Moli was in the most vulnerable position of us all he was quite in control of himself. He was now on the downhill side of the car, trapped in the back behind John, with Kelly on top of him, and a large quantity of their possessions.

"Lovelace! He said earnestly… Lovelace? Are you ok?"

John was still shocked and saying repeatedly, "That shouldn't have happened, I don't know how that happened!" Then as Moli's voice obviously crashed into his consciousness. "Ok? Ok? Yeah I'm ok." I looked down at him from my position hanging above him in the seatbelt. It was burning into my shoulder and my hip and I felt like my chest was caving in.

"Dawn, God Dawn are you ok?" he said looking up at me.

"I think so."

"Mols? Kelly? What about you two?"

"Damn it Kelly, get your elbow off of my neck," exclaimed Moli.

I felt trapped, it was unbearable. I looked around me trying to work out what was the right way up. Inside I was beginning to panic, my chest was being crushed.

"I want to get out, I've got to get out. John… John, I've got to get out, please…" I started to cry too.

"Aah! Kelly!" Moli called out in pain. I tried to turn my head around and look behind my shoulder. I could see poor old Moli, but only just. Kelly was struggling to get herself upright and Moli was squashed somewhere underneath her. She was kicking merry hell out of the poor guy in her efforts to get herself into a position where she could sit up. Moli began to flail about now desperately struggling to breathe and get free of Kelly. She had stood on about every part of him with one or other parts of her anatomy and he had had enough.

John's weight was supported by the door so he was able to get out of his seatbelt and with a little effort he was able to stand up a little. He knelt on the side of his chair and tried to push my body weight up.

"Brace yourself Dawn, otherwise you'll fall on top of me."

I pushed against the dashboard with one hand and against the back of John's seat with the other. There was a ridge of metal that ran down the middle of the car where the transmission went and I wedged my foot against this trying to take some of my weight. I was crying a lot now, I think it was the shock setting in. He pulled the metal flap which acted like a hook on the belt and it came free. Thank God John caught most of my weight, as my arm was still entangled in the strap and I think it would have broken as my weight fell under the force of gravity. With some difficulty I managed to extract myself from the seatbelt and sit on the window. The sounds coming from the back were pitiful now, Moli was obviously panicking too and grunting with the efforts he was making to move.

John tried to help them by removing some of the detritus around them into the front with us. I couldn't stop crying and shaking. John seemed unnaturally calm and was just getting on with the job of trying to help the two in the back. I stood and tried to open the door above my head. What was such an easy job when the car was in the correct position was now nigh impossible as the weight of the heavy metal door was keeping it firmly in position. John stopped to help, but even with the two of us we could only lift it a little. John returned his attention to the two in the back.

"Look Kelly, you've got to calm down," he was saying in a really gentle, but firm voice. "If you don't you're both going to get seriously hurt."

"Seriously hurt? SERIOUSLY HURT!" yelled Moli.

John laughed, relieved. "Thank Christ for that!"

"What?" said Moli.

"I thought for a moment you'd died, you haven't been that quiet since I first met you!"

"Funny, very funny! Last time you drive me anywhere Lovelace. Anyway, I am seriously hurt. Kelly you got me in the gonads at least half a dozen times, shouldn't wonder if I'll be the last of the Olivari de Molina's!" shouted Moli angrily. It may have been the most bizarre thing to do but John and Moli started laughing, then I joined in, and then Kelly too. After that Kelly and I began crying again and I think the boys did too but they would never have admitted it.

All we could do was wait, wait for someone to find us and help us. It seemed like forever. We tried to get as comfortable as we could but it was awful, and claustrophobic.

"Got a fag Lovelace?" asked Moli.

"NO!!!!!" we all shouted in unison, worrying about fire and spilt petrol, although we couldn't actually smell any, well maybe just a bit.

"I *was* joking," he tried to reassure us.

"Got a drink Mols?" responded John, not expecting him to say yes as it was just the usual reply to Moli's requests for fags.

"Well as a matter of fact," he started to say, "I happen to have a bottle of something wedged under my armpit."

"Christ! This is unbelievable," John pushed his hair away from his forehead and shook his head. "Here we are in the middle of nowhere, upside down, lucky to be alive and you've got a bottle of vodka under your armpit."

"Well you don't have to drink it. Don't force yourself on my account."

"Well you can have the first swig. I don't think any of us fancy eau de Molina."

"If you feel that way about it I'll swig the lot and then you won't have to worry."

"Moli," John said, amazed, "how is it that in the middle of a disaster you always manage to make me laugh."

"Natural talent," he replied. "But it's a very sad day today," he continued.

"It is?" questioned John.

"It's happened at last," he paused, "a Lovelace without a fag. You've changed him Dawn," he said sadly, "things will never be the same again."

Moli was heard glugging in the back and began to cough.

"Kelly?" he was obviously offering it to her. There was no reply, she obviously had refused.

"Anyone in the front want some?"

I shook my head. John answered for us both, "Not really Mols, thanks. Besides, they may want to breathalyse me."

"Do you think they will find us?" Kelly asked Moli, sounding as though she was shivering, probably with shock.

"Course they'll find us. We're right next to the road with our huge arse in the air, we must be obvious to anyone going by." It was reassuring but no one had driven by. It had seemed like ages since the accident but it could only have been a few minutes.

"What if no one comes?" I asked.

"Don't be silly Dawn. Remember all those cars that passed us on the way over, there's bound to be one along any time now." He looked at me, giving me a reassuring smile. The bump on his head had swollen up into an enormous egg shape and looked very tender.

"Does that hurt?" I asked.

"No, not really." I think he was lying, he must have had, at the very least, a headache. There were some noises outside and a loud bang on the roof. Then we saw a face pressed up against the cracked windscreen.

"You all ok?" came a concerned voice.

"Yes," we all shouted in unison. I had never in all my life been so glad to see someone.

A farmer had been driving by and had spotted the underside of the car. Getting out was quite a business though. Within minutes there seemed to be a small army of people outside trying to help us. A couple of chaps climbed onto the side of the car and with a lot of pulling, managed to get the door open. John helped me climb out. In my panic, I managed to kick him in the face. Once on the side of the car I realised how high up it was from the bank below me, it was a long jump down. When I was out John managed to pull his seat forward, it tipped up normally to allow passengers to get into the back. At this point Kelly was then able to clamber out. Moli had to wait for her to go and then it was his turn, followed by John. Everyone was so lovely and a nice lady let Kelly and I sit in her car whilst everyone lent a hand to try and help push poor old Moggy back up again, but it wasn't happening so they gave up. We were taken to the nearest farm and given cocoa and fruit cake whilst John and the farmer arranged to get the AA out. Moli absolutely charmed the farmer's wife. Well he would wouldn't he. Kelly was raising her eyes to heaven and then she laughed with me.

"So what do you think about camping Kelly? Would you do it again?" I asked, expecting the obvious answer.

"Camping? No, never ever!" Then she leaned forward and

whispered to me,"but if Moli asks me..." She left it hanging and she looked at me with shining eyes and a smile playing on her lips.

"Is it serious then?"

"Could be," she replied.

The farmer took John back to the car to await the AA. Moggy looked such a sorry state on the back of the low loader when they came back past the farm. Kelly and I retrieved our bags. They had decided that Moggy would be relayed home and we would be taken with her as far as Oxenholme station. There we would catch the train back down south.

We had all grown very fond of Moggy, and it was a real wrench to see her disappearing down the road. The AA man was very complimentary about her, and reckoned that if we had been in any other car we would all have been seriously hurt. He was also quietly confident, that with a little bit of help, Moggy would be back on the road. Well, several hundred pounds later, but definitely not a write-off.

The journey south was uneventful. We slept most of the way, we were all exhausted from the accident.We put our feet up and across to the seats on the opposite side of the train, expressly against the advice on the notice in the carriage. John and I slouched on one side and Kelly and Moli on the other. It was quite comfortable. John held on to me, and Moli held Kelly.

I woke a few times. Moli was awake and so was John. They were talking quietly.

"So what? You've seen the light at last, is that what you're telling me?"

"May have done. You know you don't have to look smug Lovelace."

"This isn't my smug face, it's really great, I'm glad you feel that way about her. Maybe now you'll get off my back."

"She is so incredible. You know, when we were at my sister's house in London… at it for hours, got a bit dry…!"

"You know you're going to have to watch the vodka intake Mols," said John concerned, not catching Moli's drift at all.

"I don't mean I needed a drink… I mean *we*… got a bit dry," he was raising his eyebrows. "Didn't know there were so many uses for natural yoghurt!"

"MOLI!" John exploded taken by surprise. I started at what I had just heard, betraying my eavesdropping and Moli immediately looked at me. He just grinned cheekily and shrugged.

Chapter 13

Dawn

We arrived in London, tired from our journey, with still another train ride ahead of us down to Kent. So we decided to spend the night, at Moli's invitation, with his sister in her flat, spending one last night together before going home and having to part again for the new term and the impending exams. We knew that this was just about the last time we four would be together like this until the summer. His sister was out but Moli reassured us she wouldn't mind.

We were all to bunk together in the living room on a sofa that turned miraculously into a bed. Girls on the bed and boys on the floor, very chivalrous, but I was happy to take the floor to be next to John. It was a very tiny flat, but its location was everything. Right in the middle of Mayfair and within striking distance of the West End or Oxford Street, well anywhere that we fancied going. John and I wanted to do a little bit of exploring on our own, so we arranged to meet up in The Marquis of Anglesey, a pub in Covent Garden. Moli and Kelly had a little bit of shopping to do, so we arranged a time to meet, then John and I grabbed a cab to St Paul's. John was ever the gentleman, walking down the street, he was always on the outside of the pavement and even when we crossed the road he made sure I was immediately on the inside.

"Looking after me, in case I wander out into the traffic?" I enquired.

"No," he said, shocked that I had mentioned it.

"My dad does that too," I added, "is it a blokey thing then?" He laughed, slipping his hand into the back pocket of my jeans so that his arm was around me as we walked.

"No, that's not the reason. It's just that a gentleman always walks on the outside of the pavement. It's something I was taught to do from very young, when walking with my mum. It goes way back to when the houses used to overhang the pavements and the slops were thrown from above into the streets below. I'm shielding you from splash back, though the only liquid that might be splashed at you today is a puddle."

"Aah, I see now," I was mightily impressed that I was walking with a gentleman, although I'd known that from the start.

We were walking from St. Paul's down Ludgate Hill. As we rounded the corner, before the final descent to the cross roads, the tower of St. Brides church could be seen riding above the roofs. It was as if there were a table upon which it stood, like a large wedding cake, tier upon tier. We walked up the rise on the far side. Although it was early evening, it was a hive of activity as some of the papers were being 'put to bed' and the print runs were beginning. John shepherded me down Bride Lane and up a series of steps into a little alley which ran alongside the graveyard, past the Old Bell Pub. As we got to the gateway we both looked up at the tower rising above us.

Not one Richard Lovelace would have recognised, his church with its square tower had burned down in the Great Fire of London in 1666 and the replacement church had been bombed in the war leaving only this tower standing. The main body of the church was new but sympathetically restored.

"It's very atmospheric in here," I said as we stood in the churchyard. "What with the noise and the hustle and bustle of Fleet Street just over there and the absolute quiet over here." John held the door open for me and we stepped inside the church. It was light and bright inside and tea was being served at the back, the West end of the Church. We shuffled around and after finding a floor plan of the original church we deduced that somewhere under the bins placed out to collect the detritus from the tea sales, Richard's body must have been laid to rest. There was nothing to mark his presence in the church, nothing. No small plaque, not one line of his beautiful poetry, not a thing to say he was once here. There was no sense of his presence either. The failing light from outside and the air itself, these were the only elements that Richard would recognise here. Canned music played and the visitors sat around in the pews talking and drinking their tea, even eating sandwiches and Kit Kat's which were also on sale. A lady sat at the back selling postcards and mugs. There were childrens' books for sale, but not so much as a stanza of Lovelace's sublime literature. But this *was* the same space where he would have worshiped, and it *was* the last place his human remains had touched. His soul was not here though, it lies interred within the pages of his poetry, awaiting another generation to seek it out and find joy in his verses. It wanders amongst the walls of Lovelace and in the chapel on the hill. It is there for anyone with romance, or loyalty in their heart but it was, sadly, not to be found here. We sat for a while, John with his arm around me.

"Are you sad you came?"

"No, no, not at all."

"But there's nothing here, no presence."

"I think you're missing something," he said looking at me. "Do you remember the tramp?" Did I remember, the stench of him was still strong in my nostrils. As we had moved past the tea sales, the smell of him had assaulted us, clawing and stale, and although he had now left the church, the smell lingered still. I am ashamed to say I had to bury my nose in my sleeve as he had passed us. He had actually bumped into John.

"This is where Richard spent the end of his life. There is some debate as to how poor he really was at the end. Some of it may have been propaganda. You know, king's loyal soldier, most handsome man in England being laid so low, but he was ill with consumption and some friends did help pay towards his upkeep. I don't know, but the tramp's presence brought that home to me. I know this isn't his church, but he was here, and I kind of like that."

"You Lovelaces'," I said, "always finding the poetry." He smiled and looked deeply into my eyes. "I don't want to go home, I feel as if once we're back and school starts and you have to study…" My stomach was churning, I couldn't bear being apart again.

"I know what you mean, it's almost like an ending." His eyes reflected back the pain in my own. "You know it's not for long though, we can still see each other at the weekends."

"But that's not what your father wants. How can you study when we just can't keep our hands off each other?" A huge wave of pain surged over me and it felt like somehow, someone had sucked the oxygen out of the atmosphere. I gasped in pain at the weight of what was in front of us. It would be back to stolen moments together, back to all those partings, all those nights trying to study and failing miserably, longing to be together and the long empty nights crying myself to sleep. It felt like the air itself was weighing down on me and the chatter around seemed to make it even more intense.

"I've got another poem for you, I think it's appropriate for where we are and how I feel about you." He took my face in his hands, and turned his searing blue eyes on me and began in a whisper.

Tell me not (Sweet) I am unkinde,
That from the Nunnerie
Of thy chaste breast, and quiet minde,
To Warre and Armes I flie.

True; a new Mistresse now I chase,
The first Foe in the Field;
And with a stronger Faith imbrace
A Sword, a Horse, a Shield.

Yet this Inconsistency is such;
As you too shall adore;
I could not love thee (Deare) so much,
Lov'd I not Honour more.

It was such a beautiful moment that we didn't speak. I gazed into his eyes, full of love, and Richard's words like a voice from the past but with so much weight of meaning for us here in the present, were so apt. It was as if he were here somewhere, awakened by the poem.

"I suppose school is a bit like you're going off to the war, to do something you have to," I said looking into his eyes.

"But it's not a war, it's school," he smiled at me gently, "and I won't be killed, and we will still see each other. It may feel like it, but it isn't life and death. I do love you Dawn, I really do." He held my face between his palms and he kissed me gently, slowly and softly.

We left the church, and Richard's ghost, and set off to find Moli and Kelly, and The Marquis of Anglesea.

*

Moli and Kelly were giggling together at the bar when we arrived. He nodded to John as we drew nearer, which I didn't understand. It was packed with well dressed people and we stood out a bit in our outdoorsy camping gear.

"We've got a treat for you Dawn," yelled Moli, cigarette clenched between his teeth. It was a little hard to be heard over the din. He pulled it from his lips. "Come on we might just make it in time." They both bundled us out of the door and turned us up the street, right to the front of the Royal Opera House. "What do you think Dawn?" Moli was grinning, I'd never seen him so delighted with himself.

"What do you mean what do I think?"

"Well you want to be an opera singer don't you? Well we're up in town and we thought you might like to go to a show," said Kelly grinning.

"What now? Dressed like this?"

"Yeah, why not," said Moli and he strode through the front doors heading for the box office. I could see the expression on the guy's face behind the glass screen and he laughed at Moli as he waved his plastic card at him. But then he was suddenly serious and was handing over tickets.

"This way," said Moli. It was obvious that Moli had been before and it wasn't long before he was leading us up a red carpeted stairway with gold everywhere. It reminded me a little of the Golden Landing at Lillesden but much, much grander. The room above was amazing with mirrors and beautiful chandeliers hanging down. We followed, getting rather odd looks from the other luxuriously clad opera goers. A guy maneuvered himself out in front of us and asked to see our tickets. Moli waved them at him. I half expected him to ask us to leave, but he smiled at Moli and began to usher us through past the queue down a dark corridor with doors to one side. He opened one of the doors for us and indicated for us to go in. I couldn't believe it, we were in the bloody Royal box!

"Sorry," said Moli, "it has a restricted view but it was all that was left, and we won't have a clue what happens on this side of the stage." He then turned to the usher and whispered to him.

"Bloody hell Moli!" I sat down in one of the comfy armchairs, bells were ringing in the background and then the lights went down. The usher reappeared with some glasses and a bottle of open champagne in a bucket. "What are we watching?" I asked.

"Don't know, I thought you could tell us that, didn't have time to ask."

"Well it could be a ballet then," I replied.

"Oh, I didn't think of that," he sounded a little disappointed.

The overture began. I didn't need any more than the first five notes of the overture.

"It's Madam Butterfly," I whispered, "one of my favourites! Moli I can't believe this!"

"It's my pleasure," he said taking my hand and then he kissed it, grinned at John and then he passed my hand to him. He turned and put his arm around Kelly, who was watching my face with delight. I looked up into John's face, I think he was in on it too. He shrugged.

"That's Moli for you!" he said.

Part Two
October 1977

Chapter 14

Lovelace

My lecture had been cancelled on the Thursday. *Fantastic!* I'd passed my A levels and got into Middlesex Polytechnic in north London and had digs nearby in Ponders End. I had decided to go straight down to Kent in Moggy and surprise Dawn. I wouldn't arrive until late but it would mean a whole extra day together, and a night. I hadn't phoned her to warn her because I wanted so badly to see the look on her face when she saw me. I knew that she would have school the next day, but I could take her in and collect her at the end of the day. I was so excited. It had been a grim week of lectures and lots of reading but as was de rigueur now I tried to get everything done ahead of deadlines so we could have time together, just me and her.

I parked the car in the extra large parking space at the corner so that she wouldn't see me drive past and spoil the surprise. It was dark now and the curtains were open. From the street outside you could see straight into the living room. My heart leapt as I saw her, and then I stopped as I recognised the guy she was talking to. *Moli!*

I don't know why I didn't just keep on walking and bound up to the door to surprise them both. I knew Moli went to see her now and again when he could get out of school. He had failed an A level and not done as well as he wanted in another, so he had stayed on an extra year to re-take and try to get better grades. There was something about the two of them here together though. It was intimate, very intimate and I was rooted to the spot, reduced to an unwilling peeping Tom. She was crying, that much was obvious and he just held her in his arms as she wept, rocking her slightly and brushing her hair. It wasn't that though, it was the fact that as they talked she pulled back and touched her stomach with a caressing stroke. He placed his hand on it too, and my mouth dropped open in shock. Clear to be seen, if that was what you were looking for, was a small bump under his hand. And then she was crying even more, and so was he, his shoulders shivered up and down as he wept. This was so personal and private, and not meant for me, I just turned and walked away.

For a long time I couldn't think of anything, I just walked and walked, I hadn't even a clue where I was going. I can't even remember if I was aware of anything, certainly not pain, there was just nothing, blank empty nothing. It wasn't until I bumped blindly into the gate at the back of the churchyard that I felt anything or became aware of where I was. But I had walked a good mile from Dawn's house. I slid down onto the floor with the kissing gate at my back, my hands on my raised knees as the images began to pass like a re-run film in front of my eyes. I watched it again as it played in slow motion. I tried to make some sense of it. Why was I shocked? Wasn't it wonderful if Dawn was pregnant? It was something we had talked about. Inconvenient yes, but a problem? No, definitely not. She knew how I would feel. Was she worried about the timing. Was it a problem with me being at college? No, we'd work it out together, that's what we had said. That wasn't it and I knew it, there was something else here, and now it all started slotting into place like some unwanted horror show just for me. Moli had been crying too, what did that mean? Had I missed something major here? I knew how Moli felt about Dawn, he had made no secret of it since he had tried to knock my block off at my house after the night Dawn and I first made love. He had thought that I had used her, that once we'd been together I'd lost interest in her. His feelings had been laid out clear as day before me. But he was my best mate… and she was the love of my life… and I thought that was how she felt about me… was I wrong? And then it hit me in the stomach like a sledge hammer. I fell forward onto my knees, unable to breathe from the blow. Pain seared white hot through my belly and I threw up violently onto the grassy path in front of me. I felt like I was going to pass out. Dawn and I hadn't made love for a while now. There had been reasons, wrong time of the month, lack of opportunity, me being at college and not being able to come down every weekend, and now I thought about it, she didn't like me to touch her any more. She pulled away and I hadn't pressed it because, well because I hadn't. But facts were facts and the maths wasn't that hard to work out. I grabbed the grass tufts on the floor in my fists as the next blow landed and again

I threw up as the pain hit me like a wall.

I didn't know how long it took before it started to show. I had noticed a slight swelling in her belly. I had wanted to ask her, but it was like some secret she was keeping from me and I knew it was hers to tell not mine to ask. I thought it was because she wanted to be sure, that she would tell me in her own time. But then I also thought it was just wishful thinking, that perhaps I had got it wrong, and that by asking I would lay myself open to yet another crass comment because she might have just put on a few pounds in weight. And then the third sledgehammer hit me... Moli! Wave after wave of pain hit again and again, and all I could do was cry out, fall on my hands and knees in the dirt and weep.

It was a long time later that I was able to pick myself up. I couldn't go back for the car, I couldn't go back in that direction, so I staggered through the kissing gate and into the fields beyond, towards a big old oak tree in the distance. I knew the tree well, Dawn and I had often come on walks over the church fields. There was a place on the far side where I could hide myself away, away from the footpath and lose myself in my misery. It was freezing, I shook so hard I thought my teeth would shatter, but I couldn't move I just sat waiting for the sun to come up.

Its pale watery gleam appeared. I had no idea of time passing. It felt like I had been there ten seconds and sometimes ten hours, but I knew when the sun rose my heart would be shattered forever. However, rise it did and I left my heart's shards scattered on the ground and walked away to find the car.

I wanted to go home, I wanted to talk to my dad, but then I knew what he would say, and I just couldn't listen to it. Mum? Well I knew she would be sad for me, but I just couldn't bear to see the triumph in her eyes. So I headed back to London, back to my digs. Dawn would be expecting me, so I had a lot of thinking to do before I phoned her, and then there was Moli. I think tears streamed down my face the whole journey. There were miles where they fell silently in a stream, then there were hours where I sat in a layby sobbing uncontrollably. Then there were the sections where I just drove as fast as Moggy would go, my foot down in blind rage. When I got to London however, I turned the car around and drove straight back to Dawn's. I had to make this all right for her, I loved her more than my life, and if I had to let her go then that was what I would do, but I wanted to make this as easy as I could for her. So I drove straight back to hers and rang the bell.

Dawn

He was standing on the doorstep, and my stomach turned over, I thought I was going to be sick there and then. How was I going to tell him this? I couldn't even admit it to myself let alone anyone else and I didn't want him to stay with me out of pity. I looked into his eyes and I just wanted him to hold me, to tell me everything was going to be all right, because when he held me it was, everything was possible and nothing bad could happen to me. But as soon as I looked at him tears fell down my cheeks and I knew I had to spare him this one.

"Hi," I said limply, "I need to talk to you."

"I need to talk to you too," he said seriously. He stepped inside and I shut the door, then he followed me up the stairs to my room. I sat on the edge of the bed, well I couldn't sit on the floor it was too uncomfortable, but I couldn't tell him that. I didn't know where to start. I looked up at him for help. He smiled at me so kindly and then said words I just couldn't comprehend.

"Look Dawn, you know I love you, but it's just becoming impossible. I have a life in London now and yours is here. I'm spending so much time on the road that I don't have time to study, and I don't want you hanging on for me until college finishes. I think it's time we stepped back from this and took some time out." I just gasped, more tears falling down my cheeks. I bit my lip so I didn't say something I might regret. He was finishing it, wasn't that what I was going to do? I laughed and smiled, and my heart broke inside. I couldn't speak, tears just spilled down my cheeks. He came up to me and knelt before me, just like he had when he had asked me to marry him, and he took my hand in his.

"I'll always love you Dawn," he was crying too, "it's just that things have changed, I've been seeing someone and although we're not together yet…" His words stabbed me like a knife. 'NO' I screamed inside my head. So he had found someone, too much of a gentleman he needed to finish with me first. But wasn't that what I was always expecting? It was too good to be true, I always knew it couldn't last, he wasn't for me. It had been some unbelievably lucky mistake that I had ever had him at all.

"Its ok…" I managed to get out, "really it's ok. You don't have to explain, really you don't because I've been seeing someone too." I don't know where that one came from, but it seemed as good a thing to say as any. He looked down and nodded. We were both crying now. He looked up into my eyes and I just threw my arms around his neck. We hugged so tight. *Oh God I loved him so much, how had it come to this nightmare*? But I had to let him go now. I let go of him, looked down at my ring, slowly slid it off and put it in his hand.

"No Dawn it's yours."

"Not any more," I said pressing it into his palm. He nodded and slipped it onto his little finger. Then he stood up. I couldn't look him in the eyes, I didn't want him to read anything my soul was saying. And he went. I think I forgot to breathe because I passed out.

Lovelace

There was a ring at the door, it was pretty early in the morning and I grabbed my jeans and pulled them on, zipping them up, but without doing up the belt. Moli was standing in the doorway. I didn't invite him in.

"You look like shit!" he said looking me up and down.

"Probably!" I said coolly in reply. "What do you want?" I wanted to be angry with him, but truth be known I couldn't muster it up. I wanted them to be happy but I didn't want my nose rubbing in it.

"Look what the fuck are you up to Lovelace? I've spoken to Dawn, and I just don't get it."

"What is there to get? I've moved on, that's it, there is no more," I tried to stay impassive.

"I don't believe this. You know your timing's crap, she's got a lot on her plate at the moment and you've just abandoned her!"

"Where the fuck do you get off telling me what I should and shouldn't do?" I yelled at him. "You love her, you have my blessing, you sort it out!" Just at that moment Francis walked past in a state of undress wearing only her knickers and t-shirt. "Hey Francis, come and say hi to an old friend of mine." I spat out the words 'old friend.' Francis came over and I draped my arm around her. "Moli meet Francis."

"Pleased to meet you," she said and then giggled and backed out from under my arm and back into the digs. Moli shook his head disapproving.

"Christ, you don't waste any time do you? So much for 'the love of your life'… I don't know you… I just don't know you," he said quietly shaking his head.

"You don't know me, YOU DON'T KNOW ME!" I yelled at him. "Well I sure as fuck don't recognise you either you bastard, going behind my back." And he thumped me full in the face with all his might and I blacked out.

I woke up probably only seconds later but Moli was gone. Francis was slapping my face gently and Chris her boyfriend was trying to drag me away from the door.

"I thought you said he was your friend," she said, as I came too.

"Yeah, I thought so too," I said sadly.

Chapter 15

Dawn

I wasn't aware of time passing, my stomach was getting bigger and bigger at an alarming rate. The doctor confirmed the worst and I was booked in as an emergency. Moli was great, he would come and sit with me after school when he could. He didn't talk much, he was just there, for company, and I was so grateful. Having him near really was a comfort, it was somehow like I had a small piece of John with me. When I had the operation he stayed with Mum and Dad outside and as I came out of theatre he was there waiting, holding my hand telling me everything was ok, but of course it wasn't. When I looked into his eyes it was John my soul yearned for. So I pretended and closed my eyes and held his hand to my face, pretending that John was there, touching me. I cried silent tears in the ward, daring not to make a sound, trying not to disturb the others in there. I couldn't move as they had put an epidural into my spine to prevent any pain, so I lay there staring at the ceiling yearning for him, knowing he would never come.

"Please let me tell him, Dawn, this is unbearable, he'd come if he knew," Moli kept saying. I couldn't answer him, I could only shake my head. He'd found someone else, it wasn't me he wanted any more, and I knew he would come if I asked, but I couldn't do that to him, I had to let him go. He didn't need to know any of this. None of it was his fault, things just happen don't they? Well this was how the cookie had crumbled for me. I had decided not to tell him and that was a good decision. This way only I was hurting, and Moli. *Poor Moli.* I knew he had been to see John, but he wouldn't tell me what had happened. I gathered from the way he spoke that John wasn't alone, but I couldn't listen to that. I imagined his eyes looking into hers and the tears spilled fresh down my face. I wonder how much water one person can cry? Moli held me gently and cuddled me. *Oh God Moli I just want to die, I can't bear the pain of not having him...* But of course I stayed silent, with my thoughts unsaid in my head. And Moli? Moli just held me, wonderful steadfast Moli.

One day Mrs Butters in the bed next door to me was taken for her operation. She was lovely, she chatted to me and called me 'little darling'. She didn't come back. They told me she had been moved to another ward, but I knew she had died. I was the only one on the ward under the age of seventy and so Moli's visits were like a life line to me. I knew Moli loved me, and I knew this was torture for him, so eventually I tried to stop him from coming too. Mum kept letting him in though, every now and again, and I just held on to him in silence.

"He'll be back Dawn, I know it, I know him, he'll be back," he told me. Did I want him back? What a silly question that was, I would have crawled over broken glass to see him once more. But I didn't want to see pity in his eyes and I knew I couldn't see him because I would have begged, I would have groveled on the floor for just a few more seconds with him. I even wondered why had I bothered. Why was it I had had the operation? I didn't want a life any more because it had ended as he left my room that day. Life now was in limbo, an existence, waiting for the sun to come back and knowing that it never would. Some days he came to me in dreams, kissed me and smiled at me, his eyes creasing up, but then I would dread having to turn over because I knew he wasn't there. It would be like the first day he had left, and a new grief, a new mourning would begin for something that was gone forever.

I wanted to help Moli out, I knew he was waiting for me to turn to him, but that would not have been fair. I loved Moli but not like that, and though I knew he would have me any way I asked, I couldn't do that to him, he deserved better.

Then there were my wonderful parents. So that was why I smiled, ate at mealtimes, existed from one moment to the next, went through the motions, because they loved me and I loved them. But that was all I had to give and anything more? I didn't have any answers to that.

Lovelace

College was a bit like another school but worse. Then I had had Dawn to look forward to seeing, to work for a future. Now I couldn't concentrate on work and I had nothing to look forward to either. What was the point? Everyone in college was looking to find someone, and I knew I would never ever find anyone even close to my Dawn. Yeah I went out, Chris and Francis were always dragging me out to parties and pubs, but all I seemed to do was get drunk. I even woke up with a girl in my bed once. Haven't a clue how she got there, but I do know I was too drunk to do anything, and she wasn't impressed with me the next morning, but there again my hangover was so bad I didn't really care. I didn't really care about anything, especially not myself.

Dad had made a surprise visit to see me. He wanted to know why I hadn't been in touch, why I hadn't come to see them when I came down to see Dawn. He'd rung Dawn's parents and they had told him we had split up. I got the disapproving speech, but again I was drunk and not really listening. He had wandered around the house picking up dirty plates etc. Yeah my room was a mess, so much for my obsessive compulsive tidiness, I didn't even care enough to wash and shave. He kept telling me how disappointed he was with me, but what could he say to me that I hadn't already said to myself over and over? But that was the problem, I felt my life was over. What did I have now? He didn't understand, and I didn't really care about anything any more. I stopped going to college, and my grades which had been two-ones and firsts had petered out. I tried to think. When had this happened, why hadn't I seen it coming? Moli. I thought I knew him, but the Moli I knew could never have done this. Maybe it was just too much, they were overcome with their feelings for each other and couldn't tell me. I think my lowest moment was when I sat in the bathroom with my razor in my hand. It wouldn't hurt much and then the pain would go and I could sleep, could rest from the torment. I wasn't frightened it was as if a huge calm had come over me. But then I thought about my Dad, and how much he loved me and Mum, and I realised what a selfish pathetic bastard I was. I hated myself in that moment and just wanted to hurt myself, to feel some physical pain because at that moment I felt nothing. So I dug the razor hard into my hand and held it as tight as I could, I just needed to feel, feel something.

Dad turned up one afternoon at the end of my bed with Carl in tow, threw my clothes at me and told me to be down in the car in five minutes. He then left Carl hovering over me. I grabbed a few things and Carl manhandled me down the stairs, I was still so drunk from the night before. We didn't say anything all the way back home, so I helped myself to the whisky in the car and drank myself back into oblivion. Once at home I went straight up to my room. Well not really, I went straight up to the attic, pulled the mattress onto the floor and threw myself on it. I looked up at the ceiling remembering my first time here with Dawn, and tears just slid down my face. How long was it now? Quite a few months had passed, she must be getting near her time. I tortured myself thinking of her holding a baby, our baby, my baby. Then I pictured Moli with her, and it wasn't my baby any more, it was his, and I knew that she was lost forever.

Mum came up to talk to me. "John, I don't know how to tell you this."

"What?" I said barely interested, "isn't this what you both

wanted? Aren't you happy it all turned out like you thought it would? Well, well done Mum, you were right all along. You told me so, isn't that what you want to say? 'I told you so?' Well congratulations to you both." My voice was heavy with sarcasm.

"John, that's not what I want to say..."

"No? Mmph," I snorted, "you know I don't want to hear this," and I stormed out of the attic, out of the house and found myself where? Sitting in the Lovelace chapel weeping and praying. Then my dad was there with his arm around me, and he just held me whilst I cried. After I stopped crying I just leaned into his warm embrace.

"Why did you give up on her John? If you feel like this what on earth could have made you give her up?"

"Love!" I answered. "Because I love her, and because I wasn't what she wanted any more." I smiled at him knowing we were about to have another stupid conversation that he just couldn't understand. And the pain, the pain in my chest was threatening to crush me.

"And you know that do you?" he asked. "How do you know that? Did she tell you?"

I nodded looking down. I looked up at him tired. I didn't want to go through it all, it was too painful, so I didn't say anything.

"John, when was the last time you spoke to Dawn?"

I shrugged. "I don't know, months ago now."

"So you don't know then?" he said concerned.

"Yeah, I know," I said resigned.

"You do?" he sounded really surprised.

"It's not mine Dad, she found someone else but she couldn't tell me, so I said I'd found someone else to make it easier for her."

"And did she tell you that she didn't love you before you said you'd found someone else, or after?"

"What does it matter Dad? She found someone else, she fell in love, she's having their baby." Oh God I was going to have to spell it out to him. I could hardly breathe as I spoke. "I saw them Dad, I saw her in his arms and I love them both. What could I do?"

He sighed. "I presume you mean Moli?" I nodded. "For God's sake John! She's not pregnant, and she's not in love with Moli, though if she is by now that's your own fault. She's been very ill."

"What? What do you mean?" I couldn't take it in. "Ill, what's wrong with her? Dad? What's wrong?"

"Cancer," he whispered. I looked at him dumbfounded.

"No!" I shouted, my voice ringing in the church. "NO!" I couldn't think, my heart was hammering in my chest and my breath was catching in my throat. "Not Dawn, not my baby, please God no. Dad?" I looked at him in agony, begging him to take it back, but I could see in his eyes it was the truth. "Oh dear God, what have I done?" I put my head in my hands tearing at my hair. "Where is she Dad? How long have you known? Where is she?" I was desperate. Here all this time I had been wallowing in my own self pity whilst my beautiful baby had been suffering God knows what on her own.

"I only found out the other day, that's why I came to get you, I wasn't sure if you knew. I was leaving your mother to talk to you. As to where she is, she's at home at the moment. But I don't think she wanted you to know about any of this. For God's sake why don't you young people talk to each other!" he said crossly. Then he stood up. "Come on, I'll take you in the car, but not before you have a shower and put some clean clothes on, you smell like a distillery!"

We didn't phone ahead, I wasn't sure if she would see me, and I didn't think her parents would be too thrilled about me turning up either, but I didn't care about that I just had to see her, to make sure she was alright. Well I knew she wasn't alright but I just had to see her. She answered the door, which surprised me, there was no baby, there was no bump. She didn't say anything to me she was obviously shocked to see it was me. I was about to speak when she just threw herself at me, arms around my neck and I just held on tight. We couldn't speak to each other, there were no words for this, we just rubbed our faces in each others hair and clung on to one another crying and stroking. But in those few moments together we said a hundred things to each other without uttering a sound.

"Dawn," I said, "I'm..."

"Don't say it," she said, "don't say your sorry." We'd been here before and we both laughed at the memory, the conversation we had had when my dad had found out about our first night together.

"I'm so in love with you," I continued and gazed into her beautiful brown eyes.

"I love you too," she said smiling widely. Then pain and hurt crossed both our faces, and we just held on tight again until the wave of sadness left.

"Is your dad in the car? Does he want to come in?" she invited.

"Well…" I hesitated.

"You can't leave him in the car. It's ok you know, it's about time our parents met don't you think?" I smiled and nodded. I put her down and we walked to the car together. Dad got out and followed us back down the drive.

She introduced Dad to her parents. They were very gracious considering they thought I had left their daughter for another woman whilst she then was coping with cancer on her own. I flinched at the thought. I had to talk to her, but we were in the middle of introductions and polite conversation. Dawn's dad went out to make some tea whilst her mum sat in an armchair. The bed had gone from the living room, so I reckoned her back was getting better. Dawn sat with her legs curled up on the settee next to me holding my hand and arm with her head nestled on my shoulder. Dad broached the subject.

"And how are you Dawn? We've only just found out about your illness."

"I'm fine now," she said staring into my eyes, but that wasn't what she was saying and I knew it. There was a sadness there and fear. She held on to my hand and buried her face in my shoulder. The conversation sort of dried up until Dawn's dad came in with the tea.

"Look I need to apologise for my behaviour," I said, "to

everyone, including you Dad, but especially to you Dawn and your parents. I have excuses, I thought you were in love with Moli." She looked shocked. "I came to see you a day early and I saw you together, I thought you were… well it doesn't matter now what I thought. I was wrong, but I told you I'd found someone else, and that wasn't true, there's never been anyone else Dawn and there never will be, can you forgive me?" I looked at her. She took my hand and pulled at the ring on my little finger. "That's mine," she said smiling at me. We kissed there and then in front of everyone and I didn't care a jot. Neither did she.

"Tea?" her dad said, and everyone broke out laughing.

*

Dad left some time later. I was invited to stay and we had loads to talk about. It was a small house though and I was given a sleeping bag to spend the night on the sofa. Dawn's parents went to bed and we stayed up with the log fire burning cheerfully in the grate. We lay on the sofa in each other's arms with just the firelight flickering. I didn't want to ask her, I figured she would tell me when she was ready.

"It began in the night, I had lots of stomach pain and I couldn't let you touch me. When it got really bad I told Mum. Mum said it was colic and that it kills horses." She laughed at the thought. "But then it went on and on, so I went to the doctors. I didn't know how to tell you, so I didn't. Moli came round and he made a joke about me putting on weight and I burst into tears and told him the truth. It was a cyst in my womb, and the speed it grew was incredible. I was so scared, and I didn't want you to know. I didn't want you to worry after your mother and everything, and with you being away at college. So when you said you'd found someone else I lied too."

"Did you know I was lying?" I asked.

"It's easier to believe that you're not loved rather than you are. At times I thought, hoped you'd been lying, but then when Moli came to see you… He didn't tell me much about the girl in your digs but…" She left it hanging.

"That was Chris's girlfriend, I let Moli think she was with me."

"Aah," she said nodding. "Well, to be honest I just couldn't cope with any of it. I certainly couldn't deal with other people's fears. I couldn't even think the word let alone say it, so I just got on with it. I had an operation… they put me on a cancer ward with all the old people… There was one lady, she was lovely. She was really sweet and chatted to me… and then one day she wasn't there any more." I squeezed her hand and rested my head on hers. "They say it's very rare but curable, but I may have to have chemotherapy. We're waiting to find out." She swallowed hard. "But I lost my ovary on one side." A tear slid down her cheek. "If I have chemo…" she didn't finish that sentence, but I knew she was talking about being infertile. "And my stomach isn't pretty any more, she said putting a protective arm over her belly. And I missed you so much." Tears slid silently down her cheeks.

"Oh God Dawn," she looked up at me and I gently wiped the tears from her cheeks. "I should have been there, oh baby, I don't care about any of that I just want you to be ok." I touched her stomach then, gently laying my hand over her arm, I looked into her eyes and said, "You're the most beautiful person in the whole world." She looked at me and hesitated then she got up and undid her jeans, pulling up her shirt. The scar was huge, but neat if rather raw and angry, it ran the length of her belly from just below her pubic hair to above her navel. "Does it hurt?" I asked.

"Sometimes," she said. "They say I can have sex, but I don't know..." Her voice dropped. "I'm scared," she confessed. "And up until now that's not something I have had to think about." She smiled a little coyly. I touched the scar gently, running my finger down its length and then pulled her forward and kissed her on it. She let her jeans slide down to the floor and stepped out of them. I held my arms open for her and she snuggled back into my chest and I pulled the sleeping bag over her to keep her warm.

"What about Moli? Have you seen him?"

"Yeah, Moli's been great. He came with me and my parents to the hospital, and he's been like a big brother, lots of cuddles and love. You know he never gave up on you, he said you'd be back."

"You know he's in love with you," I said. I thought it only fair that she knew.

"Yeah, I know, but I'm in love with someone else. He loves you too," she said smiling gently at me.

"He hit me you know," she looked around at me shocked.

"When?"

"When he came up to London to see me. When I pretended Francis and I were an item. Laid me out cold."

"Impressive," she laughed and turned looking me in the eyes. Her eyes were liquid.

"I thought I'd lost you forever. Oh God I'm such a fool," I whispered.

"So am I, I should have told you. Moli wanted to tell you, but I wouldn't let him, I made him promise." Her eyes reflected the flames in the firelight.

We kissed, it was soft and warm and so sensual, and then I just held on tight to her as she lay in my arms.

We meant to separate, she to her room and me to… well the couch where we were, but we just couldn't let go of each other, and we fell asleep in each others arms in the dying firelight. I woke in the early hours of the morning, Dawn was crying in her sleep, I shook her gently.

"Dawn, Dawn, it's just a dream." She woke with a start her face awash with tears, she threw her arms around me kissing me desperately, and all the desperate longing for her flowed out of me as I kissed her back. If I had wanted her before, it was nothing compared to now, and she was pulling me on top of her. She had her arms around my neck pulling me down.

"Please John, please," she urged me. I pulled back to look at her face. "Please…" she pleaded.

"Dawn?" I shook my head. "I can't… I'll hurt you."

She pushed me away and turned onto her side pulling her knees to her chest holding her arm across her stomach crying. It was obvious. I had rejected her and she thought I didn't want her.

"Dawn? Oh God Dawn, don't cry, please don't cry, you have no idea how much I want to. I love you Dawn." She didn't turn around, so I just curled around her back and held her whilst she cried, until she fell asleep.

Her dad was up early the next morning, he was making tea for everyone. He must have tiptoed through the lounge because the first I knew there was a hand shaking my shoulder and a large mug of tea was being offered to me. I sat up wide awake immediately. I was embarrassed and taken by surprise, Dawn was stirring next to me. I was confused, was he going to give me a mug and then thump me when my hands were full? He smiled at me, obviously enjoying my confusion.

"Look John," he said clearing his throat. "You're engaged, she loves you, and I'm not a hypocrite. But if you break her heart..."

"I won't," I said "you have my word."

"Oh and by the way…" he paused. "You're still fully clothed!"

Dawn sat up next to me, and she smiled up at me eyeing my tea.

"Ooh, is there any for me?" she asked, totally oblivious to any embarrassment. Her dad handed her a mug too, chuckled and set off up the stairs with the tea tray in his hand.

"What did he mean by that?" I asked her. She sipped her tea and smiled.

"It means he was impressed you hadn't got your kit off, but you can stay in my room from now on."

"Are you sure?" I asked not sure in the least.

"Don't worry, he and I had that conversation a long time

ago," she smiled at me and giggled.

We didn't really have a plan, we were just staying close to Dawn's house awaiting the dreaded arrival of the letter, the letter that our lives were on hold for. All I knew was I had to be there for Dawn, to help her in any way I could, and survive the nightmare which gaped all around us. It was coming to the end of term and I would have to contact college at some point, but I just needed a few days to get my head around this and to wait and see what was going to happen next. Dawn was already back attending school after her operation, but it was the weekend so we had a couple of days to find each other again. My car was still in London so we were stuck near to the house. Dawn wasn't in pain but walking too far was uncomfortable for her. We spent most of the time in her room. She lay on the bed under my arm.

"Ok..." she said exasperated, "you're like a coiled spring."

"What?" I tried to sound innocent.

"You just can't stand it can you?" she said laughing at me. "Go on then, if you must, but don't touch my drawing board, I know it doesn't look like it but I know where all the different pens are."

"Is it that obvious?" I asked.

She sat up and looked at me with her dreamy chocolate eyes.

"Yes! You know you must be the only student in the history of there being students to have a neat and tidy room." I looked down shame faced. "What? You're not telling me your room has something out of place are you?" I thought about the unholy mess I had left back at my digs. Chris and Francis had thought they had died and gone to heaven when I had moved in, I was happy to do all the cleaning. But over the last few months the whole place had deteriorated into a dirty slum, mainly of my making.

"Well you wouldn't have recognised me over the last few months," I said looking down. "I sort of lost the will to live, or at least care about where and how I lived."

"What? Left your shoes out? Or, oh my God, don't tell me, you didn't make your bed!" She was teasing me. I looked up at her and tried to smile, remembering the pain and loss of not having her in my life. She leaned over to me and touched the frown lines on my brow. I took her hand in mine and kissed her palm and then pulled her close enveloping her in my arms.

"I'm such a fool." I said.

"So am I," she replied. I kissed her, she smiled mischievously. "I should have let you tidy my room up long ago," she said. I snorted a laugh and let go of her.

"Ok then," I said shoving her away and jumping up off the bed. "Lets start with the bookshelf!"

She threw her head back and laughed and then made herself comfortable whilst I busied myself about her room. Books all upright, I remembered they were in order of her favourites. Puccini first, so I just made sure they all stood correctly. The piles of music I tidied into neat stacks. Then it was the records.

"You know if these are original recordings you should at least keep them in their sleeves to stop them getting scratched."

"If you're going to criticise then the deals off," she said screwing her face up and trying to look cross, and then dissolving into giggles.

I lined all the vinyl up on edge too and then went around the room collecting up armfuls of her clothes. I hesitated by her wardrobe and looked at her.

"Dare I open it?" I asked.

"On your head be it," she replied looking at me a little strangely.

I gingerly opened the door peaking over the top of the mountain of clothes I had in my arms. Inside the hangers were all neatly arranged, jumpers folded neatly on their shelves and all the shoes were lined up in rows. I was staggered, and then I felt her hand on my shoulder. "Well I had nothing to do either, and I was miserable." I dropped the pile of clothes right there on the floor and picked her up around the waist and held her tight burying my face in her shoulder. She threw back her head and I kissed her neck gently. Her perfume filled my senses and I luxuriated in her heady scent. Then I picked her up like a baby and carried her to the bed. I looked into her eyes, she had a serious look on her face.

"What?" I whispered. "What is it?"

Dawn

"I want to make love," I said to him, worry probably all over my face. I didn't know what he would say, whether or not he would want me like that now. I was scared of his answer too. If it was a yes, I was terrified about what it would be like after the operation, what if it hurt? What if it wasn't the same between us any more? But if it was no, would it be because he didn't find me attractive, scarred as I now was? I just knew I wanted to be close to him, to feel him inside me, to possess me and never let go, to take me in his arms and make me feel safe. I looked tentatively into his eyes, afraid of what I might see there. His eyes creased up and he smiled gently at me.

"So do I," he whispered and kissed me so gently on the lips that I unknowingly held my breath, only breathing out when he moved back. "Dawn, I don't want to be unromantic about this, but we need to talk first."

"Why?" I asked puzzled.

"Because I'm scared too," he said stroking my hair gently. "I need to know what they did to you, I mean, it's going to hurt however gentle I am. I need to know where your wounds are, are there wounds I can't see? And you're going to have to be brutally honest with me. You've got to tell me if I touch you somewhere and you don't like it, or if it hurts too much. We need to take it really slowly, and you have to know that no matter how far we get, I will stop if you need me to."

His eyes were so beautiful, he was so beautiful. It was so easy to talk, I could tell him anything, there was nothing I couldn't tell him, nothing that was too personal. He loved me with every part of his being and I him. So he laid me on a towel and we gently began our journey back to where we had been.

It was painful… and he hardly touched me. He moved so slowly as if I were made of the most fragile glass, but alongside the pain was the most exquisite warmth, and I did feel safe. I felt one with him again, and it was as if we had never been apart. All that longing for him and here I was enveloped in his strong arms, part of him, belonging to him again. We didn't really get anywhere and in time it must have been only a few minutes. I didn't have to ask him to stop because he seemed to know, but that didn't matter to me and I know it didn't matter to him either. I knew now that whatever I had to face, whatever we had to face, we could do it because we had each other.

Chapter 16

Lovelace

We had arranged to meet up with Moli. Dawn's mum was lending us the MG as my car was still up in London. We were going to pick him up from school and go down the George. I was thrilled, I was insured fully comprehensive, so with Dawn's mum's permission I got the drive of my life. It was fantastic. It had overdrive which had to be explained to me, and Dawn's mum did look a little dubious as I set off, but I knew it was her pride and joy so I didn't want to thrash it like Dawn's dad seemed to do. God knows how we were going to collect Moli though, as it was a two seater. Dawn assured me that she and her sister could get in it with one person in the tiny space at the back behind the seats. I was dubious, there was barely enough room for a small child let alone Moli or Dawn, but who was I to argue? It was great to drive, though a lot heavier than I had imagined, but it cornered beautifully and with the fitted racing seats, you hardly moved. I decelerated going into the quad. It seemed odd being back, sneaking into school rather than sneaking out of it like before. I drove up to Lancaster House and swung the car around. Moli appeared from nowhere. He jumped out of the boot room window, landing almost in front of the bonnet. I swerved to avoid a rather nasty Italian mess.

"Shit Mols talk about making an entrance!" The hood was down as it was quite a balmy night and he clambered into the back and wedged his hips in the space behind the seats.

"Thank God I've been on a diet!" he said sarcastically, and we sped off out of the quad and down around the corner into the village. I parked the car out the front of the pub and Mols skipped off around the back whilst Dawn and I, for the first time ever, went in the correct way, up the steps and through the front door of the pub. I ordered the drinks at the bar whilst Dawn went towards the back to find Moli. I arrived at our old table balancing three pints of lager between my hands to find Moli behind the high backed seats, lighting up, or rather attempting to light up his cigarette. Dawn had gone off to the loo, but maybe she was giving us a bit of space. I put the drinks down on the table and went for my lighter. It ignited immediately, as it always did. Moli eyed it up and then looked up at me.

"It's still ancient," he said as he bent forward to suck on its flame.

"It still works!" I said with a slight laugh. He drew deeply on his cigarette and nodded but didn't look at me. He got straight to the point.

"So, you thought Dawn and I...?" I felt ashamed and dropped my eyes down. "Well you know you couldn't blame her if she did. I mean I'm much more attractive than you Lovelace, and then of course there's the Italian title, Countess Dawn..." I looked up at him, he was eyeing me sideways, grinning, enjoying it and taking another deep drag on his cigarette.

"Bastard, go on then, make me suffer," I said grinning at him.

"Don't have to old man," he said, his face suddenly changing and looking at me seriously. I raised my eyebrow. "Don't forget I came to see you. I think I've seen enough self-flagellation in that direction."

I snorted agreement and nodded. "You mean I didn't fool you then?"

"Maybe for a bit. Enjoyed thumping you though!"

"Yeah well remember it, cause you won't be getting another opportunity." He laughed in response. "Look Mols..." I didn't know where to start. I had so much I needed to say to him, so much to apologise for.

"You don't have to say it," he said. I looked up at him, he shrugged. "But you can give me that damned lighter. Am I the only one that's noticed you've given up smoking? I haven't seen you have one since you met her!"

I laughed and pulled the lighter from my jeans pocket. "Yeah you are actually, but I still smoke other people's when I can..." I leaned over and grabbed the cigarette from his lips and took a drag. Then I tossed him the lighter, which he caught, and took another deep drag. Oh my God it was good, my deep craving locked in, and then I handed it back to him reluctantly.

"How's she doing?" he asked seriously.

I blew out between my lips. I didn't know what to say.

"Okay... Well how are you doing then?"

I looked down and all the air huffed out of my lungs as if I had been winded. I put my elbow on the table and ran my fingers through the front of my hair.

"Christ Mols…" I felt like I had a knife in my guts.

He put a hand on my shoulder in a gesture of sympathy and then waived a fresh cigarette at me. "Medicinal!" he said. I laughed and took it, put it between my lips and then reached into my jeans for my lighter. Quick as a flash he lit *his* lighter in front of me. We both looked at it and laughed.

Dawn came in from the loos and sat down, eyeing both of us.

"Ok what are you both talking about then?"

"Moli was telling me how attractive he was, and extolling his virtues!"

"Oh yes!" she said, "and what would those be?"

"Best mate in the whole world," I said and lifted my pint to him, "and a cocky bastard to boot!" Moli lifted his glass to mine and we clunked them together.

"To all cocky bastards," said Dawn, and we all clunked our glasses again and sniggered.

Dawn

It was great being together in the pub, it was incredibly cosy in our private space around the back, and I was so relieved that things appeared to be as tight as ever between John and Moli. Whatever they had been saying before I came back seemed to have cleared the air. It was a slow evening so Harry decided to have a lock in which meant that we could go into the public bar where the big fire was burning in the inglenook and play darts. John did all the maths as both Moli and I were useless at counting backwards. I played on both sides as we didn't have even numbers and both of them claimed their need was greatest. I happened to be a bit of a demon when it came to getting a double to start and a double to finish. I couldn't seem to hit much else but doubles were a piece of cake as long as I didn't go over my limit of two pints, after that I became more and more of a liability. John was taking his throw and Moli came up behind me and put both his arms around me, I leaned back into him. He leant his head against mine.

"Told you he'd be back."

I smiled and squeezed his forearm as it crossed in front of me.

"Keep me in the loop will you?" he asked.

"I couldn't have made it this far without you Moli, you've been great."

"Yeah well, I'm kinda fond of you both. Besides which, it seems you two just can't manage without me." I laughed.

"Interfering with the opposition again?" John called from where he was writing the score on the chalk board.

"She's on my side Lovelace, she's just pretending to help you out cause you're so useless at darts."

"Well if I'm so useless at darts, why is it that we've nearly won and you're so far behind?"

"I'm saving myself for a big finish," and he let go of me and meandered slightly towards the oche. "What do I need then Lovelace? You tell me and I'll get it."

John laughed. "Ok well you could go out on a bull and a double top."

"Right," he said screwing up his eyes, "I'll get the bull and then it's down to you Dawn."

It was a Kentish board, there were no trebles and there was no outer bull, the chances of Moli getting a bull in his state were extremely remote to say the least. The bull was tiny.

He wavered about for so long that John volunteered to point to it. Moli's eyes gleamed and he smiled widely with his enormous grin, clenching his cigarette between his teeth.

"Yeah if you wouldn't mind that would be really helpful," he said gleefully.

"Come to think of it," retorted John, "I really think the only safe place to stand is behind you." He moved back to where I was standing next to his pint. Moli took aim for the third time. But just as he let go of his dart he hiccupped. We couldn't believe it.

"You jammy bastard!" said John. I was whooping and clapping. It sailed cleanly into the bullseye.

"What can I tell you Lovelace, you either have it or you don't, and I, my friend, have it!" He hiccupped again. He dropped his other two darts at his feet and then picked them up. John took his turn leaving himself on double one.

"Madhouse," he announced exasperated.

"Come on Dawn, it's now up to you baby!" Moli said smiling as he leaned against the wall. He took his cigarette from his lips and blew a smoke ring.

"Talk about no pressure then!" I said. I lined up the dart with the double top and threw. It hit the wire and bounced out, landing at Moli's feet.

"Hey watch it, I know I have a magnetic personality but…"

The next one slid outside the wire.

"Aw," said Moli.

We all held our breath for the final dart.

"Do you know I think we should call it a draw," I said dropping my arm and looking at both boys. They looked at each other and shook their heads.

"Naaah…" they both said.

I laughed and turned back to the board and aimed. It flew into the double twenty.

"Traitor!" yelled John laughing.

"That's my girl," said Moli and he came up to me to kiss me. He paused ever so slightly as he looked at my lips and then looked me in the eye. He smiled and kissed me on the cheek.

We sat around the log fire to finish our pints. I sat back and quietly watched John and Moli chatting and laughing together. I was so glad he had such a close friend.

We delivered the slightly inebriated Moli back to the quad and I helped John to stuff him back through the boot room window. He landed rather heavily on the other side, but he was waving back at us within minutes and we left the quad as quietly as an MG can.

"John?" I said curiously playing with an idea in my head. "When did you first go to boarding school?"

"When I was six. I went to prep school first and then my parents looked around at all the public schools and chose this one for me, why?"

"You were only a baby." I thought about how small six really was. "How did you cope? Did you cry?"

"Of course I did. I hated it, well I hated it for the first few weeks of every term. I wrote rotten letters to my parents telling them how miserable I was, begging them to come and get me. But then we were all in the same boat. Later I grew to love it. Don't forget I was an only child and though I had my mates in the village I was still on my own a lot. School was a lot of fun. Well most of the time. It could be a bit brutal at times too."

"Can I ask you something?"

"What?"

"I mean you don't have to answer it if you don't want to."

"What do you want to know?"

"Or you can lie if you prefer."

He slowed the car down.

"Okay…" he dragged it out suspiciously, "what is it you want to know?"

"Well… Look you can tell me if this is none of my business."

He pulled the car to a standstill and turned off the engine.

"Spit it out then."

He turned to me, arm on the back of his seat. Eyes shining in the moonlight with a mischievous grin on his face. He obviously had some idea about what I was going to say. He wasn't going to help me out though, I had started this and he was going to enjoy watching me squirm.

"Well… you're very pretty… for a boy," *Oh God why had I started this?* I wondered, I wasn't even sure now why I was asking, or whether I even wanted to know the answer. What if I didn't like what I heard, what was I going to do then? *You idiot, you didn't think this one out did you?* I looked at him he was trying not to laugh at me.

"That's extremely kind of you," he said smiling finding it very difficult not to laugh but still not helping me out of my hole.

"Well you are." I added.

"I had curly blonde hair too when I was little… keep digging," he said smiling from ear to ear now.

"Ok," I said resigning myself. It was obvious now that he knew what I wanted to know. "Did anyone ever touch you?"

"No!" he said firmly then smiling again. "Not in that way anyway, but it did go on."

"In what way then?" I asked relieved in one way but now not happy at all and shocked.

"Well there's a reason people left me alone, I was a little bruiser. I thumped people first. Mostly they were bigger than me, and I got a bit of a reputation. Then later on I thumped anyone who was a bully or who picked on anyone smaller than themselves, even if I was the smallest of them all. There was a nasty incident in the quad once, in my first year. A group of third formers had got a new boy on the floor, they were chanting 'Milk him, milk him.' Poor guy, I just didn't even think about it. There were around five third formers on top of him, I just waded in and started punching anyone and everyone who came within reach. Then Moli joined in too and we all got lined up and caned for fighting. I didn't have much trouble with the boys at all after that. But there was one master who was obviously a bit of a sadist, he liked to hit me. Every French lesson for any reason I would get hit. Once he had to hit the whole class to catch me out, but when my turn came he hit me harder than the rest." He shrugged.

"Oh my God John, that's awful, didn't you tell anyone?" I was horrified.

"You didn't tell you just got on with it."

"You said *it* went on…"

"Yeah, some people experimented sexually. Some just needed affection no matter how they got it, and then there were some genuine cases, and of course there was occasional abuse, but that can happen anywhere." He shrugged, and then turned his piercingly beautiful blue eyes on me shining with amusement. "But no, no one ever laid a finger on me in *that* way," he smiled at me and brushed my hair from my forehead. "No one but you, and you can ask me anything."

"Was Moli the boy on the deck?" He was taken aback and shifted his gaze from me to the side hesitating. He didn't speak but the answer was obvious.

He paused and smiled again. "What about you?"

"I …" I paused. I wasn't expecting this. I closed my mouth.

"What? Dawn? Did something happen to you?"

"Well… not really… Well yes actually," I suddenly found myself getting cross. I was cross because I was going to make an excuse, an excuse that I had made ever since it had happened. "I used to have a job in a shop and I did all the shelf stacking, you know. The manager used to come along and reach past me. He was always brushing against my breasts. I didn't like it but I used to think it was a mistake and that it was my fault for not leaning back. Then he used to push behind me, rubbing himself on me as he moved past. Again I used to think it was my fault. God I am so stupid, I was thirteen and I always thought it was my fault! I've only just realised it was him, he was touching me up! He even touched me between the legs once, I wonder what excuse I made up for him for that?" I shivered. "Bastard!" I said out loud I was really cross, cross with myself too. I looked at John, he was frowning. I suddenly felt panicked and vulnerable, what was he thinking of me? He already knew that I'd slept with Pete Penfold at barely sixteen years of age, and he was less than impressed with his character. That he'd hit me repeatedly before we split up and then there was something else, something I hadn't told him about. I suddenly felt ashamed, dirty, not good enough. I looked down, I couldn't look at him.

"Dawn, it's not you fault." He was trying to get me to look at him. "Dawn? Look, things happen it doesn't make it your fault, you were a kid, I was a kid, it's neither of our faults."

"Where is this guy now anyway?" he enquired.

"By the kissing gate," I said. He laughed understanding where he was. He was in the churchyard, six feet under.

"Ok then, we'll go and jump on him tomorrow eh?" I looked up at him and laughed. He hadn't got a clue how attractive he was, I couldn't understand how I had struck it so lucky. I was besotted, simply besotted with him and it must have shown on my face.

He smiled at me as if I were some incredible prize that he'd won. He wound his arm around me. "God I love you so much, you are so beautiful," he said, and he kissed me in a way that turned all my bones to jelly.

"Dear God," I said, "who taught you to kiss like that?"
He laughed at me and smiled.
"You did," he replied, and kissed me again.

Chapter 17

Lovelace

The letter landed on the mat. We both heard the letterbox rattling and the thump as it landed. Dawn got up and walked through the hall to the door. She stood just staring at it sitting there. I came up behind her and put my hand gently on her shoulder.

"Dawn?" she didn't move. "Do you want me to get it?" She didn't move or say anything, and then the telephone suddenly started ringing. She spun around and just clung on to me burying her face in my chest. I picked up the phone with one hand, as it was right by me and reeled off her telephone number, whilst I held on to her with the other arm. It was the surgery. "Dawn... they want to talk to you." She wouldn't let go of me and she wouldn't look up. Her mum came up behind me and took the phone from my hand. I put both my arms around her and rested my cheek on the top of her head and just held her.

We could hear her mum responding to the caller, but we couldn't hear what she was saying. After a short while Dawn's mum returned and put the phone back on the cradle. I looked at her over the top of Dawn's head. Dawn hadn't moved. Her expression said it all. Chemo, she had to have chemotherapy, and I pulled her tighter to me and rubbed my cheek in her hair. Her mum pushed gently past us to get to the letter and picked it up. She pressed it into my hand and then she squeezed Dawn's shoulders.

"I'll go and make some tea," she said eyes glistening. She kissed Dawn on the back of the head, and then went towards the kitchen.

I was suddenly aware that Dawn had gone all limp, I was holding all her weight in my arms and she was slipping towards the ground. I grabbed her tight and pulled her out the hall towards the settee and then lowered her onto it, controlling her descent as best I could manage, since I was almost dropping her.

"Lois! LOIS help!" I called out to her mum in the kitchen. Her mum came rushing in and gave me directions to put her feet in the air. I pulled her flat on the sofa and then stood holding her feet up. My heart was pounding. Her mum was pulling the cushions out from under her and loosening her jeans. Dawn was coming round though. Relief and adrenaline were pumping through me.

"Dawn? Dawn?" her mum was saying to her. She began to thrash her head too and fro.

"Mum? Mum? Where's John?"

"He's here darling, just take it easy, you passed out," she moved back. "Don't crowd her, she needs air," she instructed, but moved back away from her so that I could sit by her. I looked at her mum feeling guilty that I was taking her place.

She smiled gently at me and put a reassuring hand on my shoulder. "It's ok, she needs you," and she patted me, then she went back out to get the tea.

I stroked her cheek.

"Hell of a time to take a nap," I said smiling at her. Dawn smiled at me and a tear snuck out from the edge of her eyelid and ran towards her ear. I caught it on my finger. The letter brushed her cheek as I held it in my hand.

"What does it say?" she asked.

I opened the crumpled letter in my fist.

"It says you have an appointment to see Dr Wilde in London to discuss your chemotherapy." I choked on the last word, and looked at her. "It's on Tuesday. I'd like to go with you… if that's what you want?" She nodded vigorously and held out her arms to me. I knelt on the floor and put my arm under her head and my head on her chest and listened to her breathing.

*

We all went up to the hospital together. They did lots of tests, filling her with radioactive dye and took a load of blood. It was exhausting going from one department to another, and Dawn was not the greatest giver of blood either. Every time a needle came near her, her veins dived for cover. By the time they punctured her for the twelfth time even my stomach was beginning to turn over. They tried beating her hands repeatedly, putting her arms in hot water, you name it, but by the end she was just beside herself with tiredness and stress. Dr Wilde was lovely, he was like a big friendly teddy bear, but what he was saying wasn't very friendly at all. Basically they were going to poison her within an inch of her life, and hopefully get any cancer cells that had managed to escape into her system. He said fantastic things like it was curable, very rare, excellent success rates, but her hair would fall out by the third session and she would be very ill after treatments. There would be six in all with two weeks between each one, and that her periods *should* come back after it all finished and that she *should* be able to have children. There was talk of egg collection and the possibility of freezing them.

Dr Wilde eyed us both and said "Fertilized eggs we freeze but usually the problem is the lack of a partner, especially with someone of your age?"

"Well that's no problem," I said, giving Dawns shoulder a squeeze, "if that's what you want?" Dawn was nodding desperately. But after a few phone calls and a twenty minute wait it became obvious that he was ruling this out.

"I'm sorry Dawn, but the drugs to increase the number of eggs in your womb would encourage the cancer cells to grow too, at this point it's just not a good idea. There's also the question of waiting and delaying the chemotherapy while we wait for your eggs. And it's also now imperative that you don't get pregnant." He looked up at us both. I held on tight to Dawn's hand and nodded. By now it was getting too much for Dawn and when we eventually emerged at the end of it all, she just clung on to me and cried her heart out. At that point that was the only thing I wanted to do too, but I couldn't, I had to hold it together. I could do this, I could do this for her, though

I was being tortured inside I had to be strong. God knows how I managed but I also knew that this was only a fraction of the pain that was to come. I looked over to her mum, she was clinging on to Dawn's dad and they were both crying too.

We were given some helpful telephone numbers of people to talk to, and directed to an orange house, Maggie's, in the corner of the hospital grounds. Dawn's dad went off to feed the meter again, which was an exorbitant amount for even part of an hour, and we had already been there most of the day. Getting cancer was expensive! The rest of us went off to find 'Maggie's.' We were all extremely dubious about it from the outside. All it looked like was an orange prefab with a glass roof hovering above it. We went around the side, but there were no notices or signs anywhere. A lady and her husband came out, she was wearing a headscarf obviously covering the lack of hair, so we enquired, 'was this 'Maggie's?'

Inside it was amazing, sheltered as it was from the Fulham Palace Road by a protective wall, inside it was a million miles away from the London City streets and the hospital we had spent all day in. The first thing you encountered was a huge, calm, green, inviting kitchen area, with an enormous island in the centre. It was like one of those kitchens from a TV cooking programme. Down one side was a massive farmhouse table with comfy chairs all around. This was the heart of the building. There was a large group of people doing knitting and some others just eating cake and chatting over cups of tea. Beyond that was a covered courtyard garden with another outside table and benches, and a further window which looked out onto its own garden within the hospital grounds.

A lady approached us and made us tea and we sat down just off the kitchen in a small library area with designer chairs, all really comfortable. Then we met the most amazing person, Bonnie who explained what this place was all about, but mostly she talked and guided all of us carefully through what was ahead of us. She listened to Dawn, and Dawn began the process of taking it all in, she didn't cover anything up, but she gave sound factual information. At the end of it, it was as if a huge weight had been lifted from us all. Most of all Dawn had found a home, a refuge to go to when she needed to get off the cancer ward. It was a place of safety and sanctuary, somewhere we could all relax and spend some normal hours away from the nightmare of chemotherapy and cancer. Then her mum and dad set off back to Kent, and Dawn and I made our way back through the city and then out on the tube to my digs.

Dawn was all in when we got to the house. Chris and Francis were out, but thankfully they had made some inroads into the devastation I had left behind me, and at least the communal areas were back to, well not up to my usual standard, but back to normal for most people. My room was another matter though. Dawn just stood at the door and gasped.

Dawn

"Are you sure this is your room?" I said, obviously horrified. I just couldn't hide it. I have to say the only word to describe it was squalid, and it didn't smell too savoury either. And I remembered the joke I had made that he had forgotten to make his bed or left his shoes out. What sort of unimaginable pain had he been in to live like this? *My John, my beautiful love.* Oh dear Lord what had he been going through month after month on his own? *How could I have done this to him?* I looked at him and squeezed his hand.

"Pretty deep wound huh?" As I held his hand I felt a slight bump at the base of his thumb. I looked down and saw a scar. It had obviously been deep but with thin lines like a star. My thumb gently rubbed over it. I looked up at him for an explanation. He pulled his hand from mine not meeting my eyes and nodded.

"But mended now," he smiled. "Go on, you make tea and I'll try to do something with this." I didn't really see what he would be able to do with it especially after the sort of day we had just had. We were both exhausted and all I wanted to do was sleep, but I really didn't fancy his room at all. I put the kettle on but I must have fallen asleep on the sofa. I woke up with him looking down at me concerned.

"What's the time?" I enquired. "Ten o'clock!" I had been asleep for four hours, John looked all done in. "What have you been doing all this time? You haven't been doing your room for four hours have you?" I gasped.

"Well it took rather a long time to get it into that state. It's not too bad now, though it's a bit chilly as I've had the windows open. I went back upstairs to see what he had been up to. I think most of his stuff he had thrown into bin bags and put out with the rubbish. His records were all in place again, and all the surfaces had been washed down and there was a strong pine fresh smell everywhere with a mix of wax polish. He had hoovered every inch of the place and there was fresh bedding. The curtains that had been half hanging down were neatly on the rail now. The smell of unwashed adolescent was gone and I could have sworn he had popped out to the Co-op down the road and bought new pillows and a duvet whilst I had been sleeping. I smiled at him.

"Better?" I asked.

"Much better," he said smiling at me.

"Can we go to bed now?" I asked, somewhat desperate. He laughed and nodded his head.

I think we fell asleep as soon as our heads touched the pillows. Oh and yes they were definitely new! I awoke the next morning with John's arms wrapped around me feeling his exquisite soft skin on me. I got up to go to the bathroom. Whilst I had been gone he had stirred but not woken, he was lying naked on the bed. My God he was beautiful. I had drawn lots of nudes for my art and I found myself running my artist's eye over him. He lay like an alabaster David on the sheets, his perfectly sculptured chest led the eye to the rounded strong muscles of his shoulders and arms. A thin line of hair drew the eye down his stomach from above his navel to his groin. I smiled at his erection as I realised he was going to wake up with the usual morning lust. His hips were so slim and his thighs thick and powerful. He was truly beautiful.

I looked about the room to see if I could spot any paper or a pencil. There was a pad of A3 ledger papers on his desk with pink and blue lines ruled on one side. I turned over a sheet to discover that it was blank on the other side. *Great!* Now all I needed was a pencil, which I found in the top drawer. I used a tray as a drawing board and perched myself on his desk to get a good view of him from above but I wasn't high enough. I looked about and eyed up the wardrobe. The room had a very high ceiling and the wardrobe was an old one and very sturdy, so up I went, with a little difficulty I must say, but from there I had a wonderful view of him. He was even more beautiful because his face was turned towards me and I lost myself in the sheer pleasure of looking at him and drawing him. I have to say that when I finished, I was extremely pleased with it. He really looked real, suspended somehow in another world. I was just doing his eyes wishing they were open so that I could capture his most beautiful feature, when he did open his eyes. He looked at me and smiled and then he looked confused.

"What the hell are you doing up there?" he said.

"Appreciating the view," I replied with a giggle.

He looked down at himself and smiled, propping himself up on his elbows. "And do you like what you see?" he asked suggestively, tensing and relaxing so his penis waved gently at me.

"Well it's not bad," I said teasing. "Course I've seen a lot of nude models, helps if the proportions are right."

"Oh yes? And how are my proportions then?"

"Well a little bit large in some areas," I said, laughing and attempting to clamber down.

"Oh they are, are they?" he said getting up to help me down.

"Yeah, a bag of frozen peas might help that swelling!"

He grabbed me around the waist. "You're not going anywhere near me with a bag of frozen peas," he said. He pulled me on top of him back onto the bed.

"Well then I think you might have a little bit of a problem."

"I wouldn't exactly call it a problem would you?" he said smiling.

"Well no, I think I might be able to help you out," he pulled my face to his gently and we kissed as best we could because we both found the whole thing so amusing. Then I moved slowly down his body kissing him as I went then taking him in my mouth.

"Aah… dear God," he moaned and writhed under me.

I had never done this before and wasn't really sure to begin with how I felt about it. It tasted a little salty, but as he moved and groaned it became so sensual. He smelt sexy too and what with the rocking motion, he was really turning me on, but he was huge and he was moving about a little too much. I was tempted to bite him which made me smile and then laugh, and then he grabbed my shoulders and threw me on my back. He wasn't laughing now, he was so wound up I could see he was barely holding himself in check, he wanted to take me there and then, roughly and powerfully like we had in the past. I held my breath. I hadn't meant to get him in this state and I panicked, I knew I wasn't ready for this. He looked at me frowning. "Dawn… I would never hurt you… Don't you trust me? Please don't look at me like that."

"Like what?" I said surprised.

"Frightened… you're frightened of me." Hurt and pain

crossed his face and he rolled away from me onto his back with an arm over his eyes.

I was shocked, I didn't know what to say to him but he was right.

"Its not you John… its everything. Really it's not you, I love you."

He turned his eyes to me, they were glistening with tears. He looked at me examining my face. I thought he was checking to see if I was lying. He wasn't, his words took me by surprise.

"That's not it," he said still searching my face. "You've been here before. Maybe not exactly the same…" I was shocked and said nothing. He sat up on the bed moving backwards away from me, into the pillows so they supported him upright and he looked at me and waited. He was right. I thought back. What had started as fun had quickly moved to something I didn't want, something with a violent edge. I had tried but I had been powerless to stop it as it became more and more ugly, I was so naive, it was something I just shut my eyes and endured. But I had been willing to start with, so it wasn't rape, was it? It was my own fault. Later I had taken him to the Lillesden dance where I met John for the first time, *how incredibly stupid was that?* Then when I told him it was over, he had hit me, punched me in the stomach and back. I didn't want to remember I didn't want to go back there because it was so ugly and dark and… yes it frightened me. I clutched my knees tight into my chest. I looked up at John.

"It's ok," he said, he had obviously been reading my face as I had been going over it. "You don't have to tell me if you don't want to, I think I can fill in the bits I don't know. I just wish I'd punched him a lot harder." He held his arms out to me and I eagerly latched on to him, holding on like a drowning woman.

*

I can't say that the first time was anything to write home about really. I also can't pretend that it was about anything much more than curiosity, from my side anyway. Did I think it was love? No not really. I can't even claim that, but I was swept away by the emotions, and I did think he was really sweet, I really liked him. I probably could make a case to myself that at that precise moment I thought it could be love. But it was a disaster on all fronts. Neither of us knew anything other than the basic mechanics. There was a lot of fumbling and jabbing. Pain, I do remember that it hurt a little, but not as bad as I expected and once goal was reached he stopped moving. It didn't occur to me until much later that he had probably finished as soon as he entered, but I hadn't heard or read anything about premature ejaculation. I can't even say that I was disappointed, as I had no real expectation of anything. I think in hindsight he must have hardly even got through the front door. The cuddling afterwards was lovely though and I began to think that was more likely what it was all about. But I was beginning to have doubts about what we had done. Pity I didn't think more a little bit earlier.

The second time however, was an entirely different matter. We had been out walking through the fields and it had all begun innocently enough with kissing and touching. When it looked like we were heading in the direction of sex I was again quite happy about it. We were out of doors and though no one would have found us, there was an element of excitement in that possibility too. But the kissing was becoming harder and more urgent. I remember thinking 'This is supposed to be beautiful,' and my passions were not being ignited as his obviously were. I remember trying to turn my head away, and that was when it all began to become uglier and uglier. The more I tried to avoid his kissing the tighter he held my face in his hand. His whole body weight had me pinned on the ground but I wasn't worried about that. I was a tomboy, more than a match for anyone if I so chose, and I was choosing now! His tongue was now probing, assaulting me and his grip around my face was vice like. I made noises of protest, but it just seemed to excite him more. It was time to get out of this!

God I was so naive. He may have been tall but he was somewhat on the skinny side, and I had this unshakable belief that I could take care of myself against anyone. Well that was what I had always been told. How wrong I was. His weight pressed down on me. When I got my face free I began to shout at him, "Pete No… No… Stop…" He held my arms and raised himself above me.

"You're saying no but you mean yes," and he laughed at me. It was a power thing and he was high as a kite on it.

"No I'm saying no and I mean no, get off me." Well that is what I was trying to say but only the 'no' got out. He cut off anything more with his tongue, again pressing violently into my mouth. I struggled, I really did, I couldn't believe how strong he was, and it dawned on me like a sledgehammer… I wasn't strong enough… and it was as if that was the bitterest thing of all, my weakness. My strength was sapping away at an alarming speed, another humiliation. Then all too quickly my jeans were around my thighs and he was battering against me. In his excitement he was having difficulty finding his goal, but it didn't take him long. This time it really hurt and it made me cry out. Maybe he was thinking I was enjoying this, it just hurt more and more.

Then something happened, I just switched off. I removed myself from the scene. There was a large dandelion clock just in front of my face and I concentrated on the delicate feathers at the tips, following the stems to the seed at the bottom. It swayed with a rhythm until all of a sudden it exploded and the seeds were lifted up onto the breeze. I came back to reality with Pete collapsing, his full weight onto my chest his climax achieved and his energy spent. I remember feeling tears trickling into my ears and beginning to tickle.

What had just happened? Did I consent to this? Yes I did, to begin with. *Oh God, then its my fault, not his, I didn't make it clear, I must have egged him on, I didn't fight hard enough, didn't make it clear enough.* He must have thought I was enjoying it. He rolled from on top of me squashing my dandelion. Then he was angry with me for bleeding and marking his T shirt. My pants were torn, but I was wearing white trousers. How was I to get home? I quickly rolled the remnants of my knickers into a pad and pulled up my jeans. I just wanted to cover myself up deny anything had happened. I didn't want to move because it hurt, like a sharp burning. Pete was so cross, he didn't want to be near me now or look at me. He was storming off over the field yelling at me to sort myself out and hurry up. I think I was in shock because I just got up and followed him like a fool.

Nearing my house he slowed down and started talking about the Lillesden Dance, how he was looking forward to seeing the faces on the sixth formers when he turned up with me. Not that he had looked me in the eye since the field. Do you know I would have said anything to get away from him at that moment. I wanted to be by myself, I needed a bath, I had to wash, oh and it hurt so much. I had tied my jumper around my waist so that it hung down covering me from behind. I felt sure I was bleeding through my jeans. I had been trying to walk without moving my thighs too much, walking as much as possible from the knees.

Up in the bathroom I ran the water hotter and hotter. I almost scalded myself getting in. Then the burning made me feel as though I was somehow cleaning what had happened away from me, taking off that layer of skin that had been soiled. I hugged my knees going over it. Was it my fault? He'd certainly made me feel like it was. I buried my head in my arms and began to cry. Gradually bit by bit the crying became more and more hysterical. Then I heard Mum at the bottom of the stairs calling up to me.

"Dawn? Are you all right love?"

The word love cut right through me. My mum, my lovely mum. I wanted to cry out to her but I couldn't, *what would she think of me?*

"I'm fine, just vocal exercises, sorry Mum."

"Sounds awful Dawn, I thought you were really upset," and I heard the lounge door close behind her. I took the nail brush and scrubbed until it was as painful on the outside as on the inside. The bath water had turned pink and now I really didn't know where to put myself. I climbed out the bath and pulled the plug and began to run another.

Chapter 18

Lovelace

I had to go in to college, I had an appointment with the Dean of the faculty to explain my situation. It looked like they were rather keen to kick me off my course. Well who could blame them, I was going to be missing a whole lot more with Dawn being ill, so I was expecting the worst really. Chris and Francis, my housemates, were in when we got up. They had crept in during the early hours from some party in town, and they were going to look after Dawn in the union bar until I could meet up with them later. They loved Dawn straight away and whisked her away whilst I went off to chat to the Dean.

The chat was rather illuminating. The facts were that I had passed all six subjects, some better than others but not the *one* compulsory subject, and he made it perfectly clear what he thought about public school boys and the fact I was taking up the place of someone more deserving. I pointed out that I had earned my place just like everyone else by gaining the appropriate grades, but I could see where we were headed. The fact that I had a double first grade and a two-one for three of the subjects was cutting no ice with him, so I went for reason.

Four other students had failed five out of the seven subjects passing only two to my six. Admittedly they had all passed the one compulsory subject but he still wasn't having any of it. So I played what I thought was my trump card. A student in the house next door to ours, had passed the compulsory subject on retake, but had been caught cheating red handed in the exam room and she had still been let through onto the next year of the course. The injustice astounded me and it degenerated into a yelling match. I have to say that though he wielded all the power, my arguments ran circles around him, and he obviously had never had to defend his position so vehemently before. It was a lost cause though, he was a bigot and the intensity of his hatred for everything I stood for was obvious but I left his office with my head held high.

When I reached the bar it was spreading all around the college like wildfire! Apparently you could hear every word outside, and a rather large crowd had gathered to enjoy the fireworks on the Dean's lawn underneath his office window. There had also been rather loud cheering as I finally lost my cool, and at my ruder comments about him. I had been oblivious to all this though in the heat of the exchange. When I arrived in the union bar, everyone began cheering, buying me pints and clapping me on the back. The union representative wanted me to take it further but I already had one fight ahead of me, getting Dawn through chemo, and that was far more important to me. Chris was rather more help though, he had failed his course earlier in the term too and was suggesting I switch campus and course to Humanities which was really appealing. English and History, yeah I really fancied that. Sod B.A. Business Studies, I could do accounting any time afterwards. The only reason I had chosen my course anyway was because it gave the maximum exemptions in the Chartered Accountancy exams. It wasn't what I was really interested in, even though I appeared to be good at it. But English and History, that really excited me Tudors, Civil War and Poetry, Lovelace and Shakespeare, couldn't be better.

The Union chap let us use his phone and I had an appointment that afternoon with the Humanities guy, and off we went. By 3.00 I had got myself onto a brilliant course, something I would have given my right arm to do, that is if I had thought about doing that subject in the first place. By this time my reputation was spreading amongst the colleges for telling the Dean what I thought of him. I think even the Humanities guy had got wind of it, he seemed genuinely amused by the whole situation. I was going to have to re-start in September though and that suited me just fine. I would have to get some sort of job until then, but I could have time being with Dawn and that was the main thing. Meanwhile Dawn had discovered that there was a Music and Performance course at one of the other campus' and she was setting her sights firmly on that. We'd be at college together, live together and finish together, couldn't pan out better if we'd tried. That would have been however, if she had applied in the first place, which of course she hadn't.

I gave Dad a ring. He wasn't pleased about the shift from what he saw as a useful degree to something in the 'arts,' but he was pleased I had sorted things out and that I was still at college. My room was paid up for the rest of the year, and

Dad was happy to keep my allowance going until Dawn was through her treatment, then I could get a job. But Dawn was going to be very ill right through the run up to her exams, and not leaving her in any fit state for auditions. So I decided as I had been so successful with my own course, I would have a bash and see if we could sort something out for her whilst we were in the vicinity.

We drove down the long drive through the golf course and up the other side into the trees. The college itself was a stately home, once owned by a Sassoon, it was beautiful and to one side was the Orangery which stood at the far end of a swimming pool, this was the music school. We parked the car by a really grim looking students union. How they got planning permission for a concrete monstrosity like that on a site like this was beyond me. We went around the side to see if we could find anyone inside the music school. Dawn was rather dubious.

"It just doesn't work like this for singing," she said, "you have to prepare, and I have no music, no one is going to listen to me."

"Well it has to be worth a try," I said, pulling her by the hand. Dawn hadn't applied for any colleges, she, like me, had just been surviving one day to the next, not really wanting to think about a future on her own, and not really believing she had one with her illness.

We paddled around inside going up and down the corridors. It was like the Mari Celeste, only inside the odd practice rooms could you hear signs of life, musical instruments being played and a couple of singers trilling. There was an office with a Professor's name on it, it was probably empty but I thought we should try all the doors. I knocked and a voice said 'come in' so we did. Inside was a rather elegant lady, bit like one of Mum's bridge chums. She was smiling warmly at us enquiring with her expression. I smiled and introduced myself and Dawn.

"Lovelace," she said, what a beautiful name, "any relation to the poet?" I smiled and so did Dawn.

"Well, I live in his house," I said, "but the name is a coincidence as far as we know." She was lovely, she invited us in to sit down and she listened to us and offered us coffee. She had a little machine in the corner and was having some anyway. Truth be known I think she had hit a low point in the day and was glad of the company and the distraction. It turned out that no one was in except for the students in the practice rooms, and she was only there because it was more peaceful than at her own home. There was some form of study week going on and no one was on site.

"There's nothing I can do," she said. "Dawn you must know, that you have to be called for audition and prepare a selection of pieces from different composers and eras, but then I can see that you do know all this my dear. Why don't you apply for two years time? Most of the places for next year have been allocated. Or you could always try for a late entry for the last auditions for this coming year, they're in a month's time. They've all been filled at the moment but you might get a last minute cancellation."

"It doesn't matter," said Dawn, standing up. "It was very kind of you to listen to us."

"What do you mean it doesn't matter?" I said rising to my feet. "You don't understand, she hasn't just got a pretty voice, she has an *amazing* voice, and she can't audition in a month's time. And to wait for two years..." I stopped before I said anything personal about Dawn that she wouldn't want me to say. I looked at the professor lady, she was smiling sympathetically. "You hear this all the time don't you?" I said calmly huffing out a resigned laugh. "Everyone who steps in here thinks they have an amazing voice." She nodded gently.

"But she could have applied at the correct time with everyone else. Why didn't you Dawn?" Dawn didn't answer. I hadn't mentioned the cancer and I knew that Dawn wasn't going to mention it either.

"She was ill," I said, "but I can see that you hear that a lot too." I smiled acknowledging the futility of it and nodded in defeat. I could have cried for her but I couldn't have said about the cancer, it wasn't for me to say. I took Dawn's hand in mine and smiled up at the lady. "Thank you, thank you for giving us your time."

"It's rather refreshing you know," she said, "to see two people so much in love." I smiled a little taken aback. "And you are named after my favourite poet, are you a Richard?" I shook my head.

"No, a John Richard," I replied. I shrugged. "Dad didn't want me to be a Dick!" She laughed out in surprise at my answer.

"Oh all right I'll hear her, but that's all," she said. "As I said, there are *no* places and I don't take people on privately, but

I may be able to point you in someone else's direction, or to advise you to give it up."

"I'll wait outside," I said, squeezing Dawn's hand. I didn't want to put her off so I disappeared outside the doors. I expected to hear a song, but I forgot, well I wasn't really aware, that you have to warm up a voice. So I sat on the floor and the piano went up and down the scales, getting higher and higher all the time. Then the vowels changed, it was ay, then ee, then eye, then ah, eh, I, etc., over and over. Then after what seemed ages of all sorts of silly little runs and things, she started to sing.

Dawn

I was really nervous, though she tried to put me at ease.

"What would you sing if you had the choice of anything?" She asked. I thought about it, it wasn't hard.

"'Plurez mez yeux' by Massinett from Le Cid." She raised an eyebrow at me.

"Rather an unusual choice, rather a huge piece too. You need incredible range and power for that one," she said, "and I'm not sure if I can play it either from sight reading, but I do have it. How old are you Dawn?" She went to her wall of scores and took it down.

"I'm seventeen."

"I doubt you've got the emotional experience for that one either."

"Oh you'd be surprised," I replied. She raised an eyebrow at me.

"What about something Italian?"

"Puccini, Ghianni Schicci, 'Oh mio babbino caro?'"

"Ok that's better I know I can play that one well. Some German lieder or some latin perhaps?"

"Faure, Faure's Requiem?" I responded.

"Right," she said landing them on the edge of the little baby grand piano. "Help me find them then Dawn."

I picked up the Requiem and went through the index looking for Pie Jesu, whilst she tackled Le Cid. I actually hadn't a clue where it came in the opera, I just knew the aria. I hoped she wasn't going to ask me too much about the background to each song.

"Where did you meet?" she asked me. I was a little surprised by the personal question.

"At a school dance," I replied.

"Well let's start with this one then, because I'd bet you know about love, but is it the kind you would throw yourself off a bridge for?" She was talking about Gianni Schicci one of my favourite operas. She raised her eyebrow again at me, smiled, and began the introduction. I let the music flow through me. It was easy. I imagined pleading with my father, Oh mio babino caro, to let me marry John. Then in the middle of the piece came the bit where the character threatens to go to the Ponte Vecchio and throw herself into the river Arno if he refuses her permission. Yeah I knew what that kind of love was like, and the music just swept me up. Then came the end where she begs for pity. I remembered the longing I had to have John back in my life again.

There was a long silence at the end, and I looked at her face trying to gauge her response. I'd never sung to anyone before who really knew what they were listening for, I'd just always been better than everyone else. Was this the point where she was going to let me down gently, tell me to not waste my time? I couldn't tell anything from her expression. She had her eyebrows raised and she blew out air from her mouth.

"Ok then, let's go straight for the Le Cid." She changed scores and looked at me seriously. "You're going to just have to carry on if I make a mistake… and I will," she said, " but don't wait for me I'll catch you up. I'm not a pianist, I'm a singer, or rather I was," she added. She struggled valiantly through the introduction, which I have to say really was fiendish to play, but despite the errors it really did get me in the mood. "Plurez, plurez mex yeuxes, tombe triste rosea." I knew enough not to get over emotional with the piece. I had once put so much into it I had actually cried, but then my throat had knotted and tightened up and I was unable to hit the top notes and it had all become a strangled mess. But it was a piece I could just play with the power of my voice, reigning it in then letting it go, and the range. It swept right up and then right down into my chest register. I loved it and it was packed with powerful emotion. I only had to tap into a fraction of the emotion and pain that I had felt when I had had to give John up, still keeping that little bit detached so that my voice could work properly, but enough to breathe real life into the words. I also knew John was listening outside and I wanted him to feel the despair I had felt. It was cruel in some ways, if I'd thought about it coldly like that, but it was what I needed to do for the piece, this was what

I did to produce what I had to.

"Well!" she said.

"Well?" I asked still unsure what she was going to say.

"Do you want to do the Faure?" she asked.

"Do you want me to?" I replied, not sure whether she had had enough or whether I was being placated.

"I'd love you to," she said with a smile, "but again it's quite a gear change from the last piece."

"That's ok," I said.

"Hang on a minute," she got up. "Let's go into the Orangerie, the acoustics are a lot better in there." She went to the door with the score in her hand. John was sitting on the floor outside with a strange look on his face.

"Come on dear," she said to him as I followed her out, "you come and have a listen properly."

"You sounded amazing," he whispered, and took my hand as we followed her down the corridor.

Inside the Orangerie was a huge grande piano and the swimming pool reflected its shimmering light into the inside of the building through the enormous French doors and onto the walls and ceiling. John looked around for a corner to hide in, there wasn't one. She took him by the elbow and put him in the middle of the space.

"Now," she said, "I want you to sing to him." John smiled at me apologetically, he was probably remembering what I had said to him in the Lovelace chapel. He sat down on the polished wooden floor and leaned back, his two arms supporting his weight behind him with one knee bent up in front of him the other leg outstretched. He shrugged at me and smiled.

She began to play, and I was back in the Lovelace Chapel, back where we got engaged, back looking into his dreamy eyes as he waited for my reply. This time I whispered it back to him in a hushed prayer, and I don't think I took my eyes from his for a second, not even when it finished. Then we both erupted into the same blistering smile we had in the chapel.

"Well," she said, "you do have an amazing voice and there will be a place for you. I don't know how we'll manage it, but we'll cobble something together for you. That was quite extraordinary Dawn. You have an incredible instrument. What did you think?" She said turning to John, still sat on the floor looking at me, and he quoted from Lovelace's poems.

"So did she move; so did she sing
Like the Harmonious spheres that bring
Unto their Rounds their musick's ayd;
Which she performed such a way,
As all th'inamour'd world will say
The Graces daunced, and Apollo play'd"

"Lovelace," he added looking now in her direction, just so she understood.

"No higher praise indeed," she said. "Now Dawn, I'd like you to attend the auditions in a month's time even though we're full."

I froze. She noticed it. John jumped up and was by my side immediately, taking my hand in his. I felt suddenly exposed and vulnerable.

"Now come on Dawn, you've just sung to the person it's

probably most difficult to sing to…"

"It's not that," I said quietly, "I'll be too ill by then… But I'll be better for the beginning of term," I added hopefully. "I have ...ancer." I hadn't said the word before and the initial letter just disappeared down my throat as if saying it made it real and if by keeping it unsaid it didn't exist. John squeezed my hand and looked me in the eyes checking to see if I was all right. I reassured him with a smile.

"Oh my dear," she said, "well then September it is! I'll have to contact you, and you're going to have to fill in some paper work. Can you come back after study week?" I nodded.

"Ok, then lets go and have another coffee and get some details." We followed her back to her office.

*

I think we grinned all the way home, well back to John's digs and then Chris and Francis came in and we ordered a Chinese. I couldn't believe it. I was in, in a music college to do singing and performance, and John and I would be able to be together. This was just too incredible for words. After the Chinese John walked me to a pay phone so I could tell my parents.

"So," I said, as I walked along beside John holding his hand.

"So?"

"So all I have to do now is get through this next bit!"

"Yep!" he said looking down and rubbing the ring on my finger with his thumb absent mindedly.

"You're miles away," I said watching him. "What are you thinking?"

"I'm thinking about you… and me. Dawn if I ask you something will you tell me the truth?"

"Will I want to lie?"

"You might, you might not want to hurt me."

"How badly would you be hurt?"

"I don't really know," he said looking down.

"Will you leave me?"

"No," he laughed, now looking up at me. "No, never!"

"Will you not like me?"

"No, that's impossible."

"Well it looks like I'm pretty safe then?"

He looked up through his eyelashes and my stomach did it's usual back flip.

"Do you know how I react when you look at me like that?"

"No, so tell me then." He said pulling me close and pushing my lips apart with his, pressing his tongue inside my smile. We kissed gently and rhythmically. I pulled away.

"I can't tell you anything with your tongue inside my mouth I grinned."

"Uhuh!" He said, smiling and kissing me seductively again.

"Ok, I promise to tell you the truth, what do you want to know?"

He stopped smiling and looked seriously into my eyes still holding me as if he were going to kiss me again.

"I want to know how you feel about marrying me." I smiled widely at him.

"That's easy, you've already asked me and if you remember I said yes!" He was so close I rubbed my nose up and down his, resting our foreheads together, waiting for him to speak.

"I don't mean in a few years, I mean now, how do you feel about marrying me now?"

"Are you serious? Is this your big worry?"

"Yes," he said moving back from me. "Dawn, I don't want to wait until we've finished college, and I don't want to wait until we've saved up or got a deposit for a house, or got our first jobs, I want to marry you now!"

"Why the rush? Are you trying to tell me you're pregnant?" I laughed at my own joke, but he didn't, his face just looked pained as he tried to smile casually to cover it up.

"So are you trying to say no then?" He said hesitantly, looking down again. "It's too soon, you want to wait?" He looked up at me, his lashes sweeping slowly upwards.

"No…" I said slowly, "do you… do you think I'm going to die?" I said searching his eyes.

"What?" he gasped. It was as if I had branded him with a hot iron. "Oh my God Dawn! No, no I don't think you're going to die. Oh Jesus Dawn I never even thought! Oh God I'm sorry, I'm so sorry." He dropped to his knees as if a scythe had cut his legs from under him. I couldn't have hurt him more if I had run him through with a sabre. I moved towards him and he threw his arms around my waist and clung on to me like a small boy crying. "Oh God forgive me Dawn I never meant that…"

I dropped onto my knees too and looked into his desperate face.

"Then why?" I said.

"Because I love you so much," he said sobbing, "I just love

you so much."

I flung my arms around his neck and started crying too. "Oh God I love you too, I really do. Please don't cry John, I'm sorry too." And we just clung on to each other. All the emotions held in check about the cancer and how we felt about each other just spilled over. Maybe it was what we both really needed, a damned good weep.

That night we lay in each other's arms looking at the ceiling in silence. He had his head on mine.

"So I never gave you my answer," I said.

"It doesn't matter Dawn, really it doesn't, it's fine. I know you love me, it can wait, I was just being silly." It was convincing, the painful edge was carefully buried. If I hadn't known his beautiful soul you would never have noticed.

"Look, John," I said turning to him so that I could look him in the eyes. "If I'm honest I didn't care when I married you, I knew we would get married one day, that's all I needed to know. I never thought about when, that was never important, it was just knowing that we would and that you'd asked me. I didn't care if it was tomorrow, next week, next year whenever, but you do, and if it matters to you, then it matters to me too. The answer is yes I want to marry you, and yes I want to marry you now, whenever you choose, and however you want to do it. Be it in a church or a chapel, in a tent or on a beach. All I care about is the guy in the suit, and you'd better turn up." I looked at his dazzling eyes, tears were welling in the corners of them. "And that's the honest truth. I love you, you big softie!" He laughed in response.

"Don't tell anyone, you'll ruin my hard fought reputation," he said, rolling over, and we kissed and touched and made love.

Chapter 19

Lovelace

It was raining. Today of all days, how could it be raining? Soft rain was falling and there was only a couple of hours to go. Moli was wandering about in his tail coat and waistcoat, top hat, socks, underpants but no trousers.

"Erhem…!" I coughed, he looked up questioning.

"Forgotten something? Or is this a new fashion?"

"Don't worry Lovelace, Mrs. B. is just pressing them for me, though I do think this look has a lot to be said for it."

"Dear God!" I exclaimed.

"Just think Lovelace if you get married like this then that's one less item to take off later!"

"You'll get yourself arrested, wedding or no wedding."

"Well that'll get me out of having to do the speech then! Here, look what I've got." He pulled a small hip flask from his pocket. "A little bit of vodka, just in case you need a little Dutch courage!"

"If *I* need Dutch courage?" I raised an eyebrow.

"Well Dawn may need some too, if I can get her drunk

enough she may marry me instead!" He began chuckling. I threw several things from the wash stand at him.

"Hey watch the suit… joking, only joking," he laughed. "You know I look better in this than you do," he said admiring himself in the mirror. He grabbed his shades and put them on too.

My hands were shaking, I couldn't get the cuff links through the double cuff holes. Moli came to my aid, cigarette held between his lips, still wearing the shades.

"Good God Lovelace, you getting nervous already, thought you'd be cool as a cucumber, this is what you want right?" I just looked at him. "Ok, ok, I just have to check, it's my job as best man you know. Don't want to screw it up." He held my jacket for me and I put my arms in. "You know you aren't half bad, I could marry you myself," he said. I laughed.

"You're too hairy for me Mols, much as I love you." I replied. He looked at his watch.

"Come on Lovelace, time's a ticking! And I've got a jar lined up for you at the pub before you have to face the music. Rather convenient that pub right opposite the church. You can have one before you go in, and then after you've come out! Now that's my kinda church."

We wandered downstairs to the kitchen where Mrs. B was indeed pressing his trousers.

Moli jumped into them fresh off the ironing board.

"Oooh, a tad on the warm side Mrs. B!" he said as he did up the flies and hopped about trying to avoid the hot zip with his tackle. Mrs. B laughed. Then she turned to me.

"John… you look so handsome." She sighed with her head on one side, eyes glistening. She had cut some roses from the climber on the side of the house. She popped one into my button hole securing it with a pin at the back and then did the same for Moli. The scent was heady, quite amazing for such a tiny bloom.

"Thanks Mrs. B," and I kissed her on the cheek. She grinned and blushed.

It was a small wedding, and by small I mean really small. Dawn's parents were going to be there, her sister and boyfriend, Dawn's best friend Jenny Pickles from school, my parents, Mrs. B and Moli and Kelly. Chris and Francis had driven down from London and my old football mate from the village Ulrich, and his girlfriend Michie. That was it sixteen of us in total. Moli and I were walking to the church from my house. Well no, we were walking to the pub first.The bells were ringing as we walked up the hill towards the church and at that moment it stopped raining. With the sun came a beautiful rainbow over the church tower. I got Moli to take a picture of it as I was sure it would disappear before Dawn got here. Moli was true to his word, there was a pint ready drawn and awaiting us on the bar. Chris, the owner, wanted a kiss and a cuddle from us both before she would let us pick them up.

"Did she grab your arse too Lovelace?" Moli wanted to know "or was it just me?"

I laughed at him. "It's the suits isn't it Chris?" I called to her.

"No," she laughed, "it's gorgeous, fresh young meat, and I'll grab it any chance I get!" We all laughed. "Everything's ready for later lads." She indicated to the tables arranged down the room to one side of the bar for our wedding breakfast, then it was to be back to my house for drinks and cake and some chilling out with our guests. After that, Dawn and I were going to drive to Rye in Moggy for a weekend in the Mermaid Hotel. Monday back home and Tuesday? Tuesday didn't exist, not today. We reached the church and the vicar greeted us warmly.

"This is very exciting, a Lovelace wedding in the Lovelace Chapel," he said. Inside the pews had been re-arranged slightly, pushed further over into the main isle so that Dawn had her own little isle to walk down to the chapel. It was going to be a tight squeeze in such a small space, but there was room for us all, just. Mum and Dad arrived with Mrs. B and Kelly, and then Jenny and Dawn's mum came in followed by Dawn's sister and boyfriend. We all greeted each other with kisses and hugs. Chris and Francis were introducing themselves to Ulrich and Michie. I went and had a quick word.

Ulrich hugged me warmly and introduced me to Michie who was utterly delightful. We swapped information on the Chelsea results and how his fishing was going. Michie's eyes raised to the ceiling as Ulrich launched into the latest 'one that got away' story.

"Save it for later," she said sighing, and we all laughed.

"What's the time?" I asked Moli.

"She's not even late yet, don't panic, she'll be here."

He grabbed me by the shoulders and began steering me towards the chapel steps. He plonked me down in my chair and then sat next to me. "You know if I didn't know you better

Lovelace, I'd say you were about to pass out!"

"I feel sick. " I couldn't help it I was shaking like a leaf. I dropped my head down, where was all the oxygen?

"For God's sake Lovelace, do you want a wee tot to steady the nerves?"

"No, I…" and at that moment the organist began to play the overture from Tannhauser, Dawn's choice.

Moli nudged me and we stood up at the front. We both turned around together to look.

I gasped, I heard Moli gasp too and all my nerves dissolved. She was absolutely blindingly beautiful, I had never seen her looking more radiant. She burst into a huge smile as our eyes locked, and then just as had happened when we had first met everyone else faded away and it was just me and her. As her hand was passed to me it felt like we two were inside a huge bubble, separate and still somehow, from everything but the vows we were making. We made our vows to each other and before God and in front of our families and friends and then I slipped the ring onto her finger and she in turn put one on mine. Our hands were wrapped in the priests stole, together forever. Dawn's dad read the love passage from the bible, Corinthians 13 and my dad read 'To Althea, from Prison' by Richard Lovelace. When we signed our names in the register the organist played Pie Jesu by Faure and then we walked into the sunshine to Toccata by Widor. Moli took some photos and we then went to the pub for bangers and mash with Kentish apple pie and the award winning village ice-cream. I held her hand so tight, I just didn't want to let go of her for an instant.

She was mine and I was hers. Could they see it now? Well if they couldn't they were blind.

We walked slowly down the hill back to the house. Mum and Dad had gone ahead in the car, which Dawn had used to come to the church. Everyone else had gone ahead of us. We stopped in the middle of the road level with the bottom of the churchyard and just stared into each other's eyes smiling and laughing with sheer joy.

"I love you Mrs. Lovelace," I said smiling.

"Oh, I have a beautiful name," she said.

"You've always had a beautiful name," I replied.

"Did you see the rainbow?" she asked. I nodded, I couldn't speak she was so beautiful. She put her arms around my neck and kissed me. I lifted her up in my arms and carried her like a baby over to the style at the bottom of the churchyard. It was a little damp but protected by the trees above. I sat down with her on my knee and we just held each other, sharing a quiet intimate moment together as we played with the rings on each other's fingers. They had come as a pair, with a free set of teaspoons, though what we were going to do with the teaspoons I hadn't a clue, we didn't even possess a teacup. Dawn thought it appropriate though as I loved tea so much. Then I looked into her eyes and we kissed and we could have been back at the top of the George steps that very first time we kissed. And we held on tight as we had then to catch our breath. We walked slowly down the hill to the house holding hands together. As we reached the front steps we were greeted by a shower of confetti. I led Dawn into the drawing room. On one side of the room was a coffee table with lots of presents stacked around it, and on the other side was a table with the wedding cake and some champagne glasses and a few bottles of champagne in coolers. Moli was busy taking charge and handing out the glasses. He brought two glasses over to us.

"You remember you asked me something once Lovelace? If I'd noticed anything odd about you two?" I nodded remembering the day in the Prefects' bathroom after the Lillesden dance. He was suddenly deadly serious. "Well you know when you made your vows back there? There was definitely something, something really there. I can't describe it but it was almost something you could touch, like a… glass wall, with you two on the other side of it," and then he laughed, embarrassed by what he had said and knocked back his glass of champagne in one. "Stupid!" He shook his head dismissing the idea and swigged more champagne. "Bloody hell! That's better than vodka, want another?" I nodded. Dawn and I looked into each other's eyes.

"So there was something there, did you feel it too?" She asked me. I smiled at her.

"You know I did," I replied.

"What do you think it was?"

"Love," I said taking her in my arms, and I didn't care that everyone in the room was watching us, I just kissed her passionately.

Moli started clearing his throat and began banging his flute with a spoon. We sat around in the comfy armchairs and sofas which had been moved back to leave a space to dance, Dawn sat on my knee. Moli took the floor, his speech had everyone in hysterics, even my mum, but really I can't for the life of me remember what he said. I just felt really humbled that I had such a fantastic friend. Dawn's dad made the briefest speech I have ever heard. I think it was all of three sentences, something about standing up, paying up, and shutting up! Then it was my turn.

I thanked everyone for coming, for my parents in hosting the wedding, for Dawn's parents for giving me their most precious daughter. To Mols, and his well timed right hook and that I was undeserving of such a loyal friend. And then I spoke to Dawn.

"Thank you for searching me out. You have shown me places I could not have imagined in my wildest dreams. You are my soul, my life, my love, and my heart is unconditionally yours forever." I held up my glass in a toast. "Dawn," everyone joined me "Dawn." Then I kissed her again, and everyone clapped.

Because there were so few people there it was so easy to really relax and enjoy ourselves. There was time to talk to everyone properly and they all seemed to get on so well. Dawn and Michie hit it off big time, they seemed to share the same sense of the ridiculous. I hadn't met her friend Jenny before either. She was truly lovely too, she was a bit like Moli for me, you know that amazing streak of loyalty and it was obvious she adored Dawn. There was even a small football game in the walled garden. The lads were a little competitive and the girls cheated by trying to distract us. Even Dad joined in and Mrs B. Mum got into the spirit of things too, and every now and then blew a whistle. I think Moli had produced it for her and she was our armchair umpire. Not that she had a clue about the offside rule. We called it a draw after Dawn hid the ball under her beautiful wedding gown and wouldn't give it back until I'd kissed her to her satisfaction. At which point she ran off with it, under her skirts somewhere, over the goal line and claimed it as a goal. It was blisteringly hot now and we chilled out on the patio, inside the drawing room I could hear 'Wishing Well' by Free on the reel to reel. Moli had put together an amazing compilation of all our favourite hits. I held out my hand to Dawn and she took it and we went inside. I held her in my arms as we swayed slowly to the fantastic riffs of Free. Moli cut in at the end of the record, saying 'I had a lifetime to do that and it was his turn,' so I reluctantly handed her over and asked Kelly to dance.

"How you doing Kelly?"

"I'm great, really great... and you're handsome, really handsome... and I'm drunk! What is it about morning suits? I even fancy your dad in his." She smiled and we both laughed comfortably together.

"Hey what's this?" I said turning her hand over. I had hold of her hand and could feel the ring on her finger as I held it. I looked at it, it was huge, and I mean huge. An enormous square emerald surrounded by an amazing amount of diamonds, obviously genuine and equally obviously a priceless Italian heirloom. I looked at her face, she was glowing with pleasure. "Is this what I think it is?" I asked. She nodded enthusiastically. "Does Dawn know?" I looked over to Moli and Dawn, he had obviously just told her. She was jumping up and down kissing him on the cheek and hugging him in excitement. "That's fantastic Kelly, that's really fantastic," I kissed her on the cheek, picked her up with one arm and spun her around. "When did he ask you?" I said, placing her back down on the floor.

"Not long after you announced your wedding date," she stood still and looked up at me. "I know how he feels about Dawn, I've known for ages. But I know he loves me too and I love him, you can understand that can't you?" I looked into her questioning eyes and hugged her tight.

"Yeah, I can understand that, I'm really happy for you both, you couldn't have chosen better. Bastard never told me though." I yelled it loudly at him as Dawn was dragging him by the hand in my direction. "Congratulations mate," I said hugging him tight and then winding him on the back. "Oh dear… was that a bit too hard?" We all laughed as Moli gasped for air. Dawn ran and popped her head out of the french windows.

"Everybody in please," she yelled into the garden, "and bring your glasses!" I went and grabbed a couple more bottles of champagne to top people up. It didn't take long for everyone to get in and top up their glasses. "We've just heard that Moli and Kelly have got engaged," announced Dawn, there were lots of hearty congratulations and burbling.

"To Moli and Kelly." Everyone raised their glasses and in unison toasted Moli and Kelly.

"Thank you kindly one and all!" said Moli raising his glass in a gesture of acceptance. "But now I think it's time to cut the cake, so if you would charge your glasses again," Moli announced, reverting to his role as best man. "Dawn and John." We sliced the cake and then the music went on again.

We went upstairs to change and I have to say I could scarcely keep my hands off her, especially when I saw what she had on underneath her gown.

"Dear God this isn't fair!" I complained as her dress fell revealing suspenders and stockings, but we had a drive ahead and guests downstairs. I reluctantly let her change into her going away outfit after she promised faithfully to put it all back on again for me later, so that I could then take it off.

"What about Moli and Kelly, eh?" I said, incredulous.

"Oh it's brilliant, I'm so pleased for them. You kept it quiet?" she said looking at me under her eyebrows as she pulled off a stocking.

"I didn't know, he didn't tell me, the dark horse. Still we're not joined at the hip you know, he can be mysterious at times."

"Really?" she looked up. "Like when?"

"Like about how he feels about you," I looked up at her and smiled. "He never talks about it, and I can only imagine what it costs him, I don't think I could be that loyal, and then I went and accused him…" I looked down ashamed again, reliving that moment when I saw them together. So innocent, and I had twisted it into something else.

"You could be that loyal. You were prepared to give me up when you thought I was in love with him, no matter what it cost you. He forgave you long ago, you know, but at some point you have to forgive yourself."

"You're very wise Mrs. Lovelace," I said, taking her in my arms.

"What about Kelly?" she asked.

"He loves her, and she loves him, they're going to be ok. She told me."

"What? She knows?"

"Well Dawn she's not stupid, and anyway you're a married lady now, two's company, three's a crowd and all that."

"John... that's not one of the reasons why you wanted to marry me is it? I mean you know how I feel about you... you know that I've never felt about Moli like that. I'm not going to say I don't love him because I do, just not like that!"

I took both her hands in mine.

"No, that's not why I wanted to marry you. I know you love me." I pulled her to the bed to sit. "When I'm with you, I don't know, I feel like there was some space in me before that wasn't filled. But even when we were together there was an infinitesimal space between us... God does this sound stupid or what?"

"No it doesn't, go on," she encouraged.

"Well, when we were in our bubble that tiny space was gone and for the first time I was whole." I looked into her chocolaty gaze. She was smiling at me. I looked down smiling at myself. "Don't laugh at me, please, I know I sound like an imbecile."

"I'm not laughing at you. Now your going to think I'm just saying this, but you've just described how it felt for me today. I thought we were as close as you could get, but something weird happened in the Church, maybe that's what they mean about two becoming one. I wasn't even aware of the space until it suddenly wasn't there any more." I leaned her back on the bed and kissed her as I had never kissed her before. We became lost in a world of passion and sensations. Until there was a loud knock at the door.

"Lovelace, put your pants on and get your arse back downstairs, that's what tonight's for."

It was Moli. We both laughed. God how I loved her. She was straight back into her jeans.

We spent ages saying goodbye to everyone and then we ran the gauntlet of the confetti and jumped into Moggy. Moli had tied all sorts of paraphernalia to the rear bumper and God alone knows where he obtained a three foot polystyrene silver horseshoe with a homemade 'just married' sign across it. Apparently they came in pairs because he had wedged another one on the bulbous nose of the Morris' bonnet. Later down the road we discovered several kippers sitting on the engine and pennies in the hubcaps. A few friendly motorists offered their help when they saw us retrieving cooked fish from the inside of the engine compartment. We were soon on our way again though. Moli and Kelly had promised they would join us for supper at the Mermaid later, although they were rather dubious about it and took some persuading.

"Well we're not inviting you into the bridal suite, but it would just be good to share some time together." I had said to Moli. "You could use it as an excuse to be romantic," I said nudging him.

"Listen I don't need any advice from you on how to be romantic. I'm Italian for Christ's sake, it's in the blood," said Moli laughing. "Ok, I'll book a room, but not in the Mermaid, don't want to listen to you two thrashing around all night, I'll be doing some thrashing around of my own," he said winking at me.

Chapter 20

Lovelace

The lady on reception looked at us a little bemused. Well, I suppose we looked like a couple of school kids, which was almost what we were, but she seemed to take a shine to Dawn, which I could hardly blame her for. The porter took our bags up and we were alone Mr. & Mrs. Lovelace. The bed was a half poster, it had tall posts at each corner. There was a large chest at the foot and above it a very large and substantial beam. I couldn't believe it, in a trice Dawn was on the box and upside down hanging from the beam.

"Well you just have to," she said from her inverted position in the centre of the ceiling. I collapsed backwards onto the bed in hysterics. She did a neat little handstand onto the box and landed beside me on the bed.

"I had no idea you were a contortionist, or are you a bat? I married a bat!" I said shaking with mirth.

"There's a lot you don't know about me, you'd better start finding out," and she pulled my collar bringing my face to hers.

Dinner was sumptuous, and it had been a very long time since the bangers and mash. The waiters were incredible, aprons almost down to the floor, and so many of them, each with their own individual job to do. Dawn loved it.

"It's so beautiful with the linen fold panelling, painted walls and heavy beams. How did you find it?"

"Well Mum and Dad took me on a holiday once visiting loads of old coaching Inns along the south coast, and this was the first one, the closest to home."

"I bet there are lots of ghosts," her eyes were shining. When we got to the coffee Dawn pin holed the Maitre Dee and he delighted in tales of sword fighting and other things that went bump in the night.

"They're not going to come are they?" Dawn was disappointed.

"Well he said they would, but maybe they thought better of it, maybe they thought we didn't mean it or that they would be intruding."

"But we wouldn't have asked them if we hadn't meant it. He'd know that wouldn't he?"

I took her hand over the table and smiled at her.

At which point a cheeky grin appeared behind the waiter.

"Moli! We'd given you up." I clapped him on the back and hugged him. "Kelly was looking a little uncomfortable until Dawn threw herself at her and hugged her tight."

"Oh this is brilliant, now the day is perfect," she said, and hugged Moli too and kissed him.

"Well we weren't sure whether you really meant it, whether you wanted to be alone. But I decided you might need some expert advice so…" We all laughed.

"Have you eaten?" Dawn asked. They hadn't so the kitchen made up an amazing array of sandwiches for them which we took into the snug with some more hot coffee. Later we went and sat in the little courtyard outside around the mermaid fountain. It was brilliant, Moli was on blistering form and so was Dawn for that matter. We had a wedding post mortem, reliving it all again from a different perspective. Then we just had fun with lots of amusing banter. We had to be asked to keep the noise down as the courtyard had rooms all around it, so we went back inside and sat around an enormous fireplace in the bar drinking brandy into the early hours. The night porter let Moli and Kelly out later. They had made some sort of arrangement to get back into their hotel, and I led my beautiful bride upstairs to the bedroom. I scooped her up outside the door and ducking our heads popped her onto the bed, where we both fell back exhausted.

"I'm knackered!" said Dawn, and I laughed my head off. I was too. "I suppose if we don't do it now, we might be disappointed in years to come."

"So is that what it's come to then, I marry you and a few hours later you've gone off sex for life? I should have left you as a wanton." I turned to her laughing.

"Listen, it's all up to you, if you can muster something up then I'll gladly oblige."

"You are such a romantic Dawn, really I had no idea." I responded sarcastically.

"Well come on then," she began groping in my trousers, "let's see what… Oh!" she said in surprise smiling.

"I'm eighteen, it's an automatic thing!" I said grinning.

"Oh, whose the romantic now then? And I thought it was because of me. Well if it's so automatic perhaps we can get a machine to take care of you." Her eyes were amazing, dazzling with wicked amusement. "Maybe a hoover nozzle!" she suggested, giggling.

I stood up and took off my shirt and then the rest of my clothes as she watched. She smiled as I stood naked in front of her.

"Well maybe not," she said rising off the bed and standing in front of me. "I don't think the nozzle would be able to cope!" She held up both her arms above her head smiling at me and I pulled her top off over the top of her head. Then I felt for the clasp on her bra. She smiled as I fumbled, then she took my hand and placed it round the front to where it unhooked.

"New bra, new layout! Just keeping you on your toes!" she said smiling. I smiled back at her and ran my finger tips down her sides. She shivered.

"Are you cold?" I asked. She shook her head in reply. I knelt down and undid her jeans and slid them down over her thighs. They dropped and she stepped out of them. I slid down her sexy knickers.

"You're supposed to appreciate those," she said.

"I'd rather appreciate what's inside them," I said kissing her stomach scar gently and moving down. I explored her with my tongue holding on to her hips with my hands. She opened her legs for me. She tasted of sex. I stood up and lifted her onto the bed. She wrapped her legs around me. I held her in my arms and pushed into her. She moaned. I knew I had hurt her, I felt her tense and then relax. I looked into her eyes.

"Go on," she encouraged, "please." I moved slowly feeling her tense and relax with each movement. I hesitated, this was painful for her. "Oh God please don't stop please."

"Dawn?"

"Trust me, I'm all right, just don't stop." I moved as slowly as I could, she put her hand on the small of my back guiding me with the pressure of her hand until I was as deep in her as I could possibly go. We made love slowly and as gently as I could guided by her touch until we were both there, together on the brink of our orgasm. She held her hand still and I stopped. Ah... Dear God... It was excruciating, but I could have waited there for her forever, and then she pushed her finger gently into my back moving her hips forward allowing my final push, and we came together. She held on to my hips, preventing me from moving.

"Don't, don't move," she whispered. So we slept welded together like the one being we had become.

I woke the next morning with my wife in my arms. I couldn't believe it, my wife, I said it over and over in my head and found myself smiling and laughing to myself.

"What's so funny?" said a sleepy head next to me. I looked over at her. Her hair was sticking up everywhere, her eyes were a little puffy and she was just beautiful and mine. I pulled her closer into my arms and began kissing her along her neck and down her arms.

"Does this happen to you every morning? Or is it just when I'm around?"

"Most mornings," I said, moving to her breasts.

"What the hell did you do at school then?" she asked smiling.

I stopped and looked at her, waiting for her to catch up.

"Oh…" She said cottoning on. "Would that be why your biceps are so well formed then?"

I laughed. "That and we played a lot of rugby, and there were also a lot of cold early morning swims and cross country runs. Or you just wait for it to pass."

"God you poor things, all that pent up frustration."

"Every fifteen seconds, or so they say."

"What?" she said incredulous.

"That's supposed to be how often guys my age think about sex, every fifteen seconds."

"Dear God, its surprising you can speak coherently. You must have been permanently exhausted from one activity or another!"

We laughed together.

"Are you all right… I mean after last night?" I asked her seriously.

"No…" she said turning to me eyes sparkling, "I think you need to practice a bit harder, you've not quite got it right yet," she said teasing and smiling.

"Is that right?" and we began where we had left off a few hours earlier.

We were late down for breakfast, but we managed to get in just in time. We had the restaurant to ourselves though, the last guest was just leaving as we arrived. I think we had everything on the menu we were so famished, and we giggled about needing to keep up our energy levels.

"Well what do you want to do, we have a whole day together?"

Moli and Kelly were going to meet us at the hotel for Sunday lunch, then they were going back, Kelly to Lillesden and Moli to Quentin's, back to their respective boarding schools. We had today and one more night before going back to Dawn's house.

"Can we go and explore?" she said excitedly.

"Sounds great!" So that's what we did. We first traversed the cobbled streets, finding a fantastic 'Tuck Shop' that sold sweets by the quarter pound. Dawn went mad buying all sorts of things she hadn't seen in years. Then we wandered through the churchyard over to the old gatehouse beyond. From the top of the gatehouse there was an amazing view of the marsh all the way to the sea. Inside the tower was a small cell. We sat in there together.

"What are you thinking?" she asked.

"I was just thinking about Richard Lovelace imprisoned and what it must have been like for him."

"I'm glad he was in love, I think you can stand just about anything if the reason is love." Dawn said looking at the ring on her hand. "Was it Amerantha he was in love with?"

"No, one knows her real name you know. But he wasn't just in love with his lady, he loved his king and his country. 'I could not love thee dere so much loved I not honour more.' It all made him the man he was." I replied.

"You know you're not so different from him," she said

looking up at me. I laughed. "No I mean it. You're all honour and loyalty to your friend and love for me," she looked down.

"What? What's wrong Dawn?"

Tears were falling down her cheeks. I didn't press her, I knew what was wrong, fear of what was ahead of her. I sat on the floor of the tiny cell with her between my legs in front of me with my arms around her. As she wept silently I whispered a couple of Richard's lines to her and hummed gently in her ear and held her tight. We were in there for ages, so long in fact that the curator came to find us. When he came to the door though and saw us he kindly nodded and backed out leaving us to our solitude. It was very cosy for a cell, but also a chill was setting in. I couldn't take the chance of Dawn getting ill now so reluctantly I made to move. "Simon the Pieman is just down the road," how about we warm up with a cup of tea? What do you feel like today?"

"Earl Grey," that was a surprise usually it was PG tips, bog standard.

I was so pleased to see Moli and Kelly when we got back to the Mermaid. They were having a pre-lunch drink in the snug. Dawn went upstairs to have a quick bath. She had got a bit chilled and wanted to warm up. Kelly went with her to chat and keep an eye on her, bless her. They had both picked up on the mood immediately.

"Jesus Lovelace, what can I do for you?" I laughed and looked out of the window in despair as if somehow there might be an answer outside in the sunshine. I looked at him in the eyes and in them I saw my own pain reflected back, equally raw, brothers in torment, but mine was permissible, how must he be suffer-ing too?

"Listen, Moli, do you want to be there too?" He shook his head and looked away to the window.

"You're a lot braver than I am Lovelace, this is one time I don't envy you. She won't want me there, and I couldn't bear to see her suffer and feel a helpless intruder, not unless she asks specifically for me that is... but she won't. I'll be there for you though, any time night or day if you need me." I looked at him and he turned to me with glistening eyes. "I'm not *in love* with you, it's much easier." We both snorted in sympathy with one another. What a bizarre situation it was, the three of us. Moli and I, both in love with Dawn. Then there was the added complication that he was also in love with Kelly. Who said being in love was easy? At least it wasn't for Moli. The waiter came in to see if we wanted drinks.

"Two Ricards please," he ordered, "trust me you'll enjoy." I nodded in agreement. He was right, the aniseed drink was wonderful and warming and I could feel a buzz from it which somehow dulled the aching pain in my chest.

We talked of old rugby matches, the time when the whole team was coming towards Mols and he threw his head from side to side using it like a mace, scattering the opposition in all directions, leaving himself a clear run to score under the posts. The time he broke my nose in the scrum leaving it flattened all over my face, and then obligingly broke it again the following season almost completely rectifying the flattened proboscis back to its original position with hardly a flaw to show for it.

We talked of fights we had got into together, of trips to the pub and the almost ritual verbal abuse which followed on the return journey, which almost invariably ended with me getting extremely fed up with him and throwing him over the wall next to the track. He would land in the rose bushes below and have to walk all the way around back to the house. The one time he annoyed me a little too early, I have never sobered up so quickly in my life. I had picked him up and thrown him over the wall as was usual only to realise that we were not at a point of a mere five foot drop on the other side, but one of over twenty foot to the rifle ranges below. I remember searching the rifle ranges with my eyes looking for a dead body sprawled on the ground at the base of the wall, only to find that Moli had been so drunk that he had literally bounced and was up and staggering off on the long walk around, none the worse for his long drop!

Then there was the time the school was three hundred years old and we had spent a whole week almost, locked in the George with an old boy of the school and his glamorous wife. He had been head of Lancaster house and was buying drinks for anyone in Lancaster. I think almost the whole house was in the bar and as we all drank vodka and lime at the time, the entire bar on both sides was covered with drinks, you could not have got another glass on there. We spent the whole week completely legless. On the last day his wife decided she wanted to see a swimming race, so Moli and I obliged. He drove up in his Jensen Healy Interceptor whilst we staggered up the hill. Mols and I stripped down to our underwear but as I dived in my underpants flew off. I was half way down the pool by the time I realised and had to go back for them. Moli meanwhile, was slowly meandering up the pool and I was easily able to beat him, underpants in hand. I then had to go back to rescue Moli who had completely lost his sense of direction and was going back down the first lane again. In the end Moli wedged himself into the Interceptor and refused to get out, pledging undying loyalty and love to the guy's wife and his car. We had to remove him by force, great times!

By the time Dawn and Kelly re-joined us our spirits were well and truly up again and we were ready for lunch.

"Here, I almost forgot," said Moli reaching under the couch on which he sat. "This is from Kelly and I." He pulled out a large box from underneath the couch wrapped beautifully in cream and gold paper with all sorts of cellophane and lacy bows attached.

"We heard you were in need!" Kelly said.

"Ooh, do we open it now?" asked Dawn.

"Well it is a wedding present, and you are married, unless it's all off that is?" said Moli looking hopeful in a playful way. Dawn dived in.

"Come on, it's for you too," she said excitedly. I was just so grateful to see her smiling again, so I helpfully held onto the bits of paper as she shredded the wrappings. "Oh my goodness," exclaimed Dawn. "How did you know?"

"Well we heard you had a set of spoons and needed something to go with them," said Kelly looking at Moli and smiling in a conspiratorial way. From inside the box Dawn retrieved a beautiful bone china Wedgwood teapot and milk jug.

“I couldn’t let you run off with Lovelace without the means to keep him fuelled. Sex will only get him so far, tea gets him the rest of the way.” Moli added.

“There are cups and saucers too!” she said excitedly.

“There are a couple of mugs at home for you too,” said Moli “But we left those for you to pick up later. Oh and this is for you too Lovelace.” He threw me a box, which was very light. Inside were all sorts of teas, about fifty different ones in all, some of which I had never heard of.

“That’s great Mols, Kelly.” I leaned forward to give her a kiss on the cheek. “I’ll have to save up hard for your wedding present though,” Moli raised an eyebrow enquiring. “A still for making vodka!” He laughed and Kelly tutted. We all went in to lunch.

Dawn

As expected the Mermaid excelled itself. Sunday lunch was everything a Sunday roast should be, but done to the utmost perfection. Moli and Kelly had to rush off before coffee as they both had to get back to school. We waved them off and then returned to our cosy room to have our coffee. I was determined, I was not going to allow myself any more self pity, fear, fright or whatever. There wasn’t much of our honeymoon left and I wasn’t going to let anything spoil what remained of it. So I carefully packed my fears away, leaving John lying on the bed and went into our little bathroom. Whilst I had been up with Kelly earlier I had hidden my wedding undergarments under the towels, so when I emerged I had the satisfaction of seeing

John's eyes literally pop out in surprise.

Lovelace

"Ye Gods woman, I think I just died and ended up in heaven."

"I don't think they do this sort of thing in heaven," said Dawn smiling wickedly.

"No? Well they do now because this is definitely my view of heaven," I said, leaping off the bed and taking her in my arms. "Oh my God you are so beautiful Dawn." I kissed her gently running my fingers down her spine. She automatically arched her back and threw her head back. I continued kissing her down her neck to her collar bone. She tasted incredible, smelt incredible and looked incredible, like the most amazing Christmas package all tied up with lace and satin. She was an eighteen year old's wildest fantasy come true and she loved *me* of all people. The textures were amazing. Her skin underneath the satin, I couldn't tell which was the softest, the sexiest. Her nipples rose hard against the soft fabric as they brushed against it.

"Is this all for me?" I asked dreamily.

"All for you," she whispered seductively. Her mouth hung open slightly and she pulled my leather belt free, loosening me from the confines of my jeans and pants. "Take your time."

"Take my time! You have to be joking," I said pushing her back onto the bed and sliding easily into her. "What have you done?" I asked in surprise.

"Well do you know it's amazing what Kelly carries around in her handbag. I had a little chat with her and she gave me something," I looked at her questioning. "Don't worry, it's not yoghurt!" We laughed so much we became disengaged.

Chapter 21

Dawn

Leaving the Mermaid was a real wrench. We found a book in the lounge with comments in it and so left our thanks to the staff there, vowing to return. Then we clambered aboard little Moggy and set off back to John's house. We were going there first to open presents etc and then it would be back to my house to stay the night. The sun was shining and little Moggy pootled along making her usual happy sound.

"You know I'm sure this car is talking to us," I said happily to John.

"Oh yes? I think you may have to translate for me, what is she saying?"

"She's saying, 'if you're thinking of trading me in for an MG, think again.'" John took my hand and we laughed.

To say the journey back to John's was uneventful would not be the truth. We talked and laughed comfortably together, we sang and were very silly and we sat in silence just enjoying each other's proximity. It was the perfect way to end our honeymoon, just us two, well three including Moggy, who had taken to farting when you decelerated, which caused much amusement and hilarity. She was fast acquiring a whole personality of her own. I was in Elysium and couldn't take my eyes off John whose glorious profile I could just stare at, and there was nothing he could do about it either.

"What are you doing?" he said trying to watch the road and me in one glance.

"Looking at you." He laughed in response.

"You're putting me off," he said putting his hand on my thigh.

I took his hand and guided it further up my leg, and slid my own hand onto his thigh.

"You're going to cause an accident," he said, retrieving his hand and blowing out his breath hard.

"You know you're going to have to get used to this, you're very easily distracted Mr. Lovelace." I said teasing him.

The car suddenly lurched into a siding and pulled up to a sharp halt.

"Now look here Mrs. Lovelace," he was trying to be stern, but it just wasn't washing. He grabbed me by the collar and kissed me roughly, but that was no good it just aroused an equally passionate response in me and within seconds we were out of breath and frustrated in the front seats of the car. "How do you think people manage to get anything done? I can't even drive from A to B without needing to touch you." I looked into his dreamy eyes. "I'll try to be good," I said, but I knew it was a broken promise before it left my lips.

There was a gentle tapping at the window. We both looked

around startled. Adrenaline began to pump through me. It was a policeman. John wound the window down.

"May I see your driving license Sir?" he enquired. John fumbled in his back pocket for his wallet. "Madame!" He acknowledged me with a look. "Are you all right?" he enquired.

"Err yes thank you," I answered a little embarrassed.

"Is there a problem?" John asked.

"Well sir, you appeared to leave the road at some speed back there. And your eyes are rather red. Are you taking any medication Sir? Any drugs of any sort?" I bit my lip and stifled a giggle. "Would you care to get out of the vehicle Sir?" John was not being invited, he was being instructed, so he got out of the car. I couldn't really hear what was being said but after what seemed forever John got back into the car laughing his head off.

"What? What happened? What did he say?"

"I told him I hadn't had a lot of sleep... That I was on my honeymoon."

"Did he believe you?"

"No, I had to show him my marriage license."

"And?" I said desperate to know the outcome.

"And he said I was to drive home slowly and carefully and learn to pace myself. That 'a lifetime was a long time and that I shouldn't blow it and crash on my honeymoon.' Then he nodded knowingly and said 'Good luck'." I laughed with him.

"Ok I promise I'll leave you alone while your driving," I said. Then I amended it. "Well I'll try very hard at least!" The police car pulled out in front of us, and we followed laughing but a little chastened by the event.

We arrived at Lovelace. Ooh that sounded lovely, very grand, but rather special too. I was a Lovelace too now and I liked it. I got it now, how they felt about that link with the past however tentative. John swung me up in his arms to carry me over the threshold.

"I know it's not our threshold, but it's as good as any," he said, popping a kiss onto my lips.

"Watch your back," I said. "I have plans for you later, and you'll need to be fighting fit!" He laughed and dropped me gently on the mat inside the hall.

"Mum, Dad!" he called down the hallway. He opened the door to the drawing room, his dad rose from his chair by the fireplace to come and greet us with a smile. He took me warmly in his embrace and kissed me on the cheek.

"My dear," he said. For the first time ever I really felt like I had a granddad of my own. He turned to John. "John," and shock of shock, they hugged. It was lovely and really natural, as if that was what they always did. John's mum came in and smiled at me. Well she was trying at least, so I helped her out and went over and gave her a hug and a kiss on the cheek. She was a little taken aback but despite that she did respond a little. John kissed his mum on the cheek too, she was much more comfortable with that I noted. We sat down and swapped notes on the Mermaid whilst they all had a sherry. *Yuck!* Then John's dad, Charles, *I was allowed to call him that now*, reminded John about the presents, so he ferried them over from the table in the corner of the room. We sat on the floor reading the cards and opening them together. People had been so generous, there were some lovely things. John made sure all the cards were carefully put into the boxes with the presents so that we would know later who gave us what when it came to writing our thank you cards.

"I'll make a list later," he said.

Dinner was lovely and the conversation light until John's mum started asking questions about me and what would be happening tomorrow, and the downward spiral began. John tried to head her off each time, trying to get the conversation onto something else, but it seemed she was unable to talk about anything else. Well, in her defence she was probably trying to be interested but she seemed to have no comprehension as to how it was making me feel. I became more and more silent, and my answers were becoming monosyllabic, hardly a chatty new daughter in law. Charles jumped in on the bandwagon too and it was like an assault from both sides with me in the middle. I'm sure they didn't mean it like that but Jesus, what bride wants to talk about her impending hospitalisation and all the horrors ahead of her on her honeymoon? I looked across at John for help. He looked at me with his head slightly on one side and smiled apologetically, and that alone raised my spirits.

"Look, Mum, Dad, I know you both mean well but were going to have to face all this soon enough, can we leave this for just today?"

"Oh Dawn!" his dad said, putting his knife and fork down. "How very unfeeling of us, of course you don't want to talk about this today of all days, I'm so sorry my dear." I smiled at him.

"Well you need to think about what's going to happen. I mean you need to be prepared don't you?" Continued his mum.

I looked down at my plate. Was she that unfeeling, was she doing it on purpose or was she unintelligent? I couldn't decide. But I felt whatever I said it was going to be wrong. John was there again for me, my saviour.

"Tomorrow Mum… tomorrow will be soon enough… this is still our honeymoon." His mum continued eating, she didn't comment, but she was very tense.

They tried to teach me bridge later on, but they took it so seriously and I couldn't remember what any of the bidding or numbers meant. It made no sense at all to me. I think John was a little disappointed, it turned out that he was captain of the bridge team at school and something of a prodigy at it. I was a disaster area when it came to cards and though I did try to begin with it began to stress me out somewhat as they obviously couldn't grasp what my problem was. It was obvious to them what to call and when I played the wrong card I could feel the tension. I excused myself to go to the toilet and once the door was locked I found myself in tears. Tears of frustration, disappointment at letting John down and appearing to be so thick. Well it was simple maths wasn't it? Tears of misery like some mighty weight decended and began to press down on me from which I was unable to escape. There was a gentle knock at the door.

"Dawn, are you ok?" it was John.

I didn't want him to think I was a baby. Poor guy. I was always in tears for something or other. So I couldn't play bridge, so what? They wouldn't make much of a fist at singing an aria either. I stood up determined and gave the loo a flush for good measure.

"Yes I'm fine!" I said as I opened the door. John looked concerned.

"Look I'm sorry about the cards, I thought it would be fun, something we could all do together." I slid my arms around his gorgeous slim waist.

"You married the wrong sister if it's a card sharp you want, I think I reached my limit with snap at about six years old. But I'll give it another go." I can't have sounded too enthusiastic as he hugged me tight.

"Don't worry, they've packed it all away, you're off the hook," he said, smiling gently at me and kissing my frown lines.

"No really, I will have another try, but maybe you could teach me on our own, then there might be less pressure."

"Less pressure, but other distractions!" he laughed and gave me one of his beautiful soft kisses that left me gasping for more.

"Ok well I'll sit with a bag over my head, will that help?" He looked at me his eyes narrowing and smiled.

"Well, not really, it's sort of the whole package that I find distracting." We laughed together kissing, and then his mum came down the hall and I let go of him startled. John didn't let go of me though, which was nice.

"We wondered if you were staying to supper, or are you planning to eat at Dawn's? You'll have a long day tomorrow." She said.

"No I think we need to be getting off shortly." John replied rather a clipped manner.

"We'll just tidy up the presents and then I think we'll be off."

She nodded to him and walked on towards the kitchen. He held my shoulders. "I'm sorry," he said apologising for her. "She doesn't mean it."

"It's ok," I replied, but I didn't feel it was ok.Thick! I like to think she was thick, rather than the alternative. I helped John carry the presents upstairs to the attic. We were shocked when we went inside. The baby lamb furniture had gone and there was a small double bed inside, the whole room had been redecorated and was now no longer a child's old nursery it was a proper bedroom. The rocking horse was still in situ but it had been transformed into a room for us.

"Did they do this for us?" I asked, but knowing the answer.

"I wonder when they got all this done? Must have been a rush!" replied John.

"Listen John… I'm going to go and talk to your mum." He looked at me worried. "It's all right I'm not going to have a go at her, but I think we need to clear the air a bit? I know she loves you, and so do I, so that's something we have in common. What do you think?" He nodded.

"But I'll be nearby… in case you need some help ok?"

"No, I'll do this alone… I'll be fine… really." He looked unsure but he smiled at me.

"Ok I'll finish up the presents," and he kissed me on the cheek and disappeared down the stairs. I followed him down and then turned to the back of the house towards the kitchen. She was inside sitting at the kitchen table stirring a cup of tea.

She looked up at me surprised as I entered the room but there was no welcoming smile. I was suddenly stumped. What the hell did I call her? I knew her name was Marie but she hadn't given me permission to use her name, so I suppose I was stuck with Mrs. Lovelace, but that sounded so formal and wrong. I avoided it.

"The room is beautiful," I said tentatively. "It was very kind of you."

"It was Charles' idea. He said you would prefer that room as it's furthest away and more separate from the rest of the house, though the other bedrooms are much larger and more comfortable."

"He was right, we love that room… it was still very kind of you to go to so much trouble for us."

"I was very sad to see the nursery go." She looked at me as she took a sip of her tea. Did she mean she was sad about the nursery or was it that her baby, John, now had someone of his own? "I'm surprised you've been in that part of the house before," she continued, obviously not surprised in the least and now alluding to our night together. I flushed hot. Ok, so this was not going to be as easy as I had imagined. I looked at her, she was pleased at my reaction. I thought I would try our common ground.

"You know I love John very much."

"Yes he's quite a catch isn't he." It was a statement not a question and it was obvious now what she thought of me. I was some nasty little gold digger out for what I could get. "I expect it will be turned back into a nursery quite soon." She added.

Right, not only a gold digger but pregnant within the year. I can honestly say that I just felt sad, sad for her that she couldn't see how much we loved each other, how happy we were together, how happy John was, after all she loved him too. Couldn't she see that?

"I make him happy," I said gently.

She made a derisory snort down her nose. I wanted to cry, but I was damned if I was going to give her that satisfaction. "He'll always love you too, you're his mum." I was unaware of the thin ice I had crept onto.

"You *know* he's adopted," she stated as if I was making a point, "he's not *our…* " At this point Charles swept hotly into the kitchen and brought his fist down onto the kitchen table with a slam making her saucer jump.

"*Is* my son!" he stated vehemently. He hadn't shouted but the statement was absolute. I stood there shocked, I didn't know what to do or say. I looked in panic to the door. John was standing there. I didn't know how much either of them had heard. *Oh God,* I felt awful, this was his family and whether I meant it or not I was driving a wedge between them all.

He came over to me and took both my hands in his holding them wide apart and kissed me on the forehead. Then he looked me straight in the eyes and said, "Dawn, will you wait for me in the drawing room please." His face was serious, I opened my mouth to say lots of things. "Please Dawn," and his eyes were so intense. So I left them in the kitchen. John closed the door behind me and I wandered down the passageway to… which one was the drawing room?

It was about twenty minutes later when John returned. I searched his face, but he just smiled at me gently.

"Come on," he said. "Its getting late, it's about time we got off to your place." He held out his hand to me. I wanted to ask him questions, I wanted to say I was sorry. I did none of those, I just took his hand and followed him out of the house.

He didn't say anything as we drove along, and my stomach was getting more and more knotted up. I was scared to ask him anything about it. I was hoping he would say something, but he didn't, he didn't say anything. I on the other hand was getting myself into a right state. I felt sick and the weight descending on me was pushing my lungs, constricting my breathing. I was having a full scale panic attack and I wanted to get out, I needed air and space, I just had to get away.

"John, can you stop the car please," I begged him but already I had left it too late.

"Why? What's wrong Dawn?"

"Please, please, stop the car, I have to get out!" I felt trapped, like the time when I had been held in the seatbelt when Moggy had overturned. "Please John, please stop the car!" My voice had risen in pitch I was beginning to feel hysterical. I'd already got my seatbelt off. John was slowing up, looking for a place to stop, but I'd pulled the door handle and the door was swinging open.

"Jesus Christ Dawn!" he yelled at me. Leaning over, he grabbed me around the waist with one arm, as the heavy car door swung outward violently. I had hold of the handle and had John's arm not been around me it would have pulled me out of the car. John held on to me, drawing to a stop in the side of the road. The car behind overtook and gave a loud blast on his horn as he went past. John let go of me to pull the break on, and I was out of the door, blindly staggering over a farmer's field. Where was the oxygen, there was none out here and I couldn't breathe, and the fact that I was crying wasn't helping either. I think I passed out.

I woke up in John's arms, breathing restored almost to normal.

"Dawn! Thank Christ! My God you scared me." Then he shouted angrily at me "What the fuck were you playing at trying to get out of a moving car?" All the weight came crashing in on me again as I struggled to get out of his arms. He held on to me as I fought to get away, crying and panting, but he was too strong for me and he held me close, trying to calm me down, talking gently to me, hushing me. I was fighting as hard as I could, gasping for air, and then he pulled me really tight holding my face inside his jacket. What was he doing? There was less air in here, and as it was I couldn't breathe. His voice was gentle though and he was trying to get me to breathe slower. In the absence of anything else he was cutting down my oxygen intake to stop me hyperventilating. I couldn't escape him his grip was too tight, so I began to give in and as I did that my breathing began to slow and I began to feel better. I just clung on to him and pulled him as tight as I could. I felt his face on the top of my head, he was whispering gently to me, hushing me, telling me how much he loved me. Then I opened my eyes and I was staring into his.

"Better now?" he asked me. I nodded my head. "I'm sorry I shouted at you, it's just you scared me so much. I'm good at this though," he said smiling at me, stroking my hair. I raised an eyebrow. "I'm going for the record," I still didn't understand. "Worst ending to a first date in history and now the worst ending to a honeymoon!" I smiled. "Well at least one thing's certain," he paused.

"What's that?" I croaked, my voice husky now.

"Things can only get better?" he added hopefully.

"Is everything all right here?" came a voice I vaguely recognised. We both looked up into the face of the policeman who had pulled us over earlier in the day. He put his hands on his hips as he recognised us. "Don't tell me," he said smiling, "first lovers' tiff? I had reports the young lady was being attacked!" We both looked at each other and burst out laughing.

The policeman made John wait in Moggy while he interviewed me, well he was just making sure I was ok and that I wasn't really being attacked. He was really sweet and then he asked John to join me in the back of his police car. He had a flask of cocoa which he poured out and shared with us whilst he gave us some sagely wisdom devised from thirty years of marriage.

"Always talk things through, no matter how long it takes, never go to sleep on an argument. There are no problems, no matter how big you think they are that can't be solved if you really want them to be. Love is precious, don't take it for granted, look after it, nurture it, work at it, treasure it and you will have it all your lives."

"You're wife is a very lucky lady," I said.

"I am a very lucky man!" he replied. "We met at school and we haven't had a day apart since. Now I hope you two can manage the next thirty years without any more help from me," he said smiling kindly, "and I know you are going to be all right Dawn. I'll be praying for you." I leaned forward over the front seat of the car and kissed him on the cheek. "Go on now you two, and for goodness sake drive carefully!" The policeman left us, but we were not in a very secure place to have a chat.

"Were only ten minutes from the George," said John, "What say you to dropping in there, we can talk things over… if you want?"

"Sounds good," I said, and so we set off for the George.

Chapter 22

Lovelace

We sat around the back in our usual place. Harry had very kindly made us some tea in large mugs. I stared at her, and held her fingers in one hand gently rubbing them with mine, she was so strong in some ways but fragile beyond belief in others. I wasn't sure how much to tell her after the incident in the car. Christ that had frightened me. I knew she was trying with all her might to bury her fears of what was ahead of her, and that the cracks were beginning to show, and I just couldn't believe how my own mum had treated her today. I wanted to protect her, to tell her everything was going to be all right, but that would have been a waste of my breath, because I didn't have the power to make it so. Knowing what was ahead of us was one thing but Dawn was the one who was going to have to live through it and I felt helpless. The other sad thing was that from this conversation onwards our honeymoon would definitely be over. Tomorrow had arrived earlier than we expected.

"John I'm so sorry, I don't want to cause problems between you and your family."

"You haven't, and it may have escaped your notice but you are my family, the most important part of my family. I pointed that out to them both. I don't want to have to choose between them and you. I told them that I loved them both, but if they make me I will choose, and it will be you. Dad apologised again for all the talk at the table, for upsetting you, and for the bridge. And Mum…" I paused, uncertain about how to put it.

"Go on… I can take it," she said as if she somehow knew what she was going to hear.

"She thinks you see me as a good thing, a meal ticket." She dropped her head and nodded.

"Yeah I thought as much," she mumbled.

"Dawn, look at it from her point of view, she thinks I haven't had the opportunities to meet other people, and in some ways she's right."

Dawn

Oh my God it was as if I had been struck across the face. I was stunned, he obviously registered the fact. "Dawn, please let me finish," I looked at him numb.

"Do you regret it? Do you think you made a mistake?" I could hardly breathe. He couldn't know what he held in his words, it was like waiting for my life to end. I held my breath. Tears rushed to the corners of my eyes and my head was buzzing. The door to the bar opened and a cool rush of air blew in. I looked up and Moli was standing in the doorway.

"Hi guy's, what are you doing in here?" I looked at him unable to speak. John ignored him.

"Of course I don't regret it, of course I haven't made a mistake. Haven't you been listening to anything I've been saying. Why is it so hard for you to believe that I love you? Feel free to chip in any time here Moli," he invited exasperated.

"Because she's living on a knife edge, and any minute she feels like she's going to fall off. Because she doesn't think she deserves to be loved. Because she can't believe that love like this exists for her and she thinks at any moment it's going to disappear, and when it does she will cease to exist. Should you be needing any more marriage guidance I'll be in the main bar." He walked around the corner into the bar leaving us looking at each other.

"Dawn," he said gently, "I could wander this planet a lifetime, and never find anyone like you. Don't blame me because I found the love of my life without even having to leave school. I love you more than my life and nothing is going to change that." I smiled at him.

"I'm sorry... I'm insecure... neurotic... terrified..." I stuttered.

"Beautiful," he added, "and I wouldn't change a thing about you." His eyelashes swept upwards and his blue eyes were such a deep colour and so full of love. He put his arms around me and hugged me tight rubbing his cheek against mine. "Now do you want to go home, or should we speak to our councillor first?" I laughed.

"No go and tell him it's safe to come back." John got up to go and fetch Moli.

"Jeesus Lovelace… you've been married a few short hours and your bent on screwing it up already. I should write a book you know, fill it with my pearls of wisdom, you're need is obviously great!" He took a deep drag on his cigarette, picked up his pint from the bar and followed me back to where I had left Dawn. "Listen you two, I just put my rates up from a pint an hour, to a vodka per twenty minute session. Have you managed to have any fun since I left you both?"

I took great delight in telling him about our near arrest and our double encounter with the police which he found highly amusing, especially when I told him about the policeman thinking I was attacking Dawn.

"And you thought my technique was bad!" he said laughing his head off. "I am going to be serious though. You've just done the most amazing thing, getting married. Two people more right for each other I don't think I'll ever meet, but *please*, next time you doubt it, get out that piece of paper and check the signatures eh?" We all laughed.

We went back to school with Moli and followed him in through the boot room window. He had promised to make us tea in his show. His show was on the ground floor now and very near to the boot room, so we didn't have far to go. Moli put a record on low, 'Your Song,' and we were just sipping our tea when his door opened. A rather short handsome youth came in without knocking.

"Hi, and who are you?" I said not recognising him.

"I'm the boss man round here and who are you?" It wasn't Tubby who was now in another house, it was a new junior Housemaster and he was not pleased to have us in his house late at night, or at all really. John obviously recognised him as he had sat up immediately he came into the room. Moli had jumped to his feet. "What's going on here?" he demanded of Moli.

"Well sir, they're on their honeymoon and I was the best man if you remember, and I'm serving tea, would you like some?" he enquired turning on all his charm.

"Hi, Lovelace err, congratulations. This is most irregular, but," he said thawing, "I suppose we don't get this happening very often do we?" He held out his hand for John to shake, which he did if a little reluctantly.

"Thank you Sir, err Mr. Luckhurst. Can I introduce you to my wife, Dawn." I stood up and took his hand. He smiled warmly at us. He can't have been a housemaster before because he didn't look that much older than us.

"Listen," he said, "I'll give you an hour and then I want you out of here ok?" He backed out of the room.

"Thank you Sir," Moli called after him.

John was rather quiet after that. I caught him looking at Moli a couple of times but Moli was averting his gaze. It felt like something wasn't being said. We didn't stay the hour, we finished up our tea and Moli waved us off from the boot room.

"Ok, what was all that about?" I asked. "You could cut the

atmosphere with a knife."

"What? I don't know what you mean," he replied casually.

"Aw come on John, I'm not stupid. Something upset you after the master came in. Don't you like him or something, did he cane you?" he didn't reply so I continued. "He can't be much older than us, has he been at the school long?" John didn't answer. "John?" I asked waiting, it was obvious he wasn't going to talk to me.

"Just leave it Dawn." He said firmly. And then I twigged.

"No…" I said incredulous, "Moli…? Since when? Why would he? What about Kelly…? John? What about you… did you and he …?" My chest was full of butterflies. I didn't know how to feel about this. But we'd had this conversation, hadn't we? And I'd believed him. Had he lied to me?

"No," he said firmly pulling up the car in a gateway. "No Moli and I have never had a relationship like that."

"Well like what then, cause I think you need to tell me just what it *was*, and *is* like!"

He sighed, resigned.

"We're like brothers," he said, "but more than that, because you don't get to choose your brother. He understands me completely and I he, we don't have to explain things, we just know. We have a bond of shared experiences, school, not sexual. I don't know, what more can I tell you? What else do you want to know?"

"You don't approve do you?"

"What?" he looked at me surprised, he paused for a long time. "No, no I don't… but I understand," he added.

"Ok well explain it to me, because I sure as hell don't understand."

"Well he's essentially a simple soul, he craves affection, love, whatever, and he'll take it in whatever form he can get it. His mother died when he was three, his father was always away working, he has four sisters and he was their longed for son and heir, but there was no one home to love him, so he was sent to school at the age of three."

"Three! That's barbaric!" I couldn't believe it.

"Not when there's no one else to look after you. Then his dad died when he was thirteen in our first year. So you see, he craves love, affection, closeness. He appears aloof but he's not, and yes if I had been that way inclined we probably would have been lovers, but that's not me."

"Should I feel jealous?"

"Would you be jealous if he were my brother?"

"No of course not," I replied.

"Well then. You know being adopted gives me a whole different perspective on you blood related people. You have sisters and brothers whom you love or hate, you have parents you either love to bits or can't abide to be near. Blood to me means nothing but a link with the past, the passing on of chromosomes, touching history, but what's important to me is love, here and now. Loyalty and honour I suppose. And I don't feel very loyal talking about my friend…" His voice dropped and he trailed off looking out of the side window of the car.

"What about Kelly? How does she fit in?"

He sighed and looked at me. "He loves her… but she's not

here is she? He's a year behind with all his friends gone."

"Shouldn't he tell her? I mean…"

"She knows…" he looked into my startled face. "She knows and she doesn't care… she loves him warts n'all. What about you?"

"What do you mean?" I was confused, I didn't know what he was getting at. "I mean how do you feel about him, now that you know, because it's obvious that you don't approve either." I thought about it, for about a second and then realised that it made no difference at all to me. I shrugged and looked him straight in the eyes.

"I love him too, I'm sad for him I suppose, desperately looking for affection, but I understand too now. Who knows what any of us would do if we had been in his shoes. But he does have Kelly and I don't approve of him having a lover, it's still a betrayal." He pursed his lips together and nodded.

"Yeah I know, I agree, but then we don't know if they're lovers or buddies. Could just be a late night vodka session, and I sure as hell am not going to ask! He'll tell me anyway at some point."

"Then how did you know?" I asked intrigued.

"Well it's a given thing, you always, *always* knock before entering a show. I mean Moli would never enter my show without knocking and vice versa, and it's very late, and Luckhurst is an old boy with a dangerous twinkle in his eye and a rather dubious reputation. But then Moli is eighteen and probably the only person in the school nearest to Luckhurst's age, and they know each other well. I don't know… yeah I do, it's the familiarity of that missing knock."

"You know when I say I don't approve, it isn't that I mind homosexuality, not if that's the way you are, it's just the in between status I don't understand, not if he really loves Kelly. I mean would it be the same if I was in love with him? You say he loves me but would he still want guy's as well?" John didn't answer. "Are you choosing not to answer or don't you know the answer?"

"A bit of both I suppose. For me it's clear cut, I love you, I won't ever want anyone else. But not everyone starts from the same point. He thinks it's like that for him, you're the one. But as he can't have you he's fallen in love with Kelly, so immediately he's in love with two people. And that's not including me, because he loves me too like a brother, though he fancies he loves me in the other way too when it suits him. He doesn't see it as a betrayal. And affection from someone else, well that's just sex, with nothing to do with love except in that moment of closeness, at least I think that's what he meant. I don't know, he's tried to explain it to me but for me sex and love are intrinsically linked. One is the ultimate expression of the other I can't separate the two… I think he can, and I don't fancy blokes, gender doesn't matter to him." He shrugged.

"So what is it that you don't approve of? You can't be against homosexuality are you?

"God no… I suppose it's casual sex I don't approve of. I don't really care who it's with so long as it's meaningful and an expression of love between two consenting adults. But I can see that's because of how I view sex and love, and I can see that there are other viewpoints. I suppose that as long as everyone knows and is ok with it then it's no one else's business, but relationships develop and your viewpoint changes all the time, and I can see people getting hurt. Maybe the answer is just not to judge other people and accept them as they are. I don't know, it's really late to be analysing all this kind of stuff." He looked at me for permission to start the car.

"I couldn't share you with anyone else, I want all of you forever 'and forsaking all others keep ye only unto her as long as ye both shall live'." I had put both my arms around his neck and swung myself between him and the steering wheel.

"I do," he replied, "'and forsaking all others keep ye only unto him as long as ye both shall live.'" He quoted back at me.

"I do." I replied. Then he gently kissed me and we moved together sealing our vows.

Chapter 23

Lovelace

I don't think either of us slept, rather we rested together in each other's arms, just holding each other close. I was worried for Moli. What was it I really disapproved of? I think it was people getting hurt, and the more people involved, the more chance of someone getting seriously hurt. And that someone? Well that would be Moli. He would never have Dawn, which is what he wanted most, he could never have me, which is also what he occasionally thought he craved and I could see him driving Kelly away over a relationship which didn't matter a hoot. Why was it so clear to me when he couldn't see it himself? He seemed to have his finger on the pulse when it came to Dawn and myself, but his relationships? Maybe I should write a book for him and he one for me.

I stroked Dawn's hair with my fingers, pulling gently at the thick waves of hair on her head, her beautiful hair, my beautiful baby. I knew that this was the thing that frightened her the most. She was terrified of losing it, yet it seemed such a little price to me.

"It will grow back, it's not forever."

"But it's such a big part of me, my confidence, my personality, how I feel about myself. I won't be the same."

"You'll be the same to me, I love *you* Dawn, your very essence, not your hair."

She was awake, I had held her in my arms so many times asleep. That wonderful deep breathing and complete surrender of body weight made me feel like her protective guardian, but tonight her breathing was shallower, and though she was relaxed in my arms there was still that tension of being conscious. I put my face into her waves, she smelt of apple blossom and soapy bubbles and it was so soft, like laying your head on a silky cloud. She felt my face with her fingers and then searched for my lips in the dark with hers. We felt our way gently with our noses. Our lips met softly and the chemical reaction in my body ignited immediately. I held her chin gently caressing the soft skin of her face, she rolled over facing away from me and I curled around her. She pushed her bottom into my lap, rubbing me. We had never made love this way round before, she rubbed herself against me repeatedly urging me on then guiding me in. I pushed her over onto her stomach her back felt like satin. Oh my, so many textures, so many sensations, my senses were on overload. We made love all night, in one position or another. I really don't know where we found the energy but we never reached our goal. It was as if should we stop, our time would run out. It made me feel alive and as long as we made love we would live forever the two of us together, as long as we didn't stop.

But then the room became lighter, and I heard her parent's alarm next door, and we rose in silence to get ready for the day ahead.

We went up in Moggy as I had to get the car to London anyway, Dawn's parents were going to catch the train home. Dawn sat in the back with her mum, it can't have been that comfortable for them, and her dad who was over six foot sat next to me in the front. We managed to find a parking space with ease and I helped Dawn crawl out from the back whilst Dawn's dad helped her mum escape on the other side. I slung Dawn's bag over my shoulder and then put my arm around her. She felt so small this morning, so fragile as we walked slowly to the hospital doors.

We had an appointment first at the clinic with Dr Wilde but before that, the first of the blood collection for the day. There was a really young guy in the clinic taking blood, I recognised him from one of the times before. He had spotted Dawn and when it came to her turn he was quick to volunteer to take her blood. I explained about the disappearing vein thing but he was chirpy and confident that he could get blood from a stone, and he was right. First time straight in and masses of little files were duly filled. Dawn was so grateful. He gave us some pointers for places to try if they had trouble on the ward. He was great and Dawn relaxed a bit. Then it was a bit of a wait to see Dr Wilde. He was really great too, he explained about the chemo and how it would work and some of the side effects, one of which was deafness which passed Dawn's parents by as they didn't react, but Dawn did.

"What? But I sing," said Dawn in a small voice. I squeezed her hand.

"A very rare reaction, hardly ever happens, but we can do something if it does, watch out for buzzing in the ears." A string of other nasty side effects were explained, from sores in the mouth to diarrhoea and other such pleasant things. But all that aside he obviously knew what he was talking about and what else could we do but trust him completely, which we did. All things going according to plan she should be out in three days, session one completed.

We went to the ward but there was no bed for her and so we had to wait around for about an hour in the patients' TV room. After a bed was found for her it was another series of tests from weighing her, to blood pressure, temperature etc. etc. We discovered that her chemo would be one of the last to be made up and brought up to the ward, so we went off for lunch buying some sandwiches to take to Maggie's, being told to be back by four.

Just in that short time it was such a relief not to be on the ward. We helped ourselves to mugs of tea and took over a quiet corner of one of the sitting rooms and had our sandwiches. Bonnie was great, she offered Dawn a relaxing massage before she went to the ward, but Dawn wasn't really interested in leaving me for a second. She talked about wigs and gave Dawn some leaflets and then booked a day when she would be in next with the wig guy so that Dawn would have something to wear before she lost her hair. I must admit we had quite a laugh, we even found some amusing books in the library and we took turns reading out jokes. The knitting group had returned outside and had brought with them masses of cakes which they were offering around, but eventually we had to go back to the ward.

Dawn was prepped with a cannula and then the bags of poison arrived. I held her in my arms as the yellow liquid dripped drop by drop down towards her hand, then she buried her head in my chest and wept. Then we were all told we had to go whilst the patients had their meal, Dawn went into a tailspin and so I was allowed to stay, but her parents had to go. That was the first real wrench for her. She didn't know London, she knew where she was but it was as if she had been dumped somewhere foreign and unfamiliar and was then going to be ill and feel more vulnerable than she had ever been in her life, in these strange surroundings, and at some point I was going to have to leave her too. We lay together on the bed with Dawn clinging on to me for dear life and as the clock slowly ticked round, her grip seemed to tighten.

"It's horrible," she explained, "it feels like something is alive and crawling under my skin."

All too soon I was being asked to leave and the doors were locked behind me. My beautiful girl was left alone in a strange place to face her fears on her own. I sat outside by the lifts for ages, I just couldn't leave her, I didn't know what to do. About an hour later I had made it as far as the ground floor of the hospital but I still couldn't leave her, I felt like I was abandoning her. God I wished Moli was here, but then that wouldn't have been fair on him, knowing this was going on was bad enough for him. I phoned her parents to let them know she was ok and that I had left, and then I phoned Moli.

"Lovelace? How are you doing? How's Dawn?"

I filled him in and then I found that I was crying. I couldn't speak without giving it away, so I said nothing. He was great, he chatted to me about all sorts of rubbish from school, he didn't require any response from me, he knew I couldn't, so he just burbled on and on about nothing in particular making me laugh here and there. Then he spoke about Luckhurst. It was what I thought, vodka, late night talks and the possibility of more. I sighed.

"Why is it you see my life so clearly and you're about to fuck yours up so completely?" I asked.

"What do you mean? She knows, Kelly knows I like guys too."

"Yeah she knows, but you can only rub her face in it so many times before she won't take any more. It's about time you decided what's really important and choose sides. You're eighteen now for Christ's sake and engaged. Time to stop being such a self indulgent bastard before someone really gets hurt. You once thought I was as shallow, you're in danger of not even getting the soles of your feet wet here." There was a long pause.

"So... how long have you thought like this then?"

"Always," I replied, "I just was never in a corner like this before, maybe it's changed my perspective, I don't know. I just can't watch you treat Kelly like this and say nothing, bit like you couldn't bear it when you thought I was using Dawn that time... remember?" I could hear him dragging on his cigarette on the other end of the phone. Oh God I craved a cigarette now.

"Blow some of that smoke down the phone could you?" I asked, "I've never felt so desperate as I do right now!" I could hear him obliging on the other end. "Cheers, I'm imagining it," I replied.

"Always fancied I could turn you, you know."

"Fat chance! Always fancied I knew which side you were really on."

"And what side would that be?" he replied coolly.

"You know, you said as much yourself, that time back at my house with Dawn, it came straight from the heart that time and bypassed your brain. It wasn't me you fancied then, you would cheerfully have smashed that mug into my face." I could still hear him dragging on his cigarette. "Anyway, make a decision will you cause I really need a best mate right now and I'm in danger of not liking you much."

"So… no pressure then?" I said nothing in reply. "Listen Lovelace, my sister's in, go and stay at hers tonight will you? That way you won't have to go all the way out to your digs. I've only got double economics tomorrow, I'm going to skive off games and see you up in town, where will you be at about four?"

"Where the bloody hell do you think I'll be?"

"Oh yeah, right, what's the plan there then?"

"Well I get kicked out at meal times, it's sort of sacrosanct and you get locked out for about two hours. I could meet you at Maggie's. You can't miss it it's bright orange and it's in the corner of the hospital grounds, supper is from five. Oh and bring some bloody fags with you will you... and a light!" I put the phone down and wandered out of the hospital. I drove Moggy into Mayfair but I hadn't a clue what to do with her. Luckily the doorman to Melanie's block was there, he said he would find somewhere to put her so I handed him the keys and he disappeared in her, down into the back streets. She farted in protest as he decelerated which made me laugh. Melanie was in, bless her, thank God she liked me, not that she was staying in, she was off to some drinks thing to do with work. I was so tired I collapsed on her sofa and found myself covered with a blanket several hours later. I undressed in the early hours and slept like the dead.

Melanie woke me up as she was off to work and pressed a spare key into my hand and issuing instructions to feel free and make myself at home, for which I was very grateful. Then I set off myself, back to the hospital for eight o'clock opening. The nurses were great and as soon as I was spotted outside the door they let me in. I was getting lots of smiles and adoring looks. *What the hell had Dawn been saying about me?* I wondered.

I rounded the corner of the ward and there was my precious baby still hooked up to her drip, but it had changed colour it was now a clear liquid. Her smile made my heart leap and I took her in my arms kissing her gently. My heart began to race immediately, *oh it felt so good to have her in my arms,* and I realised how wretched it had felt being seperated. She clung on to me and we just held each other for ages and ages not talking, just being together. How long had we been apart? It could have been as long as all those months a while back.

"It was awful when you left, I don't think I've ever felt like that in my life. One of the young nurses came and sat with me, she's only a year older than me, she was asking me about you... she noticed the ring on my finger. I just talked about you for ages, it made me feel close to you. She was lovely, she has a boyfriend but she's having doubts about him."

"I think you may have over gilded the lily a bit, I got all sorts of strange looks when I arrived," I replied.

"Can't have done, that would be impossible," she said her dark eyes looking up at me adoringly.

"So how was it last night then?"

"I'm just exhausted, every time a bag finishes on anyone an alarm goes off and the nurses come to change it. You spend your whole night waiting for alarms to be turned off, and then mine went off at five I was just about desperate by then. This bag is a seven hour one and I should come off it at about twelve, then I think there's a couple of four hour ones, you can check on my notes. Then it's a wash out with saline and I can go home. Oh God I want to go home." She rested her head on my chest.

"Where do you want to go Dawn? I need to tell people what you want to do. Do you want to go to my digs with me, or do you want to be down at your mum and dad's or do you want to go to Lovelace?" The reaction to the last suggestion was immediate, she screwed up her nose and shook her head. Well I wasn't surprised and who could blame her.

"I just want to be with you," she said.

"Well I'll go wherever you choose," I said stroking her cheek and brushing her hair from her eyes.

"Can we go to my house then? Do you mind?"

"Why would I mind, I'll be with you. This is about you Dawn, where you feel safe and where you feel comfy." She relaxed slightly and snuggled into my shoulder.

"There goes another alarm," she said, "why don't they turn them off?"

I was puzzled I couldn't hear anything.

"You're hallucinating Dawn," must be lack of sleep.

"Don't you hear it?" she said sternly. "It's as clear as day and it's so annoying." At that moment someone's alarm did go off, it was a loud buzzing noise.

"And there's another one," she said sighing, screwing her face up. The nurse came past and turned off the alarm in the corner.

"Dawn? What do you hear now?" I asked.

"Buzzing, loud buzzing. Why doesn't she save herself a trip and turn the other one off as well?"

"Listen, I'm just going to go and have a chat with her." I kissed her on the forehead and gave her a reassuring smile and went to find a nurse.

My heart was picking up pace, Dawn could hear buzzing and I couldn't, I remembered the side effects that had been mentioned, very rare they had said, but then so was Dawn's cancer. Please God, not her hearing too. The sister on duty was reassuring, Dr Wilde would be round about eleven and she would make sure he knew and came over. I decided not to worry Dawn and wait for him to arrive.

"Am I going to have to watch you with all these nurses around?" she said with a slight smile.

"What about you and all the young doctors?" she laughed and held me tight.

"Maybe," she said, "that should keep you on your toes." I lay on the bed with her snuggled into my chest and she fell asleep. Dawn got a good couple of hours sleep until Dr Wilde arrived to check on her. He smiled when he saw her in my arms.

"I hear from the nurses that you're newly weds? It's all the gossip, not much of a honeymoon for you though is it, I'm sorry." Dawn stirred and came to. "Good morning Dawn, I hear you've got some buzzing going on." He looked at her notes. He quickly established that she had indeed got tinnitus in her ears which alarmed her somewhat. "It's very unusual for this to happen so quickly, quite extreme, but we know exactly the specific drug that causes it, cisplatin, and we can change that drug next time for its brother carboplatin. Hopefully the buzzing should die down, we're not in the business of saving your life only to destroy your career and quality of life Dawn." He gave her a huge reassuring smile. "Besides Mrs. Lovelace, after the saline, you should be good to go tomorrow afternoon." He beamed at her again and she responded, home, she could be home tomorrow!

At lunch I had to leave as usual and I meandered around the hospital shop downstairs. There were a large selection of teddy bears and one was wearing theatre scrubs. *Perfect!* He could be her hospital companion when I wasn't allowed to be there. There were no flowers allowed on the ward and her bear could come and go with her, she loved it. We spent the afternoon chatting, cuddling, and Dawn spent some of it sleeping whilst drip after drip slowly crawled in through a series of plastic pipes. I was exhausted too, just being in a hospital seemed to drain you. You were never really comfortable and when you were something would happen, some series of checks which put you back to where you were before, and there was nothing wrong with me. How much worse was it for Dawn, who's body was now under serious attack from the vile concoctions they were pouring into her.

Dinner time came and I was duly locked out and went off to find Moli.

I spotted him from a distance away, he was sitting on a bench having a cigarette outside. As he spotted me he took another out from a packet and held it end on end to his and sucked it into life for me, handing it to me as I approached ready lit.

"Thanks," I said and sat next to him.

"Not a very good advert are we?"

"What do you mean?" I asked dragging deeply.

"Well here we are, sat outside a cancer place, smoking like our lives depended on it!" We both laughed a little guiltily.

"Cheers Moli, you've no idea how great it is to see you."

"Yes I have!" he replied, draping his arm around my shoulder, looking at me sideways and smirking. "Listen, about what you were saying last night, I've been giving it some thought."

"I'm under a lot of pressure, it's none of my business."

"Well you're wrong, it is your business, you're my best mate. Well, more than that, and you're right I am self indulgent. I like to think it gives me character but it doesn't. I am shallow. I shall endeavour to be a deeper puddle from now on, won't stop me from admiring the scenery though. You know Luckhurst is nearly as pretty as you." I laughed.

"I'm sooo flattered! You only fancy me when there's nothing else around anyway," I said sarcastically. "So what are you saying? Are you giving up the guys on the side. Have you joined me, decided to embrace your masculinity and come down on my side of the fence?"

"Ok you've made me say it, I'm normal."

"Depends on your definition of normal, and Moli… you could never be called normal!"

We both laughed.

"Well now you approve of me again can I ask how our little lady is doing?"

So I told him all about it.

"You know you should try some of your poetry, try to work this through, otherwise your going to implode."

"Well Lovelace didn't write that many poems, and between him and the rest of the metaphysical poets they didn't really cover the topic of chemotherapy, there wasn't much call for it then. Death, battle, love, adultery, King and country, but not cancer."

"Well write some of your own then, you don't have to show anyone but it may help you get it out of your system."

"So is that how your going to deal with it then. When Luckhurst hands himself to you on a plate, and he will."

"Already dealt with that one, two lengths of the school pool underwater, under the covers! Freezing cold water, and the possibility of drowning if I didn't make it, brought everything into clear perspective!"

"Jesus Christ Moli!"

"Well you did it often enough without killing yourself!"

"Yeah but I'm a stronger swimmer than you, and I have some sense of direction. I bet you were half cut with vodka too!"

"Well, I was making a life changing decision, I needed some help!"

"Well next time you make a life changing decision write a fucking poem instead, it's much safer!" He looked me in the eyes and twisted his mouth to the side smiling.

"There! You do love me Lovelace."

"Never said I didn't, just not like that, and love and like are not the same thing."

"Well you like me too now, my puddle is getting deeper as we speak!"

"So have you talked to Kelly then?" I asked.

"Not yet, I need to see her face to face for this one. I'll invite her up to town this week end."

"Well get a shift on before she thinks about all this too much, you need lots of grovelling, and 'I've seen the light' stuff."

"Would you write me a poem for her then?"

"No, write your own bloody poems!" I said exasperated with him. "You don't need any anyway, just turn on your old magic and you'll be fine."

"Oh, so you do admit I have magic then?"

"Moli," I said turning to him. "You're a pain in the fucking arse, but yes I love you, and yes I like you, now can you shut the fuck up about it!"

I left Moli at the hospital doors, he was staying in town too so I would see him later. The lift took ages to come and when it did it was full of people. I had to let another three go by before I got back up to the ward, but I thought about the poetry idea. I had written poems before, usually in the style of the metaphysical poets. They had all been utter drivel! But it was a process I enjoyed. Yeah I might give that one a go, well I was completely useless to help Dawn, maybe doing something as banal as writing a poem might help. I told her about my conversation with Moli, she was delighted.

"I'm so pleased, I didn't like thinking badly of him, about hurting Kelly I mean, not because of his preferences."

"Well at long bloody last he's decided what it is he does prefer, and after his suicidal swim, he's still alive to tell the tale, hallelujah!"

"So you swam under the covers too?" she asked.

"Well yes. Got a bit dicey if a master suddenly came round to check, you had to stay under until they went, but it was incredible training. I can do three lengths in one breath if I have to."

"This doesn't impress me, this terrifies me. It amazes me you survived boarding school at all, and I'm sure you haven't told me the half of it!" She was right, I hadn't.

I left her on her last little bag of poison and then later that evening her saline would start, meaning only a few hours tomorrow morning and she would be finished. I caught the tube back to Marble Arch and then picked my way through the back streets to Melanie's place. The doorman was thrilled to see me. We had come to an arrangement, as I didn't need the car he was hiding it in all sorts of places during the time he was on duty and then using it a bit when he was off. He wanted to borrow it the next morning, goodness knows what he was doing in it. Deliveries perhaps? Well as long as they were legal, though I thought it more likely he was taking his mum out or impressing a girl. I needed it to take Dawn home though at lunch time. He promised to have it outside the hospital for me at midday, so we arranged for him to pull in by Maggie's. This suited me perfectly, and him apparently.

I was bushed and so so grateful that I didn't have the long flog out to my digs. Melanie really didn't know how much easier staying at hers made it for me, I owed her big time. I decided to cook for her and had acquired some food on the way back. I wasn't that great a cook but I fancied I did a mean risotto and there was nothing too offensive in one of those. Moli was already there ensconced in front of the television set watching Star Trek or some such sci-fi series. Melanie was in, which was novel as she always appeared to be having lunch with so and so etc. I duly served supper on trays in front of the TV.

"Domestic Goddess too, Lovelace?" Moli teased as I presented him with parmesan shavings.

"What would you have done… beans on toast?" I replied jokingly.

"Yeah probably… but with parmesan!" he replied.

Melanie took off to her bed early, which meant I could get

the fold out settee set. I was going to have to share with Moli, as I had done on many occasion before. It didn't matter a jot to me. I stripped off and got into bed.

"What's this Lovelace? The ultimate test then?" I threw a pillow at him.

"Touch me and I'll beat your brains out." I knew he was joking. I slept like a log. Moli was gone when I awoke next morning, he had taken the early train back to school. There was a message on the bed next to me.

Read some of your damned poetry late into the night Lovelace... check out page 157, Edmund Waller, I thought it rather appropriate for my situation last night. Don't worry, I didn't touch you, I've changed sides remember? Good luck with Dawn. Give her my love and I'm up in town over the weekend, so I'm around if you want me. I'll let you know how it goes with Kelly. May see you next week too?

Love an all that, ciao bello.

Moli X

I picked up the book. *The selfe-banished.*

It is not that I love you less Than when before your feet I lay,
But to prevent the sad increase Of hopeless love, I keep away.

In vaine (alas!) for every thing Which I have knowne belong to you,

Your forme does to my fancy bring And makes my old wounds bleed anew.

Who in the Spring from the new Sun Already has a Fever got,

Too late begins those shafts to shun Which Phoebus through his veines has shot.

Too late hee would the paine asswage, And to thick shadowes does retire;

About with him he beares the rage, And in his tainted blood the fire.

But vow'd I have, and never must Your banish'd servant trouble you;

For if I breake, you may mistrust The vow I made to love you too.

"Over dramatic silly arse," I laughed out loud.

Chapter 24

Lovelace

Dawn was still hooked up to her saline when I arrived and I was told had only just got to sleep, so I crept in and sat in the chair next to her bed. I watched her sleeping, my sleeping beauty. Dark circles had begun to form under her eyes. She looked so vulnerable. Then the alarm went off as the last drop went through the machine and she began to stir.

"Hi gorgeous," I whispered to her, "time to go home." She smiled sleepily at me. In reality it was several more hours before they would let her go. She had all the pipe work removed and then it was a long wait for her drugs to come up from the pharmacist. There were things she had to take to counteract the chemo chemicals and then there were anti sickness pills and a whole host of other things. She had a little book to keep with her, and I had to promise to take her to the local hospital for injections. After they were convinced we knew what we were up to, they all cheerily waved us goodbye.

Moggy was below with Stephen, the guy from Melanie's block of flats and we dropped him off at the tube. Dawn had a rug around her and her head on a pillow. She slept most of the way. I had the car heater on full blast as her feet were freezing, and I drove carefully with my precious cargo back to Kent. She was feeling really rough when we arrived, her mum had put a blow up in her room for me but Dawn was so cold, so I lay next to her to try to warm her up.

The next three days were the pits. She was so poorly, it's the only word for it, weak and ill. I spent a lot of the time with her asleep in my arms, getting her water, helping her to the toilet, you name it I did it for her. To begin with she was self conscious but she soon reached the point where dignity and all that was left way behind. I didn't mind, of course I didn't, it was just a case of getting on with it helping her through the worst bits, making her as comfortable as I could. She wasn't actually sick which was something I was expecting, but she felt so ill. I didn't really have much time to think about it. I slept when she slept, because I knew I would be up with her later. We moved at Dawn's pace and the day and night revolved around Dawn's consciousness. Her mum offered to take over, but this was the little I could do for her and I wanted to be with her. She ate very little, everything tasted different to her, and she didn't feel hungry. But by day four, after chemo, she was feeling a lot better. Only seven more days and the cycle would begin again, except she would start from a lower point and be brought down even further. Moli had phoned to check on us, but to be honest I just didn't have time to phone him. Dawn's mum kept him updated and he sent messages via her on the phone. Dawn was just beginning to look well again and back we went to London.

I went over to see Mum and Dad just before we left for the next bout of chemo. I had lunch and then I slept the rest of the afternoon on the couch. Then I set off back to Dawn's, so I didn't get much of a chance to speak to my parents. I should have made time, but there wasn't any, so things stayed uncomfortable and unsaid.

Back in London the pattern was repeated. This time a new set of chemo drugs, the upside of which, the main bag of carboplatin took only eight hours to go into her not twelve, which was a bonus. But by the time she was reaching the end of the chemo Dawn's blood count took a nose dive and she had to have a blood transfusion. They made a mess of the cannula and eventually after having eight goes, they managed to find a vein in an extremely painful and uncomfortable place, on the outside of her wrist. After an hour or so she became seriously ill, she was reacting to the blood. I had come in hoping to take her home early only to find there was no way they would let her go. She was beside herself, crying and begging me to take her home, promising not to be any trouble.

"I promise, I promise you I'll be good," she pleaded with me.

Dear God it was agony to watch, and my heart broke as I whispered, "I can't, they won't let me."

That night when I left I just sat outside the door crying. I was still there semi awake a couple of hours later when they spotted me. Dawn was in a terrible state. They had phoned Melanie's flat and she had sent Moli to look for me as he was up in town again. I stayed with her until she fell asleep in the early hours and then of course they pushed me out again, and the door was locked behind me.

The lights out by the lifts came on automatically when I pushed the lift button and there was good old Moli waiting in the dark for me. God knows how long he had been there, probably about five hours, waiting patiently. I was just dazed and tired, emotionally drained beyond belief. I slid down the wall and cried. He slid down the wall next to me and put his arm around me and we both cried together. Then he pulled out a hip flask and we had a swig of whatever liquid he had nicked from his sister, I think it was Drambuie, but whatever it was it was ambrosia. There were no tubes or busses to be had and a taxi was going to be almost impossible to find, but conjure one up Moli did, and within half an hour we were back in Mayfair. God knows what it cost him in fare or tip. Melanie had left the lights on and made the bed up for us. We took our coats and shoes off but just fell into it fully clothed.

It seemed about five minutes later and the alarm went off. We managed to find the doorman who retrieved Moggy, and Moli drove me to the hospital. The plan was he would stay with the car until I found out what was happening then I would go and tell him.

Dawn was much better but they wanted to keep an eye on her for a few more hours, so we paid for a meter and we both went up to the ward together. Moli waited outside but when she knew he was there she got all excited and asked to see him. We swapped places so that we didn't overcrowd the ward.

Moli

I prepared myself for a shock, I knew there were going to be tubes etc. and I expected her to look awful, but truth be known she looked more beautiful than I had ever seen her. She was fragile and ill obviously and from the state of Lovelace over the previous few days, and especially last night, I was at least prepared. But I wasn't prepared for the effect she had on me. God I loved her and her eyes were shining when she saw me. She held out her arms to me and I hugged her, burying my face in her neck and hair. She felt like a small bird in my arms and I didn't dare hug her too tight.

"We've come to take you home little lady," I said, "when will they let you go?" They were waiting to take her temperature again to make sure she was back to normal.

"Thank you." She whispered. "Thank you for taking care of him."

"Never could take care of himself," I replied laughing quietly.

She was so tired and lay back on the bed. She invited me to sit and hold her which I did with great pleasure. Then her consultant appeared, he was a little bemused I think to see another guy with his arms around her. He raised an eyebrow.

"We fought for her this morning and I won, but it's only temporary." He laughed.

"You can go home Dawn but I need to talk to John before you go, is he here?"

"I'll go and get him," I volunteered, and I reluctantly left her side.

John was lying on the benches outside with his arm over his

eyes, I couldn't tell whether or not it was to shade them from the light or whether it was exhaustion. I was filled with incredible pity and jealousy all at the same time and huge emotions for the pair of them. Dawn, God Dawn, and John. What a weird creature I was, and then there was Kelly. But that world wasn't reality, and sooner or later I had to come to terms with that fact. I had two incredible friends but they were like a drug to me and I had to come off it sometime or I would just stay in this tormented limbo forever. And Kelly? Kelly was a slow burn with the potential of something extraordinary, probably eclipsing the two of them in time, but I had to give that flame a chance to grow. And then there was Luckhurst, where did he fit in. He was a craving, something intense and now, and he filled a different need. I knew it wasn't long term but it wasn't flippant either. But I recognised that relationship was the least of the four, and I had, reluctantly, already let that one go.

"Lovelace, get your butt over here, the Doctor wants to talk to you." He sat up suddenly rubbing his eyes. "He says we can take her home." *Home where you can watch her torture every second of the day you poor bastard.* Suddenly I wasn't jealous of him, I just wanted to do something, anything, and like him I was trapped in impotence. We shared a look as we swapped positions, acknowledging the pain and covering it with a smile.

Lovelace

Dr Wilde wanted to make sure I would bring her straight back up to London if she was to become ill again. He didn't want her to go to the local hospital and as long as I promised that then he was willing to let her go. I sat in the back of Moggy with Dawn across my lap and Moli drove us down to Kent. She slept. He dropped us off at Dawn's and then drove Moggy to school. Well I wasn't going to need the car, and if I had to get her back to London her parents would drive.

She was definitely worse this time round, but because of that she spent much more time asleep so it was a little easier for me, which made me feel incredibly guilty. About four days later she began to pick up and she was going stir crazy, so Moli made a big round trip, collected Kelly from school, came over in Moggy for us and we all went to the George. With Dick's permission, we moved one of the big armchairs from the front of the bar around the back where we liked to sit, so that Dawn could curl up and even sleep if she needed to. Kelly was a blast. She had been going stir crazy in school too.

"I've had so many detentions and order marks this term, you know how I love cross country Dawn." She grimaced and Dawn giggled. "Well we ran the first bit, you know while the teachers were watching, then when we got around the corner we bumped into the local motorcycle crowd, so we all took advantage and joined them for a ciggy. Then they gave us a lift the whole way around. It was fantastic I've never been on a bike before. Moli you have to get one! Anyway, we got dropped at the final bend and then ran in. Problem was it was a good hour's run and we did it in about twenty minutes. We got detention and order marks against our house, and can you believe it we had to go out and run it again. I ask you now is that fair? On top of that we got a lecture on how ladies did not sit astride motorcycle machines. Babs asked how we should sit on a bicycle and she got an extra detention." We all laughed.

"Boys' cross country is a little more barbaric," said Moli, Lovelace and I were always at the back with the smokers. One year 'Git' as we called him, basically because he was a git, got the school minibus and decided he would move the tail end Charlies along a bit faster. He got us all trapped down a steep sided lane and drove the van at us. Lovelace and I managed to get up the banking but the rest of them were having to run a sprint to escape. Poor old Fatty Tubbsy looked like he was about to have a coronary when we caught them all up again."

"There was a hell of a stink in the biology room these past few weeks Dawn. The biology group have been doing their practical dissection. This year it's frogs! Unfortunately poor old Mr. Purvis hadn't given them long enough in the chloroform and as they were waiting for the mock to start they all came too and started hopping about the lab. Kim Pringle had actually started and fainted when hers came too. Some got lost underneath the floorboards and now we have essence of putrefied frog all along the corridors. Mr. Purvis has been going around in an incredible temper ever since. Luckily it wasn't rats this year eh?"

It was really fun and cosy in the back until Harry came and whispered over the back of the seats.

"Master's in, I don't know whether or not it counts for you lot though any more?" I nodded in thanks to him. We all looked at Moli to see what he wanted to do.

"It's ok I sort of negotiated myself extra privileges as I'm eighteen, legal and I'm happy to pull a few extra duties." I looked at him to check it was the truth, I could usually tell when Moli was making it up. He wasn't, but then we weren't prepared for who the Master coming in was. It was Luckhurst and as he was an old boy he knew exactly where any of his house might be lurking at the back of the bar. He was surprised to see it was us but instead of backing off he continued to advance. *Oh Christ* I thought, three of us knew who he was. Thank God Kelly didn't know him by sight, but I wasn't sure whether or not she would know the name if it was mentioned. What the fuck did I do? If she recognised the name that really would be rubbing her face right in it and it wasn't too difficult to work out how she would feel about that one. I glanced at Moli trying to gauge his reaction to the situation. I couldn't tell, he was looking down taking a drag from his cigarette. Was he cool with this?

It was too late for me to head him off, Luckhurst came right up to the back of the benches and I was going to have to introduce him at some point. I was desperately trying to remember his first name, if Moli had mentioned him to Kelly I was betting he would have used his school familiar, his surname, so I needed to avoid that.

"Hi Lovelace, just checking out the back for fugitives... Moli," he acknowledged him with more than a casual quick glance. It almost required an answer from him the way he said his name.

"Phillip," Moli replied taking a drag from his cigarette and staring him straight in the eyes as he continued to blow out his stream of smoke. Phillip! That was it, now it was just Dawn who was in danger of mentioning his surname unless that is Kelly asked for it specifically. Was Dawn up to speed with this though? There was no way I was going to get her alone and she wasn't exactly at her brightest and quickest at the moment.

"Mrs. Lovelace," he said cheerfully to Dawn, "the last time I saw you was on your honeymoon." He smiled widely at her, turning on all his charm, which I have to say was quite devastatingly effective.

"Mr…" Oh Christ, it seemed like several minutes pause and she had walked right into it. I waited for the hammer to drop. "…Boss Man," she said narrowing her eyes at him, "isn't that what you called yourself?" *Jeeeeesus Dawn!* I screamed in my head. She really had me going there, I thought it was all going to come undone. She smiled at him and her eyes quickly flicked to me and then back to him. Thank God for that, she was completely up to speed with what was going on. Now the only danger lay with Kelly.

"Yeah, I think I did refer to myself as that, just a little pretentious but you caught me on the hop!"

"Yes you did seem a bit surprised to see us," she added, I caught the edge in her voice. So did Moli and Phillip, but Kelly was completely out of the loop and so also totally unaware. *Well played Dawn*, now he was up to speed with the fact that we knew he was a master and up to no good that night, that should keep him on the back foot for a while. His mouth twisted to one side as he smiled at her in acknowledgement and he nodded his head, but his eyes were flashing with mischievous danger and he wasn't going to back off, not now he had been challenged. He turned to Kelly who was sitting, waiting for her introduction. Moli did that one thank God as I wasn't sure how he would want her introduced either. I mean he told me he and Luckhurst were over but I only had his word for it, and I wasn't sure even Moli himself knew the truth of it.

"Phillip, my fiancé Kelly Owen. Phillip is housemaster for Lancaster," he added.

"Very pleased to meet you. Moli has told me a great deal about you," she said as she held out her hand for him to shake. He took it in his.

"Has he indeed, well I'm sorry to say he hasn't kept me as well informed about you." He kissed her hand, turning on the charm like you wouldn't believe. Whether or not he found her attractive I don't know, but boy he knew what he was doing. The double message was there loud and clear for Moli, but for Kelly she was being told she was beautiful and he desired her, which he also may of done. He and Moli were alike in many respects. Moli took a deep drag of his cigarette and eyed him seriously.

"Would you care to join us, Sir?" he said pointedly, and then he smiled at him, not too sincerely. *Dear God,* he was challenging him. *For fuck's sake Moli.* I couldn't believe it because both of us knew what the answer would be. Luckhurst smiled wickedly at the bait put before him, his eyes were sparkling with the danger. He hesitated slightly and then said, "Do you know that's the best offer I've had all day, but I'll only have the one as I have to be back on duty shortly. Can I get anyone a drink?" he asked.

"That'd be great," said Moli "I think we all could do with a refill, I'll give you a hand." I laughed and Dawn chuckled too. Moli was stiffing him with a complete round of drinks and Moli was sorely amused. Luckhurst realised it too and laughed in good sport. Moli went off to the bar with him, probably to give him some instructions and head him off. I hesitated, I wanted to go too, not to check on Mols but to warn Luckhurst off, but I reckoned that Moli was able to handle it. Then I thought better of it and decided to throw my cards into the game. There was obviously some jolly banter going on when I arrived behind them, but I wanted them both to be clear where I stood.

"Listen you two, this may be a jolly game of verbal chess to you, but if either of you hurt Kelly, Moli, I'll never forgive you and Philip..." I over pronounced the word, "I'll take you down, you know I can," I paused. I had come up against him on the rugby pitch before and I was a lot younger then. "I promise you, I will." I reached past them both and took hold of Dawn's and Kelly's drinks and left them at the bar.

Luckhurst placed himself opposite Kelly and flirted outrageously with her. He never once looked in Moli's direction but he knew what he was doing, he was playing Moli as much as he dared. Kelly loved the attention, but as soon as his drink was finished he made his move to go.

"Must you go?" said Kelly who had been charmed, there was no doubt about it.

"I'm afraid Prep duty calls." Dawn, he nodded to her, "Lovelace, I don't think I'll be seeing you in the house again."

He smiled charmingly to me. Ok so I wasn't allowed back into Lancaster whilst he was in charge, well not really surprising after I had threatened him. "Moli, you are extremely fortunate with your friends and your beautiful fiancé." He was backing off from Moli, game over. He smiled at Moli. His eyes were full of regret for one split second and then he beamed at everyone. "Enjoy the rest of your evening," and he left out the back door.

"Aw, he was gorgeous," said Kelly. "Why don't we have masters like that?"

"Because they would lead you into all sorts of trouble," said Moli laughing, then he looked at me fleetingly. It was only a second, but it was a final surrender to his choice, though there was an edge of pain. Dawn saw it and asked Kelly if she would mind going with her to the toilet. Kelly was straight up and helping Dawn to her feet.

"You ok?" I asked when they were out of earshot. He shrugged and looked down and then nodded.

"Come on, I thought it was casual?" I continued.

"It's never casual, not for me anyway, it just looks it. Is that why you disapproved so much?"

"Yes, well that and because of Kelly." I added.

"Yeah, I know, I owe her more than that. Anyway, like I said, it's over, I've chosen sides and I don't regret it. But don't think it's not painful because it is. I watch your torture with Dawn, Lovelace. Luckhurst is the least of my torments." He looked at me and I suddenly realised that he didn't just love me like I thought he did, brothers and fancying me occasionally. He was in love too. I was the torment he was talking about. His face held such agony, pain and longing. I was completely taken aback.

"I... I didn't realise. God Moli I never knew... I thought it was all bravado, just talk, like brothers but closer. I mean I know you occasionally said something flippant but I never thought you were really serious."

"Why should you?" he shrugged. "How many people do you know who are in love with three... sorry, four people at the same time?" He laughed slightly and then he turned his head and looked at me again full in the eyes. He really looked at me as he must have wanted to for all those years, and I just sat and looked at him back knowing my face wasn't reciprocating in the way he so desperately wanted it to. What he could see was sympathy, which he obviously didn't want, he turned his head away to the side.

"God Lovelace I'm screwed up," he said and put his forearms on the table in front of him and his forehead on top of them. Then he looked up at me. "Promise me Lovelace, if you have kids, just don't go and die on them." Then he suddenly realised what he had said and I could see he was immediately thinking of Dawn, agony burst on his face as he realised the implication of his words. "Oh God Lovelace, I didn't mean..." and he buried his head in his arms. I knew he was crying though he didn't make a sound. My response was instinctive, I put my arm around him and my head on his.

"Mols... Mols," I shook him, "I know you didn't mean that... it's ok really, it's ok." Kelly and Dawn reappeared, I indicated to Kelly that she needed to take over from me and moved aside.

She looked at me for an explanation.

"He made a comment about his parents, he thinks he upset me, he didn't, he'll explain it to you. I'm going to take Dawn for a game of darts, eh Dawn?" Dawn was weak and wobbly and not capable of a game of anything standing up. I took her hand and we walked around to the other bar slowly.

"Shit John, what happened? Is he really that upset about Luckhurst?" I popped her up onto a bar stool and held her there gently supporting her.

"No, he really has made his decision, there's no question, Kelly is who he's in love with." I smiled reassuringly to her. "It's just a few other things came to light and he's never really mentioned his parents to me much before, let alone the fact they died and left him." She looked at me knowing there was more. "And then he thought he'd upset me." I added, she nodded.

"Like he thinks I might leave you." She stated. She wasn't asking, she knew. She put her arms around my waist and looked up at me. "You have told him I'm going to be ok haven't you?" I looked into her beautiful pale face and smiled at her brushing her hair away from her eyes.

"Well you know Mols," I said, "always looking for the drama." We both smiled and laughed quietly. I kissed her gently on the forehead and hugged her tight. Moil and Kelly came to find us some time later on. Dawn was getting really tired so we decided to go. I walked Kelly down the steps holding her hand and I left Moli to walk Dawn to the car.

Kelly was very quick on the ball, as soon as she got me on

her own.

"That was Luckhurst wasn't it?" I looked at her surprised, she didn't wait for an answer.

"It's ok, you know, I can see what the attraction is… quite fancied him myself. Just tell me John that he loves me like I love him?"

"I don't need to Kelly, you know the answer to that one." I looked at her straight in the eyes.

"Then tell me he's worth it."

"God Kelly, you don't need me to answer that one either."

"Then tell me how much *you* love him."

I opened my mouth to reply, but I didn't know what to say, how to explain it. Had I ever even really had to think about how much he meant to me? And then if I had an answer what would she read into it? I looked at her frowning searching for the right words.

"I don't know Kelly… I just do." She looked into my eyes, trying to read me, and then smiled.

"You love him very much."

I paused and then looked straight into her eyes."Yeah I do, I really do, but not like you do."

"That's ok then," she said smiling.

"You know Kelly you are truly amazing, he is so lucky to have you."

"Yeah, and he knows it," she laughed and so did I.

Moli dropped us off at Dawn's house first, she was so tired, and then he set off to take Kelly back.

"So did you have a word with Moli then?"

"Yeah I put him straight, he knows it won't be that easy to get rid of me." We laughed at that one.

"Did he mention anything else?" I asked her.

"Like what?" I didn't reply.

"Like the fact that he's in love with not just Kelly and me but you as well, like you're the love of his life, like that perhaps?" I still didn't reply. "You know John, sometimes I think you are a little thick!"

"What?"

"Yeah, really thick," she said laughing. "You can't seriously tell me that after all this time you thought he was just joking around, that it was just like brothers for him? The guy wears his heart on his sleeve way out in the open for anyone to see. So much for you knowing what each other thinks."

"Well it can't have been that obvious because you were taken by surprise with Luckhurst."

"Well, not really. If you remember way back I asked you, I thought I could see it but I just didn't want to admit it then. Once it was shoved in my face it all slotted into place, but I could see it long before."

"Well you could have told me."

"Why would it have made a difference?"

"No… I might have been a bit more sensitive though. You know he tried to tell me in a poem he left for me not so long back, but I just thought he was being an over dramatic arse. How do you keep something like that locked up for all those years. His life must have been hell and I never knew."

"Don't be so hard on yourself, I'll bet he couldn't have wished for a better friend." She said as she put her arm around me.

"You know Kelly is incredible. Considering she's only seventeen, she is amazingly mature to cope with all this and still see the truth of how he feels about her."

Dawn laughed slightly. "She understands better than you think."

"Please Dawn, don't tell me she has lesbian leanings," I said jokingly. "I'm having enough trouble with keeping abreast of this as it is, I don't think I can cope with any more complications. Why can't it just be simple like you and me? Whatever happened to that little scenario eh?"

"Well her parents got divorced when she was very young. Only about five and she has an older brother who is gay, not bisexual, so she has had a handle on that sort of thing for a good few years now. Losing her dad at a young age, is not so far away from where Moli's at. And she feels about Moli like I feel about you, and feels he's worth a bit of extra effort."

"Well let's just hope he's straight with her and doesn't blow it then." I said climbing into bed beside her and turning the lights out.

Chapter 25

Moli

I had invited Kelly up to London for the weekend. I didn't want to stay at my sister's flat. We had serious things to talk about and I didn't want Melanie poking her nose in at any inopportune moment, so I had to come up with something great. Money wasn't a problem, that was one thing I never had to worry about. I'd had a small private income from Dad since I was born and consequently when I was small I never spent anything so it had just accumulated over the years, up until now when it was extremely useful indeed. The down side of it was whenever I used it I was reminded of why I had it, and I would have traded every penny for just a few memories of my mother. Just one more year and I would have remembered something. Children of four seem to be able to recall that far back, but three? I had nothing. Well not entirely nothing, I remembered a warmth, and a colour, pale green, and a smell, her perfume... Joy it's called, very apt, as that is what I felt whenever I smelt it. It's not often but on a tube, at the theatre, the odd restaurant, oh and parties, lots of my sister's Sloane Ranger friends wore it, so I still got to indulge when they invited me along to their 'in town do's'. I used to think I should feel morose when I caught a whiff but it just made my heart sing. Joy... from what I had been told Mum might have been called that as she was a really joyful person, una persona gioiosa e piena di solare, full of light and life. Green was appropriate too, spring green, new life and all that...

Anyway, my youngest sister was working for the University of London and I had come up with a wow experience for Kelly. I was sure now, not that I wasn't before really, it's just that my life was such a complicated mess of emotions, huge emotions that I had spent a lifetime suppressing in one form or another. Packing my feelings into different compartments because that was the only way I could deal with them, and here I was at eighteen with some form of freedom at last, but finding that putting things into different boxes wasn't the way everyone else dealt with this. Everyone else seemed to have one box for love and when it went wrong they lifted the lid and away it went, then in hopped the next love and the lid was shut, one at a time. Two for a bit maybe until one or other found out and they were then back to one love again. I however kept opening up a new box, never letting the previous one go, so now I was surrounded by boxes desperately trying to hold the lids down. John's box for instance, that lid had been screwed down for years from that first day he had come and saved me from the boys in the quad. I was terrified, they had me pinned down in the middle of the quad surrounded by what I thought was the entire lower school and were humiliating me beyond belief. 'Milk him' was the cry and they were already sitting on top of me trying to get my belt undone. It wasn't hard to imagine what their intentions were. But then in came John, fists swinging. He was a first year too but he just didn't seem to care. I suppose he was my hero, not only brave but beautiful too. I loved him from that very moment, but I knew enough to keep that one hidden, and so the lid was securely shut. Friends was ok, best mates was better, but over the years it became so intense and the more it grew into a physical attraction for me, the more I had to hide it and make sure I guarded every look, every touch. My personal torment for something I could never have. Then when we reached around sixteen I tried pushing him to see which way he leant. We would joke about it, that was the worst for me. I just wanted to scream at him it wasn't a joke, that I died every time I looked at him, a little bit more each day. But to tell him how I felt? I didn't dare for fear of losing him forever. There was no question for him, babes, boobs and page three pinups in the Sun newspaper. Not that I was indifferent to them either, which seemed to confuse me even more. But he was my first love, and he never twigged, not really until just the other day. All those years of hiding it and one unguarded look had given it away. I should have trusted him as a friend, I knew now that although he would never love me as I wanted him to, he did love me. But I knew I wasn't gay entirely because there were girls over the years, and then there was the box with Dawn in it.

Oh my God Dawn... I remembered when she walked up to me that evening at the conference and introduced herself. I couldn't believe it, she walked straight up to our group, to me, and as I held her hand I lost my heart to her there and then, she was magical. Lovelace had said very little about her but he had hinted at something. He had first dibs on her, and when she turned to him… well I really couldn't blame her could I? I had hoped that he would crash and burn, he seemed bent on screwing it up all the time. Then I could console him and when the coast was clear step in. I was like a moth to a flame. I could see how they felt about each other yet I couldn't tear myself away, always hoping for her to turn to me, but even in his absence, my big moment, there was no possibility of that, and I couldn't have done it then because I knew he'd be back for her. Yes she loved me, but like a brother. Like I needed more of that kind of love! No she would never look at me the way she looked at him, and another piece of my heart was locked away in box number two.

Then there was box number three, that was probably the lid that opened and shut most normally. In and out of that one were my lovers, usually guys, probably because I was in that sort of environment but when the opportunity arose there were occasionally girls. In them I sought the kind of love I felt for Lovelace. Sometimes I thought I'd found it. Well if I'm honest every time I thought I'd found it, but they never lasted, most probably because I was too intense and scared them off. But they did satisfy a physical need in me. In those lovers they gave back to me what I so desperately needed, a desire to be loved back, not as a bloody friend! That was the box Luckhurst was in. He was just the latest in a long line, but he too would be transient, I could recognise that. So it had stopped before it had got out of hand because, I had box number four and that was far too precious to lose over something ephemeral.

Kelly, my slow burn! There was something about her I don't even know what it was now, but that casual meeting at the Lillesden Dance had put her into box number four. How she had got there I don't really know, because if I'm truly honest, to begin with she was a snog and a fumble in the dark. Then it became letters, not exactly the height of a passionate romantic encounter, but there was always something I couldn't quite let go of. We argued, sometimes violently, we had crazy sex, we laughed so much, but it was different from what John and Dawn had, I could see that so I didn't really see what was going on until the wedding date was announced. Not that that changed my feelings towards John and Dawn it just made me suddenly realise how I really felt about Kelly. In that moment of joining at John and Dawn's wedding, when they were so completely cut off from the rest of us by some invisible barrier, I could have stepped out and married Kelly there and then. It was, I think, the most amazing experience I have ever felt. It was as if she had been there all along carving her own little piece out of my heart without me really noticing, until a huge amount of it was suddenly taken and the possibilities with her suddenly seemed endless. Why would I let Luckhurst jeopardise that? But I already had, and that was what I needed to talk to her about. I just hoped I hadn't left it too late. I had told Lovelace I had dealt with this some time ago but I had just been putting it off.

Kelly

Moli wanted to meet me up in London. I knew that things were coming to a head. Yes I had his ring on my finger. I twisted it in the light of my school desk lamp and it sent hundreds of light spots over the wall and glistened flashing from each of the facets. But I didn't have Moli, not the bit I wanted. I had a piece of him and though it was enough for now, it wasn't enough for a lifetime and I could see that eventually I would crave that which I couldn't have, and eventually it would drive us apart. So, what was I going to do? How far would I go to get him? There were too many of us in this relationship, I knew that. But what did I want, what did I really want?

I counted the pills in the packet. Would you go that far Kelly? Would you trap him? Or was it a case of walking away with something of him of your own, knowing that would be all you would ever really own, his child. It didn't really bother me that I was only seventeen and just about to leave school. I never really wanted a career of any type, something would turn up along that line, but I longed for a family of my own. My family had been such a disaster area, not unlike Moli's really. But I knew I wanted Moli, I loved him beyond anything. Being with Moli was exciting and wild, unpredictable and crazy, and I felt the whole time like we were on some mad adventure. He fascinated me too, I found it exciting that he had liked guys. I could understand that I liked them too, but I couldn't cope with the fact that he carried this huge torch for Dawn. We were friends Dawn and I, close friends, but apart from bigger boobs, and I have to say arse, than me, I couldn't see why he couldn't put that one down. Or was it just that because John wanted her he had to want her too? I thought there might be a lot in that, though he himself seemed convinced it was love, love like John had for her. *Mmph*, I didn't want to accept that one, and anyway given time I thought I could kick that little idea into touch. Who was my main rival here? Well you didn't have to search long to find the answer to that one. Luckhurst and the others before weren't a problem. I could see that once he had a permanent relationship he wouldn't look around any more. But John…? Had they ever been lovers? No, John was straight as a die, all man and macho and striking to look at. He was a pretty amazing package for a girl, and for a guy who hero worshiped him. God Moli really knew how to set masochism to a whole new level. I imagined them both nude in the showers after games. Dear God, how did he survive it. How do you cover up an attraction like that in a communal shower with your ultimate wet dream soaped up and shining next to you? I'd have to ask him about that one. No, it was John who I had to deal with but I didn't know if I could. Dawn? Yes I could compete with her and win. Luckhurst? Yes easy. But John? The answer wasn't so clear cut.

I had to look amazing. I had ordered some new shoes. At first I could hardly stagger in them, but I had been practising going up and down the golden landing at school in them for weeks. We had some fantastic large mirrors up there and I had been walking up and down for hours whilst reciting poetry for English Lit. Once I had mastered walking on the flat I had then taken to going up and down the main staircase. I had used my mum's old trick of a potato wiped on the bottom of them which stopped them slipping. *Must be the starch.* Babs had dyed my hair. We had several shades of blonde, red and dark brown, and she applied them for me in streaks, I have to say it was better than a salon job. My nails were so long I had to get Babs to pull up my tights for me after I had ruined three pairs just as I got them past my thighs each time. Then there was the dress. Well I was dressing to kill or die in the attempt. I have to say that if I had wanted to show more leg it would have been an impossibility. And then I practiced bending over in the mirror. How far before you got a flash of something? How far dare I go? As I applied my make up the little row of pills winked at me on the dresser, I picked them up and ran my nails gently along the foil back. Who was I kidding, I took them religiously. If I'd wanted to deliberately get pregnant I should have stopped taking these weeks ago, and no. However much I wanted him I couldn't go that far. So I punctured the foil and swallowed it down and I knew, that if I walked away from him tonight, there would be no piece of Moli I could keep forever, he would leave my life entirely. I looked at my reflection, I looked so sad but I fought back the tears, I didn't have time to start again on my face. Babs had said my cab was here. I felt sick. This could be my last night ever with Moli. I threw up in the basin. *Oh great!* Now I had to brush my teeth again and redo my lipstick. The cab's meter was running and I'd be late for my train. I rushed to finish my lipstick, grabbed my bag and left my room as fast as my ridiculous heels could safely carry me. I wasn't going to give him up without a final fight.

Moli

I could have afforded any hotel I chose in London, but what was a hotel room? Kelly came from money too so though she would know what it cost, it would be just that, another hotel room. I had to do better than that I had to be imaginative. I had thought about a friend's dad's yacht down at the moorings at Greenwich reach, but thought it may be tempting fate. The thought of getting Kelly over the stinking Thames mud, into a flimsy tender and out to a yacht however fancy on a river running at over seven knots, filled me with alarm. I had visions of Kelly wearing stilettos and puncturing said dinghy and us both floundering about in the pitch black depths. Eventually, if we were lucky enough to reach shore, clambering out over sixty foot of thick oozing stinking mud? No not the yacht! Then there was down market, fish and chips in Leicester Square and a movie, or a Chinese meal in Soho, pint in a pub? No. My youngest sister Florence worked for the University of London in the most amazing little palace you can imagine, a real unknown treasure and I had arranged with her to have the whole building for the night. With a little bit of catering arranged from Fortnum and Masons we were set for an incredible venue at least. Well what would come of the rest of the evening was really down to Kelly and how she felt about me.

I had told Kelly to dress for dinner and I have to say I looked my best in a dinner jacket, and as I had some serious groveling to do I turned up at Charing Cross early to meet her off the train from Kent. She looked incredible. I was right about the stilettos. Pop! an inflatable dinghy would not have stood a chance! Her legs went on and on for miles, disappearing into the shortest mini dress I have ever seen. *Wow!* Well it was on the cards. She hadn't come dressed like that to ditch me.

"My God Kelly you look amazing." I said taking her hand. My pulse had raised considerably, pumping blood to areas I really didn't want it to at that precise moment. She pressed herself against me as if she was going to kiss me but she didn't, she smiled at me and whilst I was locked into her gaze, she grabbed my groin and squeezed gently but firmly.

"Did I pass the first test then?" I enquired smiling at her.

"Oh yeah!" she replied and smiled widely showing her teeth. I placed my hand on the small of her back and guided her along beside me to the waiting cab. How she didn't fall off those high heels I will never know but they had brought her eye level almost to mine which was great. She stooped to get into the cab, and I was not the gentleman. I am afraid that as I handed her into the cab, she bent, and her skirt rose even higher. I got an eyeful of the tops of her legs as they disappeared into the hem of her dress, revealing ever so briefly a quick flash of black lace. I took a sharp intake of breath and resisted the urge to touch her from behind, then followed her into the cab. She was either going to drive me to an early grave by teasing me to death, or I was on a promise, neither of which I minded at that precise moment. I knew it also to be deliberate on her behalf, as she knew full well how to get into a cab discretely, without revealing anything had she so chosen.

"Portman Square," I instructed the driver.

"Portman Square? There's nothing in Portman Square," she

stated and then added, "is there?"

"Oh yeah," I replied in the same tone that she had used earlier.

"A new club perhaps?" she started guessing. "Oh God, not a private look around the internal workings of Marks and Sparks," she grimaced.

"Phew… and I nearly thought of that one!" I answered in a sarcastic tone.

"I know, it's one of those secret sub stations where all the power for the city is produced and we have to climb down a manhole to get there?" She turned her ankle over to reveal the length of the heels she was wearing. I just gazed travelling the length of her leg with my eye. "You know if it's a sewer you could have asked me to put on wellies and bring my own peg." She was giggling, though looking a little nervous too.

"Now would I do that to you?" I looked at her out of the side of my eye teasing.

"Yes you bloody well would," she sounded a little cross, "'Camping', he said," quoting me from long ago "'it'll be fun', he said. Not to mention the freezing cold, the muddy field with a mud bath, car crash and a host of other…" I stopped her mouth with mine plunging my tongue into hers in full flow as her anger was intensifying. She resisted momentarily, and then joined me in yielding to a rather passionate and exciting embrace. I stopped and looked her in the eyes and licked my lips.

"You are perfect for the occasion," I said, "but if rubber wellies and a trip around Marks and Sparks is what turns you on, then I am sure I can arrange it given a little time?" I looked at her trying to pull off my cheeky seductive look, it worked. She batted her eyelashes in a feint at looking angry but with submission.

"Mmph… well there'd better be no manholes then either," she stated adamantly. I laughed and slid back alongside her facing forward. We were now travelling along the front of Selfridges. "Almost there, northern side please." We drove around the railings of the square to the far left hand corner on the northern side and pulled up. I paid the driver and got out first, opening and holding the door for Kelly. She looked up dubiously at the building as she got out. My God I just couldn't stop staring at her legs. The cab driver took off and we stood on the pavement her looking up at the building and me looking up and down her sexy silk clad legs.

"It's just a town house," she said. "So what's special about *this* town house?"

"I gather you're less than somewhat impressed by the exterior then?" I surmised blandly. I was rather more impressed with her exterior. "This, I will have you know is a palace, a little palace I will grant you, but a palace non the less, and tonight it belongs entirely to you." And with that I bowed and kissed her hand. "Welcome to Home House." I offered her my arm and we went up the steps to the front door. I opened the door with a large key which I produced from my pocket and took her hand to help her inside. Inside the front door was a wide entrance hall, a room in itself. There was a desk in the corner which we went and looked at.

"Oh my goodness," Kelly exclaimed, "this is from the dark ages." The desk was an old switchboard with a dial and loads of plugs on leads which you put into the correct hole to connect the caller to the appropriate phone. "Its an antique."

"I rather think the whole place is an antique," I said encouraging her on. "Come on." The doors beyond were open and as all the lights were lit you could see the staircase beyond. Marble pillars, well not marble, rather painted with a feather to look like marble, and the most elegant staircase swept up the middle of the curved room bifurcating into two further flights on either side, encircling around the curved walls in front of a painted statue in the centre. Above our heads was a glass domed ceiling.

"Oh my goodness Moli, it's beautiful. Is it really a palace? How did you find it? Is anyone else here? What…"

"Too many questions." I stated stopping her in full flow. "And the reality isn't very interesting, but basically it *is* a palace, it *is* yours for the night and we *are* entirely alone. We have it to ourselves, we can go anywhere you want, though some of the beautiful rooms are offices. We just have one proviso, that *if* we have a row we are not to throw anything as it may be a priceless antique and also it may damage the delicate fabric of the building which in itself is a priceless antique, other than that we can do anything we like." I opened the doors to the front of the stairs and led her into an exquisite blue room which was to all intents and purposes empty apart from some sofas and the pillars in each corner. There was a bottle of champagne in the centre, on the floor in a silver cooler with a couple of glasses. I watched Kelly as she entered the room. She walked through it slowly ignoring the champagne and continued on into the next room. I followed behind at a distance into another exquisite room with paintings on the walls. Beyond that room she entered a smaller green room. She wandered in front of the fireplace and ran her hand over the carved nautical implements on the relief. Then she walked out of that room round in a circle and back into the huge room containing the champagne, slowly gazing about her, mainly looking up at the ceiling and the walls.

"It's Adams isn't it?" she stated a little unsure. "I recognise some of the style, we have an Adams room at home, but it's nothing like this, and I thought that was rather grand."

"Look Kelly if you want a history lesson I am not your guy, it's pretty, that's about all I can tell you, and it was built as a palace by the Countess of Home, and nobody can afford it so the University moved in with its books, which are upstairs, and loads of students." I hesitated. "Well the students are home right now, but they don't look after it and kick the hell out of it when they have parties. Apparently in the back garden, in the God damn greenhouse I ask you, are hundreds of priceless paintings awaiting restoration. And all that stands between us and making off with a priceless work of art is a Yale lock and a ten foot brick garden wall!" I looked at her from under my fringe, standing there in the middle of the room with those endless sexy legs which I was desperate to explore in close proximity. "Are you interested in a life on the run living on the proceeds of illicit art sales?" She had her arms folded across her chest and her breasts moved slowly up and down as she breathed. She knew she looked stunning, she was standing like a model with her foot behind and her leg turned out towards me, she turned to me smiling.

"Do you know Moli, I believe every word you are telling me, and yes, if you were serious, yes I would spend my life on the run… with you." Though she was about twenty feet away from me her eyes were intense. "And besides, we wouldn't need to pick the lock either!"

"Oh yeah, how's that then?" I asked leaning against the door frame.

"Well if it's a greenhouse, then all I'd need is a brick."

I laughed out loud.

"Well we have another problem, I'm never going to get you over a ten foot wall in those shoes am I? Well at least not without damaging myself severely."

"I'd take them off… for you," she offered.

"Listen Kelly, I'm supposed to be grovelling here, and you're supposed to be making this hard for me."

"Why?" she asked, though she full well knew why.

I looked down and took a deep breath and slowly walked towards her hands in pockets.

"Why? Because I'm a bastard, because I love far too many people at the same time, because I'm an emotional mess, because I don't deserve you, and because it's taken me so long to decide what, who, it is I really want. You can stop me any time here." I invited her. I was standing in front of her now so close but she hadn't made a move to touch me. I looked up at her through my fringe.

"I'm waiting," she said.

"What for?"

"For you to tell me just what, who, it is that you really want, and Moli, I want it to be the truth, however many of us it is just tell me the truth, then I'll know what I'm facing, whether I can cope with the competition or not. And listen, I know, or at least I think I know who will always be on your list, I can cope with some of it just not all. I don't want to change you because I love you but I need you to be honest with me."

I sat down on the floor and propped my head up with my hand, elbow balanced on my knee and sighed. Then I lay back flat on the floor looking up at her.

"I thought I was just going to have to tell you about Luckhurst." I laughed and despair hit me, "but you want to take my soul…" She wanted it all, she wanted all my boxes open and I realised I was about to lose her and tears welled in my eyes. She squatted down next to me, still perfectly balanced on her heels.

"I don't want to take your soul Moli," she said gently. "I just need to read it occasionally. I need to know if I'm in there at all, how far down your list I am, who's at the top? You think I'm cool with all of this, but every name on that list is like a knife to me. Some I understand, but I'm only human Moli." Then she started shaking her head, "No, no, that's not the truth Moli… I want to be the only one that matters to you. I know that I never will be, I can live with that if it's who I think it is, but if it's anyone else I can't Moli, even though I will love you forever there's really only one name I can deal with, and I can live with that one, but only one. So tell me Moli, not now, I don't want it to be now, because I don't want to say goodbye, not yet anyway, but some time tonight, when you're ready, tell me, and until then you'd better have this." She placed her engagement ring on the floor by my head. Then she stood picking up the champagne bottle as she did and the two flutes in her other hand and walked out of the room. I could hear her heals clicking on the floor as she walked towards the stairs and then as she climbed up to the floor above.

I lay there dazed on the floor. Pick one, that was what she was saying to me, out of the four, well only three really now I had already said goodbye to Luckhurst but I hadn't even been able to tell her about that. So much for that sacrifice. In that second I had realised that I was going to lose her, he wasn't even registering in my conscience against her. But who did she want me to say. She knew I loved both Dawn and John. Which one did she think I would choose? Did she want it to be Dawn because she was female and she could compete with competition of the same sex? Or did she want it to be John because she new he would never turn to me even if he were free? How do you choose between love? Kelly, oh God, to lose Kelly? 'Grovel, tell her you've seen the light, use your magic.' Lovelace's words came flooding to me. Christ Lovelace, what do I do? I just stared at the ceiling unable to move because of the weight now bearing down on me. Choose, how could I choose? I don't know how long I lay there but eventually I got up and went looking for her.

She was in a tiny circular room with gold fabric on the walls. A small Dresden chandelier hung above the desk that occupied the centre of the room. She was sitting on the end of it looking out of the huge curved glass window which overlooked the garden and the greenhouse at the end. She didn't look up as I came in, she just stared out of the window.

"So you're telling me that out there are hundreds of priceless paintings?"

I followed her gaze to the end of the small enclosed garden.

"Yep, hundreds, all priceless. Russian religious icons, Cezanne's, Monet, you name it they've probably got it out there. Or if it's not out there now it will be at some time in the future. That's the restoration department for the Courtauld Institute of Art. Looks like the greenhouse, could do with a bit of restoration itself!"

"It's got to have an alarm on it, I mean anyone could hop over the wall."

"Well I don't think they advertise the fact, but yes anyone could."

"They must be insured." She said wistfully.

"You can't really insure something that's priceless. Anyway, who would think they would be there? No one in their right mind, so they're probably as safe as houses. The university certainly couldn't afford insurance I'll bet."

"Ask me again Moli."

"What?"

"Forget our earlier conversation and ask me again. Ask me to run away with you. How many paintings do you think we'd need for a lifetime on the run? Pretend we didn't speak, tell me you love me Moli." She broke down in tears her head dropped not looking at me. "Take me in your arms, make love to me. I don't care who you love, how many you love, what sex they are, just tell me you love me and I'll believe you, please don't let me walk away?" I stood in front of her one hand on her waist and took her chin in my hand raising her head to look at me.

"Kelly, I do love you, you know that's the truth. I don't want to lose you, God I don't want you to go." I looked into her desperate eyes and we were kissing as if our last moments on the planet had come. She opened her legs and was pulling at my flies. I pulled at her pants and they ripped under my fingers and I was in her pushing her back onto the desk. I can't say it was anything but desperation on both our parts, and violent. It was about need and trying to hold onto something that we both felt was slipping away from us. The top of her dress came down easily and she cried out under the relentless battering, but when I went to pull away she grabbed my back, digging her nails into me grabbing my neck and thrusting her hips forward harder and harder until I came deep and hard within her. Then we just lay there panting and clinging on from exhaustion.

We peeled apart without kissing, there was nothing tender at all about this. I sorted myself out in silence whilst she rearranged the top of her dress and pulled down her hem. I reached for the champagne, not for any other reason than I was thirsty. The cork flew out of my hand and hit the priceless Dresden chandelier above our heads. We both cowered waiting in shock for something to fall. We held our breath, but nothing did. We both burst into laughter and I poured the champagne out into the flutes. Handing one to her we smiled at each other, it seemed a lifetime since we had done that. It seemed a lifetime ago that we had been friends. I lifted her down from the desk and we wandered around exploring room upon room. The library was interesting. One room was blue, the stacks of books were away from the walls so that they didn't do damage, but the gold gilding and the pillars… How could anyone in their right minds allow such a place to be abused so? The next room was even more amazing, more gold and detail until the last green room at the front. Row upon row of reading desks looked so incongruous in the sumptuous surroundings. Kelly gasped at this room.

"This is so bizarre," she exclaimed, "I can hear the students now 'my college is a palace compared to yours'," she laughed. We wound our way to the next floor up. There were still some grand rooms up here. One which must have been a bedroom had hand painted wallpaper with a dark blue background and oriental birds with a silver ceiling. Another room contained hundreds of Chippendale chairs all in yellow fabric.

"Do you think they would miss a dozen or so?" Kelly enquired.

"Probably not, we could give them to Lovelace as a wedding present, something to sit on whilst they have a cup of tea!" We both giggled. We wandered down a corridor and around the bend. I knew there was food somewhere in this place, my sister had received the hamper I had ordered, but where the hell had she left it? We opened the door into the most amazing bathroom I have ever seen and this really was made from marble. It was also obviously somebody's office. The floor sloped ever so gently to a drain in the middle around which were signs of the zodiac in different coloured inlays. The bath had pillars either side and was enormous with a lion's mouth in the middle, obviously where the water came out. The ceiling was glass. There was a wooden cover on the top of the bath which was very wide and someone, obviously my sister, had made up a bed on top of it. Duvet cover and pillows, a sumptuous Romanesque boudoir and on the floor in the corner was a small hamper from Fortnum's.

"Dinner, are you hungry?" I looked at Kelly. She hadn't said much since the sex. Neither of us had said anything about it. She shook her head, tears spilling from her eyes and we were there again needing each other even more than we had before. This time it was against the wall, on the marble floor up against the side of the bath, stripping off our clothes as best we could in amongst the violence. We didn't speak after, we just curled up together on the duvet on top of the bath cover and fell asleep.

I awoke later. Kelly was gone, her clothes were on the ground so I knew she was still here somewhere. I had to find her, I had to talk to her, because I now had her answer. I wandered through the building stark naked apart from my boots, looking for her, cigarettes and lighter in hand dinner jacket over my shoulder. I found her at the bottom of the staircase wearing my shirt and shivering. She heard me coming but didn't move. I put my jacket around her shoulders and sat by her side. I offered her a cigarette, she didn't smoke often but she took one now. I lit her cigarette and then mine, then looked at the lighter in my hand and ran my thumb gently over it.

"Kelly?"

"Not yet Moli, just give me a few more minutes." She looked up at me, eyes glistening with tears. I put my arm around her and pulled her close, she laid her head on my chest.

"So the art theft is off then?" she asked. I nodded without saying anything. "Pity, I'd found an answer to the ten foot brick wall," she laughed sadly.

"Oh yeah, how would that work then?" I replied.

"Well why go over a ten foot wall when you can walk out the front door?" she said.

I snorted a small laugh down my nose, but neither of us felt like laughing. I felt I was about to lose something so precious and I didn't know how I was going to survive on the other side, and I think, no I know, she was feeling the same. We flicked the ash into the cigarette box and stubbed our cigarettes both out on the lid. The time had come to tell her. Now that awful moment was here I found that I was crying, not sobbing, just tears flowing down my cheeks and I was helpless to stop them, so I didn't.

"Kelly I love you so much…"

"But…" she added for me and she buried her face in her hands crying silently.

"You said you wanted the truth," I said quietly.

"Do you even know the truth?" She asked shouting, tears streaking her face.

"Yes, I do." I answered quietly. "Look, you said you didn't

want to change me."

"Well I lied Moli, I lied!" she snapped, getting up and walking away from me. "I lied because I want you to choose me… but you're not going to are you?" she said whispering the last bit.

"No, not first I can't." I looked down at the lighter in my hand. I could hardly see it now it was a golden blur in amongst my tears. "Even though I can never have him I can't deny he comes first and he always will. Even though he loves someone else in the same way I love him, the way I will always love him no matter what."

"And what about Dawn?" I laughed. I hadn't said his name but she knew who I was talking about.

"I do love Dawn, but she belongs to someone else, and I love you more," I said looking up into her face." She looked at me for a moment and then turned away from me and walked out of the hall away into the front room. So I had got it wrong, she had wanted me to choose Dawn. John was a guy, she felt she couldn't compete with a guy. I cried like a baby burying my face in my hands, my heart breaking. Oh my God, just how do you survive this? I thought of Dawn when John had left, now I knew the grief the unbearable grief. Then I felt Kerry's hands around my wrists, she was standing in front of me pulling my hands from my face. She took my hands in hers, she was smiling at me. I couldn't cope with that, I couldn't take her eyes so I looked down. She turned her hand over in mine and I gasped. She was wearing her engagement ring. I laughed through my tears and looked up at her, relief and joy rushing through my system, she was laughing and crying too.

"I want to get married here," she stated.

"We can do that," I replied looking into her eyes.

"And I want each of our children to be conceived on this spot!"

"We can do that too," I whispered. God she was wonderful, then we were kissing in a wild frenzy and I took her there and then at the bottom of the stairs in the middle of the floor. The only thing I could think of asking her when we'd finished was, "Do you ever take those things off?" She raised one of her slim long legs admiring the shoe for a minute and answered.

"No."

Chapter 26

Lovelace

This was the one, the session that she had been dreading. From here on in, though the next two sessions wouldn't take as long, these were the ones that would take her hair. She would just be staying in overnight, so instead of going to her home we decided that we would go to my digs and then travel down to her parents when she felt better. It was really all over that first day, but she had to have the saline wash out and that would be an overnight thing. It was beginning to get more and more difficult to find a vein. They kept puncturing her but no blood was coming out. Her poor hands were bruised and swollen, and all this just made the whole business so much harder for her. I left her at lunchtime holding onto her bear and was again locked out of the ward. I took some sandwiches down to Maggie's and hung about there until I was allowed back in. I was a bit early so I was hanging about by the door when I recognised the back of another older guy waiting outside the door.

"Dad?" he turned around to me. "What are you doing here? Is Mum with you? You didn't tell me you were coming. Oh

God it's great to see you." I threw my arms around him and he hugged me tight. It felt so good, it was as if I was a small boy and he would make everything all right for me, I clung on. But then I came back to reality, I wasn't a small boy and he couldn't do a damned thing, whether he wanted to or not. He smiled at me as I pulled away from him.

"How are you doing son?" he asked. I just nodded my head and then looked up at him. He didn't really require an answer. "How's Dawn?"

"Oh, she's doing ok, we'll be out tomorrow and I'm taking her back to my digs this time.

Where's Mum?" I asked.

"Oh she's keeping well, she's at home, I'm up in town staying at my club. I've booked a table for dinner if you'd care to join me later?"

"Well..." I hesitated, I wouldn't be leaving Dawn until late, "I'll be here until at least eight, which may mean it'll be too late for dinner." There was no way I would leave Dawn until I was forced to.

"No that's fine I'll make arrangements, you come along when you can. Do you want a room too?"

"Er... no thanks, I'm staying with Moli's sister in Mayfair and she'll be expecting me so..."

"No no, quite right, quite right," he replied.

"Are you coming in... to see Dawn?"

"If that's allowed?" he asked tentatively.

"Of course it is, she'll be delighted to see you. Come on."

We crept into the ward. Dawn was fast asleep with her teddy

bear clutched against her.

"Oh my, poor child," he exclaimed, "John, I'm so sorry I haven't been before."

"To be quite honest Dad it's a good job you didn't. But it's all right, we're getting through this, only two more sessions and it'll all be over." At which point I had to bite my lip. A surge of emotion coming from God knows where suddenly rushed up into my chest and I couldn't say another word. I became completely choked as I stood looking at her, oblivious and peacefully asleep with her bear. My dad put his hand on my shoulder, it was so comforting.

"We've let you both down… badly," he said. "Is there anything I can do for you, now?" His hand was still on my shoulder. I shook my head and leaned my head on his hand. We stayed like that for ages, just watching Dawn sleep. Then he squeezed my shoulder with his hand and said, "I'll be back for you later then. I'll wait out the front in the car at about eight, come down when you're ready, and give Dawn my love when she wakes." He kissed my head and left.

Dawn slept a long time, in fact I thought she was never going to wake up. I kept getting up to make sure she was still breathing, but she was sound asleep. I examined the bag, it looked innocuous enough, could be water even. I watched it drip by drip as it descended under the pull of gravity adding to the small reservoir further down the pipe, before it crawled slowly downwards through the jaws of the machine pushing the liquid on and on down the tube into her hand where her blood flow then sucked it in. Her fingers were holding her bear tight, she looked like a little girl, just a baby, and I saw her as my dad had. Dark circles under her eyes and her skin pale grey in colour, no blush to her cheeks, if I hadn't known better… *No*. I stopped myself before I thought the word. There was a pen and pad on her trolley so I started playing around with a few lines in my head, and suddenly it just came flowing out of me. I can't say I wrote it because it really wrote itself, but it captured how I was feeling. The title was easy: *Chemotherapy.*

No more to battle in distant war
The field far beauteous than any before,
And into the Dawn it's firey saber slicing
Indiscriminate evil advancing.

Quiet she lies, as in a state of grace
Whilst death it's mantle caresses her face,
Gravity begins then blood draws it in
To creep on the foe secreted within.

Smashing and tearing is carnage released
Beauty sleeps on whilst raped by the beast,
A standby spectator, I, shackled and chained
Whilst my baby, within my touch, is ravaged and maimed.

Quiet and quiescent must I sit and accept
My sentinel watch in dark hours have wept,
And I like a coward steal my way home
Leaving battle and field locked in and alone.

Returning at daybreak refreshed from my rest
As accomplice more poison allow I to crawl in at her wrist
And what outward signs denote such a war
Skeins of ebony litter the floor.

To Win! To Win! Is everything
But not so much as one weapon I swing.
Not one hand in her defence can I raise
But two raise I in shame to cover my face.

The fight is hers and hers alone
So sit I safe, keeping vigil, and pray she will return home.

Although her hair was still in place, I knew it was this session, this inoffensive little bag and only a matter of time till the insidious mixture in increasing amounts of chemicals would eventually burn it out at the roots. The vile process had begun. Please God it would do it's job and kill the cancer too.

She was quite buoyant when she awoke, mainly because she knew she would be going home the next day. She was sad she missed Dad. Then again all too soon the nurse was pushing me out the door and our time was up.

Dad was sitting in the back of his car pulled over on the side of the pavement. I climbed in beside him exhausted. I must have fallen asleep because the next thing I knew Dad was gently shaking me and we were outside his club. I followed him inside, the doorman took his coat, and then went into the cosy warm inner sanctum of the gentleman's club. It was filled with leather chairs and sofas. I had been before but I now knew why he came. It was like Maggie's for Dawn, a home from home, not like a hotel but somewhere where he could relax properly when he couldn't be in his own home. Privileged yes, but then who of us wouldn't have chosen this if they could? Dad was getting too old for all this, he should have retired long ago, but the firm had begged him to stay on. He led me into the dining room, it was full, I didn't expect so many people to be dining mid week but then this was London I supposed. We were shown to a table in a quieter area near the far wall and attended to by a waiter Dad obviously knew well. I was so bushed I held my head up on my hands, elbows on the table. I knew it was bad manners but I was almost beyond eating at that point. Dad didn't talk much, he just got me fed and kept me from falling asleep onto my plate.

"I'm sorry," he said, "I had no idea. I should have taken you straight back to your friend's house. How are you going to get Dawn back to your digs tomorrow?" I explained about how Moggy was 'stored' when I didn't need her. He offered to take us in the car the next day, and I gratefully accepted. "I have a couple of meetings in the morning, but after that I'm at your disposal." I arranged to meet up with him at Maggie's whenever we managed to get Dawn off her drip and then he was going to come with us to my place. He waved me goodbye from his club and sent me off in the car with Carl the chauffeur back to Mayfair.

The next day as I arrived Dawn had five minutes to go on her saline and then we were to go to Maggie's to meet the wig man. She had been allowed to order several wigs because he liked her so much, so she could see which one suited her best. We had such a laugh with the chap trying them on. I looked hideous in them all, even though I fancied myself as a rock musician in one of them. We actually got hysterical at one point when the wig man started singing and dancing in one of them. I have to say though Dawn looked absolutely gorgeous in all of them but one in particular really suited her, which was the one she chose. It was most like her own hair style if the colour was a little lighter. She was thrilled, which of course was the point and so by the time Dad arrived she was still in high spirits. Dad was great, he gave her a big bear hug when he saw her, though he was quite shocked at the speed with which she began to go downhill. We had to stop the car a couple of times as she felt so sick. She sat on the door ledge and kept saying she was sorry, and I know she was embarrassed too. I kept telling her it was all right, holding her head as she threw up into the gutter. Dad just sat back stunned, he offered to help but in reality there was nothing he could do but keep out of the way. We eventually got back to my place and Dad and I got her upstairs onto the bed. She was out of it by now and fell straight to sleep. Back downstairs Dad had got his coat off and was making me a cup of tea. There was no milk so he sent Carl off for some supplies.

"How long has it been like this?" he wanted to know. "How on earth are you going to manage? I want you to come home, you need help, let us help you."

I sighed. "Dawn wants to be with me, and I want Dawn to be

where she feels comfortable." The message was clear. She didn't feel comfortable at Lovelace. Dad nodded.

"But why haven't you gone to Dawn's home?"

"Can you imagine a journey to Kent with Dawn feeling like this? No, we'll travel down in a couple of days when she's feeling better."

"But what about you John, you're all on your own." I smiled at him.

"We're married Dad, in sickness and in health. I'll look after her she's my responsibility."

"Yes, but who will look after you? You're my responsibility too." He stated. "Look lets talk about practicalities, what *can* I do for you? Shopping? Would having Carl and the car at your disposal help you any? Let me do *something* for you, please." I sighed, trying to think.

"Ok, yeah some shopping would be good, and yes Moggy is in town so I wouldn't mind a trip in with Dawn when she's better to go and get it."

"Good, I can do that, I feel a lot better now." He said. "So my next job I think is to make sure you both feel welcome and comfortable at *your* home John. I am so sorry about that. Your mother doesn't mean it you know." I looked at him and raised an eyebrow.

"I think I made it clear Dad, either we are both welcome or I won't be coming home, and I don't know if Dawn will want to come back and I'm not going to make her." He was looking at me with a frown on his face, but he nodded.

"I'll have to sort this out," he said. I shrugged.

"Look Dad, you're welcome to stay, but I need to go and sit with Dawn."

"Right, I'll sort out some food for you." I left him downstairs and went to sit, sleep whatever. Dad was actually quite brilliant and it was great to have the company. He sent Carl off shopping with a long list and then he set about making a meal out of what he could find in the cupboards. He kept popping up with cups of tea. If I was awake he'd chat, if we were asleep he just left us, the rest of the time God alone knows what he was up to, sorting his business out I suppose. Later that evening when I came down he was getting ready to go.

"Listen John, I've got a few things to do for work over the next couple of days and I'll do those from town, but I'll be back tomorrow and see if I can give you a hand, that is if you don't mind." He looked at me hesitantly as if he wasn't sure I would want his help.

I smiled at him. "Thanks, that'd be great." He smiled gently back at me, obviously greatly pleased and relieved.

"Ok then, there's a meal for you in the oven. I don't suppose Dawn will be interested, but I've got some rather nice soup on low for her and a few little snacks that she may fancy. There's fresh milk and bread and a few other bits and bobs, and I'll take care of your lunch tomorrow, you can do breakfast. I'll be over at about ten if that's ok then you can get some sleep, I think you may be needing it by then." He smiled at me and then held his arms out.

"Thanks Dad," I said as I hugged him.

"Good." He said patting me. "I'll see you tomorrow."

He was true to his word, at ten the next day he reappeared, albeit in more casual attire, and he spent the day helping out where he could, making tea, making meals etc. With him around I really did get some quality sleep. We spent the next few days like this until Dawn began to really pick up again and then he sent Carl off to retrieve Moggy and he drove us down to Kent to Dawn's place.

Dawn's beautiful hair was now beginning to go. Her pillow was strewn with hair. Each time she slept more seemed to be on the pillow the next day. It got in her mouth, she was permanently trying to retrieve bits from down her neck. Eventually she tied a scarf around it just to keep it from annoying her so much, but she was stressing about it constantly. She persuaded me to cut it really short and although she cried she said she felt much better. But only a few days later she wanted it gone. I got a kind lady at the local hairdressers to agree to do it for her in a room around the back, so that no one would see. I sat and held her hand whilst the lady gently shaved the rest of Dawns' beautiful waves away. Tears streamed down her face the whole time, but when she had finished Dawn wiped her face and said, "Well that's that then." She felt her head with her hands and put her wig on and looked at me for my reaction. I smiled at her.

"You don't need the wig for me, you look beautiful," I didn't have to lie, it was the truth. She smiled at me. Maybe when I get used to it I won't need it." I think it was people's reactions that she was most afraid of, and she only went without her wig around the house.

Kelly was great, she had sent her a superb selection of different hats to wear, all very trendy. Goodness knows when she got time to shop for them or even where she managed to get hold of them but her parcel really brightened Dawn's day. Then it was chemo time again, and back we went. She lay asleep on the bed as I returned from lunch and she looked so breathtakingly beautiful I sat and wrote another poem.

This time her mum stayed with us and we took it in turns to sit with Dawn. There was quite a lot of time in between the bags for some reason so we spent the hours in-between at Maggie's. We took up occupation of a corner of one of the sitting rooms and Dawn curled up on a sofa and slept, so did Dawn's mum and I to be frank, but it was just so much better to be off the ward. We really felt like we were in our own front room, it was so much easier to relax, and there was tea in the kitchen whenever we liked. Thank God for this place, it was a life line to us. Dad came out again and helped and then again he ferried us back down to Kent. Only one more session to go.

We met Moli in the George again on a Saturday. He hadn't seen Dawn since she lost her hair and she was really worried about his reaction to her. She was wearing her wig but she kept pulling at the sides of it nervously. He walked into the back of the bar with a wooly hat pulled right down over his ears and a large scarf wound up fat around his neck. He sat down and began to peel off his scarf and then he pulled his hat off. He was as bald as a coot. Dawn and I gasped, his beautiful curly blonde hair was gone completely.

"What? What did you do that for?" I gasped. Dawn was just struck dumb.

"Well we had a charity day at school and I raised fifty smackers all on my own. I thought we could compare notes as it grows back." Then he was obviously suddenly panicked about what Dawn's reaction was and worried he'd done the wrong thing. He looked at her face waiting for her to say something.

"You silly arse." She said. "What if it doesn't grow back at all, your beautiful hair Moli!" He relaxed immediately.

"Course it'll grow back!" he said. "It's only hair, it's not as if I've cut anything vital off!"

"Do you possess anything vital?" she asked laughing.

"Wouldn't you like to know," he said knowingly, "you'll have to ask Kelly about that. Anyway, what do you think? I think I have a remarkably beautifully shaped head It's symmetrical which is more than I can say for a lot of people's, you'd be amazed how many asymmetrical squashed heads there are around. Lovelace for example, I don't suggest you do this you're lop sided, pretty, but definitely lop sided!"

"That's true," said Dawn, "your ears aren't level."

"Hey less of the personal comments thank you, my ears are fine and they're happy where they are," I replied jokingly.

"Well your hair covers a multitude of sins Lovelace." Dawn hesitated and then she took off her wig. She looked up at Moli slowly. He gave her the most wonderful smile, it said I love you loud and clear. She looked so vulnerable, and then he said "Your ears are lop sided too." She screwed up her mouth as if she were really cross, but she couldn't keep it up and we all burst out laughing.

"My hair will grow back but you will still be a silly arse!" she said exasperated.

"Tell you what Dawn, it's bloody cold without hair. I'm amazed at it's insulating properties I may have to borrow one of Kelly's hats.

"I'll let you have the pink one," she said.

Chapter 27

Lovelace

Dad had invited us down to Lovelace, and he had made the point that the invitation was from Mum as well. I had asked Dawn what she wanted to do, she had one more session of chemo to go and I thought we should wait until after that, but Dawn said she didn't want to think about it and that we should just go. I hadn't really talked to Mum since my visit on my own and to be honest all I had done then was really arrive, sleep and leave. Things between us were quiet I suppose, I had said very little to her since the evening when she had been so unkind to Dawn. I knew Dad was desperate for things to be right between us all. Family had always been important to him, I knew he was caught between his loyalties to Mum and to us.

We pulled up outside the house. It was Saturday evening and we were to spend the night and see how it went. I looked over to Dawn, her face was illuminated by the porch light from the front door.

"Are you ready?" I asked her taking her hand and giving it a squeeze. She was biting her lip and fiddling with the hair of her wig. I gave her a reassuring smile. She looked at me unsure but nodded anyway. "Dawn, it's going to be ok, I'll look after you, I promise." I wasn't sure at all about this. I felt the timing was wrong, I wished I'd insisted we wait until the chemo was over, but I would look after her, anything, anything at all out of place and we would walk. We reached the front steps and I rang the bell. I would normally have gone straight in, but things had changed since our wedding day. Dad opened the door, Mum was standing behind slightly to one side. God this was awkward and I could feel poor Dawn shivering as she held my hand. Dad was so thrilled to see us, he held out his arms to Dawn and she instinctively went forward into his embrace. I followed her in immediately into the hall. Mum looked hesitantly at me, as if she wasn't sure of my reaction. I went up to her and kissed her on the cheek and gave her a hug. She held on to me and then released me. Then she looked at Dawn who was now turned towards her.

"Dawn, I…" she was so uncomfortable, I wanted to say something for her, but Dawn just went straight up to her and hugged her. Mum was taken aback, she hadn't expected this, neither had I. There was an awkward moment and then Mum put her arms around her and hugged her back. Dad and I let our breath out, which we had both unknowingly been holding. It wasn't mended but it was a start.

We went into the drawing room and sat down in front of the fire. Mum excused herself to go and fetch some tea and invited Dawn to go with her. I looked at Dawn to see what she wanted to do, there was no way I was going to let her go on her own.

Mum saw the panic on my face.

"It's all right John, I've behaved badly and there are some things I need to say to Dawn. I'll say them here if you want Dawn, but I'd really rather prefer to talk to you alone, but only if you are all right with that." I looked at Dawn, she nodded and then she followed Mum out of the room. I looked at Dad.

"Do you think they'll be all right?"

He smiled at me and patted me on the shoulder. "I'm sure of it," he said and he went to the drinks cabinet to pour us out a whisky.

Dawn

I followed her down the hall. I have to admit I was terrified, not particularly because I was scared of her, I was just scared of being attacked verbally. I wanted so much to make this all right for John, he had hardly been home since he'd got married and I was the reason and I hated that. I felt that for him, being adopted, he needed his family in a way I didn't. I know that wasn't probably true, but I felt in some ways that his family was more fragile than mine. Knowing John's dad really was related to him made it feel more permanent but his mum? I know she was worried about their bond, I didn't want John to be too. As soon as we reached the kitchen she invited me to sit down and then she sat down across the table from me.

"Dawn, I need to apologise to you for the things I said to you last time you were here, and for my behaviour towards you." I didn't reply because there wasn't really anything I could say to that. She continued. "I don't know whether John has said anything about Charles and myself," she looked at me. I looked bemused. I didn't know what she meant. She continued. "We married late in life, Charles was forty-nine I was forty-four, we met through an agency. He was successful in business and needed a wife and had never really met anyone and I, well I had never had any security and I suppose that was what I was looking for. I assumed, wrongly, that that was what you were looking for in John too. We were never in love, Charles and I. I don't think I've ever experienced that but we have grown to love each other in some ways over the years. We did try for a family but I was ill and it then became impossible. John was.... Well John was all our dreams come true, something we never thought we would have, a child of our own and someone who kept us together and loved us. I suppose if I'm honest I'm scared of what you two have and jealous of how that leaves Charles and I, of John's feelings towards us not being his blood parents." She looked up at me trying to read my expression.

"You should talk to John, I mean about how he feels about being adopted. You know you have nothing to worry about, you've done a terrific job, he has no hang ups about it, he loves you both. You should really talk to him I can't believe you don't know what he feels for you, but then he's a guy and I suppose he won't tell you unless you ask. As for us, we love each other very much. I'm sorry you don't understand it but I would never want to come between him and his family, you're part of who he is and he needs you both." I shrugged, I didn't know what else to say to her. She wasn't the sort of person you could spontaneously hug, she was formal and stiff, it was just who she was, but I didn't want her to think I was stand offish. She had her hands on the table and was looking down. I put my hand on top of hers and gave it a squeeze, I felt I had to make some gesture to her. Her reaction surprised me, she grabbed it tight with both her hands and looked up at me.

"I'm so sorry, can you forgive me?" I smiled at her and said.

"There's nothing to forgive." She smiled back at me with a look that said 'yes there is and you and I both know it.' Then she got up and put the water on the boil. She directed me to plates and a cake tin and then she carried the tea tray back to the drawing room and I followed. We were never going to be bosom pals, but we were going to be ok. Later in our room I told John what had been said.

"You need to talk to your parents, tell them you love them."

"They know."

"No they don't, your dad does because he has that security of knowing you really are related to him, but your mum doesn't. You need to tell her, and I mean really spell it out to her, where she fits in now that you have me, it's important. Perhaps it's time you let your dad explain your adoption to you, it would give you an opportunity to get it all out in the open." He didn't say anything.

"John?"

"You know why I don't want to do that, I don't want to hurt them." He replied.

"But John, they are being hurt because you don't talk about it. You can't keep thinking that people know and understand what you feel, you have to tell them. It's like Moli, look at how you misinterpreted that one, and you would have sworn he knew your inner most thoughts and you his, no one does unless you tell them."

"You know my feelings."

"But John you tell me, you talk to me, and even then I worry you'll change your mind and you have to keep reassuring me that you love me. We're all paranoid about love. Remember what the policeman said. 'Don't take it for granted look after it, nurture it, work at it, treasure it and you will have it all your lives.' That doesn't just go for our love it's for all kinds of love."

"Mmmn... Maybe... I'll have a talk to Mum but the adoption... I'll have to think about it."

John got up early the next morning trying not to wake me, but of course I was aware of him as soon as he moved. I knew he was going to talk to his mum so I pretended to be asleep. He leant over me and hovered. I tried to keep really still.

"You're a terrible actress," he whispered, "but I love you." He kissed me on the eyes. I smiled but didn't open them. It was about an hour later when I went down to the kitchen. Mrs. Brownie had been making fresh drop scones and they smelled just delicious, all piled high keeping warm under a towel on the side of the Aga. Charles was helping himself too.

"How are you my dear?" he asked smiling at me. I smiled back at him, he really was lovely. I would have thought he would have had lots of girlfriends when he was younger, but then I really didn't know that much about him at all.

"I'm great," I said nodding and taking a drop scone off the Aga. "Can I ask you about your family? I don't really know that much about you." He laughed his reply.

"Of course you can, they're your family too now. I'll get some pictures out after breakfast but I can tell you now."

It was fascinating I tried to link it in with bits of history I knew. It was amazing, because of the missing generation we were straight back into the Edwardian age, an age of horses and carriages, long dresses and dressing for dinner. Gentlemen wearing hard starched collars attached with studs, walking canes with silver tops. He was a child when the Titanic sank, and he and his twin wore dresses until they were 'breached' at five. He had two older sisters and a younger brother Walter who was born four years after him. His parents had musical evenings with their friends bringing their instruments, his dad played the cello and the viola, whilst his mum was a singer and pianist. They had a town house in Chiswick, Wavenden Avenue, it sounded grand, and the boys attended Latymer, a public school which they ran to every day. Several miles there, back for lunch and then back to school again in the afternoon. He and his twin were inseparable and the two best runners in the school, winning medals and being noted in the Chiswick Gazette. Charles always came second, his brother Fredrick was faster and won the All England Public Schools flat race, they were both in the relay together. The race had to be re-run because they finished so quickly the officials didn't think the whole team had run. Fred was being considered for the Olympic games in 1928.

"One of us had the brains and was painfully shy, and the other had the looks and was charismatic." I was immediately confused, which one was he referring to as himself? He could have been either description. Though I would never have put Charles down as painfully shy, he was an MD for God's sake of a highly prestigious firm and not bad looking. Charismatic? I bet he could be in a board room.

His elder sister contracted TB which passed to his other sister Phyllis and then Fred got it. Charles went all quiet his brother, 'the better of the two,' as he described him, died aged twenty-one, and Phyllis never really recovered. He wouldn't say much more about her. I gathered he resented his older sister after that, though he didn't say it.

He talked a little, about the war, I gathered he was in the RAF but not as a flier, in administration. He had to move from one airfield because the dam busters moved in and it was all hush hush. Then he ended up in Malta and he began complaining about tomatoes and sesame bread, neither of which he could now stand, and that he got into trouble with Pussy Foster and Sir Keith Sir Park, so called as he was knighted twice. He was their ADC, but I didn't know what one of those was, so I just smiled, it sounded important. He described meeting the Pope during the war as he escorted the Bishop of Gozo for the laying on of hands and how he made a bit of a fool of himself on the way back.

"You see it took much longer on the way back and so I thought we had been kidnapped by the Germans." He laughed as he told me how the pilot had to explain to him, a RAF Lieutenant but with no knowledge of flying, about headwinds and tailwinds and why it was taking so long to get back to

Malta. "Nothing at all to do with the Germans!"

He told me a little about his friend who he accompanied into Berlin with supplies after the war, and how the Russians were handing out axes on the steps of the Reich Chancellery. He apparently took a lump of marble out of Hitler's desk. He waived a hand in the direction of an oddly shaped ashtray on the side. "Had it made into an ashtray, best thing for it," he said. On the journey they stayed in a castle and they found some iron cross certificates so they filled in one for each other and awarded themselves an iron cross. His friend Eric turned out to be an ex- prisoner of war who had escaped in a wooden horse. *Hey! They made a film of that, I had seen it on the television!* Then apparently they had flown out to the Philippines to interview prisoners of war held by the Japanese. They returned the long way around the world via America, at which point Eric (Williams) had begun to write his book *The Wooden Horse,* Charles was his proof reader!

He talked mostly about his younger brother who had been in bomb disposal in Birmingham, and who attended to a bomb. "He had only just enough time to tell everyone to get down," he said sadly, "and the bomb went off in front of him." He mentioned his brother was only just married and that she had a daughter, Juliet, that he had tried to help bring her up, but her mother had moved away to Australia. Then he looked up and smiled at me.

"Which brings us to John, who you know we adopted," and his twinkling blue eyes crinkled up at the sides, just like John's. I couldn't help but smile back at the familiar look which I loved so much. Mrs. Brownie pottered about getting lunch ready and then John came in to join us.

"I'm making frothy coffee if anyone is interested?" he announced. Everyone fancied one, even Mrs. Brownie who produced a large saucepan for him. John's dad went off to his study to look out some photos. John threw his arms around me from behind and kissed me on the cheek.

"Did you talk to your mum?"

"Yes," he answered obviously in a buoyant mood, he was almost bouncing.

"And?" I asked exasperated.

"And you were right, people should talk to each other more."

"What about your dad then? Are you going to talk to him too?"

"Yes! But, maybe not today." He said tipping coffee and sugar into the pan on top of the milk. I was disappointed, and it must have shown. He looked at me for an explanation.

"Well your dad was just telling me about his family and obviously you came up at the end, and, well, it just seemed like a bit was missing that he would have liked to talk about. I felt a bit sad for him I suppose."

"Ok, frothy coffee first, then we'll go and find him." We didn't need to he came back into the kitchen carrying armfuls of photos and spread them on the kitchen table. His mother followed behind with an armful of albums and we all sat around the kitchen table passing the photos back and forth, whilst the frothy coffee rapidly rose up the sides of the pan.

"John!" Shouted Mrs. Brownie. "Are you in charge of this

or what?" She had picked up the pan and removed it from the heat, just as it was about to boil over onto the top of the Aga. John took the pan from her apologising whilst she surveyed the kitchen table covered with photos. "Well its sandwiches for lunch if you want to continue in here or a proper Sunday Roast, but only if you remove yourselves to one of the other rooms in the house." Marie laughed picking up the albums and apologised again to Mrs. Brownie. I helped collect up the loose photographs. John put the frothy coffees onto a tray, minus Mrs. Brownies, and followed us down the hall into Charles' study.

We spread the photos all over his desk and began pouring over them again. A photo of his brother came to light, Frederick the runner. He was handsome and I could see now which twin Charles was.

"I was painfully shy," he said, "Fred was slightly older than me, only by a few minutes. He was so handsome, and he charmed everyone. I had to take elocution lessons to help me to speak. We were inseparable." There were photos of them rowing together in an eight on the Thames, in boy scout uniforms, in formal suits, in school uniforms. There was no doubt that losing his twin brother had been an enormous blow to him and that he had never got over it, even now half of him was missing. Then there was a picture of his other brother Walter and his bride Freya, and after that a photo of her on her own holding her baby Juliet. There was a picture of Charles and a little girl at a boating lake and he was helping her launch a paper boat. He looked at it for a long time and then he looked at John longingly. John was watching him too.

"Dad," John addressed him.

"Uh!" His dad was obviously miles away even though they were looking at each other.

"Do you want to tell me, about my parents?" Charles didn't seem surprised; he just smiled at John, his eyes creasing up.

"I'd love to, I'd really love to." His arm fell onto John's shoulder as if he had suddenly let go of some huge burden.

Walter's bride, Freya was alone after he died, she had no family and she was pregnant. Charles was in love with her. He didn't say that, but you didn't have to be Einstein to work that one out, his whole face said it as he talked about her. I looked at Marie. Did she know? I thought so but then again I wasn't sure. Charles had offered to marry her, to look after her and her baby, in a completely gentlemanly way, of course. What he meant was no sex, but that wasn't something he would have said straight out. But she declined his offer. *Thank God. The poor guy* I thought. Imagine being in love with someone, living with them day after day and never having the possibility of being close to them, talk about a living torment. Then suddenly I thought of Moli and I began to understand his life, being John's 'friend' year after year, and never ever being able to say how he felt about him.

Freya declined Charles' offer, he did however support her in every way that he could. He became Uncle to Juliet, though he loved her as if she were his. Then they moved away to Australia. Freya wanted to make a new life for herself and her daughter. She met a minister out there and she married him. It was obvious that Charles was heartbroken.

Years later Juliet returned to the UK a grown woman and Charles supported her financially. When she wanted to get married Charles didn't approve of her choice of husband but he gave her away at her wedding. She became pregnant and gave birth to John. But it came to light that John was not her husband's, he was the result of an affair with her husband's best friend. It was decided that she would give up the baby to save their marriage, and it did work, for a few years at least. The men saved their friendship somehow too. Huh! I thought, only a man could come up with that one and think it would work. She gives up a baby and they stay best friends and every day she has the reminder of her lover still being around. He can't give up his friend though she gives up her child? It beggars belief that anyone thought for a second that scenario would work, but apparently that is what happened. And the baby? Who could she entrust to take her precious baby? Why Charles of course, he would do anything for the daughter of the woman he loved. The daughter he would have taken as his own had her mother married him. Though with Marie in the room that one wasn't said either. I tried to put it into terms I could manage. If I was in love with Moli and had an affair, what would happen there? Would John give up Moli and vice versa? Could I give up a baby and stay with John with Moli being there the whole time reminding me of what had happened and what I had given up? Dear God, I wouldn't even give the idea a seconds room! Were they all stupid or what? Whoever thought that would work needed their brain seeing to. Or did she love both of them?

Did she realise she loved her husband the most and that was the only way she could stay with him. I mean I knew what that was like, I loved Moli, not like John but I did love him. Naah, it still was never going to work. Anyway the upshot of it all was that the marriage didn't last. *Surprise surprise!* She eventually left, and the men? Guess what? They were still best friends as far as Charles knew? *What?* Was there maybe more to it, were they ever lovers? I really was meeting myself coming back now, it was just getting too complicated for me. Juliet, John's mother, she disappeared, lost touch with the family, left her precious baby with the one man she knew would love him as his own. John was looking down at the floor. He knew about Juliet, but he didn't know about the rest of the details. When he looked up I could see he had tears in his eyes. He looked at his dad with such love I will never forget it as long as I live. His dad just looked terrified as if he didn't know what reaction to expect from John. John went up to him and touched him on the arm.

"Thanks Dad, I love you." He said, and they hugged each other so tenderly, I was so choked. I looked at his mum, her head was on one side and tears were falling down her face too, it was so intimate I hardly dare breathe and so beautiful too. Then John went and hugged his mum. "Thanks Mum, I owe you both so much." I sat as quiet as I could, my face awash and my chest full of emotion for them all. Then John came and put his arms around me and I just held him.

Chapter 28

Lovelace

With the last chemo session we were back to the original routine of several days in the hospital but this time Dawn was buoyant. It was the last session and every bag would be one more nearer to the last. She unpacked her bear and popped him on the end of her bed. I climbed onto the bed beside her and held her in my arms as they began the awful business of finding a vein. They went backwards and forwards from one hand to the other, they tried her wrists on both sides, the backs of both hands. It was horrendous. Then I remembered the blood guy downstairs. It wasn't too late and he might still be there so we did a quick disappearing act, pretending to go to the loo and scuttled down to the outpatients clinic. He was still there. He was thrilled to see Dawn and really pleased that it was going to be her last chemo session. He was still going to see her at outpatients so he could afford to be generous. He didn't have the right bits to plumb her cannula in but he knew where he could get hold of them so he disappeared vowing to return. A few minutes later he was ready to have a go.

"I have to admit it, it's hard," he said, making attempt number three.

"Well as long as you don't go over twelve attempts," said Dawn turning her head into my shoulder, "that's the record so far."

"But hey! Eureka!" he shouted as blood flowed into the syringe he was holding.

"Thank you, thank you so much," said Dawn in tears. "You just have no idea what that means," and she kissed him.

"Wow, I've never had that reaction before," he said, going red from tip to toe. "Any time Dawn, you come and see me, any time!"

We snuck back into her ward and onto the bed. The nurse who came back to have another go looked at the cannula and twisted her mouth.

"Ok, I suppose I don't blame you, but don't tell anyone will you." We both shook our heads in silent agreement. In came the big bag of poison and down it dripped.

"Last time," I whispered to her. She snuggled in to me and we talked about the upshot of the weekend's revelations.

"Do you think your mum knows how Charles felt about Freya, Walter's wife? I mean he was obviously in love with her."

"Yeah, I think she must do. You know she never liked her and now that sort of makes sense. They used to come over from Australia to visit you know, they used to stay before they lost contact. Dad would get all excited about it, now I know why, and Mum would be in a bad mood for days."

"I was trying to put it into terms that I could relate to, you know, you me and Moli and how that would work."

"And how did that work?" I asked trying to see what she was getting at.

"Not at all," she said emphatically. "You would never have made me choose between you or my baby. If you remember we did play out that scenario, you gave me up. And there would be no circumstances that I can think of when you would ever make Moli choose either, you would stand back. Even if you loved Moli like you do me, surely that would make you want to keep the baby all the more. As for them being friends not lovers, I don't know, that sort of thing was illegal then so no one would know for sure, what do you think?"

"The only way to think about it is the way it played out, the friendship was more valuable or maybe just more enduring than either of their relationships with Julia. Affairs between best friends and partners happen all the time, the problem was she got pregnant which was concrete evidence of the affair. The other guy may have felt guilty about what he had done to his friend and backed off, but there was still a baby as a reminder. We know she stayed with her husband for a few years so without the baby it did work for a time. Maybe she realised she really did love her husband. During which time he must have forgiven his friend. How she felt about the guys we don't know, but she did agree to having the baby adopted. Oh that's me!" I said realising suddenly. "Maybe she felt she had no option, no way out, maybe Brian, her husband threatened to leave her. Or maybe she didn't want to be reminded every day of her affair, mistake, whatever? We'll never really know and it's stupid to try and make sense of it, the only ones who will ever know are not here to ask. None of it matters to me, I have two amazing parents, who love me no matter who I am or what I do. I have you who I love more than my life and you love me too. And we are blessed with a fantastic friend. I only wish we didn't cause him so much pain and that it could be a simple friendship, but then life is not perfect, certainly not for Moli."

"I wonder if that is it then?"

"What do you mean by that?" I asked her uncertain what she was getting at.

"Well do you know if you are it or were there any more children?"

"That's an intriguing possibility! I never even thought about that one. I presume Dad kept in contact with the family, but there again how would he?"

"Well there you go then, you could have brothers or sisters. You may even know them and never know it. But at least we know I'm not one." We laughed together remembering when she had thought I might be her brother.

"It was lovely you know, when your dad told you your story, he wasn't hurt a bit, he was just so proud to tell you that you belonged to him. And your mum was proud too."

"I know," I acknowledged, "in future I will pay more attention to your pearls of wisdom." Dawn was becoming drowsy so she slept for a while in my arms whilst I ran though it all again in my head wondering about brothers and sisters I might or might not have.

She came to about an hour later. "I've got it, I've worked it out!"

"Worked what out?"

"Juliet, I couldn't understand it before because I was looking at it from the wrong side, or rather the wrong bloke!" I lay still waiting for her to make sense.

"I thought she was married to her John, but she wasn't, she was married to Moli! Now it makes sense!"

"It does? Cause I'm left way behind."

"No, really I've worked it out. Listen, three people, for some reason she marries her 'Moli' who she loves but isn't in love with."

"Why?"

"I don't know, could be lots of reasons, maybe she was never asked by 'John'. Maybe he was away, maybe he never told her how he felt and stood back for his friend, now I know you can understand that one!" she said stridently.

"Ok, then what?" I asked.

"So then 'John' comes back into the picture, the love of her life and they have an affair and oh my god she, 'I,' get pregnant. Their choice is to be together and hurt 'Moli,' could you do that? Imagine the guilt. And 'Moli,' I know he would still love me and want me. So noble 'John' backs out and tries to keep them together."

"You're forgetting something," I said smiling.

"What?"

"Me… the baby, what would you do?"

"I…"

"Couldn't do it," I finished her sentence for her. "But if you were back in the fifties, pressures from families, who knows. The fact is I was adopted. But no matter how much you loved 'Moli' eventually you would leave and what would be left? I'd still love 'Moli' and if he forgave me, which he would, then yes we would still be friends."

"I feel so sorry for them." She said and hugged me tight. "You're a real love child, no wonder there was magic when we met, bubbles at our wedding, you're really special."

I laughed out loud.

"Dawn, you are such a romantic, I'm only special to you silly, I'm a big hairy bloke to other people."

"Not all other people. Anyway you're mine, and you need lots of love."

"Oh I do, do I?" I said laughing looking at her adoringly. Oh my, I loved her so much she had no real idea.

"Yes, and I intend to give you lots and lots," she suddenly became exhausted, "but I'm so tired right now, and cold, please hold me John." I tucked the covers around her and held her tight. She fell asleep so abruptly in my arms I was a little alarmed. A nurse was passing and she saw my worried face and came over. She took her pulse and then smiled at me.

"Last session?" I nodded in reply to her. "We'll miss you two love birds, not enough to want to see you back though." She added strongly. "No one wants you to have to go through this again." She smiled at me. "But you've had a lot of us reassessing our relationships and a few have been coming up quite a bit short! Others have been going home and realising how lucky they are too! You two have made us all a little less complacent."

She touched Dawn's face gently. "She's just tired poor love. You take care of each other." She looked up at me and smiled again and patted my hand.

I looked at my sleeping angel in my arms. How lucky was I that she searched me out and came to the conference looking for me? I thought after the dance that I would never see her again. I began thinking about Moli, how he stood back over Dawn. Thank God it was me she loved or we could be in exactly the same position as my poor blood parents were. I never thought finding my true family would be so emotional or so complicated. And what about brothers and sisters? Well they would be half siblings probably, but I wondered also what happened to poor Juliet, where was she now? She would never contact my dad because she wouldn't know how his family felt about all this. I wondered about what had happened to her, whether I could find her, whether she would want me to. Then I too fell asleep with Dawn beside me.

I was kicked out at the end of the day as usual and made my way back to Mayfair. Dear God I was glad this wasn't going to continue for much longer. Melanie had some strange concoction for supper, she was doing experimental cooking, I was polite to begin with, but actually it was quite good in an odd sort of way.

"You know I'm going to miss you John, I've really rather enjoyed having someone here now and again and you eat absolutely anything I put in front of you which is heartening."

I laughed.

"I don't know what I would have done without you Melanie,

it's another good hour on the tube to my place, I don't think I would have ever got there some evenings."

"I've got to ask you something," she said, looking me straight in the eyes but she hesitated and then looked down.

"What?"

"Well," she hesitated, "I love my brother very much, but I don't really understand him. I used to think that you and he… well, then Dawn appears on the scene and it's obvious that he's head over heals in love with her because that's all I hear about, and then she turns out to be your girlfriend. Then your married and I expect him to be heartbroken and suddenly he's engaged to this Kelly. Then all he can talk about is you again and he seems desperate for your approval, and I really don't know who he's in love with or whether he even knows himself. I don't want to pry John, but he's my brother and I worry about him. I don't know how to help him when I can't even work out which side he bats on. I know you two are close, you don't have to tell me how close, that's none of my business, but if you can cast a little light for me I'd be grateful?"

I coughed a little, with embarrassment I suppose. "What can I tell you, he's a complicated guy," I laughed as I tried to gather my thoughts and work out what I was going to say. "Moli has a great capacity for love and a great need too. Just be there for him I guess, 'cause he leaves himself wide open for getting hurt. He really is in love with Kelly you know, I think this one is a keeper." She smiled at me and sighed.

"Pity," she said smiling, "I preferred the idea of you and Moli, maybe I just like having gorgeous guys around. Now I suppose

I'll have to make some sort of effort with this Kelly person."

"You won't have to make much effort, really, she's great and you're going to love her when you get to know her, and most importantly Moli really does love her."

"Ok, if you say he loves her…but you know you're like family to us. Just don't let anything ever spoil that will you John."

"I'll try not to." I replied laughing.

"Anyway, any time, and I mean any time you need to borrow my flat or come visit you know you are welcome. Keep the key, just remember to knock, you never know, I may not always be on my own. It will give whoever something to think about if suddenly a lovely looking young man lets himself into my flat, it'll keep them on their toes eh?"

"Any time Melanie, if you need an irate boyfriend to burst in, I'm your guy." I went to sleep really happy that night. Tomorrow would be the last day of poison then wash out and home the next day. I couldn't wait to see Dawn in the morning, even though I knew she would be rough, it was one day nearer home.

The next day I was there early again, the nurses let me in. Dawn was fast asleep. I sat in the chair with the discarded teddy in my arms. I closed my eyes, listening half heartedly to the burble of chatter going on in the ward. Two girls were chatting discussing their treatment talking about what it had been like for both of them and comparing notes. I was half tuned in to what they were saying. They both had cancer, very rare, and this was the centre of excellence in the country for this form of cancer and it's name was a 'molar pregnancy.' I opened my eyes in shock. It was a pregnancy? Had Dawn lost a baby then and I didn't know? I looked across at her still sleeping peacefully besides me. Oh my poor girl, I gently touched her hand, swollen by the chemicals and constant abuse of needles. But why hadn't she said? Surely she would have said something, told me. Maybe she didn't want to hurt me, maybe she thought she needed to keep that from me. I thought about how it made me feel, sad, desperately sad, that not only had she had to lose her ovary she had lost a baby as well. I knew it was our baby I didn't need to ask her that, but she had lost something, a chance of a future child and on top of that this creeping nightmare of cancer lurked somewhere inside her too. Why hadn't she told me? I began to cry, to grieve for some small person I would never know. Dawn opened her eyes and her smile dazzled me, I went and sat on the bed next to her.

"I love you so much Dawn," I whispered, choked.

"I love you too," and she smiled even wider.

"Dawn... why didn't you tell me there was a baby?" She looked at me puzzled. "I was listening to the girls over the other side talking about their cancer." Dawn looked over at the girls and then back at me with understanding in her eyes.

"You shouldn't eavesdrop on other people's conversations." She stated with a gentle smile. "You have added two and two together and come up with six." She gave a slight chuckle. "Good job you've given up the business studies course if that's an example of your mathematics, you'd have made a lousy accountant!"

"What do you mean?" I asked puzzled.

She took my hand in hers and looked me straight in the eyes. "I didn't have what they have. Most of the girls in here have had a molar pregnancy, I'm the only one here with dysgerminoma. It's the equivalent to testicular cancer in boys but much rarer." She put her head on one side looking at me. "Did you really think we'd lost a baby?" I nodded. "Well we haven't." The relief must have been evident on my face. "Oh you poor guy. How did you feel though, I mean about the possibility of having a baby? I mean, we don't know if I can, if I'll be able to, how would you feel about possibly never having children?" I looked into her eyes and I could see the sadness there.

I put my hands on both her shoulders and captured her eyes with mine. "Dawn, I've realised this morning that I am the luckiest man on the planet. I have you, and your treatment is over, your cured, and I get to spend the rest of my life with you, however long or short that may be I don't care I have you. I'd love to have children but that's a lottery for everyone, not only us, and if we don't, well, we'll have had all that practise." She laughed at that, "and I'll still have you, how could I ask for anything more when I already have everything. I love you and I always will." She hugged me tight around the waist.

"And the good news is," said a nurse over my shoulder, "That's a bag of saline Dawn, as soon as it's finished and you've seen Dr. Wilde, you can go. Your drugs have been cut down as you were so poorly the last time you had this selection, so they've cut a few out!"

Dawn buried her face in my lap, I knew she was crying. I have to say I was too, it was an odd mix of feelings, sadness at her suffering, anger that she had had to go through all that, joy that she was ok and had come through it, and relief that it was all over. I rubbed her back whispering, "It's over, it's all over." We could go home and begin our future together.

Chapter 29

Lovelace

Later that week we met Moli down the George.

"So how did it pan out with Kelly? You never told me, but I gather you're still together otherwise you would have said something." It was the first time I had had a chance to talk to him and he hadn't phoned or anything.

"Well..." he hesitated.

"Do you want to talk alone?" asked Dawn. "I mean I really don't mind."

"God no, you're my family you two. No it's not that, it's well... it's just a little bit early to be telling people but... she's pregnant." The look on his face said it all, he was ecstatic.

"That's fantastic, oh Moli, that's just amazing, congratulations mate." I held out my hand to him to shake and as he took it I pulled him close and hugged him. "I'm so pleased for you" I said close to his ear. He laid his head on my shoulder facing away from me and just held on tight to me and we just sat there hugging, sharing a wonderful close intimate moment, one he had probably waited all his life for. Then he looked up for Dawn and she scurried around to the other side of him and we all three sat in a big huddle just cuddling each other united in our happiness for him.

"So the old tackle works then!" I stated later on.

"Well as I've said before Lovelace, you either have it or you don't, and I HAVE IT!" we all chimed in the last bit together and laughed.

"When is it due?" I asked.

"I don't know Lovelace, how long does it take to cook a baby?"

"For God's sake you did basic biology, nine months." I replied.

"Oh really? Well once they had given me the instructions I stopped listening."

"Yeah right," I replied sarcastically, "you lost your cherry before they even gave out the instructions!"

"Well I had an enquiring mind!" Moli stated. Then I glanced at Dawn I didn't know how this news was really affecting her, but I wanted her to know I was aware.

Moli was worrying about her too. He squeezed Dawn's hand. "Dawn? Are you all right talking about this?" he asked her.

"Oh Moli I'm so happy for you both, I am, really I am." She held up her arms and hugged him tight around the neck and then she burst into tears on him so he just held her and gently rocked her. After a bit she reassured him again. "Come on Moli, I want to hear all about it."

"Well the school don't know but her parents do. She's been chucking up for the last few days and the kitchen at school have been cleaning like madmen. They think it's a bug in the catering and everyone is keeping quiet. Her parents have been remarkably cool about it. We've only a few weeks to go to the end of term and school's not about to initiate a scandal by expelling her even if they do find out. Wedding's booked up in London a month after term ends, before she gets too big and apparently I inherit some sort of mausoleum in town so we even have somewhere to live. What with the old private income we'll be ok until I can get some sort of job. I even get the small estate in Italy, so if you need somewhere to go on a cheap holiday I'm your guy, hey maybe that will be my line, 'Italian Holidays… live like a Count!' Should make some money from Brits wanting to sample my cellars!" He gave Dawn a gentle squeeze, she was tucked quietly under his arm.

"Dear God, the mind boggles at what may be lurking in your cellars Moli!" Dawn laughed joining in. "So where is the mausoleum then? Highgate cemetery by any chance?" She carried on laughing.

"Belg…" he said under his breath, coughing as he spoke.

"Where? Belgium?" I asked.

"No, Belg…" again he swallowed the address.

"Belsize Park?" I guessed.

"Belgravia" he spat out all embarrassed.

"Oh yeah! Some mausoleum Mols. Shit man did you know? I mean before?"

"Well I knew there were the odd properties waiting for me to reach twenty-five or when I married but no not really, it's all been a bit of a shock. I think the school wonders what's going on I've had solicitors visiting my show constantly over the last week, and you know what Luckhurst thinks about visitors to my show! Why, would it have tempted either of you then? No don't answer that, I know the answer to that already and I've decided to stop inviting rejection. Anyway guys I'm happy, for the first time in my life I am really, really happy. And something even rarer, I'm in love for the first time in my life with someone who actually loves me back. Which brings me to a burning question Lovelace..."

"You know I will, you don't have to ask me." I presumed it was a best man question.

"Oh great well that's the bill for the catering taken care of then," he said laughing his head off.

"Bastard!" Then I added. "Only if you want fish and chips then, that's about all I can afford." I laughed. "Dawn will provide the ketchup won't you Dawn?"

"For you Moli I'll provide Ketchup, HP and vinegar," he smiled at her.

"Moli?" she continued, "does Kelly know you've cut all your hair off?"

"Well no, I haven't had a chance to tell her yet what with all that's been going on, why?"

"How long do you think it takes to grow it back?" he just looked at her not understanding. "You're getting married and you've only got some downy fluff, there's no way you're going to make it to even a short hairstyle in time. You're going to be bald in your wedding photos do you know how she might feel about that?"

"Oh shit!" said Moli, "I think she may have me by the gonads this time!" Then Dawn kissed him on the cheek and got up. I looked at her with a worried frown. Moli looked too. "Just going to the ladies," she said smiling reassuringly at us both.

I met her in the passageway coming back, well I had to go and check on her and see if she was all right. She looked at me as she walked towards me down the hall.

"Don't be kind to me, otherwise I'll lose it, I can cry tonight but right now I need to be happy for Moli." She smiled at me, paused as she came closer and held up her hand to keep me back, and then she walked back into the bar with a smile on her face. I felt hurt that I couldn't touch her, but I understood, so I followed her back into the bar.

Moli was very drunk when we posted him in through the boot room window but he didn't have far to go on the other side to his show so we were sure he would make it unaided. I span the car in the quad and we drove home in silence.

Back at Dawn's house we went straight up to her room, we undressed and climbed into bed. Dawn faced away from me so I curled around her holding her. I knew she was wide awake but time was ticking on and on and she hadn't said a thing. I hoped she was going to talk to me but it really didn't look as if she was so I thought I'd better start it.

"Dawn? Do you want to talk about it?" I asked her.

"What am I supposed to talk about?" she replied flatly.

"Well about how you feel, about Moli and Kelly's news, anything you want Dawn just please don't shut me out!"

"Oh so this is about you and how you feel is it? Sorry I didn't realise. Well I'm thrilled, thrilled for them, and I'm jealous, jealous that we may never have that opportunity, there I've said it, is that what I'm supposed to say?" There was no emotion whatsoever in her voice it was just flat and I was taken aback. I didn't know how I was supposed to react. I knew she was hurting and that this wasn't like her, but I didn't know what the right thing to say to her was. I tried to kiss her head but she pulled away from me and rolled further away to the edge of the bed.

"Dawn?" I whispered, she made no response. "Dawn?"

"What? What is it that you want me to say?" she snapped back at me angrily.

"I don't know, but I want you to talk to me. I know you're hurting and I want to help you." I replied gently.

"Well you can't," she shot back at me. There was a pause then, "You know I don't think I can cope with you in the bed tonight I feel too ill. Please leave me alone."

"If I believed you I would go, but I don't, and I'm not going anywhere." She threw back the covers and sat up on the edge of the bed.

"Well then I suppose I'll have to sleep somewhere else then." She waivered on the side of the bed, she wasn't going to be able to stand up and I could see that.

"Dawn, if you want me to take you downstairs to the settee, I will, but I won't leave you there on your own." She was so angry she was thumping the mattress with her fists on either side of her in frustration.

"I need to go to the bathroom." She stated.

"Okay," I said slowly, but I'm not leaving you alone in there either, you can hardly stand."

"Why won't you just leave me alone!" she shouted and then she started sobbing and gasping for air. I bit my lip, I was in agony for her, I didn't know what to do. I knew she was in the most unimaginable pain and that the last thing I should do was what she was asking for. There was a knock on the bedroom door. It was Dawn's mum.

"Mum," she yelled out. Her mum opened the door.

"Are you two all right?" she asked.

"Mum," she yelled out desperately, "tell him to go away, please tell him to go away."

Her words cut into me like a knife, but I knew I couldn't feel sorry for myself, something was eating up Dawn and this wasn't about me, well I hoped it wasn't.

"Look, I'll go away if that's what you want, but only if your mum stays with you."

"I don't need you and I don't need anyone, Mum please make him go," she was crying and pleading. I looked at her mum. She came up to Dawn and crouched down.

"Dawn," she tried to get her to look at her, "Dawn it's either him or me, who do you want?"

"I don't want anybody, I just want to be left alone, please leave me alone." She curled up into a ball on the floor hugging her knees and crying. Her mum looked at me.

"I think I need to make tea and this one's down to you. I'll be downstairs, call me if you need me John," and she shut the door. I got out of bed and knelt on the floor beside her.

Dawn I want to help, but I don't know how?" I touched her on her back and she arched it away from me. *Okay* I thought, *I can sit and watch her from the other side of the room, in which case I don't see anything changing in the next hour or so or I could take the bull by the horns and see what happens.* I felt she was crying out in pain but didn't know what she wanted. I thought perhaps that asking her to talk might also be a step too far, maybe she couldn't put it into words either, so I grabbed her with both my arms and pulled her close to me. She started to fight. She kicked and struggled as best she could, but she was so weak that it didn't last long. She tried to hit me but I held on to her arms, holding her as tight as I could, as she struggled against me. Tears ran down her cheeks as I held her and she yelled at me to let her go and that she hated me. And then the fight was over and she cried in my arms as if her heart were breaking and I cried too. Then she rolled into my chest and clung on to me like a child seeking comfort. I didn't want to press her with questions so I reached out to a tape recorder on the floor by the bed and pressed play. Very quietly the gentle humming chorus from Madame Butterfly began to play. Her mum came in with two mugs of tea and smiled tenderly at me and placed her hand on my shoulder. I put my free hand on it as a thank you. She placed the mugs on the floor by me and then she tiptoed out, indicating to me that she was going back to bed. I just sat on the floor with Dawn wrapped around me in my arms listening to the gentle music. I thought I'd try and break the silence. I gently stroked her face, she wasn't looking at me but her eyes were open, staring.

"Dawn you don't have to talk, but is this about your cancer?" I didn't think she was going to respond, but she did, she nodded without speaking or looking at me. "Okay, and is this about your hair?" again she nodded. "What about Moli and Kelly, is it about them?" This time she shook her head, "But it's about the baby right?" She nodded and a tear trickled down her face. I wiped it gently away with my finger. "Is it about me Dawn?" this time she looked me in the eyes and nodded. "And you think I won't want you?" she nodded.

"You know a very wise person told me something once," I leaned forward to grab the leg of my jeans which were on the floor just about within reach. I pulled them so I could reach my wallet in the back pocket. Then one handed I tried to pull out a piece of paper, the contents of my wallet all came out together but I found the thing I was looking for. "He said, if ever one of us doubted how the other one felt about them then we should check the signatures on this." I held up our marriage certificate for her. As for your hair Dawn, I wrote a poem about that while you were asleep in hospital. I'll read it for you now." I grabbed another piece of paper that had dropped from the wallet and read it to her.

On losing her hair.

Radiant Dawn
Though art so wondrous fair
What needest thou
Of tresses of hair.

Thy inward beauty
Reflects around
Weep not for Ebony
Bestrewing the ground.

The price is paid
An empty boat crosses
Fairest Dawn
Countest not thy losses.

But rather rejoice
Though it cuts like a knife
Your hair will grow back
Its price was your life.

When I got to the last verse tears began to flow down her cheeks. "So you see Dawn your hair is the price of your life to me, infinitely more precious. As for the cancer, you have survived, and I know that in itself is going to be hard to come to terms with when others don't but that's not you fault Dawn. And a baby, do you really want a baby at the moment? I thought that was something for the future, but look at me Dawn, I was adopted, there are many ways of having a baby, and we don't even know that we can't yet. But if that's what you want as soon as we get the go ahead then by all means let's try."

"I love you." She said softly.

I smiled at her with such love. "I love you too, and now we

have a lifetime together to prove it to one another. I lifted her up in my arms and gently placed her on the bed. "Now do you want me to sleep somewhere else?" I asked. She shook her head, so I climbed into bed beside her and held her through the night.

Chapter 30

Moli

Bloody hell, marriage! Wasn't that exactly what I had said to Lovelace when he had come up with a similar scenario? Well here I was at the age of eighteen and considering something even more unimaginable than that, marriage and a baby all in one go. Cold feet? Christ yes I had cold feet, but more brought about by blind terror, not because I had any doubts about me and Kelly. I was stinking drunk as well. I thought when you got drunk your brain slowed down and thoughts got muddled. Not me, when I got drunk it was like I was on speed or something, my mind always began to race and now I had too much going round and round in my brain. I tried to sort it out by lying still on my bed, the glow from my hi-fi highlighted the outlines of my show.

Question number one: Was I happy? Yes, no question, yes. Well that was a good start.

Question number two: Did I love her? God yes. Love, lust, like all of it. Great, well I was doing well here.

Question number three: What about a baby? Did I want a

baby? Well that was sort of irrelevant now because like it or not there was going to be one. But did I want one? Yeah I really did, maybe I wouldn't have chosen now but it was amazing, *Jesus*... frightening... I don't know, scary stuff all around really.

Question four: Did I want to get married? Well yeah, sure. At eighteen? Yes? Oh God not quite so easy now... This is where the blind terror starts to creep in. *Where's my best mate when I need him?* That was what I needed right now... but was it? Bad idea to go in that direction... but too late, that was the direction I longed to go in and silent tears fell down my face and I let myself indulge in what could have been. Stored in my memory was every detail of every time we had been together and I re-ran the lot. I had seen how he looked at Dawn, that intense fire in his eyes that melted her soul, I now imagined him looking at me like that. The pain of it was unbelievable, it raked my chest from my throat down to my groin. *Why? Why do I keep torturing myself?* I knew why, because it was the only way I could have him, that was why. The only way he would respond to me the way I so desperately wanted him to, was in my imagination. Tonight was the first time he had held me in his arms and I hadn't dared turn my head to him, because I knew what his immediate reaction would be... to let go and I so wanted that moment to last as long as possible, forever if it could. But then it was better, because Dawn came round and held me too, and I was lost, forgetting the reason for that emotion which was Kelly, me and the baby, I imagined it was them loving me completely. *God now I need another drink, where do I go from here?* I thought I was able to get my head around this and now it was just getting worse. I know that drink depressed people and I was now staggering in the pits. *Air, I need air!* So I grabbed a bottle of vodka from its hiding place behind the curtain and staggered out of my room in the direction of the tower.

It's amazing how one minute you can be euphoric about the future and the next in the depths of despair but that was where I was headed as I reached the top of the tower and I hadn't even noticed. I emerged at the top and surveyed the view spread out before me. From up here it looked so beautiful, the lights from the villages and houses twinkled in the distance and I could see for miles. I looked in the direction Lovelace was and imagined that one of the lights in the distance was where he was. Then I looked further a field, way off into the horizon where I knew Kelly was. There was nowhere to sit down up here, so I climbed onto the ledge with my legs dangling over the side. I had a good head for heights and it didn't bother me that there was about a seventy foot drop under me to the hard tarmac of the quad below. I flipped up my top pocket and shook a cigarette from the pack putting it between my lips and placed the pack on the ledge beside me. I stretched out so I could get the lighter from my jeans pocket and lit up. Then as it caught the light and my eyes took in the little object my soul broke and I cried holding the small lighter against my chest, against my heart.

"Moli?" It was Luckhurst my house master.

He was up on the ledge… Christ *and* he was drunk out of his brains, he was in a really bad way. Adrenaline was pumping through me and I hadn't a clue what to do. My immediate thought was that he was going to jump. Jesus, was this my doing? Had I had a hand in this? He was crying his heart out. Oh God I wanted to put my arms around him and comfort him, he looked so alone, so broken.

"Moli?" I didn't want to startle him. He knew I was there but he didn't respond. He had his arm across his chest in some gesture of comfort holding on tight to himself and a cigarette in the other hand. His eyes were streaming and snot and saliva hung down in strands. My heart went out to him, it was agony witnessing such pain, I felt myself beginning to tear up. Had I done this to him? Should I have spotted something earlier like when he shaved his head? This wasn't just anyone, this was my Moli. Oh God, how do I help him?

"Moli? Are you all right?" God what a stupid thing to say, of course he wasn't all right. I moved slowly ahead until I was touching the wall some five feet away from him. "Do you mind if I join you?" I asked looking at him carefully for any sign that he was responding to me. His head dropped down and he turned his face away from me. I took it as a no and slowly swung my legs over the ledge too.

I thought I knew Moli pretty well, but it now struck me that I knew bugger all about him really, well nothing that was really of any help to me like what made him tick. I knew that he was eighteen and repeating his final year. That he was the only one of his year left. That may be of use. He was engaged to Kelly a very attractive girl of about seventeen. That he hung around with Lovelace from his previous year and his girlfriend Dawn, no wife now, and that she had cancer. Could be something to do with the cancer maybe? And I knew that he had found me attractive, as I did him, and I also knew from his past that he wasn't averse to male on male relationships. I had known him for many years when he was a junior and I was four years ahead of him, but he didn't know how I felt about him really. He was beautiful, but too young then, and he seemed to be welded to the hip of Lovelace. Odd that, him and Lovelace, there were never any rumours about them other than that they were friends, best friends, unlike Moli who had quite a reputation even at an early age. Then there were all those official people coming and going to his show recently, solicitors he said to do with his engagement, maybe I should have probed a bit deeper. I really didn't know what to say to him, where to pitch it, the girl, the cancer, me? So I thought I would play safe and go for the friendship.

"So where's Lovelace tonight then?" Some safe ground… he let out such a cry of agony as he breathed out that I got it immediately. "Oh God, I'm sorry Moli... I didn't know you two were…"

"We're not," he said adamantly.

"Right!" Bingo, I'd got it first hit, unrequited love, and by the sound of it years and years of it. "Does he know?" I asked. Moli looked up at me and started laughing. Okay so he knew. Now I had a real problem, Moli was laughing so much and I could see him lurching forward, he was so drunk, he only had to lose it for a second and he would be gone. I laughed along with him a bit and then said "But he's married," I was stating the obvious. Moli stopped laughing and looked at me and tears began to stream down his face again. "Jesus… her too?" Moli snorted a laugh of agreement at me and flicked his cigarette into the night sky. "Kelly?" he was smiling now and nodding. "Well no wonder there was no room for me then!" I stated, amazed by the revelation and taking my eye off the business in hand which was to stop Moli from toppling forward off the top of the tower. Our eyes locked, he steadied. Ok so he did feel something for me. "Moli," I said calmly "get off the frigging ledge." He looked down at the quad between his legs and then started laughing again, this time hysterically. "Jesus Moli! Just get off the ledge will you!" I yelled, at which point he lost his balance completely and fell backwards, thank Christ, smashing his head on the ground and leaving his legs up in the air and bent over the ledge he had been sitting on. I leapt down immediately swinging my legs back over the wall. He had his eyes shut. Was he out cold? I put my face down, cheek to his mouth and nostrils to feel if he was breathing. I looked at his chest to see it rising. *Thank God for that* I turned my face to his and he was looking at me right in the eyes. My God I wanted to kiss him, I had always wanted to kiss him, I had thought of moments like this for years and I knew he was waiting for me to do it.

"I think your life is complicated enough." I said, knowing I may regret this moment forever. God I was already regretting it. Moli turned his head away tears streaming again. I sat up with my back to the wall and picked up the packet of cigarettes that had fallen onto the roof beside me. I took out two and felt in my pocket for my matches I was beginning to shake now with the shock of it all. I struck the match a couple of times before it caught and then lit both cigarettes. I nudged him as he was looking away and handed one of the cigarettes to him. We smoked in silence, Moli still with his legs on the sill and me with my back to the wall. "How's the head? You took a pretty nasty bang there."

"I wasn't going to jump you know… might have fallen." He added beginning to snigger now.

"Bastard!" I answered. "Would have made a magnificent end to my very short career!"

"You should think about moving to an all girl's school, that is unless you'll be tempted there too!" said Moli.

"I'm twenty-two Moli, give me some credit for this evening please! Anyway, you should be at college, technically you shouldn't be off limits!"

"But I am off limits."

"Yeah… I know, you weren't much help though."

"You should be able to deal with temptation."

"You have no idea Moli." God I was thinking about how much I had thought about him over the years.

"No… I have no idea." And a tear trickled from the side of his eye towards his ear. He dragged deeply on his cigarette.

"Sorry." God how could I have said that after what I had just witnessed this evening? "So how did you get into such a mess?"

"All too easily it seems…" he paused for a long while, "…I

think I have a disease. I meet someone, I fall in love, I meet someone else, I fall in love until there's quite a party!"

"What do your parents say about all this?" There was a long pause, he didn't reply.

"What you haven't talked to them? God Moli, that's where you're going wrong."

"Y'think? Yeah… you know I should have thought of that… Yeah brilliant idea!" His voice was thick with sarcasm.

"What? Am I missing something here?" I looked at him puzzled. He just smiled at me. Then he swung his legs down, nearly taking my head off in the process and sat up cross legged next to me. We were sitting really close.

"I'm going to be a father you know."

"Really?"

"Really… and so I would never have jumped. Just so you know." He took another drag on his cigarette and blew a smoke ring or two.

"So is that what this is all about then?"

"If you like." He said calmly. "Off you go then … excellent… job done." He turned his head away from me, then flicked his cigarette over the parapet.

"Look Moli…" I hesitated, I didn't want to load him with any more pressure but if it could help him in any way? "I do know what it's like… believe me." He turned his head to me tears in his eyes.

"And did you ever get over him?"

I clamped my lips together in a resigned smile looking down, I didn't dare look up.

I looked away and took a drag on my cigarette. "No, no I never have. Love is just that isn't it? Why should it be any less for guy's?"

"Does he know?"

I snorted a laugh, *God if he only knew.* "No… no… and he never will now." I said suddenly feeling stronger and able to look him in the eyes. But as I looked at him tears began to run down my own face.

"I'm sorry," Moli held out his hand to me. I took it. "When did he die?" That took me by surprise, well maybe it was a good thing to let him assume. I shook my head dismissing the question so I didn't have to answer. I squeezed his hand tight and he pulled me to him. We put our arms around each other and held on tight and then the facade cracked in both of us and I held him in my arms as we both wept.

*

The next day I phoned Lovelace.

"Lovelace? Thank God. Listen I'm really worried about Moli and I don't seem to have any address or phone number for his parents and the office isn't open until Monday. I've got his sister's address but I don't think that's appropriate and I think maybe you're the person I need to talk to anyway. Last night he was a hell of a mess…" I filled him in on the night's events.

Moli

I woke up and Lovelace was sitting in the armchair across from me, head propped up on his hand, arm supported by the arm of the chair. He was staring at me.

"Jesus Lovelace, you gave me a fright… what the hell? Aah… I suppose Luckhurst called you." I reached for the packet of cigarettes by my bed and lit up, I held on to the lighter and put my arm behind my head checking my watch for the time as I did so. It was late, very late. Breakfast was well and truly over.

"He's worried about you." I snorted a snigger down my nose.

"He thought I was going to jump from the tower last night." I snorted another laugh down my nose as I took a drag and tried to stare Lovelace down.

"Well, were you?"

I laughed and sat up and turned to flick my ash into the ashtray beside me.

"Thought you knew me better than that Lovelace." I stared at him. God his eyes pierced into your soul. He said nothing. "Listen, Vodka crisis, that's all… I suppose I'm going to have to give it up sometime soon what with my new responsibilities and what not."

I didn't look at him, I just held on to the lighter, feeling its weight in my hand.

"Christ Moli, I thought you'd got this sorted. I thought you were happy… At least that's what you said."

I closed my eyes and rubbed my forehead with my finger and thumb, I didn't want to have this conversation with him, you know the one where he says he's in love with Dawn and I'm his best friend and I have to pull myself together… again. It was raw this morning as well and I pushed my thumb into the side of my eye in an attempt to stop anything leaking out. I nodded looking down.

"Sure, sure… How's Dawn?" I didn't look up.

"Stop trying to change the subject."

I didn't say anything, I just looked up at him straight in the eyes and took a drag on my cigarette slowly.

"Moli?"

"Look, you know it's really nice of you to pop in, but I sure as hell didn't invite you."

"So what do you think I should do then wait until they're scraping you off the quad?"

"I have an excellent head for heights," I replied calmly, taking another drag.

"You know Mols, you once told me to write poetry to stop me from imploding. It really worked for me, helped me out at some really low moments. But what's your solution for yourself? You crawl inside a bottle of vodka and either take midnight swims under the covers or climb to the top of the building and sit on the edge off your skull, and then you tell me you weren't intent on jumping. Maybe you weren't but it sounds as if you wouldn't have minded much if you fell either!"

"This your new line then Lovelace? Amateur psychology?"

"Stop trying to change the subject, GOD DAMN IT!"

"Well it's good to see I can arouse some sort of passion in you."

"For Christ's sake Moli…! This isn't a joke. You want to see passion? Well how would you like to see the passion in my finding my best friend face down in the pool or with his head staved in, is that the kind of thing you want? Or do you want to haul me on the rack with you Moli? Don't you think that I know your pain is first and foremost my fault because I can't give you what you want?" His eyes were flashing angry so angry with me, and all I could think was *God, he's beautiful, like a dark avenging angel.* All I could do was laugh and smile at him. Which was now making him furious.

"God Moli sometimes..."

"Sometimes you are so glorious... did you know that?" I looked at him laughing and smiling, which completely took the wind out of his sails.

"AAAAhhhhhhhhh... " he yelled out in frustration hands on his hips, he looked down and started laughing with me.

"Look I'm sorry Lovelace... but Luckhurst shouldn't have called you. I know it was stupid to sit on the ledge, but you know the tower... there's nowhere to take a load off." I turned seriously to him. "And yeah, I know I shouldn't indulge in what I can't have, but I'm human ok... and you're a hard act to get over, and I never am going to get over you, and to be honest I don't ever want to. So yeah, I indulge my fantasies sometimes, stops me from imploding, and then I get back to reality. It's just my reality is a bit shit scary at the moment, my best mate has rather a lot on his plate, my girlfriend is rather ill, and my fiancé is chucking up and rather a long way away..." I shrugged "So I crawled inside a bottle... shoot me."

"Don't tempt me," said Lovelace as he sat on the bed next to me. "For God's sake Mols, you've got to take care of yourself... you know you can call me... anytime."

"Any time? No. No, not any time and I have to learn to

deal with that one. You were with the right person last night. I expect she needed you a lot more than I did. And look," I said brightening up, "I promise to stay away from tall buildings and swimming pools. Next time I'll stay in my show and listen to sad FM ok?" I looked him straight in his beautiful striking blue eyes. He looked back at me with a slight smile on his lips.

"Ok" he said with a resigned laugh. We both held our hands up to each other and slapped them together.

Chapter 31

Moli

Luckhurst had been keeping rather a close eye on me since the episode in the tower, and to be honest I enjoyed his company, but I'd promised myself and Lovelace that that road was closed. But God I needed something, someone. Kelly was such a long way away and now that Dawn's chemotherapy was over Lovelace was back at his digs. He'd got a job and was busy playing house with her. Term was drawing to a close and I was trying to throw myself into house duties but that also meant that Luckhurst and I found ourselves together, a lot.

He was great, the banter was light and fun and he made me feel more like myself. Knowing we had a shared pain made me feel like I had someone on my side for a change. There again, I'm no saint and I think I would have gone back on my word to Lovelace and indulged myself if it hadn't been for the fact that Luckhurst seemed to have changed his view of me. I wasn't getting the same vibe from him as before and the come on looks had gone. He was obviously grieving, poor bastard, and I really think I was helping him out there. It was obvious too that he still craved my company, as I did his, but he had seemed to come to some sort of acceptance about this bloke of his who had died. Well it's a bit of a fait accompli when it comes to death.

I had had a rethink about my night up on the tower. What was I doing up there? Lovelace was right, oblivion had been staring me in the face and if I had fallen forward then the decision would have been made for me. I was vulnerable I could recognise that and Luckhurst was easy on the eye, and like a big brother I could rest my head against, sanctuary really. So we spent a lot of time together, burnt the midnight oil a bit, got drunk, talked. God we talked for England about music, sex, religion, A. C. Milan and a whole heap more. He didn't seem like a master to me, he was just a friend, a really close friend. Well, I had known him for years on and off. We were both in pain but it was good to have him there because he understood, he really understood in a way that Lovelace never could. I didn't feel I had to hide it or pull myself together I could properly grieve because that was what it was like and I had to get some form of closure on this I really had before I could begin my new chapter with Kelly. So I talked about Lovelace the whole time to him and he talked about Oliver, Ollie he called him. God he was crazy about him, you could see it in his eyes and I know it made him really happy to have someone he could talk to about him. I didn't remember him at all, but then I hadn't really been aware of the boys in other houses so many years ahead of us, he would never have come across my radar. That is until one day I walked into his office without knocking. The door was open and he was head down on his computer.

"With you in a minute Moli," he said without really looking up at me "have a seat." I didn't, I began to meander around his room looking at the rows and rows of school photos on the wall opposite. I paused and laughed at the one for this year, one little bugger had done the usual trick of standing on one side and running around the back as the camera swept along and appeared on the other side of the photo too grinning. There I was on the far left on the front seats sitting next to Luckhurst, teachers all in the middle and me, as I was there for an extra year. I scanned upwards to the previous year and my stomach turned in an excited leap. Longing grabbed me as I gazed at Lovelace and myself dead centre side by side standing in the first row behind the masters. The whole of the sixth form were on this row and I remembered now why we looked so amused. It had been a job to get us all there as we had been playing tricks all week. As was tradition the sixth form always came up with a few jibes and jokes to play on the rest of the school as their final farewell salute. Pearson, who was into these things, had received a large parcel of chemicals from his brother who was at university. He had in turn got it from their father's secretary, who worked at ICI, and we had aided and abetted him in turning the swimming pool a rather lurid shade of fluorescent green. It wasn't harmful, apparently it's used for dying rivers to study the effects of water flow and some such stuff and as Pearson's brother had been studying geography he had ordered it months ago for his independent field study on river confluences. He thought it was a brilliant thing to send to his brother still in school, knowing that it would be very useful for the end of term. Unfortunately, once added, the damn stuff had sunk to the bottom as the filtration system was turned off at night. The effect that we had wanted was not achieved and so Lovelace and I had stripped off and dived in as human mixers. We had been in there half the night until the full effect was achieved right into the corners. Then we had had an impromptu party with the rest of the lads finding out by Chinese whispers. Lord we were drunk and I have to say all a little green around the gills. It was obvious who had done it as the whole of the sixth form were a little off colour.

I was hit by the impact of his eyes on me and held myself back from the wall with my two hands. Luckhurst had come up behind me and put his arm around my shoulder.

"You have great taste, you know, he had to be one of the best looking guy's in your year." He said squeezing my shoulder. "And he's a great guy, you and he have quite a friendship there, at least you will always have that."

I couldn't really speak, I just stared at him caught by his eyes looking intently into mine. So I nodded in response and tried to slow my breathing down. I dragged my eyes away.

"So where's your guy then?" I began looking up at the older photos scanning over them for Luckhurst's face. He was four years older than me so I worked my way back along the wall. Luckhurst had moved back away from the photos.

"Err… I don't think he was in them, he always seemed to be ill for one reason or another."

"Oh, God I'm sorry. He was sick at school then? God that

must have been hard." Luckhurst wasn't difficult to spot though. He really was a handsome guy if not tall, and he looked really happy smiling happily out of the photo.

"Here you are… I wonder where I am… Hey look at that! I'm standing right behind you with Lovelace." I sniggered as I looked at the pair of third formers. "Should be a couple more of these." I said as my eyes scanned to the next photo. I knew where Lovelace and I were on this one, I had it at home. We'd been moved as we were too tall to stand with the others in our year and we had been put a little lower down with another year group. Far over to the left. "Good God, what are the chances of that eh? Look Luckhurst you're right in front of us again. My God we look young." Luckhurst had moved back to his desk.

"Yeah? Well what do you know. Look Moli leave that will you, I need you to run over to York House with a message for Mr Munn it's rather urgent."

"Sure, sure, just one last one…" and I froze. I knew where I was in this one too. As first years we were too small to stand and Lovelace and I were sat cross legged on the ground right on the first row this time just a little in from the right and right behind me was Luckhurst then a forth former and he wasn't smiling this time, he wasn't looking full into the camera either. His gaze had dropped, he was looking down at me. I breathed in and held my breath pausing in confusion not sure what I was looking at. I turned to look at Luckhurst. Was this a coincidence? He was sitting at his desk leaning on it, one arm in front of him lying along the desk and the other elbow on the desk, hand propping up his chin. He had his eyes closed as if he was waiting for a hammer to fall.

"Ollie," I paused. He hadn't opened his eyes or moved. "Olivari de Molina, Moli," I added. He still said nothing but he screwed up his eyes tight and then opened them and looked at me. "It's me?" But by now I knew the answer. He looked down at the desk clasping both hands together. "Shit...shit... but you said he'd died."

"No... you said he'd died. I don't know... it just seemed easier. Sorry." He added as an afterthought looking down.

"Christ..." I couldn't think, "what am I supposed to do with this?"

"Nothing." He looked up at me. "Absolutely nothing... Moli... you were never to know."

"Yeah, but I do know now. Jesus Christ, why didn't you say something?"

"Why? And add to your problems? It may have escaped your notice but I'm your housemaster, and there are rules. I love my job and I want to be good at it, and if I can make it past you I know I'll always be ok."

"I don't mean now? I mean years ago, when we were both in school. You knew what I was like!" He snorted down his nose and closed his eyes.

"Yeah I knew, but were you really? Four years is a big difference in school when I was sixteen you were only twelve, too young. Four years is nothing when you're thirty, what's the real difference between thirty and thirty-four nothing, but when I was eighteen you were only fourteen. God Moli I didn't just want you I was in love with you." He sighed. "Look, I'm really sorry you found out, more sorry than you can know. I suppose I need to tell someone. Jesus what a mess!" He put his face in his hands. I slumped down into the armchair next to the fire to think. We didn't say anything for ages. Finally I managed to gather my thoughts.

"Look," I said, looking over to him. "You've behaved impeccably. So you're gay, you can't help it if you fell in love when you were at school, who didn't? And it's not your fault I failed and decided to do an extra year."

"Christ Moli, cut the crap. You and I... Christ even Lovelace knows that if you'd said yes I'd have been all over you like a rash last term. I shouldn't be here. Maybe you were right, I should be in a girls school, no worries there." There was a long silence again. Luckhurst had his head bowed.

"Well I guess you're the only one who knows whether it's guy's in general you have a problem with or whether it's because it was me who landed back with the extra year. If it's any guy then yes, you need another job. But if it's because it was me, well I'll be gone in three weeks and you will have thrown your career away because you fell in love when you were fifteen, that hardly seems fair really." I looked over to him, he hadn't looked up. I walked out of the room.

Luckhurst

Fuck, fuck, fuck, fuck! What a bloody mess I had landed in and I couldn't blame anyone but myself. It was Moli, of course it was Moli the love of my bloody life, the guy I had dreamt about since he had started school. The guy I looked out for playing rugby, or to see where he was in the hall when the whole school were in. The guy I would sit under the tree and watch as he mucked about at breaktimes with Lovelace and the rest of his year. The guy who I had got so near to and had nearly had an affair with, that was until Lovelace had butted in. Thank God he had though. The guy who had become my friend, something I would have given my right arm for in school. Of course it was Moli. Throw my career away, yes I would have gladly thrown it away for Moli, even a brief affair would have been worth it for him. But, was I as a gay man a danger to the kids I was in charge of. No. Yes I could go to a girls school, but there would be no rugby to take, no cricket in the summer and I was a damned good cricket coach. There was no doubt I was promiscuous as a teenager, so were half the year, but I never went with anyone younger than myself, and it was always with someone who was as equally keen and up front. God did girls have this sort of trouble? No, my problem was and always would be Moli. And now I had probably lost the very best of him and me, our friendship. God I was jealous of Lovelace, he could have him on a plate, he had his unfailing friendship and he couldn't see, or rather didn't want, his love. I knew he loved him, but to have a physical relationship with Moli, to become one with him... Yeah I knew how Moli felt about Lovelace because there I was up beside him on the stake burning too, but burning for him.

I left his office, I was quite calm really. Confused a little, but there was no doubt it was me the poor guy had been in love with all these years. God I'd had affairs in school, if he'd made an approach then I would have been flattered to have an older boy interested in me. Especially Luckhurst, he was always handsome and enigmatic, he was someone we all fantasised about at some time or another, well all the guys who liked guys that was. What strength of character he had, because he had laid his soul bare when he had been talking about Ollie. *Thick, that's what I am thick*, Ollie, Moli, heavens it was so obvious now I knew.

I turned back to his room, this time I knocked and waited for an answer. There wasn't one. I knew he was still in there as I had just left him. I wasn't going away, I knocked again gently.

"Listen, it's me, can I come in?" He cleared his throat.

"Yeah, yeah, come on in… watch me burn… why not." He sounded really down. I opened the door went in and shut it behind me. He was in the armchair head propped up on one arm, one foot up on his knee. He didn't look at me he was looking out of the window to the side of the chair.

"Phillip, look, don't throw your career away, you're a really great teacher you've got nothing to be ashamed about, I'm not going to tell anyone."

"Yeah, thanks for that Moli." He was struggling to keep it together I could hear it in his voice, but he hadn't turned around. "You've got some prep to do in about twenty minutes haven't you?" He paused to steady his voice. He shifted position leaning forward and clasping his hands together tight. "Jesus Moli, get out of here will you..." I could see the tears falling. I made a move towards him, he saw it and jumped up out of the chair moving away from me, over to the window. Still not looking at me he put both hands on the window ledge. "Please Moli don't... I need you to go."

"You didn't leave me up on the tower," I replied gently.

"Christ Moli that was different... Please, please just go now eh? I'm ok. I'll see you at supper."

I walked up to him and put my hand on his shoulder. His head dropped down and he cried grasping the window ledge tightly in his hands. I put my head down on his stooped figure.

*

It was a rough three weeks. Luckhurst was obviously avoiding me and he was careful never to be alone with me. He wouldn't, or couldn't meet my gaze, and when he talked to me he was always in a rush to get somewhere, anywhere but where I was. I knew why pain was etched across his face and I know the last three weeks were seeming like an eternity to him, but I also knew he equally felt that they were running away like sand, faster than he wanted because though he couldn't bear to be near me he also couldn't bear it that I would soon be gone. I understood and tried to keep as low a profile as I could but we found we were looking out for this year's pranksters most evenings and kept bumping into one another. It was really uncomfortable for him. I knew exactly how he was feeling, he died every time he saw me. I made his heart bleed afresh and each time the pain was clear on his face. Then all of a sudden it was the last day and all the boarders were piling their things up in the quad. I helped them all pack them away into various cars, shook the sixth formers I had got to know by the hands, patted them on the back and then had spent the rest of the evening packing the last of my own stuff into my trunk. Lovelace was picking me up the next day and running me to the train station. I pulled the last of the vodka out from its hiding place behind the curtain, grabbed my mug and cigarettes and set off to climb the tower for the last time. I was pretty sure that he would be up there, and he was with his own little mini bar set out. He had his back to the wall sitting on the ground and a large bottle of Laphroaig and some soda on the ledge above him. He was well on his way to being merry and had his knees up with his arms clasped around them, cigarette between his teeth. He nodded at me as I approached.

"Do you mind if I join you?" I asked looking at him through my fringe or rather the lack of it. Since I had shaved my head there was only a sort of spiky fluff.

"Be my guest Moli, you're a free man now!" he smiled warmly at me. It was as if the last three weeks hadn't happened. I looked at my watch.

"Well not quite, but I will be in about half an hour!" We both sniggered together.

"So, when are you leaving?" He looked down as he dragged on his cigarette.

"About ten thirty tomorrow. Lovelace is picking me up with my stuff and taking me to the station."

"Aah… Lovelace." He nodded without looking at me. I sat opposite him with my legs outstretched and poured myself a vodka. I lit up and held on to the lighter.

"That's unusual," he said nodding to the lighter. "Bit of an antique that, is it gold?"

I shrugged.

"Never really thought." I looked at it carefully turning it over looking for a hallmark. There was a hallmark on the bottom of it. "What do you know," I said in surprise. I pulled it apart and there was another on the inside case. I slipped the sleeve closed again.

"Do you mind?" he asked holding his hand out.

I passed it to him. He snorted in resignation as he flipped it over and saw the beautifully scribed looping letter L in the crest on the front side.

"What did you do? Steal it off him?"

I laughed. "No, he gave it to me, but he stole it off his dad."

"Well his dad has good taste." He looked carefully at the hallmark. "It's Edwardian, it's beautiful. You know it's one of a pair?"

"No, how do you know that?"

"Well because it's a dress lighter, it's smaller than a normal one. It was made for a dinner suit, so that it wouldn't show in a pocket. I bet it has a big brother somewhere."

"I'd better tell him to look for it then. He's been bitching about not having it any more ever since he gave it to me." We laughed. "So, what did you decide, about the career I mean?"

"Well, I only have to survive another twenty minutes now."

He turned his wrist over to look at his watch, he wore it on the inside of his wrist. "And I've made it, so I'm going to stay on."

"Good," I replied vehemently. "And I can guarantee that you're going to make it." He smiled and nodded snorting in amused agreement.

"So do you mind me asking if there was ever anyone else?"

"What? Who meant anything you mean?" he looked me in the eyes and dragged on his cigarette. "No!" he smiled at me. "You're the one" he smiled even more, "the only one." He was almost laughing now with me. "Why are *you* laughing, does that make you feel good? Is that what you wanted to hear?"

I was a little self conscious and I looked down as I nodded. Yeah, that makes me feel good, yeah, I suppose selfishly that *is* what I wanted to hear. It makes me sad though too."

"Yeah, it's pretty shit isn't it, but then you'd know all about that too so..." We both laughed again. "Do you mind if I ask you a question?"

"No shoot."

"Well, Kelly, I mean with a girl... you know, does it do it for you the same as with a guy?"

I was taken aback a bit with his directness.

"So I take it from that that you've never even tried?"

He shook his head and shivered.

"Don't get me wrong, they are lovely, I love to flirt with them and they seem to like me I get a great reaction from them, but no, no way, girls, women, just don't do it for me, turn me on I mean." I took a deep breath.

"Well... no it's not the same, it's different..." I paused trying to compare the two in my mind I searched for words like 'softer,' but then there is something really soft about a strong powerful guy when he's putty in your hands. Every word I searched for had it's equal counterpart in the opposite sex. Not the same though, not less even, just different. I looked to him and raised my eyebrow, I couldn't put it into words.

"So... do you love her then?"

"Body and soul." I replied without hesitation.

"Lovelace?" I should have known he would throw that one in but it still winded me.

I shut my eyes.

"Ask me again one day, one day when you've fallen in love again with someone else and I'll ask you then how you feel about me."

"You don't need to... I know what my answer will be."

"Well then you know what my answer is then... it will always be there, he's the one."

"So do you think you'll last... with Kelly I mean?"

"Yeah, I do... but there are some things I need to put behind me first before I can move on."

"Like what?"

The bell started to strike in the clock tower to our left.

"You made it!" I said and held up my glass in toast to him.

"Yeah touch and go there for a while." He looked into my eyes deeply and laughed as he held his drink up to mine and touched glasses. I leaned forward and trailed my fingers down his beautiful face and looked back into his eyes.

"One night Phillip, that's all I can give you, and it won't even be that because you know who I will be with, I can't lie to you." He rested his face against my hand and closed his eyes.

"Oh God, what do I say?"

"You say yes, and then we can both get on with the rest of our lives." I stood up one finger wedged in the top of the vodka bottle and the rest of that hand holding onto the tumbler. I held out my free hand to him. He took it and followed me down the steps of the tower to my show.

*

It was an amazing night and I have no regrets or guilt at all. To Luckhurst's credit I didn't spend the whole night imagining I was with Lovelace, though a good deal of it I was. We didn't talk at all until early morning entwined in each others arms lying quietly feeling the time slipping away.

"Are you going to be all right after this?" I was worried about him I knew what I meant to him and didn't want to have made things worse.

"It was the gift of a lifetime, I can never regret this. You can't ever begin to imagine. This is something I thought I would never have." He turned to me and we kissed so tenderly.

"What about you? Are you ready to move on now?"

"Well I won't know that until I see him, but yes. I can't possibly spend the rest of my life where I was. God I don't know Phillip, I expect I'm just like you, hoping that somehow I've satisfied some sort of desperate need." I looked at him and we began to kiss again, and become aroused again. He paused and pulled back to look at me.

"What?" I asked.

"Can I ask something of you Moli?"

"Sure."

"This time, can I know that it's me you see?" His eyes were deep grey and beautiful, like some thick viscous liquid.

"I see you Phillip, you don't have to ask."

*

I was sitting on my trunk in the quad when Lovelace arrived. I knew Luckhurst was watching me from somewhere in the building, but we had said our goodbye. Though we both cried I felt that he was going to be ok now, I just had to get through the next few minutes with Lovelace. His little car farted as it came down the drive and I laughed out loud. Of course it was just glorious to see him after the night I had just had holding him in my arms, making love with him, I felt calm, at peace inside. He got out the car and walked towards me smiling.

"Ready to say goodbye to the old place then?" His dazzling eyes flashed at me.

Jesus he was beautiful, and I couldn't stop smiling. I wanted to laugh out loud, shout out loud so I did.

"Wahoooooo!" I threw back my head and laughed, throwing my jacket up into the air.

"God, I never thought you'd be that happy to be leaving. Good night was it last night?"

"You better believe it, the best!"

"So you're still half cut then?" He was laughing at me now too.

"Probably." He picked up one end of the trunk waiting for me to grab the other. We manhandled the huge thing and the assortment of bags into the back of his Morris, then I climbed into the front seat and Lovelace spun the car in the quad.

"Hey! Hang on." I said suddenly, taking off the seatbelt.

"What? Forgotten something?" Lovelace pulled the car up.

"Yeah, I have, just a tick." I ran back into Lancaster I knew he would be up the stairs in the window overlooking the quad. He turned around as he heard me coming. I ran up the stairs to him and took him in my arms and kissed him passionately.

"Well?" he said, smiling at me. "How was it?"

"I'm gonna be ok," I said still holding him in my arms, smiling back at him. "I really am, I can move on. Phil…" I wanted to say thank you, that he had given me what I so desperately couldn't find on my own.

"It's ok." He whispered. "Now go, have a great life."

"You too," and I kissed him one last time.

"So?" said Lovelace back in the car. "What did you forget?"

"My manners... come on get me out of here Lovelace," and we drove off to the station.

The End

About the Author

Christie H. Lovelace grew up in the Lake District, until moving south to Kent when she seven. She graduated from Birkbeck, University of London with a BSC in Geography Geology. She worked at the English National Opera, the Courtauld Institute of Art and the School of Oriental and African Studies and has even appeared briefly in the West End. She now teaches in Kent. She lives with her husband and two children.

Two's Company… is her first novel, and has been produced in collaboration with her daughter.

Addendum

In 1976 the age of consent in England was 21 years of age for members of the same sex, which would make the relationship between Moli and Luckhurst illegal. Today the age of consent is 16, in Italy the age of consent is 14. I initially wrote the book in 2012. Had the affair between Moli and Luckhurst taken place now, even though Luckhurst is in a position of trust, the affair would be legal as Moli is over the age of 18. Whether it would be considered ethical is debatable. I do not condone the breaking of the law by the characters in the book, nor do I agree with a relationship between a teacher and a pupil, however young the teacher. I put to you a scenario on how their relationship might come about. How you view this is open to discussion, you will interpret it from your own viewpoint.

Boarding school is an amazing experience for those lucky enough to attend one. I have full confidence in their dedication to protecting our children in this type of environment. My own two children, both girl and boy, attended boarding school to the age of 18 and loved it.

Lightning Source UK Ltd.
Milton Keynes UK
UKOW05f1801300813

216237UK00002B/3/P